Patience, Ambrose

by

Jud Widing

PART ONE

THE TREE WATERS ITSELF

1798

O N E

THE OLD HICKORY TREE AT THE SOUTHERN END OF Pleasance Square was celebrating its one hundred and fifth birthday on the day Aggy's father hanged from its heartiest bough. It had been planted by Peter Woldrup in 1693 as an early stab at what would come to be called 'urban renewal,' but as urbanity had not as yet had a chance to develop, let alone decay, let alone demand renewal, Woldrup called it an 'internal improvement,' which already put him quite ahead of his time. Alas, his time came and went. Woldrup dropped dead when the tree he planted had only just cleared five feet. Too small to be of much use to kids at play, or a noose on the job.

In 1704 it produced its first full bushel of nuts, though these were mockernuts, so-called for a hearty appearance that yields, after tremendous effort on the part of the hungry supplicant, to an insultingly paltry store of edible meat. In 1721 a young girl named Hazel Achene scooped up an especially boorish mocker-nut and stuffed it into the pocket sewn on the front of the dyed pastel dress of which she was so proud, where it would remain until that evening, when she would remove it from the pocket, insert it wholly into her mouth, and promptly choke to death. This was on the tree's twenty-eighth birthday.

Young Ms. Achene can be considered the first life claimed by the sinister hickory, though one may be cautioned to add 'as far as we know.' For want of Woldrup's precise cause of death, just as a for instance.

Other spirits sped towards salvation by way of Woldrup's 'internal improvement' include one Joseph Mohair, who was quite fond of the other sort of spirits, and so inspired did lay down a wager amongst like-minded imbibers that he could spur his horse into charging the mighty hickory's trunk full-bore, to the point of the guileless pony's crashing into the same. Mohair's horse, a savvy steed that answered to no name but had been tragically saddled with the sobriquet Shagbark, demonstrated that its loyalty to Mohair stretched just far enough to get a good running start; the horse got to a gallop alright, but halted a few inches from the hickory. Mohair, for reasons all his own, made no effort to grab a fistful of Shagbark's mane as he went soaring over the animal's head. This was in 1767. As Mohair lost both his bet and his head, the menace of Pleasance Square turned seventy-four.

A pattern emerges. Did the mockernuts grow ever-so-slightly

more robust at these two intervals? Did their mockeries become just a touch more vulgar on birthdays number ninety-one (Jonathan Cordwainer, falling from the highest branch and meeting all the rest on his way down) or one hundred and twenty (Miranda Ackroyd, carving the initials of her beloved into the roots with sharp knife, unsteady hand, and prominent radial artery) or one hundred and fifty-two (Leland Macy, strolling beneath the tree when a two-foot-tall beehive dropped onto his head, to the great displeasure of the bees inside)? Ought one deduce some dreadful Providence in this? Or ought one attribute the examples just submitted, along with six more yet unmentioned, to the formless god of Coincidence?

It can hardly matter at this point. In either event, the tree waters itself.

But fear not: the moribund hickory tree at the southern end of Pleasance Square will meet its demise in 1982, when a new round of 'internal improvements,' by now called 'urban beautification,' will deem Pleasance Square insufficiently pleasant. Out will come the tree, to be set upon by many pointy machines with steady hands and no names to monogram.

Thus will end the two hundred and eighty-nine year long reign of Pleasance Square's most bloodthirsty shrub.

Unless, of course, one considers the bats. As in baseball.

By the late 20th century, hickory will have been supplanted by ash as the timber of choice for bat manufacturers. Ash is lighter, facilitating a faster swing. Hickory swings slower, but its heft lands harder. And yet. Somehow, despite its obsolescence, by Providence or Coincidence, the menace will achieve renascence in fifty-sevenesence. Fifty-seven baseball bats, sluggers, slammers, equalizers, Louisville doublers, Italian restraining orders,

West Texas massages. Fifty-seven.

How many of those will be used for less-than-sportsmanlike conduct? How many will be used as props in a mortal tragedy? How many of those tragedies will be enacted on an anniversary of the day Peter Woldrup stuck a seed in the soil in 1693? How many people's lives will fall under the shadow so familiar to Pleasance Square, and how many of them will be perfectly oblivious to the font of their misfortune? How many would be devastated to learn what they're actually giving their child, as they hand them a bolt of memorious timber and enjoin them to "have fun"?

How many will suspect, and ignore, their upright hairs and ringing ears?

As before: hardly matters.

T W O

WHAT MATTERS AT PRESENT IS HAPPY RETURN NUMBER one hundred and five for the sinister hickory. For it was on that day, on October 9, 1798, that Aggy had been brought to watch the execution of her father by the man who arranged it. *Execution* isn't entirely accurate; that implies some form of judicial procedure or bureaucratic sanction. Neither applied. Aggy's father, who had to pretend his name was Henry but whose most true and secret name was Bangura, was people-shaped property. Just like Aggy, who had no surplus names to hide away and take out when she was low. She was just Aggy, and while her father could be Henry or Bangura, Aggy never saw what difference it made. Both Henry and Bangura were now dangling from a hickory tree, piss dribbling down their leg, naked toes clenching at nothing.

Was it Bangura who talked Henry into running away? Or the other way around?

Despite knowing full well that her father was not in fact two separate people occupying the same body, Aggy could only think of her father's decision to sneak off into the night *without her* as being due to some meddling Other. She was fifteen years old. She worked all the live-long day on Master Pinchwife's farm, hard work that had given her strong shoulders and powerful legs. Her dad was old as dirt, nearing his forties at this point. He'd spent the last few weeks glazing the sash panes on the hotbed, owing to a gamey ankle. And even at such a simple task, he had struggled! What labor did Henry or Bangura imagine they might be confronted by in the course of their flight, at which Aggy could not match him, or even best him?

It was impossible to think of anything beyond 'get a lady pregnant,' which was surely not a phase of the escape plan. Which left Aggy no choice but to assume that her father had failed to wake her as he departed not by necessity, but by *choice*.

And look where it had gotten him. Boys from the city slicing up his pants into pennants to take home as souvenirs. The first lynching any of them had seen, maybe. Or maybe every time was like the first time.

As word of her father's capture, and the consequences he would be facing, made their way to Aggy's ears, she felt herself torn between fury and guilt. Fury because how could she be anything *but* furious; guilty because what if she had been there to help him? Might she have helped him across the river that ultimately swept him towards capture?

It was by these thoughts that she was consumed as Master

Pinchwife ordered her to accompany him to Pleasance Square, to witness the cost of becoming "uppity." It was in this introspective frame of mind that she bore such witness, watching the mouth of the noose swing over the branch and snap back down as though already burdened, observing her father bending to thread his head through the thick ring of rope, acknowledging that he was saying something to her, nearly choking on his own tears to utter final words Aggy could neither hear nor interpret. It was while distracted by her fury and guilt that Aggy only half-attended to the hard pull of the rope that hoisted her father into the air.

If there was blessing to be found in this, it was that Aggy hadn't the presence of mind to fix the image firmly in her memory.

It looked as though her father had stopped twitching, but it was impossible to tell; the boys from the city had moved on to his shirt. Straining to reach, the brainiest of the bunch rushed over to the far end of the rope that had been run around a hook stomped into the ground, and set upon it with his knife. It was the work of several minutes, but the boy meant to see Bangura's body brought low enough for him to reach. And so he did.

Aggy watched this in a state of distraction far more focused than her previous one. There were no two contrary impulses by which to be flummoxed. There was no overriding emotion whatsoever. Now there was only the clarity of absence.

Master Pinchwife concluded a joke to the chief executioner. This Aggy knew because Master Pinchwife was laughing quite a lot, while the chief executioner was trying to laugh but was mostly looking over at Henry's corpse with something approaching envy. Aggy watched the two men who were largely responsible for her father's death – though she spared no scorn for the quickly dissipating crowd, drawn to the spectacle of an unruly tool made to suffer – but could muster up nothing. Not guilt, not even the fury with which she'd only just parted company. Aggy was aware of how strange this was, aware of all of the feelings she should be experiencing but wasn't. She could observe another emotional self from a distance, a speck on the horizon that perhaps had a name it had secreted even from Aggy, but each step towards the specter prompted from it a compensatory step back.

In all her life, Aggy had never actually made it to a horizon. She saw them every day, was surrounded by them, but never got one up close. This trip into the city was the furthest off Master Pinchwife's farm she'd ever gone. Yet the horizon remained just where it had always been.

Master Pinchwife lumbered over, still guffawing at whatever joke of his had managed to wipe the smile off the executioner's face once and for all. One look at Aggy, though, and he came to a full stop of foot and funnybone alike. He studied her for several seconds, trying to make sense of her as he might a person who *actually* found his jokes funny.

"I don't expect you find this a mirthful occasion," he announced, "but you must see things from my perspective."

He did not elaborate, nor did Aggy ask him to.

Master Pinchwife lifted his nose slightly. "Stop your mooning at me in such fashion."

Aggy wanted to ask him, as she might have on a different day, What fashion? How am I mooning? But this, too, was now consigned to the unreachable horizon. Aggy feared that she would live out the rest of her life like this, looking down to find some part of herself missing, looking up to see it slipping out into the night without her, vanishing over the far side of a rise.

Goodbye understated truculence. Tell fury and guilt I said *hi*.

Master Pinchwife slapped her upside the head. A softer slap, one whose sting would abate within minutes, as opposed to not-so-minutes. "I told you to cease your face-making!" he shouted. A new batch of boys from the city looked up from Henry's body, like jackals from a fawn. But only for a moment.

"I'm sorry," Aggy told him, bowing her head. "I'll stop at once."

Nodding, Master Pinchwife wiped his slap-happy hand on his jacket. Aggy wondered if perhaps he *had* drawn blood, but her face was too cold to yield an answer without running a hand along the offended area. And now would not be the time to check.

Checking his own hand, Master Pinchwife asked his soft palms "Do you want a scrap of your father's garments, assuming any remain?"

"No," Aggy told Master Pinchwife's hands.

Satisfied, those supple fists vanished into pockets. "Then we're going home," Master Pinchwife told her. "Collect the carriage."

Aggy did as she was told, trudging out of Pleasance Square by way of the old hickory's shadow.

T   H   R   E   E

IT WAS ONLY FOR WANT OF COMPARISON THAT THE Pinchwife estate could get away with calling itself an *estate*. Drummond, aka "Master" Pinchwife, acquired the modest plot in 1784. Acquired? Oh, but it was nearer to theft! Approaching his third year as a state assemblyman for Stringfellow County, an election that came on the heels of a respectable if not especially commendable dash around the circuit courts, it would be an understatement of proportions one could not possibly *over*state to say that Drummond fancied himself a natural negotiator. And so, when confronted with a man named George looking to sell his chunk of the country, Drummond bartered. After an hour of price-parrying and number-chucking, Drummond had emerged the breathless, flop-sweating victor. Hardly believing a dope willing to dicker away three hundred and thirty-one acres for a measly two hundred and eighty-five dollars could sign his own name on a document, let alone recognize which end of the pen was which, Drummond graced the deed with his autograph far more eagerly than his attention.

Worthy of his attention, of course, was that George had had a fill-in-the-blank deed on his person. In an alehouse, of all places, which was where said signatures had been affixed to said deed. Or perhaps Drummond's suspicions could have been raised by George's insistence that the deal be closed on *this very eve*, in whichever specie was most readily available. And on a more sober occasion, Drummond would very well have noticed these things. But whatever intoxications the whiskey could not provide were enthusiastically supplied by the high of triumph. He had negotiated for land and won his plot cheap. This was a cause for celebration! Drummond insisted on buying George another drink.

To everyone but Drummond, the conclusion of this particular plot is eminently predictable. George had never before, and would never again, answer to that name. Nor would his face be seen again in New York state. For there was something crooked about those three hundred and thirty-one acres: two hundred and fifteen of said acres, to be specific, as well as literal.

Yes, of the three hundred and thirty-one acres Drummond had purchased, a full one hundred and sixteen were arable. The other two hundred and fifteen were blighted not by woods (themselves a resource) or by swamp (which could be drained), but by hills. And not cute little hills that swell and slope in such soft repose that failing to have a picnic upon them feels a moral wrong. No, we're talking Earth warts here, tumors of dirt metastasizing upwards at improbable angles, as though the ground were trying to touch its own toes. It was topographical tomfoolery of the highest order, and something for which Drummond had no intention of standing. Which was lucky, because that was rather difficult to do most places on the property. Far more likely was to find oneself tumbling head over heels down a hill, which not incidentally was an apt way of dramatizing how Drummond came to possess such an estate.

In short: Drummond was expecting to pay a steeper price for the land than he did. But, in the end…well, you get it.

Hardly a tenable situation, for a man whose most renewable resource was his own entitlement. After getting quite a few of the area's most knowledgable farmers drunk enough to tolerate his incessant questioning, Drummond became acquainted with – then obsessed by – the concept of terrace farming. It held an immediate appeal; it was nothing short of literally reshaping the Earth to one's will. A grand staircase of soil, each step supporting a different crop! Suddenly those three hundred and thirty-one acres of up and down and up and down and sometimes flat but then up and down again didn't look like such a waste. They looked like a spatially efficient farm just waiting to be cleft from a disobedient country.

A daunting task, to be sure. But that was why God made slaves!

Very quickly, the labor Drummond drew from his father's ranks or purchased at market (paying *very close attention* to every jot and tittle) learned the difference between the *concept* of terrace farming and the *practice*. In a word: irrigation. Seed could hardly be deposited into terraces overly rich in liquid, and any soak would need to be replenished regularly. This was an engineering difficulty that Drummond rather forcefully declared to be not his problem. His problem was a dwindling pool of assets. The solution was liberal application of the bullwhip to any slave who had the temerity to report yet another failed crop.

It was from this environment that Henry/Bangura had attempted to flee, and it was to one identical that Aggy and Drummond returned that night. Identical save the lack of the former's father, of course, and the arrival of a fearful, dreadfully familiar torpor gripping the slave quarters. It would prove fleeting, Aggy knew, just as surely as it would return again.

Maybe not for her, though. She had felt a great many things in her fifteen years, but *nothing* had never been one of them. How can one be rid of *nothing*, when it takes up so much space that one has nowhere left to put *something, anything at all?*

Aggy considered this as she drove the horses up the largest and least ludicrous of the hills, atop which sat The Pinchwife Estate, that ramshackle two-story cabin painted a pretentious, peeling white. It never failed to fill Aggy with despair...until now. Just as that usual shudder of sympathy that accompanied every snap of the horses' reins suddenly left her spine unmolested.

"Goodnight!" Drummond announced *alto voce* from inside the carriage, which was his way of telling her to stop the carriage because he wanted to be let out exactly *here*.

Aggy pulled the reins and waited for the slamming of the carriage door. She shivered against the needling winds, teasing her with the northwest's meteorological leftovers. Still waiting. She looked up, imagining herself lazing in the cradle of that newborn moon. Still waiting. She looked to her right, away from the Estate and towards that part of the horizon the city saw fit to blemish on the clearest nights. It was nearly impossible to make out the dull bruise of countless torches, but some starless eves you could spot it, if only you had someone to guide you with a firm, steady finger.

For Aggy, that digit had belonged to her father. There, he'd pointed. See that bundle of stars up there? Just below that. There's the city.

Had she asked him if she'd ever get to see it one day? She had.

What had he said? Who knows.

If this threatened to feel like anything to Aggy just then, it might have been funny. I know, Dad. I do. And so did you, for a little. What do you know now, huh?

So much for mirth.

Finally, the door to the carriage slammed. Aggy turned and saw Drummond hustling towards his front door. Nary a glance back, which was only to be expected. Strange that she should even have importuned her neck with the glance. What *had* she expected?

Aggy snapped the reins and made for the stables.

F O U R

HER BED WAS A PILE OF STRAW IN THE ATTIC SPACE OF the farmhouse kitchen. She shared the confines with twel...*eleven* other slaves of varying ages and genders. They all had a little bit more room tonight. Aggy wondered how many grieved the cause of the extra space, how many instead hoped the person next to them might make an ill-fated break for freedom, and maybe take a friend while they were at it.

How many of them would never even think such a thing, would be scandalized to know that Aggy could, would, did?

Aggy paused for a moment at the top of the ladder, patient as the gloom blushed.

The contours of the space seemed to wax and wane in synchrony with Ruth's snoring; the older woman's guttural eruptions limned the low, exposed-beam ceiling of the attic, as her choked inhalations darkened the walls against which disorienting speckles of moonlight played. In and out, in and out, Ruth's snoring conducted the huddle of human bodies shivering against one another. Or so it seemed, as Aggy waited for her eyes to cotton to the darkness.

Such a sight might once have amused her. In another world.

But Aggy was not amused; all she wanted was sleep. So knowing the space as she did, knowing precisely where she could and could not place her feet, knowing how far to fold at the waist to save from whapping her head against rotten wood, she stepped off the ladder before her eyes had fully adjusted to the dark.

Her second step into the attic was onto flesh. "Ah!" cried the voice of Molly, who was young enough that even Aggy thought her a child.

"Sorry," Aggy whispered.

"Shh," someone hissed from the corner of the attic. Impossible to name someone from their sibilance, but Aggy suspected that had been Clive.

"Sorry," Aggy offered reflexively, adding "mhm" upon receiving a second shush. The question of why her gentle apology should be more distruptive than Ruth's whipsaw snoring certainly arose, but remained unposed.

"You *shh,*" Lillian shushed the shusher on Aggy's behalf, from the not-so-far side of the attic.

"I'm tryin' to sleep," the shusher snapped, confirming himself to be Clive.

"Sorry," Aggy repeated once again as she used the searching sole of her foot to audition weight-bearing surfaces. She was having a hell of a time finding anything that wasn't a human body.

"You leave off her," young Molly squeaked from nearer the ladderside of the space. "She's just back from the Square."

This silenced Clive, and the rest of the peanut gallery besides. Save Ruth, of course.

From the mess of body, a pale, slumber-drooped eye turned towards Aggy. Instantly recognizable as belonging to Elizabeth; the dull green gave it away. "Some room here," she mumbled to Aggy.

Ought to be plenty of room, Aggy wanted to say. The thought occurred not maliciously, but objectively; her father had been a large man, and now he was gone. There ought to have been at least a Henry-sized hole in the crush up here. Instead, it seemed her friends had sprawled to fill the space. For which Aggy did not blame them. She just wanted the chance to put her foot down and feel something solid. Something other than her unblooded kin. And to sleep, of course. She wanted sleep. It was all she cared about right now. The only thing.

Elizabeth shifted over as best she could; Sally, against whose back Elizabeth was already flush, proved far less willing to make space. Fortunate that Aggy was so small, then.

"Thanks," Aggy whispered to Elizabeth as she lowered herself to the floor.

"You're welcome," Molly whispered from back by the ladder.

"She wasn't talkin' to you," Lillian goaded.

"Aw," Molly whimpered.

"She was talkin' to Elizabeth."

"Thanks to you too, Molly," Aggy added.

"Y'all gotta shush up," Clive implored, his tone too plaintive to match his injunctive phrasing.

"*You* shush up," Lillian returned fire.

Just as Aggy released her body fully onto the floor of the attic, squeezing herself between Elizabeth and who she was almost certain was Sally, Ruth's snoring *burst*. The old woman, well into her thirties she was, lifted her head from the huddle. Her mouth dropped into an O, from which emerged a noise that had far more sharp bits than the aperture would suggest.

This, too, was a sight that might once have amused Aggy. Another observation from another world.

Ruth heaved herself up. Her rise jostled all of the other bodies smushed into the crawlspace, but none raised a word against her.

Far quicker to stand than she had been to lay herself to rest — old habits, and that — Aggy was back on her feet, hunched at the waist and one hand planted on the ceiling above her, by the time Ruth waded her way across the attic.

She pointed to the ladder behind Aggy.

In the same world to which mirth had been banished, Aggy was aware of trepidation. They were not permitted to leave the attic this late at night without cause. Almost *certainly*, they would not have been welcome in the kitchens had they not some specific task to accomplish there. But these were thoughts for a far-off world. And in truth, there was little risk to descending; the Pinchwifes' interest in cooking lay with the raw ingredients (specifically the vegetables they could grow and sell) and the ready meals (specifically those that included as few vegetables as possible). All of the messy middle bits, as with the irrigation dilemma, were deemed beneath Pinchwife consideration. This was a job for the slaves, as the messy middle sections of life so often were.

And there are few messier, more middle-y sections of a house than the kitchen.

So Aggy lead the way down the ladder.

Ruth's first question once they had descended: "Did you watch?"

Aggy nodded.

Ruth sighed and nodded. Disappointment, but not in Aggy.

"Master wanted me to," Aggy pre-emptively protested.

Hhhh was the sound that Ruth made. Air escaping her nostrils, as she frowned for (as opposed to *at*) Aggy, shaking her head. And then, unsurprisingly, she closed in.

A small stature had never stopped Ruth from giving hugs big enough to scaffold a revivalist's tent, and provide a greater sense of comfort besides. Even knowing this, Aggy noted a dull surprise at the way Ruth's embrace seemed to not only close in from all sides, but, somehow, from above and below as well.

This would have been the time to cry. A great big hug from a great small lady, that's the sort of thing that really starts the waterworks, bursts the dam and drowns the mental landscape in pent-up emotion. But Aggy merely stood, wrapped up in Ruth's arms, waiting for something to strike her. A feeling. A thought. A hand. Anything.

Nothing did. And perhaps this perplexed Ruth even more than Aggy, because she didn't do or say anything for a few minutes. They just stood there, Ruth's arms locked around Aggy's shoulders.

Aggy cracked her eyelids a hair. Ruth's eyes were wide open, staring into some unimaginable distance. Awaiting a flood that would be long in coming.

And so it was that the first thing Aggy felt after the death of her father was feeling bad about not feeling bad enough to help Ruth help her not feel bad anymore.

Tentatively, Aggy lifted her hand and brought it gently to rest on Ruth's head. She did this again. And again.

"There there," Aggy cooed. "It's alright."

Ruth squeezed Aggy tighter, burying her face in the young woman's décolletage.

"It's okay," Aggy informed her. She thought she felt Ruth's body shudder once or twice, but the older woman could easily have been shifting her weight, nothing more. "There there."

F I V E

AGGY WAS PICKING WHAT MISTRESS PINCHWIFE CALLED the "winter apples" when Jesse found her.

Jesse held a privileged position on the farm, acting as a personal butler and valet to Master (save those occassions when Drummond insisted Jesse hand off the horses to a young girl, that she might squire her Master to her own father's lynching). Which position naturally afforded him a level of comfort scarcely imaginable to his fellow slaves. Which comfort naturally engendered resentment. Which resentment often found itself diluted by pity, because while it was unclear what Jesse had done to earn such a desirable role, it was clear that merit had played little to no role in the nomination. Where pity found purchase was that Jesse was quite clearly aware that he was bad at everything, and he tried *oh* so earnestly to be better. It was impossible to resent a guy like that *too* much, at least when he was in front of you.

But, as there had been no grand epiphanies or revelations in the sleepless hours since Aggy had been uncoupled from her only blooded kin, resentment and pity were equally inaccessible to her. She had nothing for Jesse but tenuous half-attention.

"Scuse me," Jesse began, "sorry to disturb you."

Aggy shrugged and shook her head: no big deal.

Hands hooked above his navel as though clutching the brim of an invisible hat, Jesse got down to business: "That's a fine bushel you've picked, for as long as you've been at it."

"What does he want, Jesse?"

Patience, Ambrose

Jesse burped slightly. It was a little tic that burbled up whenever Jesse heard another slave talking about Master Drummond in any manner they would never risk in their Master's presence. "He wants to see you on the porch."

Aggy sighed and took a glance at her basket. Maybe a third full of apples. The apples were Mistress' particular fascination; anything less than a full basket by sundown meant, at the very least, a slap on the cheek from her. That was the *very* least. Aggy just had to hope Master accounted for the cause for her shortfall, i.e. him. She certainly hadn't the gaul to do it herself. That went far beyond understated truculence, educating a Pinchwife like that.

Shivers played her bones like a washboard mere seconds after she'd ceased her labors. Damn this frayed hopsack frock with which she'd been sent to the field; movement was all that kept the chill away in the cold seasons.

So of course Master wanted to meet on the porch. Not inside, where a fire might be drawn. He wanted to bundle up in his coats and watch her vibrate as he extemporized about, what, probably Job again, Master loved telling his slaves about Job, like you think *you've* got it rough, you heard about this Job guy? What a Job. *Joke.*

But Master called, and Aggy had to answer. Whatever he wanted to say to her, wherever he wanted her standing as he said it, however long it took him to say, Aggy had to listen. This, too, as it happens, if you can believe it, is why God made slaves. So they were told, whenever Job was getting a much-deserved break from his eternal recurrence.

Why hadn't she started walking to the Estate? Why was she just standing here in the cold, letting her jaw chatter and snap away like a woodpecker with a deadline? What was she waiting for, Master to come to her? Boy, if she said that to Jesse, he might sick up his entire stomach – not just the contents, but the whole kit and kaboodle.

This amused her, this image. Not enough to make her smile. Just enough to make the terrace-wending trek back to the Estate a little warmer than it might otherwise have been.

A cutting chill nonetheless accompanied her, as she noticed the way her fellow slaves paused in their labors to watch her progress. How Lillian turned her head, that perpetual smirk falling into something terribly *soft* as she clapped eyes on Aggy. How Holly, straining on tiptoes to reach those few apples left to lower boughs, nearly ran towards Aggy upon seeing the direction in which she was headed…and how a mournful Ruth stopped the young girl before she'd had a chance to leap from the terrace.

Aggy recalled an episode in which she and a few of the others had attempted to dissuade another young slave called John from making such a leap. He'd been no more than five or six years old at the time, possessed of the same jovial self-destructive spirit as most every boy his age. In the end, Ruth had been the one to keep him from the jump, with nothing more than her words and the wisdom they so manifestly possessed. Poor John was still and all taken not a year later, found late one February in the orchard, frozen against a dead trunk. Why he had been there, nobody had ever managed to divine.

It had been quite some time since Aggy had thought about him. For a moment, she wondered what had brought him to mind. At which point it became obvious: the faces she had just now seen Ruth, Lillian, Sally, and the others making were precisely the same faces she had seen directed towards John atop the terrace. Towards a child on the precipice of tragedy.

Given the distance still left to cover, she had plenty of time to imagine herself in the orchard, late one February.

SHE WAS GREETED, UPON REACHING THE PORCH, BY nobody. Had she taken an atypically long time to get here from the orchard? She didn't think so, but it wouldn't exactly be out of character for Master to have a less-than-comprehensive grasp of how long it took to navigate the property. So where had he gone?

She stood just in front of the bottom step; to ascend unbidden would be as good as a dry run for mounting the steps to Saint Peter's gate.

But she had been bidden, hadn't she?

Bidden by *Jesse*, though. It took an invite from a Pinchwife directly to get a slave up the steps.

Right?

Aggy thought about her bushel just sitting in the orchard, unattended…she imagined another slave, probably Clive, that son of a bitch, pinching the apples from her basket and tossing them into his, so he could sneak off and have a very cold nap somewhere. She hoped he froze to death, that cunting cock-sucker piece of fucking shit and then Aggy was on her knees before the steps of the Estate, racked by violent sobs that grabbed her by the shoulders and throttled, clutching the heart she'd hoped was lost to an imagined distance, slamming her forehead against the unyielding, frozen earth, not praying but wishing. Wishing the world would just crack open and swallow her up already.

"Aggy!" Master shouted before he was even fully out his front door. "What on God's good Earth am I to make of this display?"

Try as she might, Aggy could find no words capable of containing her grief.

Master turned around to study his front door. Having reached a decision, he turned back to Aggy and scampered down the stairs. "Alright! Alright!" he declared on the way down. "Quiet now! Shut up!" He reached the earthen landing and walked directly to the ever-shrinking Aggy. "Why are you not expressing your displeasures out in the field, where your din may prove salubrious to the taming of your fellow laborers, and incidentally where their pachydermous ears might save mine from this rumpus? Not that my ears are pachydermous, I hasten to add. Quite regular in shape and size, as you can well see." Master reached up behind his ears and gave them both three flaps.

Still struggling to control her sobs, Aggy stared up at the man who had just killed her father in front of her, the man who *owned* her, flapping his ears with his fingers. In that moment, she came as close to extemporizing a full sociopolitical treatise as any human on the planet ever had.

His oratory (sharpened by the state assembly, honed by his marital dissembling) having failed him, Master made recourse to more immediate means of coercion: "If you don't stop your wailing, I shall kick you quite hard."

Aggy didn't fall altogether silent, but did manage to find some words down in her grieving deep. "I'm sorry, Master. You called for me."

"Pah! I did no such…" He touched a finger to his chin and grimaced at nothing in particular. "Jesse told you to come *now*, did he?"

"W…" Aggy snuffled and cursed her own weakness, only obliquely recognizing the strength that this implied. "Was I not supposed to?"

Master tutted and shook his head at the ground, planting his hands on his hips. "No, Aggy, you were not. I wanted to speak with you this evening, after the sun had fallen."

"Oh! I'm so sorry!" Aggy felt more sobs swelling in her throat. Evidently Master saw them too, as his eyes flared with something astoundingly like (but surely not) fear.

"It's alright!" Master shouted. "It's fine! Just...go back to the orchard. Pick what apples you can. I shall have a word with your Mistress about your idiot grief, and petition that she judge your day's yield accordingly. Failing that, I shall simply inform her that your pitiful bounty is a consequence of Jesse's meddling. She has never once found that an implausible account," he added, to himself more than Aggy.

Aggy wondered why, then, Jesse was kept around the farm, let alone retained as arguably Master's most trusted confidante. And then she thought about the tone Master had taken for his self-directed aside. That knowing, almost mischievous tone.

That was probably as close to an answer as she could ever hope for.

S   I   X

IN HINDSIGHT, THAT ANSWER WAS ALSO A WARNING.

Aggy had returned to the orchard to find her basket of apples precisely as she had left it. Perhaps, had it been emptied, the grief which had visited her at the threshold of the Estate may have circled back to run its course. But the basket was full, or at least as full as it had been, and that was a stroke of good luck that made it impossible for Aggy to fully access her anguish once more. Simple enough to cry about a dead dad when you had images of empty baskets swirling around your mind, but a full basket and a full casket rather balanced each other out. Not that Aggy's father was getting either.

So she picked until she couldn't see her hands before her eyes, and plodded back towards the kitchen by what little light the moon saw fit to yield. Slowly slowly she moved, to curb (though not eliminate) the inevitable indignities of walking into low-hanging branches or tripping over roots.

Once, she put her leading foot down to discover the planet missing. Nearly walked off one of the ziggurat's steps, she had. The fall could have broken her neck. Had she taken it. She reiterated that thought to herself the rest of the way back to the Estate. Impossible to parse the inflection from the echo, though; an internal monologue was such a slippery monotone.

Aggy followed the same rule that had kept her safe since childhood: if she was close enough to the Estate itself that she'd need to look up to take in the entire edifice, it was time to look down. Avert her eyes, lest she scuff the spotless white exterior with her attention. Fill her sight with nothing but her own two feet shod in rotting leather, the scabrous knuckles of her toes, the naked dirt before her; anything at all, to spare those pale steps to the front porch from her peripheral vision.

Aggy pondered her way around the house, to the back door which faced, yet kept apart from, the kitchens above which the owned people lived. And she kept her eyes down down *down* as she placed her far-from-full basket before a waiting Mistress Pinchwife. The Mistress' arms were tightly folded across the sheer plunge of her boastful muslin, her mouth knotted like string left in a pocket. Aggy knew this, from the way the planet seemed to buckle around her. Bowing. This was not a woman who had ever put a foot down without finding something upon which to tread. It helped, of course, that she would never hesitate to tread upon living bodies.

But apparently, incredibly, unbelievably, Master had actually followed through with his assurance that he would reason with the Mistress. For all she had to say to Aggy was, "Tomorrow we shall keep focused on our work, hm?" and then, with a shooing wave of the hand, Aggy was dismissed.

From that particular task, that was. There were so many others with which Aggy had to busy herself in the service of supper: for the Masters, a light repast of that most unusual transatlantic delicacy, potatoes, roasted with salt and a small portion of butter, and let's certainly not forget the fresh-pressed cider, that's why God made apples after all; for the Mustangs a just-slightly-heartier mix of oats sourced from an impossibly distant land called Ohio and some peas and hemp seed which were just up from tiers four and two of the westernmost terrace, the only one that could sustain grain growth by means inexplicable. Then it was back to the apples for Aggy, grinding down the post-press pulps to mix with pig grease (from the farm of Master's son) and rosewater, the rose being of Mistress' autumn-scolded garden and the water being just any old water, Mistress always demanded fresh water from the well because she could *tell* but one day Aggy forgot and used water that had collected in a bucket during a storm and Mistress hadn't noticed…anyway, *that* apple slop concoction was then applied to Mistress' face, as she had gotten the notion into her head that such a slop might bring vitality back into her visage. And it was after this application, then, and *only* then, that Aggy was dismissed for the night...to clean up, because making dinner and pulping apples and doing anything at all with pig grease makes an unholy mess that can only be exorcised with a comparable measure of elbow grease, and why does one think God made the slaves, hm?

So Aggy set to work sanctifying her abominable wake, which is to say scrubbing and rubbing and scraping and sweating, just as all the other slaves were, sweeping and spiffing and buffing and pushing a lot of dust under furniture and carpets, all to make right the things they made wrong, to keep the Pinchwifes from making them gone.

Also falling into that category was Aggy's *final* final task for the night (save checking up on the horses and the farm's sparse livestock an hour or two prior to cockcrow, cockcrow being metaphorical as there were no cocks on the property): returning to the porch to speak with Master. Who had always been quite fond of crowing over himself, come to think of it.

This time, mercifully, the porch was occupied by Master, bundled in his coats just as Aggy had expected him to be. "You've got all that whinnying out of your system, I trust," mumbled the bundle.

"Yes," Aggy lied, without quite knowing it.

"Can't hear you, girl. Present yourself."

One by one, Aggy mounted the front steps. Back doors, slaves could come and go with far less ceremony. Granted that Mistress was not darkening the threshold, of course. But there was no conditional to walking up the front steps. It was unheard of, for someone of Aggy's stock. Easier to imagine a horse mounting these steps, than a slave. Funnier, as well. By quite a lot.

And yet...she had been up once before, though the reason

that had carried her up these stairs was lost to her. Perhaps it had been a dream. Were the world a kinder place, Aggy might have believed that it had been a dream. In any event, she could remember how each of the eight steps felt beneath her bare feet, the way some of the boards held firm or sagged or shifted. How some groaned in disappointment that a dray should be climbing them while others thrilled at the elevation of such filth. How she felt a sharp prick on the third step from the top and had assumed she would find a splinter sticking out of her right foot later but, oh glorious day, there was no splinter to be found. Such were the most wondrous days of her youth, be they dreamt or lived: when there were no splinters.

Now, here, on this night, the steps were not as she remember-ed them. They each seemed to sag in the same dull fashion, differing only in their depth. All groaned, though their groans seemed motivated by grievances more individualized and speci-fic than simply 'disappointment.' All of them jabbed at her soles as she walked, some quite certainly drawing blood. If there should be no splinters later tonight, she vowed…but had noth-ing to offer her God. For now she was on the porch, and He had abandoned her.

"Sit," Master called, as he parted the bundle and patted his lap.

S E V E N

"IS THIS SOMETHING YOU WANT?" HE KEPT ASKING. "IS this what you desire?" Never before had Master sought Aggy's opinion, and yet, now that he was leading her to the bedroom from which his wife was mysteriously absent, Master had grown almost comically solicitous.

Even in her youth and inexperience, Aggy was not the least bit confounded by Master's actions. This was not a question of obtaining consent. Consent had and would never come between them; so deeply engrained was the coercion, Aggy could imagine Master actually fooling himself into believing a slave's assent was freely offered. Sometimes. But not this time, she was sure. This was about pretext. Master's preference for the slave girls who retained a youthful face through physical maturation was well known on the farm, to nearly everyone save Mistress – though Aggy could only infer that by her lack of comment on the matter. Perhaps she, too, knew, in which case Master's peccadillos were an open secret that all kept only from themselves. That Master imagined these illicit encounters to be the will of the victim was similarly understood, along with the consequences visited upon those foolish enough to accept the pretense at face value and demur. It was but a half day's ride to Spoons Creek, which sluiced past the Master's son's swine farm on the way to draining into the Allegheny River, which poured itself into the Ohio, and suddenly one was on the mythic Mississippi, being whisked ever southwards into cotton country. An old friend of Aggy's called Margaret had one day complained of Master's advances, and boasted of rebuffing the same. The next day she was gone. A week or so after this, Jesse solemnly relayed her fate between small burps; she had been sold to a cotton plantation in a place called Tennessee, allegedly the newest state admitted to the Union.

Aggy had disbelieved both Margaret and Jesse at the time, a fact which she could now hardly believe. All at once, though, the sequence of events announced itself as an unspoken law of the Estate: Master's sexual impositions, when "consented" to "freely," were burdens to be borne for a night and never repeated. Yet advances rebuffed would see any girl steely enough to wear the mantle of young woman manacled and sold down the river.

Which was what Master was hoping for, Aggy realized. There were no obvious hints, no whispered assurances that she could always say no, no allusions to what befell the others. But somehow, she could just tell, smell, *feel* that Master wanted her to say no. It was in the way he paused between each button, gawped and boggled even as he disrobed himself. He had prepared for battle, only to discover too late that he'd forgotten to declare war.

He wanted to sell her away. To make a Margaret of her. This, Aggy deduced *in situ*. What baffled her, and where she rested her attention as Master drew too near to take in (the eyes averted themselves on reflex, of course), was why the man contrived a pretext to be rid of her. Why he sought to extort a rebuff. He was accountable to no one; it was inconceivable he would be sharing this with the Mistress. So why this awful pretense, to be known only to himself and his victim?

Impossible though it seemed, Aggy decided that it went some ways beyond the beastly triumph of the act. Of battering her against a headboard still crowned with a single strand of his wife's hair. This, Aggy decided, was what contrition looked like in a man incapable of fully experiencing it. Master regretted hanging Aggy's father. At the very least, he lamented bringing her to witness it. Each time he saw her stung him anew, then, but simply selling her would force him to tacitly acknowledge what he had done to so stir his own conscience. Which was beyond his grasp. And thus, the ruse. The rape.

But if this was true – and Aggy chose to believe that it was, if for no other reason than it leavened the world's cruelty with comprehensibility – Master had failed to take into account the position this put Aggy in. Though who would have expected him to do otherwise? He saw her as something less than human.

So be it. Here was the greatest achievement of her little life of dehumanizaitons; whatever she was, she would outsmart the bastard. For if she was correct – and she was, damn it all, she was – if she rebuffed him at any point, even now, as he grunted out question marks, she would be sold, and Master would be rid of his guilt on grounds that preserved his goodly image of himself. Without his having to truly face what he had done.

But if Aggy endured…Master would be stuck with her, at least until such time as he mustered up the courage to stare his regret straight in the eye.

Prior to selling her off, that was. For Aggy had no illusions as to how this ended for her. In tragedy, yes. In agony, or if she should find a backlog of fortune awaiting her, swift death.

But she could pull Drummond Pinchwife along with her. An emotional suicide pact.

Victory to she who feared not death.

"Yes," she whispered to him, trying hard to keep her voice steady.

Drummond hesitated for a moment, pulling his head back from her neck. "What?" he asked. He could scarcely have sounded more incredulous – more *lost* – if Aggy had announced she would be campaigning for his seat on the state assembly next year.

In that moment, she knew she was right. She'd seen straight

through him. Made him insubstantial.

Right here, right now, she owned the moment. It was the first and only thing she had ever possessed.

It was horrible. It was currency.

"I want this," she confirmed.

Ah, but here was the tragic and hideous punchline: that it should be in this moment that Aggy first felt anything warm after the execution of her father. For what else could she feel as she gazed upon Drummond's stupid fucking face? That look of idiot offense, of being lost and hurt and yes *bested*, of finally knowing how it felt to want something and not get it?

That face was one she had seen far too often, in any surface that threw a reflection. In the eyes of people who shared her lot. But it was not one she had ever seen on such a pale visage. Had she ever suspected a white face capable of such contortions? She tried to hold it in her mind as she bit her tongue, for no other reason than to keep from laughing, from crying.

E I G H T

MASTER FINISHED ABOUT TWENTY-THREE SECONDS AFTER he started, at which point he simply pulled out, got up, opened the door and pointed to the hall. Aggy collected her garments and withdrew.

When she returned to the kitchen attic, everyone was lying precisely as Aggy would have expected them to be. Huddles in the dark. Yet…something struck Aggy as incorrect. There was an excess of absence here; Ruth did not snore, the rest did not shiver.

They were awake, Aggy realized. Awake and waiting. Yet no one rose to meet her, to embrace her, to console her.

This was surely not for a lack of concern; quite the opposite. Aggy knew she could have stirred anyone here – yes, even Clive – and found a sympathetic ear. But she neither needed nor wanted comfort. She'd already had that, in the form of Master's fleeting expression of dipshit defeat. She was not a victim entire tonight. That was a thought to carry her into sleep.

Upon waking, she discovered herself to have been inducted into the world of adulthood. Which for any woman on the Estate who was not Mistress Martha, meant learning the full width and breadth of their Master's inhumanity. Whether she wanted to or not.

She didn't, for what it was worth. But she listened, for it was clear the others found succor in these confessions.

Ruth, true to form, was the one most burdened by memories of Drummond's other victims. Some of the stories Aggy was familiar with to some extent (typically the conclusion, for youth had spared her the bulk of the tragedy); others she was hearing for the first time. In each account, the sequence Aggy had intuited played itself out. Drummond had his way; if met with opposition, he sold the troublesome woman off.

It broke Aggy's heart, to hear a litany of names she had never heard before, imagining the human lives they signified. Imagining the torment to which those people were now being subjected.

But the worst was yet to come; Aggy's friends had still to testify.

Sally confessed that she was among the same unhappy number as Aggy and the women in Ruth's tales, though she averred that by some miracle she did not get pregnant. The word choice seemed bleakly comic; Aggy could not help but wonder if Sally had taken the lessons of Job a bit too closely to heart, if it made sense to call not getting pregnant as a result of a rape a "miracle," when a more punctual, proactive sort of divine intercession would have been a much preferred method of contraception. But this, she kept to herself.

Molly, the child who Aggy could not bear to imagine suffering so much as a scrape, had benefited from no divine favor at any point in the process: Drummond had gotten her pregnant, a fact Molly intuited from her first missed period (which was itself hard to miss, given how new and novel the whole phenomenon had still been). She, however, made the mistake of communicating this to Drummond; he had smiled and assured her it would all be okay, if she could only keep this between them. The following evening he bade her follow him to the edge of the property. She awoke ten hours later with two cracked ribs and no life inside her. In this, she was yet more fortunate than Margaret; she was not taken to the river.

The commonality between these tales, putting their catalyst to one side, was clear enough: to speak out was to conjure yet more devious acts from the demon of the Estate.

"I'm so sorry," Aggy told them, knowing no other words in that instant.

"Hey," Lillian snapped. "You don't apologize."

Sally placed a hand on Aggy's shoulder.

Aggy sniffed, nodded, and placed a hand over top of Sally's.

"You don't apologize," Lillian repeated, more softly this time.

"I wish so much ill upon him," Elizabeth mumbled to herself. "None befalls, though I do wish it."

"Keep wishin'," Sally told her. "Can't hurt."

"That's just the problem," Elizabeth replied, casting a mournful glance Aggy's way.

Aggy saw the glance, but couldn't bring herself to return it. Which she regretted, along with quite a few other things, as that comforting clutch dissolved and the morning progressed. All day she braced, not for anything in particular, just for *anything*. For lovely though it was to imagine Drummond in psychological distress – not to mention flattering to fancy herself as having outmaneuvered him into that position – Aggy feared how unpredictable this could make him. For how might such a stupid, vain man react after mulling on his disgrace for a long, lonely night? Would he have reconciled with his contrition, and so come to her with shackles and a bill of sale despite her acquiescence? Would she be setting laundry out on the line and feel a bullwhip slashing across her back? Or would Master open the second-story window of his bedroom and announce emancipation for all his slaves, and then dive out headfirst? Nothing seemed impossible.

Before the sun was even halfway to overhead, Aggy's neck was killing her; every unusual sound she heard elicited a forceful cranking of her head in that direction, with the full expectation of encountering an entire posse galloping towards her. But no, the metallic *shnk* she heard down at the stables was simply the wind knocking the stirrups of a post-hung saddle together like chimes, just as the leaden *thmp* she heard out in the orchard was nothing more than an overripe apple leaping its death.

Around high noon, though, Aggy finally heard a meaningful noise. She'd grabbed a wide pail and hiked out to the well on the edge of the property, drawing water for the crops on a high terrace back near the house (behold, the wonders of Master's irrigation system), when she heard the unmistakable sound of Mistress screaming at Jesse.

Aggy's hand slid from the pump; she crept nearer the edge of the hill facing the road, following the music of her Mistress' displeasure. After some seconds the carriage appeared through a small copse. Despite its regal, deep-blue exterior, the carriage bounced along the dirt road like it was scared of a bee that wouldn't leave it alone, each dip and buck occasioning a similar change in Mistress' pitched keening. More constant, though, was the mortified expression chiseled into Jesse's visage, which held steady as the Mistress unleashed her fury:

"…me there, and now we're stuck in a rut, by God as my witness I shall [unintelligible]…"

And then they were out of earshot.

Amusing though the sight ought to have been, Aggy watched the carriage's passing with mounting dread. Obviously Master wouldn't tell Mistress what he'd done last night…but if he were in a state of heightened agitation, some kind of comeuppance coma, might the needling of a highly piqued Mistress bring friction to his kindling?

Immediately after having this thought, she kicked herself that she should still be so naïve.

To confirm her suspicions, she cornered Jesse the soonest she could, which was not an hour and some after he had returned with Mistress. Aggy found him putzing around the Estate, kicking at little drifts of soil. He spotted her as she approached, and recognized himself as *found*, which was to say, as being sought. Thus commenced a small chase, concluded when Aggy had nearly run Jesse to the edge of the woods leading to Spoons

Creek – and, more proximately, upon her shouting "goddamnit, quit your runnin', you big dumbass!" The verbal abuse halted Jesse, which went halfway to telling Aggy what she needed to know.

"How come you took Mistress off the Estate?" Aggy demanded, in pursuit of that second half.

"Family business?" Jesse replied, slipping no fewer than three little belches into those five syllables.

Fired by a confidence she knew was not wholly hers (though who could say from whom she had taken it), Aggy rose onto her tippytoes and jabbed a finger into Jesse's chest. "You tell me how come."

Jesse's eyes flared wider. "B..." *urp*. "Bedbugs."

Aggy cocked her head slightly. "And how's one night over the hill gonna fix that?"

"What do you mean?"

"I *mean*," Aggy snapped, quietly astonished by her own tenacity, "I didn't see nobody tossin' out Mistress' bed entire."

Jesse appeared to fully recapitulate a portion of his most recent meal. "Lord, no. Mistress' bed? The thought of touchin' such a...no, I'm far from fit."

"So it's still up there?"

"Strikes me as you say."

"So the bed's got the bugs is still there."

Jesse nodded, reducing his discomfort to a low, if sustained, gurgle.

"*So*," Aggy pressed, "why'd you take Mistress off for the night?"

"Bedbugs," Jesse replied, with all the confidence of a man who has learned his lessons by rote.

Patience, Ambrose

Which took Aggy the rest of the way to having her suspicions confirmed; Master retained Jesse's services in such an intimate capacity because Jesse was the eminently desirable combination of incompetent and precise. He would dutifully (if not expertly) execute any command issued to him, and never once question the wisdom nor the motive of it. Facilitator and scapegoat, wingman and fallguy, his very real ineptitude was the most perfectly plausible excuse to cover for Master's indiscretions. *Bedbugs in the bed?* Aggy could imagine the bastard saying to Mistress. *Is that what Jesse told you? Of course not, just a terrific misunderstanding. So sorry to hear he got you stuck in a rut for the night. No, I couldn't dream of selling him. Far too loyal. Don't you have something else you could be doing, other than giving me an earful, dear?*

And would Mistress press the point beyond that? Or would she have spent all her energies chewing out Jesse, and so retire to the nearest surface that was both recumbent and upholstered? What would happen if she didn't?

All day, different fears percolated, like bubbles in Mistress' rosewater pig grease, a new one taking its first breath, swelling and expanding as it drew strength from Aggy's manifold paranoias and insecurities, until ultimately popping beneath the well-reasoned tip of a good point just as another rose to take its place.

The final pinprick was, fittingly enough, Master himself. Just as the sun was nearing the horizon, as Aggy was trudging back towards the orchard, she spotted a bundled Master staring at the sky.

With eerie immediacy, he looked down and met her eye, as though he'd been expecting her.

She froze, and began trembling before the chill had a chance to fall.

Master nodded once and looked back up at the sky.

And that, as it turned out, was that.

N   I   N   E

EVERYTHING WENT BACK TO NORMAL. THE WINTER SEASON was approaching, and the final apple harvest had to be collected before the frost arrived and brought about the applecalypse. So October aged like a true philosopher, growing darker and colder by the day. Meanwhile, the punishment for anything less than a full basket of apples by sundown escalated from flagellation with a riding crop to lashes by the whip, to hanging by one's wrists, bound behind the back.

For a time, Aggy watched in horror as her friends (and some less-than-friends) suffered these fates. Poor Sally, for whom wit was so often quicker on the draw than discretion, suffered a shoulder dislocation from the lattermost punishment. Her crime had been having a go at juggling a few of the apples. Frivolous, Mistress had decreed, and so Maser had fetched the rope.

It turned Aggy's stomach, and it was increasingly common that she should be awakened from precious sleep by a dreadful, pinching nausea. By day, the ache grew diffuse but no less aggressive, sapping her appetite and making work increasingly challenging. She began to suffer nasal delusions, by which the apples she was stuffing into pies and tarts, or cooking down into apple butter to be tucked away and forgotten in the arctic dark of the farmhouse cellar (so reminiscent of the attic just above), came to smell more and more sour to her. She raised these concerns to Ruth one night, who insisted, along with the others tucked away in the attic, that the apples and their byproducts gave nothing but sweet perfumes. So even sweetness had forsaken Aggy, it seemed.

At some point…well, actually at a very specific yet arbitrary point, October 31st became November 1st. Aggy was awake for the moment, and as always found herself underwhelmed. It was a new month because that was just the way it was. But nothing was actually new. It was still the same unending, inescapable day to her. Nothing noteworthy really happened until November 3rd.

By then, the harvest was over. Which in no way signaled a dearth of work to be done. It simply meant that the urgency of the work had abated, and so the severity of the punishments for work deemed insufficient had relaxed ever so slightly. What took the place of harvest was a mild panic over preservation; root crops had to be buried, to protect them against the unforgiving New York winters. No less strenuous from a labor perspective, this work, though easier for being done out from under the shadow of the switch.

And yet, it was while merely shoveling over the onions that Aggy had her first truly overwhelming bout of nausea.

It started as just a feeling, abstract and unformed, like an instant of premonitory dread she had once felt immediately prior to being shat upon by a passing yellow warbler. Except this time, the metaphorical shit came from within. It felt as though it was going to burst out of every orifice it could find, this indigestive devil, until it changed its mind and contracted upon itself with such force that Aggy was sure she'd permanently shrunk an inch in every direction.

Dropping the shovel, she fell to her hands and knees and moaned. Moaning was hardly how she liked to conduct herself

– she'd been making a conscious effort to clutch every shred of dignity she could close to heart, since that night a few weeks ago – but this one escaped her far more successfully than her father had the farm.

And then arrived the followers of Moan-ses, the breadbasket exodus, let my people go. She vomited once before she had the presence of mind to not stand *right* over top the onions. Crawling to the side, she vomited for the second time directly onto the head of the shovel. This load had some blood in it. And as she was investigating that, here came the third wave with a little bit more blood than the last, presumably out of courtesy so that next time she wouldn't have to be bent so far over the curved head of the shovel that her upchuck splashed back in her face. When it was all over, she slumped to the side – *not* the side where she'd hurled the first time – and lay on her back, panting, shivering.

Later, who knew how much later other than it had been long enough for the shadows of the higher terrace to stretch out and embrace her, Aggy pushed herself to her feet, stabilizing the ascent with a hand against the rough stone wall of the terrace beside her. Once she felt steady, she did her best to bury her sick, clean off the end of the shovel, clean up her hands, and finish burying the onions. But time, like everything else in the world that didn't sleep in the attic of the kitchens, was against her. So she settled for doing an admittedly rather poor job that at least *looked* like it might have been good. Were the onions well-covered enough to survive the winter? She'd find out next year. And maybe by then, nobody would be able to remember who had serviced this particular terrace. Or maybe she'd be dead. God, she was hungry.

Patience, Ambrose

She returned to the kitchens later than she should have, and so entered to meet a rather cross-looking Ruth hard at work slicing some of the remaining apples into narrow slivers to be dried over the cookstove. I.e., Aggy's job.

"Ruth," Aggy whimpered.

Ruth looked up. Her cross expression straightened out in an insant. "What in…what happened to you?"

Aggy took a few staggering steps into the kitchen and slumped into the sole chair against the far wall. Wooden but comfortably carved, this was not a chair meant for slaves to sit in, but not one Mistress had ever availed herself of either. So for whom was this chair meant? Aggy didn't know. She didn't care. Thus and so: she sat.

"I'm dying," she mumbled into her hands. Under Ruth's questioning, she explained what had happened in the field, how quickly the sickness had taken her. Then, after some tender prodding from Ruth, as well as Molly and Elizabeth as they arrived in the kitchens to help prepare the evening's repast, Aggy went on to detail her experiences over the last few weeks, the wildly fluctuating moods and nausea and hunger and dizziness, her slow but atypical weight gain, the mutiny of her senses.

What she did *not* remind them of, for it had no need of being said out loud, was what had occurred one bleak evening in October, what had preceded these escalating symptoms.

Ruth did her best to wipe the sweetness of the apples from her hands, knowing Aggy would find the scent bitter and rotten. The effort was unsuccessful, but Aggy recognized the intention, and appreciated it.

"Aggy," Ruth whispered to the young woman's pinched, dewy eyes. And that was all. Because here was another thing that had no need of being said aloud.

T E N

BACK IN OCTOBER, DRUMMOND PINCHWIFE HAD TAKEN about twenty-three seconds to climax inside of Aggy. In so doing, he released precisely one hundred and sixteen million sperm into her vagina. This was a sperm count on the lower end of the spectrum, but largely in keeping with that of a man of his age and health. It was also exactly one million times the number of acres of arable land he'd had on his property, prior to constructing his terrible terraces. Make of that what you will. As for the sperm, they had no time to concern themselves over numerical serendipity, let alone their abominable genesis: they were a gaggle of mindless cyclopses with a race to run.

It would be, if you'll excuse the pun, premature to name the sperm that will emerge victorious from this race. Suffice it to say that we would not be disappointed if we should focus our attention on *this* particular runner and say no more about it. Watch it as it collects its bearings amongst the wintry swirl of its competitors for selfhood. Talk about culture shock, talk about fish out of water! But it's worse than just immigrating to a new nation without a visitor's bureau. The liquid in Aggy's vagina, like that of all women, has a low pH content that renders it acidic. Her reading is 3.9, which is on the lower, more acidic end. Maybe that doesn't matter, but who's to say what will and won't be important? Perhaps a higher-pH stock would have advantaged an otherwise formidable challenger to our pro(state)tagonist, were the also-ran not too busy being disintegrated by ladyacid.

Patience, Ambrose

And so our white-tailed hero rushes to face its next challenge, the Ordeal of the Cervix. Aggy is, unbeknownst to all, on this October evening bang in the middle of that brief period of ovulation which sees the Cervix opening its doors and diluting its mucusy membrane into something a bit more swimmable. But the passage to the uterus is far from clear – witness our favored sperm zipping through and between the imposing, fleshy outcroppings of the endocervix, zooming past millions and millions of its loadmates who have been dashed upon the invisible crags of hardened mucus, snagged in the folds of the cervix! Does our lead catch on one of these, potentially condemned to a slow expiration as nothing more than one among millions? Do they find their not-so-footing and push onwards, rejoining the frantic dash towards an uncertain end, and unknown rewards? Does it make it to the uterus, surfing the muscular contractions, hanging ten towards the fallopian tubes?

It must and it does and it has; how else could it be bustling into the rhythmic surging of the cilia, a million and one little hairs heaving the sperm towards the uterus? Hundreds of dome-headed contestants become entangled in their microscopic escort, while those who remain kick into overdrive, wagging their little tails harder and faster than ever before.

At last, they round a corner: we see the egg! Aggy's egg, glistening in the itty bitty distance. Squeezing past the corona radiata, poking at the zona pellucida until the zona says *alright already* and releases enzymes that allow the sperm to burrow inside. From there it's simply a matter of who can wiggle through to the outer membrane of the egg itself. Our sperm vies with but a few others to be the first through. There are some that seem to be making greater headway, it's still anybody's game…and ours is through!

It connects with the egg, fuses with the membrane, and is absorbed. This is where the *real* fun begins.

But…what's this we see, panning off to the right? A second egg, being fertilized by a second sperm that has made the same perilous journey? Gosh, what a reveal!

Does it reduce the value of a life, to go from being the only successful sperm out of one hundred and sixteen million, to being one of two? Or, viewed from the other side, is it more a buy-one-get-one miracle to have two viable eggs ready and waiting?

Hardly matters. A more meaningful question is; what would Aggy have made of this adventure unfolding inside of her, and would she have been somewhat delighted, or wholly mortified, to know that she was going to be delivering not one not three but *two* little bundles come next summer?

Again: hardly mattered. What mattered to the mother herself was the demon that had planted the seed. Master. *Drummond.* Which made the child(ren) what, half-owned, half-owner?

And what if she could choose? What if Aggy could, by some impossible application of will, deliver what she believed to be her only child according to her whim? Would she birth something pale like its father, to be whisked over the ever-vanishing horizon and raised in resplendent ignorance? Or would she choose a child who looked like her, like *her* father, like the only people who had ever demonstrated a capacity for kindness…and so doom the child to all of the agonies which attended such a life?

That was a question that mattered. Whether or not it led to an answer that had any actual practical application, whether the life of her offspring could be as proscribed as she imagined, whether this was the kind of question that would even make sense when this next wave of nausea had passed over her...the answer still matt-ered. This mattered.

This was the first conviction she ever held in the second part of her life, the one that had begun on October 9th under the old hickory in Pleasance Square.

1799

O N E

ON THE FIRST OF JANUARY, AS DRUMMOND WAS LEAVING to attend the regular session of the twenty-second state legislature, one could at least *pretend* to not notice Aggy's pregnancy, as long as one was not Aggy herself. This Drummond did, despite Martha's incessant, astute outbursts.

"Is Aggy receiving more generous portions, do you think?" Martha would ask.

To this, Drummond would invariably reply "Hah?"

"Surely you've noticed her ballooning midsection? Or is this merely my imagination?"

"Huh?"

And so it went, Drummond playing dumb, playing for time, until he could go to Albany and play politics with his pals. A reasonable enough strategy in the short-term, but one with a wheelbarrow of deficiencies in the long term. All of which revealed themselves to Drummond at the exact moment Jesse took up the reins and started the carriage down the winding road from the Estate.

"Fucking heck," Drummond castigated himself. Why hadn't he simply agreed with Martha – yes, now that you mention it, Aggy certainly *does* seem to be expanding at an alarming rate – and then hypothesized on who the father might be? Well, that'd have saved him some grief at least until the baby popped out. Then, he'd just have to hope it skewed swarthy. If it didn't, well, he'd dream up a nameless white rascal and compel Aggy to recall the night said rascal came in through the window. Only…the attic didn't have a window. "Fucking heck and *then* some!"

He slammed his fist against the door of the carriage. From up top, Jesse said "woaaaaaah" to the horses. The carriage slowed.

"Goddamnit!" Drummond swung open the door. "Don't stop!"

"What's the matter, Master?" Jesse inquired.

"Keep going!"

"Did you want to tell me something?"

"NO!"

"Ah, I'm sorry." Jesse sat back in his seat and apologized to the horses too.

Drummond fumed. If only Jesse had lighter skin. This was just the sort of fuck-up for which the man's shoulders had been sculpted. Was it too late to just *sell* Aggy? He feared that it was – Martha had caught the scent of something rotten. An overly enthusiastic attempt to resolve the situation would be as good as admitting guilt. He needed to be craftier than…well, himself.

Problem was, he was just so damn crafty! Every time he tried to come up with something he might not otherwise have come up with, he'd already come up with it.

The terraces of the property's eastern reach rattled past the window. Drummond watched them, his mind rattling right along with them.

T W O

BY THE THIRD WEEK OF JANUARY, THE QUESTION WAS NO longer whether or not Aggy was with child; what Mistress Martha wanted to know now was, who by?

On this, Aggy remained tight-lipped. Not to protect Drummond – that was the *last* thing she cared about. Nor was it for the sake of the unborn child, whom Aggy could not help but resent. It was to protect herself.

If Martha knew that she was about to have a new mulatto half-child-in-law, what might the woman do? Aggy couldn't pretend to know "Mistress" as anything more than a cruel, aloof woman whose passion for apples alternated between spiritual and carnal. Would she try to take the child for herself, and raise it as her own? Would she have the child carted off, to be buried in one of the countless barren plots that had swallowed so many seeds and given so little in return? Would she have Aggy herself placed in such a grave? Or, that most frightening of possibilities, sold down south? Eager though imagination was to innovate on oblivion, Aggy knew perfectly well her nightmares turned on a spit of truth: no good came of naming a father. So Aggy held her peace, confident that her atticmates would do the same. She had less faith in Jesse, fresh back from dropping Drummond in Albany (and more to the point, still understandably nervy about the ride home, as slaves riding solo tended to happen upon those most inclined to make their lives even more horrible than usual), following suit…though it occurred to her that the man might genuinely fail to connect the night he had shepherded Mistress from the plague of fictive bedbugs with Aggy's ever-expanding midsection.

Aggy's friends mercifully indulged her in ignoring the child. The only time anyone had ever made direct reference to it in Aggy's presence was one evening when Molly asked if she might place her hand on Aggy's stomach to feel the child kicking. Aggy growled her demurral, than whispered her apology. But the simple fact was that a secret was best kept between two parties, and from the beginning, this had been stretched between far more. Which left Aggy eager to imagine the sad fact of this life inside her went no further than the three people to whom it was of immediate concern; the mother, the father, and the child. The rotten, half-breed child that Aggy was terrified that she might learn to love.

(What she didn't know, of course, was that she'd get two chances to realize her worst fears. Which just goes to show, there's always something worse. Fear-wise.)

Speaking of worse: the vomiting, the hunger, the chills and sweats, all of these developed a real can-do attitude as January wore out its welcome. This translated to a can't-do disposition on Aggy's part; the number of tasks she could successfully undertake dwindled day by day, until finally she was of little use to anyone who didn't need help flattening a rug.

One day in early February, Mistress made her very first-ever trip up the ladder to the kitchen attic, where Aggy had taken to squirreling herself away for the most unbearable spasms of agony. Miserable as she was, Aggy was distantly amused by the racket Mistress made as she struggled to ascend; it sounded as though this might have been the woman's first time up *any* ladder, full-stop.

Mistress's head popped primly over the lip of the entrance, chin nearly resting on the wooden boards. "What in, I musn't say it, oh, but I must, for I simply cannot overstate the case, what in the *Lord's name* are you doing curled around your own stomach in so selfish a fashion, when I have a coat in need of mending and a regrettable shortage of steady hands possessed of the requisite skill, well?"

"I'm sorry," Aggy lied. She continued more honestly: "I've never felt so much pain. I think the baby might be sick."

"You tell me who the father is, I might fetch you a doctor."

Back to dishonesty: "I don't know, Mistress. Honest." She coughed.

"How should such a thing be possible, hm?"

"It was dark."

Mistress sneezed and shook her head. "And my heavens, is this where you put all the dust you've swept from the floor? Up in this sty? Or *did* sweep, prior to you succumbing to indulgent indolence! Oh!" This last outburst Mistress added as she lost her footing and slipped off the ladder, landing in the kitchen with a mighty crash.

Aggy hadn't had much to smile about in the last few months, so she did her best to remember everything about this moment as it was. Maybe, that way, she could keep *this* smile close at hand.

T   H   R   E   E

DESPITE IT SO FORCEFULLY COMMANDING HER ATTEN-
tion, Aggy remained oblivious to the nitty-gritty of what was
actually happening in her uterus. Which just goes to show, she's
no different from the rest of us.

What was happening was: her two little tummygoblins, tethered to the same placenta by two thick umbilical cords, were well
on their way to becoming people. The hearts had been pumping
away for a few weeks, all their little fingers and toes were capped
with budding nails, they'd even started pissing into the fluid and
sucking their thumbs. No lungs yet, nor eyelashes, nor dreams.
Classic, by-the-book bottom-of-the-second-trimester, in other
words.

But then, there was the other thing.

The two little almost-creatures, finding themselves well met
in the ovum, were loathe to part. That's pure rationalization, of
course, but how else to explain the third umbilical cord, stretching not from placenta to child, but from baby navel to baby
navel? An extra yolk sac, an extra splash of allantois? Sufficient,
perhaps. But somehow lacking.

Whatever the cause, the two children were twice joined,
sharing the placenta of their mother, swapping nutrients with
each other through the crowded bypass of their belly buttons.
An aberration, a fluke, not the sort of thing one expects to see.
But also not the sort of thing one can simply ignore for being
impossible. There they are, dizygotic twins tethered to each

other as surely as their mother. Brother and sister, there, it's been said, the cat's out of the bag. It's a boy, it's a girl. Only one of them can be 'expected.' Aggy will imagine the sex of her child, as mothers sometimes do, becoming more attached to the idea of one than the other. Will her body unconsciously feed that one a little bit more? Will the favored child share that gift with its unexpected sibling? Will they learn, perhaps, to rely on each other more readily than anyone or anything, including their own mother, before their brains have developed much past what even a trout would consider "a bit slow"?

No, of course not. That's impossible.

F   O   U   R

CLIMBING THE LADDER UP TO THE ATTIC WAS BECOMING MORE and more of a challenge by the day. Were it not for the swell of her midsection, Aggy would have sworn the dense little life inside her was anywhere but; the image she couldn't shake was one of a chain cinched around her midsection, some six feet of links leading to a colossal tree stump freshly cut and culled from the Earth. Weight at distance, dragged across a frozen landscape. Or, as the case may be, up a ladder.

She took the final rung of the climb with a heroic grunt, then fell to the floor and crawled across the attic. Much easier, to drag that invisible millstone up after her.

"What are you doin'?" asked Molly's voice.

Aggy started. She froze, then kicked herself; stasis was a poor response to surprise. "I'm…" she considered attempting to explain that her baby felt like dead weight at the end of a lead, but decided that a girl as young as Molly couldn't possibly understand.

Then she remembered what Molly had told her, about being lured out to the field by Drummond…and suddenly it was the thought of seeing comprehension on such a soft face that terrified Aggy.

"I'm just tired," Aggy finally replied. She turned over and lay flat on her back, closing her eyes and sighing.

"Mhm," Molly agreed.

Aggy took another breath, then opened her eyes and turned to glance at Molly. At the young girl sitting alone in the gloom of the attic. "What are you doin' up here?"

Molly shrugged. "I guess I'm j-"

"Hey!" Sally shouted as her head popped up into the attic.

This time, Aggy jumped. Which made her feel a touch better about her previous freeze-up. "Don't shout!" Aggy shouted. "No call for it!"

"I'm surprised," Sally elaborated, a touch of embarrassment in her tone, "that's call for it."

"She's too tired to work," Molly explained on Aggy's behalf, not unsympathetically.

"Too…" Sally narrowed her eyes, then climbed the rest of the way into the attic. "Too tired to work?"

"Yeah," Aggy grunted, flopping back down to the floor. "Tired and sick besides. I'm with *child*, Sally." She lifted her head. "Anyway, what are *you* doin' here?"

"What am I…" Sally pressed a hand to her chest, then pointed it at Aggy. "I saw you headin' this way, and came to see why that should be, at this hour."

"Playin' Overseer, then. Is what you're d-"

"I'm not *playin' Overseer*. I'm..."

Aggy nodded. "You're overseein' my labors."

"I'm..." Sally suppressed a small laugh. "Fine, then." The smile vanished. "I just don't wanna see you put to the lash."

Aggy sucked air through her nostrils, then let her head flop gently to the floor of the attic. "Let her try. No room to swing the damn thing up here."

"Mistress can fetch someone to drag you out," Molly chimed in, solemn beyond what her years ought to have allowed.

The three young women glanced at one another, refusing to dignify the obvious; Drummond could not know of this. Him being off at the legislature made for a slightly less fraught few weeks on the Estate, but Mistress had never shied from issuing him, before he'd had a chance to set his bags down, a full report on what she believed were the slaves' lapses in Protestant work ethic. And oh, did the man ever relish the opportunity to reacquaint himself with corporal punishment. What a release it must have been, after struggling through such a long period of civility.

Aggy opened her mouth, then shook her head. "I..." she tried to push herself upright again.

A bolt of lightning struck the center of her forehead. Her stomach clenched.

The child within her kicked.

Kicked hard enough to shift her whole body.

Aggy settled back to the floor, uttering a sigh that was something more of a sob.

Sally and Molly glanced at one another. Then back to Aggy. In as much as she had the attention to spare for them, she had to imagine they had no idea what they ought to say to her. Which certainly tracked; she had no words for them either. This wasn't something that had happened on the Estate before. A victim of the Master, carrying a child of his to term. There was no precedent.

"Mistress knows you're with child," Molly ventured. "Right?"

"She does," Aggy nodded. "Seen me up here, t-"

"Not suspecting the father," Sally amended, "surely."

Aggy shook her head. "I can't fathom she suspects."

Molly nodded. "Then…she'll have to see how it is you're too tired and sick to work. Having been with child herself."

Sally thought about that. "I hope so," she mumbled. The three sat together in silence for several seconds. Then, all but whispering "I shall try her," Sally turned and descended the ladder.

Aggy did her best to quell the panic rising inside of her. Relying on Mistress for mercy. Oh, what a world.

Yet what else was there to do? Nothing. As ever, she was at the mercy of those ill-disposed towards the same.

She listened to Sally tromp through the kitchens and leave, closing the door gently behind her. Only once Sally was gone did Aggy think to turn to Molly. "So," she asked her, "what *are* you doin' up here?"

"I wanted to keep ya company," Molly replied.

"…but you was up here before I."

Molly considered that, then sighed and said "there was a black bird wouldn't leave me alone. So I'm hidin' 'til he goes away."

Aggy smiled, but said nothing. And the two hid together, until Molly recovered her courage.

F I V E

REMARKABLY, MISTRESS DID TAKE A KIND OF MERCY ON Aggy, leaving her up in the attic and limiting her authoritarian intrusions to standing at the base of the ladder and shouting things like "indulge in theatrics as you must, you prima twice over, both donna and gravida!" The cost of this dispensation, however, was that Aggy's provisions were cut by two-thirds. While undoubtedly a profound nutritional blow, the quality of her experience scarcely changed, *vis a vis* hunger. Her appetite had grown only more and more insatiable, and no amount of food could propitiate whatever gurgling beast lay coiled in her belly. So, sure, what did it matter to her if there were only a third as many sacrifices to cast into the bottomless pit? Starving was starving.

But if her belly went empty (ignoring that it felt so full of baby it was fit to burst at any minute), she had other things to fill her up. Heartwise, awww, in a cute way.

Aggy's friends went out of their way to help her in whatever way they could. Sneaking her a whole baked sweet potato (thank you, Sally), singing her a song (thank you, Ruth), cutting her hair (thank you, Molly, but *careful* with those shears); it was more kindness than Aggy had ever known, stuffed into just a few weeks. More than anything, it terrified her, though she couldn't say why. Until, that was, her erstwhile, not-quite-nemesis Clive came bearing a strip of cured pork belly. Aggy had never even known pork belly was in need of a cure, though one taste was enough to convince her of its wisdom. She could not begin to imagine how Clive might have acquired such a precious comestible. So she thanked him profusely, but as he slipped back down to the kitchen, a rather hopeless explanation for this outpouring of kindness occurred to Aggy. And, having occurred, made a bed of her skull.

This was the untenable generosity extended to the mortally ill. They all, each and every one of them, believed that Aggy was going to die in child birth, if she even made it that far. She was awful sickly as it was, wasn't she? Yes, she was. And so, her friends were doing nothing more than trying to make her as comfortable as they could. Until the end came.

She felt hard tears stinging the corners of her eyes, and she blinked them into oblivion. It hurt, by God, being written off as a dead woman who simply hadn't gotten the bad news yet, by the only people who hadn't already written her off as less-than-human to begin with.

As the days passed, Mistress' eruptions from the bottom of the ladder grew both more common and more voluble; it wasn't long before she had taken to making increasingly specific (and so, transparently idle) threats, nattering about the going price for a strong child these days. Strangely enough, this gave the impression that Martha was perhaps the only person on the property who actually believed Aggy was going to carry the child to term. Odd to say, but Aggy found this horribly touching. In precisely the same way as a parapalegic must welcome the return of sensation below the waist, even if the occasion for feeling was being trod upon by a dressage horse.

So yeah, that hurt. But Aggy had borne more pain than this. *This* was all but a negligible garnish on the porridge of torment that was her life at present. Take food from the hungry, heap misery upon the suffering, what difference did it make to her? She could handle it. Always had.

And always will, she decided.

S I X

OK, PERHAPS SHE'D SPOKEN TOO SOON: HERE WAS AN imposition she hadn't the fortitude to bear.

"Folks are sayin' I'm the father," the top of Jesse's head informed Aggy from the entrance to the attic.

This roused Aggy from her torpor as nothing else had. "What?" She pushed up onto her elbows. "Who's sayin' that?"

The rest of Jesse's face slid up into view. "All kinds of folks."

"...who's sa-"

"Mistress told me she suspected it," Jesse interrupted belchingly, "yes."

"Well," Aggy sighed, knowing the answer before the question had been asked, "did you tell her it wasn't you?"

"After my own fashion, I suppose."

Aggy tilted her chin just a touch towards the floor.

"No," Jesse amended, "I did not."

Aggy tried to sit up more fully, but hadn't the strength. "Well," she grunted from near-prostration, "you be sure she doesn't rope you into the middle of this." The order curdled on her tongue; Drummond's deed had been possible, in no small part, thanks to Jesse's bedbug misdirection. Which already put him squarely in the middle. Still, Aggy believed even a man as obsequious as Jesse would have dabbled with defiance, had he known what the consequences of his actions would be.

"Of course not," Jesse replied. He sighed, then glared intently at his left elbow. "Only…"

"…" Aggy said to fill the silence.

"…" Jesse replied.

"…only what?"

"Only," Jesse burped, "I had to make sure."

"…you had to make sure of what?"

"That it wasn't me in the middle of this."

Oh, dear. Aggy was hardly in the proper headspace, or *any*-space, to be consoling someone. Still, she could take a run at it: "you didn't know," she assured him, softly as she could.

"Oh Lord," Jesse gasped, "I knew it!" He curled up into himself, slamming his forehead into his waiting palms. "I can't fully tell you how sorry am I, Aggy!"

"No way he could've told you what he meant to do," Aggy cooed. "I know you wouldn't have done it, if ya'd known."

"Huh?" Jesse asked, lifting his snot-glazed grimace from his hands. "Who told me to what?"

"Drumm-"

Urp.

Aggy sighed. "Master."

"What'd he tell me?"

"About the bedbugs."

"What bedbugs?"

"The…in Mistress' bed. The bedbugs."

Jesse glanced around the attic, as though for a clue. "What's the gotta do with…huh?"

"You…" Aggy blinked hard, a woman seeking to banish a mirage. "You took her off the Estate that night. Sayin' bedbugs."

"Sayin'…what night?"

"The night…" Aggy shook her head. "What are you talkin' about?"

"How I put you in a family way. *Bedbugs,*" Jesse enunciated, implying a question without properly asking one.

"…" Aggy replied.

"I am so sorry," he reiterated, inching closer to her, manifestly struggling not to let the pain of dragging himself across the bare planks of the attic floor show on his face.

"…" Aggy emphasized.

"I ain't sure I'm fit to be a dad, only I'll tr-"

"*Jesse.*"

He halted, sighing in relief. "Yeah?"

Aggy felt it so imperative that she wave her arms in front of her face that she forgot to compensate for the loss of her elbow bolsters. She crashed down onto her back. Jesse launched himself to her side before Aggy had finished her first little bounce off the floorboards sodden by her perspiration.

"I just figure I oughta tell you," Jesse explained to her as he cupped her hands in his, "that I've always been a little sweet on ya. I'm just some kinda shy, but, well, I never thought I'd be gettin' ya in a family way!"

"Listen to me," Aggy said as softly as she could, shifting her hands so that hers now cradled his, "you did not get me pregnant."

"But…" Jesse studied his own hands, as though checking his mental math. "But I'm sweet on ya."

Aggy shook her head. "Who taught you about babymakin'?"

"Master did."

"And what'd he tell ya?"

"A man's sweet on a lady, so an angel does a miracle in her

belly."

Aggy coughed softly. "…do you, m-*hm*, ah…do you know what sex is?"

"Sin, ain't it?"

Aggy took a deep breath, closed her eyes, and extricated herself from the situation the only way she knew how:

"Do you know why Drummond al-"

"Urp."

"-ways has you ferrying Mistress off the property for reasons that only get you yelled at?"

"Because he tells me to?"

"That's not a reason."

Jesse shrugged.

"Well," Aggy informed him, "what happens when you're off is the thing makes for a baby some months later."

Jesse cocked his head slightly. "I don't see what you mean."

So, to the lasting displeasure of them both, she elaborated.

S E V E N

BY THE TIME FEBRUARY HAD SLIPPED INTO MARCH, AGGY would have traded anything in the world to feel mere pain again.

Aggy had been buried alive, she didn't think she had been or maybe she'd dreamt it, but then how could she feel the clods of dirt dropping onto her head, one after another after another? Lucidity would return to her like a relapse, plunging her into a fear so all-consuming it seemed a physical presence in the room with her, a dreadful swine as black and lonely as midnight, staring at her with beady little eyes that had seen the deaths of stars and found them uninspiring, uninspired. Martha would take her baby from her. Her boy. Ambrose, she would call him. Where had that name come from? There was no way to know, no way to find out, from down here in the bottom of a grave, being buried buried buried

Alive. Up. Awake. She was clear. Just not for long. Down there, that was where the pain lived. Up here was fear. Fear above, pain below, her between. This was no way to live. This was not living. This was self-inflicted. This was her fault. She had let this happen. She had made this happen. It was her fault. Fear above, pain

Below. Dirt grinding between her teeth, earthworms crawling through her hair, clump another shovelful, her chest collapsing, clump soil pouring into her ears and burying her brain, clump clump cl

Up. This was Hell. She had created it. How could there be this much suffering in the world? How had it all fallen upon her? Fear above pain below. She could not stop the pain. The pain had burrowed into her hollowed her out made a nest had a baby named Ambrose he was a sweet boy she would lose him. Ambrose. It was a beautiful name. Where had it come from? She didn't know. All she knew was that she didn't want to lose him. That was the fear. That she would love him. Sorry, *lose* him. Fear above. That was the fear? Then the fear was hers. She didn't have to be

Low. Cl. Too much dirt atop. Cl. What was a little more dirt less food more hurt more hurt more hurt she couldn't take it. She had to. She couldn't. Something poking her back. Fingers. Cold fingers. Hands from even lower, burrowing up and grabbing. Pulling. Pulling her further down. No. Please. Please.

Please. Anything. Just make them stop. Make them go

Above. Who cared. What mattered. Why fight. Why struggle. It happens with you. Someone tells Mistress. Martha. She takes your Ambrose. Master's Ambrose. Drummond. Bastard. All without you. Happens to you. Not with you. Not for you. Ha. Never for you. So let him go. No Ambrose, no fear. Let them have him. Martha. Drummond. Death. Whoever. Let Ambrose be an it again. Let them have it. Let her be without fear. Let her have nothing above. Let have her respite from

Below.

E I G H T

INSIDE. THE MID-SECTION, TO BE SPECIFIC. THE WOMB with a view. When last we left our amnionauts, they had taken the small, impossible step of cinching themselves together, one to the other, by way of a second umbilicus. How did this happen? What made them so special, that they should be transgressing natural laws before they'd even worked out how to open both eyes at once?

One might as well ask the question of the two sperm who beat out millions of other applicants to get the gig. What made these two particular sperm so special? And as long as we're navel-gazing, what made this particular species so special, or this particular planet, this galaxy, this universe?

Silly question, right? Because the mere act of posing it is a performance of the answer.

But leave the cosmos to one side and zoom aaaaaaall the way back in to Aggy's tummy. Something else is happening. If you had a lot of questions before, hoo boy, just you wait.

Aggy's body, at this stage only intermittently in contact with her mind, has perhaps taken it upon itself to eliminate the cause of her fear. Or maybe Aggy herself has performed a kind of psychoscopic surgery. Or maybe it was simply a matter of one mostly-formed foot kicking a bit too hard against the edge of its world. Whatever the cause, the effect remains: the umbilical cord which had been connecting the twins to their mother is now floating freely in the nutrient soup. The plug has been pulled, the kibosh has been put, the fate has been sealed. So long Ambrose, goodbye Untitled Sister, we hardly knew ye.

But not so fast. The placenta may have unburdened itself of the two babies, but what did they need that squishy little diva for anyway? They'd gotten about all they needed from it, dried the damn thing out. No, they couldn't be kicked out – they were leaving of their own accord! The world was *full* of placentas, it only stood to reason. They'd find another in good time. And until then, they had each other.

What sort of fetal attraction was this? Twins, tethered together but floating free in the maternal airlock, awaiting explosive decompression? Heading into their third trimester with only the other to feed them? A recipe for disaster, surely. If the twins survive at all, their lives will no doubt have more in common with the farm's produce than the people who tend it. Anything else would be, quite simply, impossible.

As before, our enceinte interlude concludes with an abstract premonition: not so much, with the herbaceous babies. The impossible will suffice, as before. And why not? Why should one content oneself with just a single impossibility? Why not push at any boundary one finds? Pliability in one is an aberration. Two?

That looks a bit more like a pattern.

N I N E

APRIL FOURTH WAS A DAY OF UPS AND DOWN, ABOVES and belows. The aboves, curiously, were not so fraught with terror as they had once been, the belows not quite so deep. Perhaps it was simply the reassurance of Martha failing to rattle the ladder with threats and promises, which of course meant that word of her husband's infidelity had failed to reach her, in which case Martha might not bother taking the child away. Perhaps, perhaps…only no, Aggy could dismiss that out of hand. This eerie equanimity was something more fundamental than that. It was…solitude. Despite the continued swelling of her midsection, Aggy had lost any sense of a life inside of her. This could well have signaled that she and her child had finally found concord…but she didn't believe that was the case. There was such an absence to her days, now. A pair of glassy little eyes had been staring over her shoulder for months now, judging her, damning her…now gone, withdrawn to regions and for reasons unknown.

Had the child sensed that never again would it know comfort as it now did? Or had the comforts never been worth sticking around for in the first place? Maybe the child had died of malnourishment. That certainly seemed plausible; Aggy's appetite was beginning to return to her, as was the satisfaction she derived from her rations, now reduced once again by half. Even with less food than before (her friends didn't have quite as much to share now that they were returning to the fields and terraces;

they needed that food, and Aggy was happy to let them have it), and even with less life inside of her, Aggy felt more full than she had in quite a long time.

This was relief, she realized. She didn't want the baby. Only no, that didn't fully capture it; had the baby been born and spirited away, Aggy would have shattered on the spot. No, what she preferred, what she had always wanted but never had the courage to actively wish for, was a stillbirth. For what kind of a life could a mulatto child have? What did it have to look forward to? Desperate sips of air in a lifetime of drowning? No. This was not something into which to deliver a life. This was not a world in which one could be said to live at all.

Had she willed herself into a miscarriage? Horrible though that was to countenance, the thought was, yes, a relief. Poor child. Poor, unhappy child. Aggy couldn't help but envy the creature its misfortune.

Although, she supposed it didn't quite count as misfortune, if it had been she to inflict it upon th-

A tug from the navel.

Aggy flinched. Looked down at her stomach.

Not a tug from without.

That had been a nudge. From within.

A kick.

No.

Aggy glanced down at her stomach, lifting the thin hopsack for a view of naked flesh. She glared at her own form, daring the creature within to stir. Praying that it wouldn't. Knowing, in an instant of dreadful uncertainty, that it would.

Another kick.

And unless Aggy was very much mistaken…she had seen the

skin of her belly bulge, ever so slightly.

Hell and damnation! Alive! The alien was still alive! God, but if she were not so incapacitated (the agony had abated, yes, but not *vanished),* she might well have tried to terminate the pregnancy herself. For the child's sake. Why not, when the horrors of this life so greatly outweighed the pleasures?

She glanced over at the edge of the attic's floorboards, where the ladder poked up through that square aperture. It was so small, she wasn't certain if her stomach could fit through.

It was only in weighing the idea that Aggy was aware of having had it at all. But yes…what better way to spare the child its suffering, than by cutting it off at the pass, as it were? And what a wonderful booby prize, if her own unhappy tale should be brought to a close at the same instant…

Using the blanket beneath her back as a runner, Aggy bent her right knee and reoriented herself. So her shoulders and head were pointing straight at the hole. This would be the way to do it. She could just scoot herself over there, watch the termite-nibbled beams of the ceiling pass over her like good fortune, and wait for the drop. She wouldn't see it coming. It would just happen, and then it would be over. Above or below, she would go to one and stay there. And that seemed easier, not having to hope for the other, knowing there was finally no hope for anything else.

Bending both knees now, she planted her feet flat on the floor and pushed.

Her stomach lifted. The back of her head levered down against the wood. Those were the only parts of her that moved.

Some runner the blanket was. Aggy put her feet back down, took a deep breath, and started shimmying towards the drop, wriggling like a worm from

Down. The pain held her down but Aggy was on a mission now, she had something to work towards. The final drop. And she wouldn't be able to drop if she couldn't get

Up. Gasping for air, wiping sweat from her face, cursing the young Drummond devouring her from the inside out, she shimmied shimmied shimmied until she felt the rough-hewn wood beneath her head fall away.

The hole. She was at the hole. But she had not fallen through. Its edge dug into the meat below her neck.

It had not happened. It was not over.

There was no deliberation. In a single moment, she knew: she couldn't go through with this.

She'd only had time to get three or four good sobs in before she heard Ruth asking, "Heavens Aggy, is it time?"

"No," Aggy managed between heaves.

"Then what are you doing?"

"I don't know!"

"Did you hear?"

Aggy rolled onto her right shoulder and craned her neck, getting a look straight down into the kitchens, onto Ruth's upturned face. So this was what it felt like to be God – looking down, the power of life and death in your hand. Even if it was only hers, and the baby's. Even if, in truth, she lacked the courage to have much of a grip on death.

"Hear what?" she asked.

Ruth narrowed her eyes at Aggy for a moment, scanning the scene, wondering why else Aggy would have dragged herself to the drop like this…but mercifully, she let the moment pass. "Master's back, and he's got somethin' to tell us seems really kinda, uh, somethin'. He wants to see us all at the Estate about an hour hence."

"Does he know I'm, um…"

Ruth nodded. "He told us *everybody*. I mentioned you were shut up in the attic, and he leaned on the word."

Everybody. Aggy's stomach dropped. Oh, how she envied it.

T E N

IT WAS HARD WORK, GETTING AGGY OUT OF THE ATTIC. Clive and Jesse were fetched from the Estate, the latter refusing to come until he received verbal permission from Martha to do so (there was certainly a joke in that, but Aggy wasn't in the mood to find it). They climbed up the ladder, each taking a shoulder and holding on as Aggy swung her legs over the drop. From the kitchen, Ruth helped guide each foot to the next rung of the ladder, using her body as a means of support when Aggy had made it further down than the men up top could keep hold from above. At that point, Sally joined Ruth in spotting the end of Aggy's descent.

The women stepped back, then rushed forward as Aggy went tilting backwards. Her legs had wasted away from disuse, her back gone limp. The tears so recently abandoned were quickly recovered; it hadn't even occurred to Aggy that there would be a physical cost to her seclusion. No time to wallow, though; she'd have to take her tears to go. Clive ducked under one of her arms, Jesse under the other, and then they were off, Aggy's legs dangling between her escorts.

Ruth swung the door open, and by golly the hits just kept on coming. Sheltered from the elements for going on four months, Aggy had forgotten just how aggressive the natural world could be. Bugs buzzing birds screaming wind howling buds exploding clouds threatening and over it all the sun burning blazing blinding. A moan escaped her. Either nobody heard it, or they were all too tactful to acknowledge having heard it.

So nobody heard it, then.

E L E V E N

ALL HANDS GATHERED AT THE BASE OF THE STEPS. AGGY viewed these small wooden mockeries of the field's terraces with trepidation; the memory of her last ascent, and what had awaited her at the top, remained a memory with blood on its fangs. Should she be beckoned up them yet again, the physical challenge of heaving her parturient bulk would be the least of her obstacles.

Drummond was nowhere to be seen on the porch, presumably in the service of making a grand entrance once his audience had fully assembled. Aggy scanned the windows, looking for a pink piggy face peeking out from behind a curtain. She didn't see one, but that didn't mean there wasn't one to see.

She was rather glad to be balanced between two men of middling strength. Each, she hoped, would chalk her trembling up to the weakness of the other. Because she *was* trembling, oh yes she was.

For there was only one piece of news momentous enough to warrant such a formal, all-hands announcement: Drummond intended to declare his paternity. What did this mean? It obviously wouldn't come as much of a shock to anybody except Martha, who was likewise absent from view. Wouldn't it be a humiliation to her? What would she do then? What would Drummond do? Why in God's name was he doing this? What did he stand to gain? She prayed that he would only take the child from her, leave her be, leave her *here*. Anything, as long as he didn't send her south.

And then she remembered Job. So she stopped praying.

First-story window on the far left: a curtain rustled. Oink oink.

The front door swung open. Drummond emerged, looking a bit more heavyset and a whole lot paler…but otherwise precisely as he had appeared in Aggy's nightmares almost every night this year. If anything, the slab of his cap-shadowed forehead seemed to have dug itself a few new little divots, the better to cast a disapproving gloom. Disapproval of what? Why, whatever he happened to be looking at in any given moment. Of course.

He clutched the lapels of his off-cream jacket; both the fidget and the flogger were new affectations. Picked up from his well-to-do buddies on the legislature, perhaps? Whatever this new look was intended to be, Aggy was fairly sure he was doing it wrong. Drummond looked like nothing so much as someone who had thrown on the whitest items of clothing he had, regardless of how well their hues suited one another, and sauntered down to the courthouse in the hopes of selling live chickens to the departing barristers.

Drummond's grey little fists balled up right at his clavicle, like somebody had just tucked him in for bed. Thusly cuddled, he took a moment to survey his very literally captive audience, slowly tracking across each of them in turn. It wasn't until he'd turned towards Aggy that she clocked the expression on his face.

Patience, Ambrose

Furrowed brow, pursed lips, drawn jaw. Frustration. Drummond was frustrated.

That didn't bode well. Perhaps he was making this announcement because Martha *had* found out, and sought to mitigate her own embarrassment by making a spectacle of her spite? Who's going to be looking at the jilted woman, after all, when there's a perfectly good lynching happening just over yonder?

"You ok?" Clive whispered from beside her.

Aggy didn't ask what he meant. She knew. Her trembling was getting even worse.

"Yea, it is the twenty-second state legislature that has lately concluded," Drummond began without ceremony, "and, um… well, put it this way, when you hear tell of the Bank of the Manhattan Company, you remember that *I* was instrumental in the chartering of the same. This is a limited salve, but one which I must nonetheless apply to a most grievous wound our state has suffered."

He took a deep breath, and then shocked them all by sitting down on the top step and removing his cocked felt hat.

A few of the slaves, Aggy included, gasped. It wasn't so much the action as his demeanor; this was as casual as anyone had ever seen Drummond, and more casual than most imagined him capable of being.

"Terrible news out of Albany, I'm afraid to report," he continued, "though I admit it may not find such unfavorable ears amongst yourselves, particularly upon first hearing, I will elucidate the reasons this news bears ill for us all immediately after relaying said news to you. So I will remind you to contain yourselves, knowing full well such feats of impulse control are inimical to your savage nature."

Aggy had stopped trembling; she felt what little attention she was managing to muster slingshotting between her ears and the very center of her brain. What the hell was he talking about? That this was *not* about his having sired a child with Aggy was clear. Alright, she was safe, at least on that count. So what the hell *was* this about?

"A bill was passed," Drummond finally resumed, phrasing his announcement with delicate, handwashing precision, "which goes by the name…" he sighed and rolled his eyes and slapped his hat and waved it and put it on his head and took it off and sighed again and stomped his feet and cracked his neck and tried to take his hat off again but found it still and already in his hand and so he put it back on his head and so this time succeeded in taking it off again and sighed again and stomped his feet again and sighed again and said "it's a gradual emancipation act."

To this there were no gasps or shouts or laughter or tears. There was only listening. Eye-popping, neck-stretching, jaw-dropping kinds of listening. Listening so loud you could hardly hear a damn thing over it.

"What this means for *you*," Drummond continued, "is that you are legally no longer slaves." He paused, as though expecting a whooping ruckus, expecting them to strip naked and run howling into the woods, expecting them to do something other than sear him with their fulminant attention. Finally he resumed: "You are not slaves…you are indentured servants."

Astonishingly enough, it was Jesse who spoke up first. "What's the difference?" he asked.

Drummond smiled. "*Indentured servant* takes longer to say." The lupine grin burned off quickly. "That's a semantic parsing I'm all too happy to oblige. Where I take umbrage with the motion, which I must unfortunately call a bill, is, um, well, the emancipation part." He paused, swallowed, and looked at his hat. "Children born on or after the fourth of July this year shall be released from indenture on their twenty-eighty birthday. Twenty-fifth, if they should be a girl."

Aggy felt like she was going back Below again. She shook her head and bit her lip, fighting to stay Above.

"Upon the lapsing of that indenture…" Drummond sighed. "They will be free."

Whatever little knuckle of brainpower had been slamming around Aggy's skull lost its mojo. Her jaw flapped open, but no sound emerged.

Drummond's pinched little mouth also gawped open. He left it in a loose 'O' for a moment, as his eyes drifted slowly over his chattel.

They fell upon Aggy…except, no. They didn't. They slid right over her. As though she were just one face among many. As though the words Drummond had just spoken applied to her in precisely the same way they applied to everyone else: not at all.

It didn't register to Aggy as an especially willfull action, or a message meant for only her. Drummond was simply…allowing his eyes to drift over his chattel.

He had forgotten about her, Aggy realized. He had completely forgotten.

Without another word, Drummond heaved himself to his feet, turned around, and walked back into the house, slamming the door behind him.

Aggy wanted to collapse. She wanted so desperately to fall, to be low, to be plunged into the Earth itself. But for once, the ground was just too far away.

T W E L V E

IT HAD BEEN...FALL? EARLY WINTER? AGGY COULDN'T recall the date of conception, which dismayed her twice over. Once because it made it nearly impossible to predict when her child might come due. Twice because it meant she'd failed to remember the date of her father's hanging.

But why would she? What use were dates to her? Every day was, at bottom, identical: wake up and do what the Pinchwifes tell you to do. She'd internalized the broad annual rhythms of reap and sow, yes, but ultimately the decision of when to perform any given task in that process fell to someone else. There was no percentage in fretting over days and dates, and until now she'd never even imagined that might change.

In a way, she supposed, it hadn't. Ruth assured her that most babies are born around nine months after conception. But that was just an approximation, and babies were rarely considerate enough to consult Mommy about the most auspicious time to pop out and say hello. When it was time, it would be time. So even if Aggy knew exactly when Drummond had raped her, and could project nine months out to see if the approximate delivery date fell before or after July fourth...well, so what? It wasn't as though she could wait until the baby's head slithered out, perhaps in late June, then persuade it to crawl back inside and just take it easy for another week or two. The baby would mark the time of its arrival, and would not be gainsaid.

If only one could make a preemie see reason! What greater, more forceful case could there be for a fetal filibuster than freedom? How absurd it was, that emancipation should ultimately fall to an accident of birth, whether or not one was born before or after an arbitrary date?

(Not arbitrary, Aggy later found out from Jesse. When he told her what the fourth of July meant for the country as a whole, the irony of it all made her dizzy.)

Yet how could she fail to fret over anything that offered liberation for her bloodline? Or, she thought in her lowest moments back up in the attic, thinking of her father swinging from an old hickory tree, *from* her bloodline?

In her nightmares, she watched Drummond's gaze pass swiftly over her. A searing light in the darkness. Except, no, it was precisely the opposite: a beam of shadow cutting through a cloudless day.

He had forgotten. And why *would* he remember? Aggy had simply been one more victim joining the many. The damned fool had likely convinced himself the child would die inside of her, and so allowed himself to forget.

Oh, how she wished she could still feel her child. It was alive, that she knew for a fact…but since that night in the attic, she could no longer *feel* it. She just hoped it could still feel her. That it wasn't too late.

Hold on, she whispered to her child every morning and every night. Hold on. Independence day is coming for those it forgot the first time around. If only you can hold on. I'm sorry that I let you go, I'm not as strong as you have to be. Ambrose. My sweet Ambrose. Have patience.

Hold on.

Jud Widing

T H I R T E E N

A LITTLE LATE FOR THAT, OF COURSE. THE LITTLE BUN-dles weren't so little anymore: six odd pounds and growing. Shorn from their mother, from the placenta they had been sharing, Ambrose and Sister (Working Title) had only seemed to benefit from their unbreakable, umbilical relationship. Their central nervous systems had just about finished laying wire. The lungs had inflated, ready to get pumping. And most importantly, their brains had developed a little something extra. No new lobes or cortices, nothing quite so dramatic. Just a third and final impossibility, to cap off the fat-chance trilogy of their gestation.

Push in through their teeny tiny ear, wend down the external auditory canal, punch through the tympanic membrane, swirl around the cochlea, and proceed into the auditory cortex. From there we have an entire brain to play in, to explore, to be dazzled by! What a miraculous little machine, capable of such beauty, such power, such unspeakable cruelty. A tool like any other, then, unique only in being both engine and operator. But that's not why we're here. We're here for this spot right *here*, at the top of the head and a little ways back. The parietal lobe, the bit that takes disparate sensory inputs and weaves them into a coherent, navigable experience. Looks pink and squishy like any other part of the brain, yes, this is true. And the boundaries between lobes aren't so well-defined as colored diagrams might have you believe. This is also true.

But a third truth, and a third impossibility, is this extra-wrinkly tonsure of the kiddies' parietal lobes, where the folds are deeper and more tightly packed than they tend to be in other humans. Nothing dramatic, nothing worthy of a swelling orchestra or act break. Just a few extra wrinkles, common to the early term twins, and likewise unique. Ho-hum, move along, nothing of note to see here.

How all things grand and massive begin, in other words.

F O U R T E E N

JUNE WAS A SWEAT-DRENCHED BLUR OF ANXIETY AND confusion. Aggy wanted Ambrose to wait, to be born after the fourth of July. Now she wanted him *out*, get *out* of there you one-hundred pound intruder! Now she wanted him dead, she couldn't possibly condemn him to a life of servitude because there was no *way* he could hold on, she could feel him pounding on the lining of her uterus with his little fists, maybe grey like Drummond's, shrieking let me *out* let me *out*. Now *she* wanted to be dead. Now she needed to live to see him born after the fourth, and then she could die. Now she needed to keep her son, to raise him as her own even if she could never be free as he could, would never be. Now she needed him to wait. Have patience. Hold on.

The pain, the trips to Below, had grown less generalized. Gone were the funereal fugues, the days passed at the bottom of a hole. In their place were sharp abdominal pains, muscle spasms in her once-again decommissioned legs, sores on her back. More quotidian agonies, ones she found unbearable one day, a blessed distraction the next.

Of a less variable nature was her loneliness; as work on the farm grew more ample and arduous, her friends, yes they were all her friends, even Clive, even Jesse, she believed it, her friends had little to no time to come up and visit her. When they did, the muggy gloom of the attic inevitably put them to sleep. Elizabeth had a gift for succumbing to slumber in the middle of a sentence, and picking up right where she left off upon waking. This was the whole of Aggy's amusement now. Even that most cherished memory of Mistress taking her tumble from the ladder had ceased to divert; all withered in a deep shade. Ache was too soft a word. As was any other.

Drummond had, it seemed, still not managed to recall the fact that the very pregnant slave wasting away above his kitchens was on the threshold of delivering his issue. Not once did the bastard come to see her. She had never expected him to, even if he had remembered; it would have been so contrary to his entire disposition, there had never been a chance in hell, and even if there had, she'd have spat in his eye had he dared to show it…yet and still, despite everything stacked against his making any attempt to check in on Aggy, his failure to do so surprised her. He'd not made even a token effort to offer the Estate as a venue for the birth of his child…not that she'd have been able to go in her condition. Not that she would have, were she able. Just…well, leave it. She would have Ambrose in this attic.

Which meant if she died in childbirth up here…she would already have seen the sky, the horizon, for the very last time. Without having known it.

The thought wasn't entirely disturbing.

Of course, it was equally possible that Drummond had very *much* remembered the role he had played in putting Aggy up in the attic. Just as it was possible he had gotten wind of just how common was the knowledge of the child's paternity. Could that explain his keeping such distance between them? Aggy didn't know, no longer cared to speculate. She was truly alone in this endeavor. Not even her child was on her side, not entirely – she couldn't explain why she felt this, why she *knew* this, but she did. And she couldn't blame him – she had denied him her love, only to force it once more upon him, so many times now. For reasons entirely uncoupled from any person the boy could ever grow up to be. And he'd not even been born! What right did she have, pretending to motherhood? She wanted them to take the child from her, let him be free elsewhere. She wanted to raise the child, give him a chance to make different mistakes than her own father had made. She wanted him to hold on.

She wanted this to be over.

FIFTEEN

AGGY SCARCELY HAD A CHANCE TO SPEAK WITH HER friends when they came in for the evening – most were asleep before they'd fully squeezed in amongst one another.

And yet here they were, waking her up in the middle of the night.

"Hruh?" Aggy wondered as she felt a firm hand giving her shoulder a hard time.

In the dark, she saw her fellow lodgers all standing, hunched beneath the low ceiling, shifting their weight from foot to foot. Odd. People didn't usually stand in here. The ceiling was so very low, after all.

They were whispering to each other, but Aggy couldn't make

out what they were saying. She could hear bare feet slapping frantically against the floor of the kitchen below. Someone running away.

"Aggy," cooed the Ruth-shaped shadow, "it's happening."

"Hruh?!" Collecting herself, Aggy felt the straw beneath her: it was matted, wet. "I pissed myself?"

The shadows chuckled uneasily. Their whispering made it difficult to tell one voice from another.

"It's not pee."

"Your water broke."

"The baby's coming."

"Sally went to fetch Master."

"It's happening." That was Ruth again.

Aggy's first thought was *no it's not*. It couldn't be. Despite her having been pregnant for what felt like an eternity, it was impossible that she was going to give birth tonight. She wasn't the type of person to give birth. She hadn't at any point in her previous fifteen years…*sixteen*, she realized with a start. She'd been born in April. As she was bobbing up down above below, she'd grown another year older. And yet, she felt no different. Numbers and dates, all things meaningless. Except for when they weren't.

She was having her baby. Ambrose was coming. Tonight. *Now.*

"What day is it?" she asked the room.

The room was silent. Just the creaking of wood, the hush of the wind. Which was her answer. There was no way they weren't all acutely aware of what she was asking. Not answering was answering: it was not the fourth of July.

"Um…" a voice that sounded like Sally's, but couldn't have been because she was off fetching Master for some goddamned reason, said, "I'm really sorry."

Aggy sighed. Her eyes had adjusted to the darkness enough to make out Ruth's face as she knelt down and leaned in.

"It's the third, Aggy," Ruth told her. "It's the third of July."

"…" Aggy felt her jaw clenching so tightly her entire skull seemed to be collapsing. "Late or early?"

"Late," Ruth whispered.

"…" Aggy replied. "Oh my God. Oh *God*," she cried, crunching over her condemned child, into something approaching an upright seat. Oh, if only she could keep leaning forward, crushing the life within her, before it suffered the indignity of existence. The third of July! And late, at that! Hours shy of freedom! "No!" Aggy shrieked. "No no no! That's not fair!"

"Relaaaaaax," Ruth sighed. "Just take it easy. We can do this. *You* can do this."

"What time is it?" Aggy demanded. "It is near midnight? He can hold on! Ambrose can hold on!"

A ball of light rose from the kitchen. A candle, born by Drummond. Seeing the father of her child, her *owner*, only strengthened Aggy's resolve. She would hold on. Ambrose would hold on. He would wait, be patient, and so be free.

If her child could be free, that would be enough for Aggy.

"Someone's birthin' up here?" Drummond demanded. He lifted the candle into the attic, squinted at Aggy…and looked to come within a hair's breadth of passing out.

That was it, right there. The moment Drummond remembered what he'd done. Or, at the very least, came to recognize the consequences of it.

"Drummond!" she screamed, drawing sharp intakes of breath around the room. Master Pinchwife had always been quite clear, he never wanted to hear a slave refer to him by his first name.

Yet he gave no indication of finding this shocking. He was already as shocked as he could manage, it seemed, standing on the ladder, only half his body in the attic proper, staring at Aggy as though she were sprouting wings.

"Drummond," she growled, "what time is it?!"

More mute ogling. Aggy couldn't help but wonder if the ogre had ever seen a child delivered before. Perhaps he'd excused himself for the duration of Martha's labor. For the arrival of the child he *more or less* counted as his own.

And yet, here he was. Just staring.

Aggy choked on her own saliva, and coughed. "What time is it, you stupid bastard?!"

That got a reaction, from Drummond as well as the assembled. Aggy knew she would regret saying that, but at the moment, she didn't care. And incredibly…Drummond seemed to understand this. Without much more than a dirty look, he fished a silver hunter pocket watch from the folds of his waistcoat. "Quarter to ten," he monotoned. Thick as he was, he, too, knew precisely why Aggy was asking.

"You keep that clock near at hand!" She screamed as the hoof of a bible-black mare punched through her stomach. Ruth told her to breathe and push, breathe and push. Aggy couldn't decide which she wanted to do less.

S I X T E E N

ALL HANDS ON DECK, ALL HANDS ON DECK, THIS IS *NOT* a drill.

Patience, Ambrose

The twins could feel that something was expected of them, something for which they had been preparing for their entire kinda-lives, something for which they were wholly unprepared. Something was pulling them, pushing them, wanted them *out*, wanted them to *stay*. In the face of contradictory instructions, waiting seemed the safest course. And so they kicked back and relaxed, lolling in the…say, where was their wonderful bath going?

A beam of what the hell was that it was like what they saw flickering outside their bubble world sometimes but now it was cutting through let's call it *light*, who invited light here, both twins told the other that *they* certainly hadn't, this was their clubhouse and they'd always preferred to keep the lights *off*, only it had found a way in and was tearing itself an entrance, further and further open with each passing second, which wasn't how things were done around here, not in the least, and was this how things were going to be now? Ambrose and TBD had always consulted each other on every decision, where they would float and when, whose limbs would go where, and in each case they had always reached effortless agreement. But now there was a new variable, a new player in the game, *light*, and now what the hell else was this racket? Something that was like light but for the ears, loud shrill yodely warbling let's call it screaming *noise*. Two intruders! How could they keep all manner of things in perfect balance, when there were so many new things being thrown haphazardly into their world? This was how things were going to be now, huh?

They were just undertaking an umbilical back-and-forth on the matter when the light and sound and heat and stink and awful ate Ambrose alive.

SEVENTEEN

"IT'S A BOY!" RUTH LAUGHED.

"I know," Aggy averred, her head heavier than her neck could manage. Her mouth hung open as she ground the back of her skull into the straw. "Ambrose, his name is Ambrose."

"Ambrose," Ruth repeated approvingly. "You did it Aggy! Ambrose is alive!" She tried to show the twitching, mewling infant to Aggy, but the mother wasn't in a celebratory mood. Not yet.

"What time is it?!" she snarled at Drummond, who had not moved from his spot halfway up the ladder. "What time is it, and don't you lie to me!"

Drummond flattened his lips and pulled out the watch. He cracked open the silver face, its convoluted filigree both clutching for and swatting away the candlelight. Slowly, terribly, his lips curled into a malign crescent. Points up.

Aggy shrieked so loudly, the gurgling Ambrose fell still. It was a long, largely incoherent oath the mother uttered. The only comprehensible portions seemed variations on the theme of "no."

Ruth quickly tied a small string around the umbilical cord and cut it with a knife she'd had Elizabeth fetch from the kitchen, one that would need a *very* good wash tomorrow morning.

The moment the blade severed the cord, Ambrose *screamed,* a terrifying, unnervingly mature howl that clashed with Aggy's in nightmarish disharmony.

For a brief second, Ruth seemed rudderless, as though she'd

just that instant woken up from a *very* strange dream to find herself delivering a child. Then the second elapsed. Ruth handed Ambrose off to Molly, who nearly burst into tears as she attempted to wipe the viscera from the boy's body.

Resuming a kneeling position near Aggy's head, Ruth clapped her hands onto the unhappy mother's cheeks and torqued her head up towards hers. Aggy's eyes boggled, the scream drying up in her throat. Ambrose's lamentations redoubled, a dutiful son taking up his mother's slack.

"You gotta push out the afterbirth," Ruth said. "You're so close. Just push."

"Ah!" Drummond giggled. "Midnight! Just now!" He swung his hands at one another, as though of a mind to clap, before realizing his hands were quite full with a little bit of fire. "Happy fourth of July everyone," he mumbled with labored cheer as he placed the candle down on the floorboard. Curtly, with a far more sinister sort of pleasure, he gestured to Molly. "Bring the boy here, let us have a look at my newest little increase!"

Aggy screamed and pushed. She imagined shooting her afterbirth out with such force that it splatted onto Drummond's face, knocked him off the ladder, and sent him tumbling headfirst down to a broken neck.

E I G H T E E N

AMBROSE'S SISTER REMAINED UNBORN IN THE WOMB, experiencing the horrors of the outside world though the cord. Just as she knew, she just *knew*, Ambrose was still experiencing their quiet world through the same. Perhaps this was an order they could maintain, trading places from time to time. This could be an agreeable state of affairs. No, it wasn't *all* bad. Though she would miss her brother dearly.

And then, catastrophe. Her lifeline was severed. Ambrose's absence gained sudden weight and texture. It was suffocating.

She could hear him screaming, had never heard his voice but she just *knew* it was him. Try as she might, she could not cry out for him.

Not in here, at least.

A quiet and perfect world this was indeed, but only for its being shared. To be alone was to be imprisoned. Isolation was incarceration was immiseration.

However unappealing the world outside may have seemed, it was the world in which her only friend now resided. It was one into which he had been dragged; she, on the other hand, would be barging her way in, whether that world wanted her or not.

She felt a slight tug towards the light, but it wasn't nearly strong enough for her liking. So she set her soft little shoulder and charged.

N I N E T E E N

AGGY WAS PUSHING, HER EYES LOCKED ON DRUMMOND AS he waved ever more violently towards Molly.

"Give me the damn child," he commanded.

Molly just stared at him. "I can't hear what you're saying, over this boy's ruckus. I imagine he'll quiet down once he's back in his mother's arms."

"GIVE ME THE BOY!"

"What? I can't make out a word you're saying!"

Drummond shook his head and stepped up the final rungs of the ladder. Molly took a step back as the other women put themselves between their Master and his son, who was both his child and his chattel.

"PUSH HIM!" Aggy screamed.

No one moved to follow the order – there were still some lines they couldn't imagine crossing – but all the same Drummond swung himself up and away from the hole as quickly as he could.

"Did mine fucking ears just deceive me?" he yelled at Aggy, as he landed in the attic on all fours.

"I said I'M PUSHING!"

And so she was.

Ruth gasped. Everyone turned to see what the gasping was about. They followed her gaze towards Aggy's southern passage. More gasps.

Aggy could feel the afterbirth crowning. Wasn't that what was supposed to be happening?

"What?" she cried. "What's wrong with it?"

A dozen-odd faces boggled at her, shadows dancing across some, others backlit by the tiny flame.

"WHAT?!" Her latest interrogatory swelled into another guttural cry; the damn thing was still coming. How big was this fucking afterbirth?

Ruth fell to her knees between Aggy's bent legs, putting a hand on either thigh.

"Relax," she repeated a tone identical to the one with which she'd coached Ambrose out. "There's another baby coming. So you know what you have to do. Breathe and push. Breathe and push."

Tears fell from Aggy's eyes. "Another?!" She was terrified she wouldn't be able to do it again, to push another child out, to feel it tearing her open, shredding her to ribbons…

But it was the fourth of July. Independence day.

She would have a free child. A child who would *become* free, at any rate. One child free twenty-eight years from now, twenty-five if they should be a girl. The other a slave for life, with no hope for freedom, no hope.

She couldn't make sense of it, couldn't wrap her head around the absurdity of it all. Two children, their births separated by mere minutes, marked for two wholly divergent fates by a piece of paper, signed by a few dozen men in an Albany meeting hall.

But she would have time enough to take the snarl of elation and hatred and relief and terror and hope and despair, and parse it for sense, later. For now, she had to push and breathe, push and oh *Christ*.

The baby slid out as though it had gotten a running start. Like it had been *fighting* its way out. Must have been because everything down there had gotten stretched out after Ambrose. Must have been.

Ruth, quicker than her years entitled her to be, rushed to take the disconcertingly-still newborn in her arms. "Get me some string," she bade the room, "something to tie off the cord."

"Uhhh," they all said.

"String!" Ruth snapped. Then she saw what the uhhh was about. She followed the girl's umbilicus, tracing it all the way to the point at which she had cut it following Ambrose's birth.

The same cord, strung between the two children, with nothing connecting them to the mother.

Patience, Ambrose

Ruth paused for a moment, her hand still outstretched, mouth agape, staring at the impossibility.

Something to think on later.

"String," Ruth whispered.

Lillian tore a strip of cloth off her shirt and handed it to Ruth. More for the sake of procedure than anything, Ruth tied it around the cord and cut.

Clearing her throat, Ruth knelt next to Aggy and placed a hand on her shoulder. "It's a girl," she said.

"Free at twenty-five," the new mother whispered, her head flopping from side to side, eyes fixed on the ceiling. "Free at twenty-five. Free free free." She lifted her head and fixed her gaze directly on Drummond, who was crouching beside the drop, motionless. "Happy fourth of July," she grumbled at him.

Drummond simply stared back at her. Shorn of bluster, Aggy could finally study the man to the quick. She found him small, so small. It was only in trying to make himself larger that he became dangerous.

Still, Aggy held eye contact with the man who believed himself her Master, and announced "I want to see my children now."

Drummond did nothing to intervene as Molly and Lillian brought Aggy her babies. As the new mother cradled one in the crook of each arm, Ambrose stopped crying, and his sister started fidgeting as a newborn ought to. If Aggy didn't know better, she'd say they both had smiles on their faces.

"What's her name?" Ruth asked.

Aggy smiled. Wasn't it obvious? She looked to her daughter, free at twenty-five for no other reason than the meridiem had ticked from post to ante, and cooed, "Patience."

T W E N T Y

PATIENCE AND AMBROSE LAY CURLED IN THEIR MOTHER'S arms, seemingly indifferent to the affection raining down upon them. Their tiny, seeking hands instead reached for one another's. Aggy held them tighter, to bring them closer together. It was remarkable, she reflected, how two newborns so fresh they'd yet to dry had the strength to grasp at each other like that. All the while, their innocent little faces radiated peaceful contentment, as though a long-sought prize had finally been won.

On the less-sunny side of things, the children were each far lighter of skin than their mother. Darker of skin than their father, yes, but that wasn't Aggy's concern. They were unmistakably mixed-race children, swarthy enough to invite persecution, pale enough to be stigmatized by their fellow persecutees. Aggy's heart sank. Her children had been branded with the indignity of their conception, the tragedy of their ancestry.

Without meaning to, she slackened her arms ever so slightly, letting the children slump away from her breast. And each other.

Patience and Ambrose threw their heads back and wailed in synchrony.

Aggy shook her own head. Yes, her children might well cry. Ambrose in her right hand, a slave (sorry, *indentured servant*) for life. Patience in her left, property for a score and five years, then suddenly, inexplicably free. What did that mean? What sorts of lives would they be able to lead? The mother joined her children in weeping; that misfortune lay ahead for each them was the only guarantee. But, then again, they came by that honestly; what other fortune had Aggy herself ever known, besides mis-?

She looked around the attic. Drummond had fucked off, perhaps to fetch a free hand to help snatch the babies away, perhaps to leave Aggy the wailing children until such time as they were no longer wailing.

All that remained were her friends. Ruth, Molly, Sally, Elizabeth, Lillian…

Not all misfortune, then. Just enough to obscure the other sort, more often than not.

But that wouldn't last. Drummond would be back by morning. With people of his own. Not friends. No, men like Drummond didn't have friends.

But men like Drummond always knew more men like Drummond.

Yes, Drummond and the men like him would be back. Soon. And they would pry the children from Aggy's hands, grab them by the heels and swing them into those exposed beams in the ceiling…

Aggy banished the vision, and found herself happy in spite of it. Yes, happy. For she was here, in this moment, surrounded by friends.

And she was here, in this moment, holding her children. Not Drummond's children. They were hers, and hers alone.

She looked down at them.

Neither returned her gaze. They were, if Aggy was not very much mistaken, staring intently at each other. Reaching for each other, even, their slick, soft hands flailing about in the empty space between them.

Aggy brought the twins closer together. At which point, they ceased their mewling, greeting one another with satisfied silence.

They did not need her. This was the most horrible, most wonderful gift of all; Aggy's children did not need her. They only needed each other. Which she had given them.

Which she could give them.

Aggy's perfectly happy moment, as all moments are wont to do, passed.

She looked up at her friends. The words caught in her throat, but she fought them out all the same:

"My babies can't stay here."

Aggy's friends did not contradict her. They just nodded, and waited to hear how they could help. While Aggy waited for a bright idea.

In the short term, they all decided it seemed a good start to help Aggy out of the attic.

T W E N T Y - O N E

PATIENCE AND AMBROSE WOULD HAVE BEEN HARD-pressed to articulate the nature of their bond, and not just because they were still pre-linguistic slug-nuggets. Although, an argument could be made that "goo boo bloo goo" said more about their mysterious connection than any series of more commonly understood words could.

So, then, for those of a more interpretive mind: goo boo bloo goo.

For the rest: the pull between these two twins was stronger than mere affection, stronger than the simple yearning for things familiar. This was deeper, something born of that extra little wrinkley bit in the back of their brains. One might stop short of calling it supernatural, but that's just a semantic bias. So call it supernormal, and be careful not to let any daylight cleave the word in twain.

Think of the feeling of walking into a room and not being able to remember why you came in, but being very easily able to acess the urgency with which you entered. Think of threading a hand into a pocket and finding only more pocket where there ought to have been a billfold, and rushing back to the saloon at which you are *certain* you left it, hoping vainly that tonight the establishment might inexplicably be host to only the most community-minded of drunkards. Think of needing desperately to use the privy, and realizing that circumstances have conspired to keep you from such a facility for the foreseeable future.

The sensation which arose in the empty space between Patience and Ambrose, in those moments when their mother's hustling tore them apart, wasn't quite like any of that. It sort of was, but not quite.

Mostly, it was like goo boo bloo goo.

But when they were together? When Aggy's friends had finished bucket-brigading these strange babies down the ladder, and delivered them into the same set of cradled arms? It was something beyond fulfillment, and also not at all similar to it. It was the purpose of knowing why you walked into the room, the unreflective satisfaction of finding your wallet precisely where you left it (with a few bills you'd forgotten were in there to boot), and you can fill in the scatological happy ending yourself. It was a kind of, alright, if you insist, super*normal* harmony. Not that everything was going to be alright, that they would be happy no matter what if only they could stick together, no, nothing of that sort. It was just that, if they stuck together, maybe, everything *could* be alright. It was hope, and everything that comes with it. The good and the bad, the goo and bloo.

TWENTY-TWO

"STOP!" AGGY CRIED. "STOP, STOP, STOP." SHE WAVED HER hand frantically to be pulled back up into the attic. Away from her children, who had been safely lowered to the kitchen below.

Even as the red receded from the corners of her vision, Aggy couldn't help but notice how indifferent the fragile little twins were to being separated from their mother. Not the least bit curious where she'd gotten to; they were perfectly happy mooning at each other in Molly's arms.

"What's wrong?" Sally asked, placing a supporting hand under Aggy's head.

"I can't," Aggy panted. "Hurts."

From below, Lillian poked her head out around the ladder and called up into the attic: "She comin' or what?"

"Kiddin' me?" Ruth mumbled. She lay a soft palm on Aggy's shoulder and peered down into the kitchens. "She just birthed a child, damn you!"

"Two children," Aggy corrected through a grimace.

"Two children, that's right." Ruth studied the ladder, then Aggy. "Two children," she repeated absent-mindedly to herself.

"Where does it hurt?" Elizabeth asked, pointing unhelpfully between Aggy's legs. "There?"

"For a start," Aggy gasped back. The truth was, she couldn't have pinpointed the pain if her life depended on it; she had sunk into a sea of needles, each point possessed of a mind and a thirst.

They jabbed themselves into her eyes, beneath her fingernails, rode each breath into her lungs. It was all pain. All pain.

"Gettin' down the ladder's gonna be the hardest part," Ruth lied. "We just gotta…"

Aggy rolled her head around, settling into a solid glare sent Ruth's way.

Ruth shrugged, then nodded.

"Gettin' down *could* be the easy part," Molly suggested from below, the babies stirring against her chest as she spoke. "Could line somethin' cushioned up, you plop on down."

"Nobody's ploppin' tonight," Ruth answered on Aggy's behalf.

Aggy took a deep breath, bared her teeth, and snapped out her conviction: "I can manage the ladder."

Ruth studied the new mother's face as she sat upright and scooted herself towards the drop to the kitchens. "You certain of that?"

"I got no choice."

Just as Aggy got her feet over the drop, the kitchen beneath them erupted with shouts.

"Hey!" Lillian shouted, her attention snapping towards the rear door to the kitchens, her face following it out of Aggy's view.

"What's…oh *Lord,"* a man's voice thundered.

"No!" Aggy heard Lillian cry. "Get out!"

Molly held the babies more tightly to her chest, taking a fearful step backwards as she kept her gaze locked on whatever Lillian had rushed to.

That was all more than enough to get Aggy down the ladder, needle-sea be damned. She all but skipped the last two rungs, landing heavily in the kitchen…and collapsing onto the floor.

Before Aggy knew what had happened, Ruth was down the ladder and by her side, putting herself in between Aggy and the new arrival: Jesse.

"Back!" Ruth screamed at him.

"I'm no harm!" Jesse shrieked.

Molly seemed to be trying to say something, but all she was managing were a series of choked sobs.

Aggy, meanwhile, had eyes only for her children. The two still-slick babes in Molly's arms, who could scarcely have been more at peace in a well-padded pram. Despite the screaming, the sobbing, the shaking of the body against which they reposed…they were calm.

And, for once, they were staring at their mother. Both still reached for one another with their flailing feet – Aggy wondered if they were even aware of doing that, before realizing that newborn babies probably aren't aware of doing *anything* – but they had finally had their fill of one another's faces, and now studied their mother. Prostrate on the floor, wrapped around the legs of a ladder. Their mother.

They stared at her, and she at them.

The noise in the room escalated. Someone began throwing something at someone else. But Aggy wasn't paying attention. All she could see were her children.

And how those four little eyes, those two little smiles, those twenty searching fingers, changed everything.

"Oh," Aggy sighed. Which said it all.

TWENTY-THREE

TO LOVE SOMEONE ONLY GAVE THE WORLD SOMETHING TO TAKE from you. So Aggy had believed, before she had stared into the patient eyes of her children. But now? Now that she had experienced the futility of attempting to cauterize those wonderous wounds that love inflicted? She recognized the failure of perspective to which she'd been committed. Love for someone else was a gift, one you could give *yourself.* And if you could give it to yourself, nobody could take it from you. They may take what you love, and that might burn you alive.

But, all the same, fire was a terrific source of energy.

Aggy loved her daughter, she realized. She loved her son. And this truth she arrived at only by learning from their example, from seeing the love they had for each other. In seeing it, Aggy recognized it in herself. Recognized that it was distinct from the pain for which she had, until now, mistaken it.

This wasn't self-interest misinterpreted, it wasn't romanticized indigestion. It was the scariest, biggest, dumbest, most important feeling a person could have, could ever *hope* to have.

Oh, but here was the cruelest joke of them all. The punchline that would knock Aggy out for good. The only way she could embrace the love her children had taught her *was to let them go.* Only this was release of a physical kind, rather than the emotional one she had tried and failed. She would have to hold them in her heart, even as she pushed them from her body.

Fine. This she would do.

But…there remained the eagerness, the *need*, for them to

know. Aggy wanted them to know…what? Not necessarily who their mother was, or even who their *father* was, though these were hardly irrelevant. No, she simply wanted to send them out into the world with a fuller understanding of themselves, knowing themselves to be embraced by the love that had triumphed over the ignominy of their conception…

Oh, to hell with it: she wanted them to know that their mother either loved them or liked them a whole lot, or at least had some sort of positive feeling towards them, even if their father was more a bastard than either could ever be. She wanted them to know that she was a failure in her maternal obligations, having not the slightest idea how to sooth their blistering hearts save to bring them nearer one another, and that not a day would go by that would bring her reprieve from that; she would not allow it. She wanted them to know that she hated herself for how she had given up on whatever they had been in the womb, how she had abandoned them in her heart purely to protect herself…most of all, she wanted her children to know what she herself was only now discovering, late in the day but hopefully not *too* late, that defining love by imagined ends rather than immediate means could only close one off. All roads ended in a great, lightless con-traction, and good fortune could only be constructed on the graves of those who had suffered sufficiently to shore up the foundation. All of this, Aggy knew to a near-moral certainty.

But, if all of that was true (as it most certainly was), then… what was the harm in lighting a fire or two?

After all, who knew what might happen with just that much more fire in the world?

Aggy smiled at her children, and felt the world reconstruct itself around them. It was no kinder for this reconstruction, but at least now Aggy could see the seams.

She smiled. "Jesse," she whispered.

Jesse finished ducking from the path of a large pan Ruth had lately thrown at him, then said "I've not come for ruckus!"

"You hush," Aggy told him, staring her injunction around the room. All complied. Rising to an unsteady kneel and returning her attention to Jesse, Aggy asked "Drummond tell you somethin' I oughta know?"

"Gone to fetch some men," Jesse replied quickly.

Sally gasped. Ruth shook her head.

Aggy ignored them. "How long'll he be?"

Jesse shrugged. "Some hours. They ain't near, but nor're they far."

"Before sun-up?"

"To a certainty," Jesse nodded gravely.

I will never see my babies in sunlight, Aggy realized. The thought could have toppled her, had she been standing. But curiously, from a kneel it had the opposite effect: gripping the legs of the ladder, Aggy heaved herself the rest of the way to her feet, and asked Jesse "you helpin' me, or hinderin'?"

Jesse burped and blinked at the same time. That done, he struck a much steelier pose. "Helpin'."

Aggy nodded, then turned to the rest of her friends around the room.

So much fire here. It was a wonder they'd never burned the Estate to ashes.

Ah, but one dream at a time.

"My babies can't stay here," Aggy repeated.

"I can fetch the wagon," Jesse suggested, his voice cracking with nervous excitement. "Have it r-"

"No," Aggy cut him off. "They'll have us back before this time again tomorrow."

"Big ruts," Elizabeth mumbled as she belatedly clomped down the ladder. "Easy trail."

"Oh," Jesse frowned.

"Fly through the woods," Lillian suggested.

Again, Aggy shook her head. "I am in no condition."

"So…" Jesse scratched at his neck. "How're you gonna get ou-"

"I'm not," Aggy whispered. Slowly, she looked around the kitchens.

Everyone alternated their attentions between Aggy's eyes and their own feet.

"You want one of us to run off with them," Ruth finally replied, in a tone that wasn't entirely a question.

"It's the only way," Aggy told her.

"I'm your man," Jesse volunteered.

"I need your help for somethin' else," Aggy told him.

"So…" Jesse's head jutted out as he blinked, a deep gurgle rising in his belly.

"Anybody who takes 'em," Lillian scoffed, "what, you expect 'em to raise 'em?"

"Person who takes 'em is gonna get hunted," Ruth informed Aggy. "That's a mighty ask."

Aggy blinked dew from her eyes. "I'd do it if I could. But I ain't fit for it. And I go no other ideas."

Sally sighed, forceful enough to silence everyone in the kitchen.

All eyes snapped towards her.

"Ah…" Sally mumbled, pulling her eyes from the counters

opposite the back door, "I might have got an idea here."

Aggy didn't have to ask what it was. She gave Sally space, and bless her heart, the girl filled it.

TWENTY-FOUR

THE *HOW* OF SECRETING AGGY'S CHILDREN FROM THE ESTATE was, in a certain sense, provided by none other than Drummond himself.

One winter ago, while clearing the road to the Estate of snow, Sally had slipped on a patch of ice and landed hard on her wrist. Fearing it broken, her mind naturally turned to the consequences of becoming unproductive on the Pinchwife Estate (i.e. no longer being on the Pinchwife Estate), which naturally sent her tumbling into sputtering terror. Aggy and Ruth had done their best to comfort her, a process that Aggy remembered well – long nights of tending to the offended joint and reassuring Sally that, no, in fact, it wasn't broken, likely just sprained. What Aggy did not remember, for having never been privy to, was the afternoon following the injury, when Drummond had come thundering over to a Sally back at work with the shovel, and groaning with each spadeful of snow she heaved off the road. Naturally, Drummond had Jesse following at his heel, to serve as both threat and protection as he demanded to know why the byway of his property should still be shrouded in winter.

"Even though I had the damn shovel yet in my hands," Sally harrumphed to Aggy and the rest in the kitchens.

Which was not, of course, what she had said on the day. No, last winter all she had said was "I had a spill, Sir," with downcast eyes.

"It's for this that you wail so?" Drummond had scoffed. "And what of Job, hm? From whom all was taken?" Drummond had bent at the waist, his hands planted on his knees – in the kitchens, Sally reenacted the gesture, and even at this distance it filled Aggy with indignant rage.

"Did he cry?" Drummond had demanded, talking once more of Job. "Did he poison his God's ear with vain lamentations? Or did he return to his tasks, confident that the Lord would set all aright in the fullness of time?"

"Technically," Jesse had apparently burped from behind Drummond, "Job 30:20 says that Job done both of those things. He says 'I cry unto thee, and thou dost...'" here, Sally claimed Jesse had caught Drummond's razor-sharp gaze that said *the lord hath hardened my heart unto you* and wisely fallen to silence.

Aggy cocked an eyebrow across the kitchens. "That true?" she asked Jesse.

Jesse cocked his entire head. "What's true?"

"You talkin' back to him."

"That wasn't..." Jesse scratched his chin, emitting something halfway between a burp and a sigh. "Wasn't talkin' back. Just Bible stuff, that was."

"Hm," Aggy nodded softly.

"I'm sayin' this," Sally continued, before going on to explain why she was mentioning the incident at all: mulling over the misfortunes of Drummond's favorite biblical figure had naturally set Sally's mind to perusing the halls of God's other protagonists. And way down there, all the way at the other end of this heavenly pass, was Drummond's *least* favorite Bible boy, the one Aggy had really only ever heard about from her fellow slaves: Moses.

Moses, the deliverer. Moses, the prophet. Moses, the foundling. The foundling on the Nile. Naturally, Sally had picked Jesse's biblically-literate brain about Moses for nothing more than the pleasure of hearing a good yarn, but…that was an idea, wasn't it? Spoons Creek, just a half day's ride away, was no Nile…

"But it might could do," Sally concluded.

"…" everyone replied in unison.

"That way none of us gotta go on the run," Sally whispered as a postscript. "Because anybody who runs…they'll get caught in time."

"Are you," Aggy clarified, "suggestin' we put my babies in a basket and plop 'em in the river?"

"Nobody's ploppin'," Ruth growled.

"We won't *plop* 'em," Sally piggybacked, more defensive than she perhaps ought to have been. "Just…" she pantomimed gently consigning a basket into creekwaters. *"Place* 'em."

"Spoons Creek is the body what carried Margaret south," Lillian noted flatly.

"Anybody who gets caught is followin' her," Elizabeth submitted.

"Allegheny," Jesse recited, "to Ohio, to Mississip."

Sally shrugged. "The kids get that far down, they got bigger problems'n hittin' cotton country. But that's why I'm sugge-"

"Cotton country?" Molly asked, pulling the mucus-bubbling kiddies nearer to her bosom.

"Just hope somebody plucks 'em outta the river, then?" Lillian grumbled. "You're killin' those kids, you do that."

"They don't exactly got sunnier days ahead if they stay here," Sally shot back.

"Cloudy day's better'n bein' dead."

Sally had a riposte for that, and Lillian wasn't one to back down from a challenge; the two women launched into a full-tilt argument.

But Aggy wasn't listening. Instead, she stepped softly towards Molly, her legs unsteady beneath her, but bolstered by something more than musculature. She extended her arms.

Molly nodded, then carefully transferred the newborns to their mother's arms.

What struck Aggy first was how warm her children were. It was like cradling two loaves of bread, fresh from the oven and a little undercooked besides. An altogether pleasant sensation, it was.

Feeling suddenly scientific, Aggy slowly juked her elbows out to the sides, separating the twins' game of footsie and putting just a few inches of distance in between them.

The results were instantaneous, unmistakable; the moment they lost contact with one another, Patience and Ambrose set to whimpering, mewling, tending quickly towards proper tears.

Aggy reunited them, bringing her arms back in far enough to allow toe-to-toe contact. No surprises here: the children soften-ed, smiles once more lighting up their faces.

Faces which they turned to look up at their mother, affixing her with a breathtakingly cogent sort of smile. Two smiles, in fact. Though they looked like perfect reflections of a single ex-pression.

Aggy smiled back at them. It was the sort of trembling smile that required getting the teeth involved.

"Hey," Aggy calmly called to Sally and Lillian, still spitting venom at one another. "Quit that."

Sally tripped through the first half of an insult already in progress, then hung her head and said "sorry."

Lillian just shrugged, which was the best one could hope for from her.

Satisfied, Aggy jutted her chin at Sally. "We need somethin' could hold 'em both at once."

Sally took a moment to process that thought, making a few experimental grunts before recovering the faculty of speech. "On...on, um, in the river?"

"Aggy," Ruth gasped, her tone a counsel.

For once, Aggy ignored Ruth. "If we put 'em together... they'll come through alright."

"They're babies," Elizabeth pointed out, as though it was a secret she couldn't keep to herself any longer.

"I can run 'em," Molly insisted, audibly losing confidence in herself as she spoke. "I can...run..."

"You're too young to run 'em," Sally insisted.

"It's just runnin'!"

"It's *not* just runnin'," several women informed Molly at once.

Aggy ignored these voices, keeping her eyes fixed firmly on Sally, her heart with her children.

Slowly, Sally nodded. She pointed across the room. To a large basket Aggy and the other women who worked the apple orchards knew *all* too well, with deep, tightly-woven sides, and a thick handle sweeping over top.

It would fit the twins quite comfortably, with room for more than a few insulating blankets.

Aggy shivered. If Patience and Ambrose noticed, they didn't let on. "Okay," she whispered, nodding softly. "Okay."

"Aggy," Ruth repeated, more forcefully.

"Are you plannin' on fightin' me here?" Aggy demanded of

Ruth.

"…no."

"You wanna lend a hand?"

Ruth sighed, then nodded.

Aggy flashed a smile, then jerked her chin towards the basket. "Then help ready that."

"I can run it," Jesse once again insisted.

As before, Aggy shook her head. "No. I need you elsewhere." She paused, then summoned Molly with a nod. Carefully, Aggy passed her children to the young woman (no longer a girl), studying them with tight-jawed objectivity once they were in Molly's arms.

"As I think on it," Aggy added to Jesse, "I can use your help twice over."

Jesse stood up straighter; it was a miracle he managed to avoid snapping off a salute.

TWENTY-FIVE

TWO SCRIBBLES ON A SCRAP OF PAPER. THAT WAS ALL AGGY could give to her children. She knew it wasn't enough…but all the same, it was everything.

"Which one's which?" Aggy asked, for what she resolved would be the final time.

Jesse pointed to the squiggle with which he had blighted the top portion of the scrap. "This one's Patience." He traced his finger along the first letter. "This here's the *P*. Makes the *puh* sound."

Aggy nodded, then pointed to the squiggle below Patience's

name. "Ambrose."

"That's so," Jesse nodded.

Emotion welled up within Aggy, but she caught it before it had a chance to get much higher than her throat. Now wasn't the time. Just a few more hours. Then she could feel all of this. Would have little else to occupy her.

She recalled a time, after first returning from Pleasance Square, when she'd had quite the opposite problem. Of feeling nothing. Of wishing she could feel *anything*. The thought made her smile. Which signaled a feeling, like all the others. One she was glad she could feel. Like, yes, all of the others.

Even the ones that would have to wait.

Aggy sighed and took up the scrap of paper, the one Jesse had torn from a Bible he had fetched from his little cabin behind the Estate. It was a blank page, from the very front of the book, one which bore no scripture that might distract from its purpose.

Patience and Ambrose would take their names with them down the river. Aggy had nothing else to offer.

Besides a chance at a better life, of course. A life at all.

Aggy took the scrap and placed it in the basket Sally and Ruth had prepared. It was a mess of blankets and kerchiefs, sourced from places Aggy would prefer not to know. Most were clean, the women had assured Aggy, and that would have to be good enough.

"How're you gonna keep that note dry?" Lillian demanded, yet another of the needling questions she'd taken to asking. Better that than trying to convince Aggy not to go through with this, as she had for the first hour.

Aggy nodded Molly over. The young woman, weeping as though on Aggy's behalf, brought the children and placed them gently in the basket. Careful to minimize their separation; the eerie connection between Patience and Ambrose had not been lost on her.

Aggy smiled down at her twins, but found that expression flickering into something darker in the face of…an illusion, certainly. It couldn't have been anything more than a trick of light that made Patience appear noticeably, well, lighter than her brother. *Drastically* more pale, really. As though the same pen which had signed the children's fates into law had moved on to scribble down a thought or two about the specifics of their sk…

An illusion, certainly. A trick of the light.

Aggy shook her head, then took the scrap of paper from Jesse and placed it in the makeshift crib, tucking it just beneath the twins' feet. "If the page gets wet here," Aggy sighed, once more struggling to keep her throat from clenching shut, "they'll have worse to worry over than losin' their names."

"They already do," Lillian rasped.

Molly stepped forward, all but body-checking Lillian. "What do you want her to do, huh?"

"It's alright," Aggy told Molly.

"Gotta get the kiddies out," the young woman groused.

"Soonish," Jesse added, glancing out the window, at the deep mauve just beginning to leaven the night.

Aggy nodded. "I ken the dangers well," she told Lillian. "But I got faith."

Jesse bowed his head. "I can lead us in prayer. Go-"

"Quit that."

"-d…uh?"

Aggy shook his head at him. "You and I got shit to do."

Jesse let his clasped hands fall slowly to his sides. "I was…

prayin'."

"Yeah, I saw. How's that been workin' for ya?"

To assuage Jesse's confusion, Ruth patted him on the shoulder and said "she didn't mean faith the way you mean it."

"Sure I did," Aggy countered. "I'm just aimin' it somewhere different."

Taking a deep breath, needing to tense her entire body just to keep from collapsing, Aggy turned to face her children for the very last time. Patience, Ambrose.

They smiled up at her. As if to let her know, they would be alright. As long as they had one another, they would come through just fine.

Aggy wanted nothing more than to lean over, to stick her head into the basket and kiss them each on the forehead. If she did, though, she knew perfectly well the sides would come off. She would fall apart. And now was not the time. Their lives depended on Aggy keeping it together.

If she *didn't* kiss them goodbye, meanwhile, she would merely regret it for the rest of her life. Which was bound to be quite a short stretch of time.

An obvious choice, then.

"Take them," Aggy whispered.

Not needing to be told twice, Sally — who had volunteered herself as the fleetest of foot, and despite that long-ago sprain, surely was — snapped up the basket and hustled out the door.

Aggy watched Sally go. Listened to her footsteps pounding into oblivion. Listened, in vain, for any sign of distress on the part of her children, for being taken from their mother.

Nothing of the sort, naturally. For they still had each other. There was a distant sting to that, but more than anything, Aggy found it the greatest blessing of her life.

She was aware of her friends stepping forward to comfort her. Of understanding hands reaching for her shoulder. As with the kiss; she could not afford the succor.

"Time," was all she said to Jesse. Fortunately, he found that word far less confusing than Aggy's use of *faith*; he followed her out the door as she went to meet her Master, her Mistress, and likely her Maker, resolved to deny each of them their self-appointed titles.

TWENTY-SIX

PATIENCE AND AMBROSE WERE A MAD METRONOME SETting the pace for Sally's flight through the woods. The inertia of each stride swung the newborns further from one another in the basket, now closer, now further. And with each swing that rolled the infants apart, a thin mewling rose up from their chests, only to fall once more as they crashed back into one another on the next swing. Given how soft and fresh they were, Sally might have expected them to be more distressed by their reunions – had she not been prepared for this by the incredulous whispers of Molly and Ruth. It was the first time Sally had personally witnessed the spooky supernormality of the kiddies' connection up close and personal, and there was a part of her that was grateful it would be the last. Why that should be the case was difficult to parse, particularly when one's attention was more immediately focused on not taking a header over a hill and spilling the children into the dirt.

Spoons Creek was a half day's ride on horseback. So Jesse had insisted. How long would it be on foot, then, with a fragile burden at that? And how long would it be before Master sent someone out in pursuit? It had certainly occurred to Sally, that volunteering for this particular adventure had put her in great jeopardy, perhaps to the point of scratching an 'X' on her own death warrant. But prior to this moment, the consequences of that decision had been a delightful abstraction.

Death was much more palpable here, sprinting through a thick wood lit by little more than the velvet intimations of sunrise.

Yet as she glanced down at the children in the basket now slung over her right arm…she did not for a moment consider abandoning the endeavor. This, too, was something on which she could not quite bring reason to bear.

So she ran on, periodically gasping in terror at the thought of what would befall her when Master returned with his pique up, only to notice her absence.

Of course, it also hadn't occurred to her just how effective Aggy's diversion would prove to be.

TWENTY-SEVEN

THE STAIRS WERE THE FIRST THING TO TRULY GIVE HER PAUSE. Aggy halted at the bottom of them, lifting her gaze to the porch of the Estate. From which Drummond had once summoned her, one cold and unhappy night in October.

She considered the steps. Whether or not her attic-withered legs would be strong enough to carry her up. Or…yes, whether there might not be greater delight found in remaining just where she was. Down here.

"You in need of a helpin' hand up?" Jesse asked from beside her.

She opened her mouth to respond…but paused, narrowing her eyes. "You hear that?" she asked.

Jesse shook his head.

Aggy lifted a finger towards the heavens, then turned back towards the main road into the Estate.

The ziggurat slashes were just fading into relief against the lightening sky. The low roll of land between them, though, and the path threading along it, were yet invisible.

Still, Aggy knew the clop-and-rattle of a posse when she heard one.

"They're comin' up the road," she told Jesse.

He frowned, then scratched his nose and burped quietly. More of a hiccup, really. "This ain't somethin' we gotta do."

"Too late to say so." Aggy nodded sadly, then jerked her chin towards the stairs to the Estate. "Please."

Jesse nodded sadly, then mounted the first step. He paused, and turned around. "You oughta come up. We can b-"

"No," Aggy shook her head. "I want her comin' down *here.*"

Jesse mouthed the words to himself, then turned his attention towards the void of horizon along which his Master was hustling, with ill-intent and men of like mind. He sighed once, burped twice, and double-timed it up into the Estate.

The door slammed shut behind him. And Aggy was alone.

In the silence of a coming sunrise, she found herself combating the strange feeling of having overreacted. Hard to sustain a sense of dread, after all, when one was surrounded by birds whistling into a crisp, crimson morning. Was Drummond really on his way here to take Aggy's children, to do who knew what with them? Was she herself truly in danger of being spirited off to a fate identical to, or perhaps worse than, the one that had befallen her father?

Aggy laughed to herself. *At* herself. Classic bottom-of-the-stairs thinking, this was. And once upon a time, she might have imagined the best way to counter it was by climbing to the top. Now, though, she knew better. The problem wasn't one's position relative to those little wooden steps; it was the steps themselves.

Just as the sound of approaching horses resolved itself enough for Aggy to guess at the number of mounts (six, she'd venture), the front door to the Estate swung open. Out came Martha Pinchwife, the veins in her neck betraying a full-voiced reprimand, already locked and loaded. Following close behind was the inevitable target of her scorn, poor Jesse. Poor, courageous Jesse.

His incompetence would be his salvation, Aggy thought with no joy; nobody would believe him intelligent enough to have knowingly aided in any of this.

Martha stumbled slightly at the top of the steps, as she spotted Aggy waiting at the bottom. "Oh, you've hatched. Good. Have you the foggiest what it is this buffoon wishes to show me?"

"Come down," Aggy called to her. As she heard it, she had to concede the calm of her voice registered as far more threatening than any barking or bellowing could have.

Martha stared at Aggy for a moment, the cords in her throat dissolving, replaced by veins bulging out of her forehead. "What?"

"I got somethin' to tell you," Aggy called. "Come down."

"Something to…" Martha's mouth flapped noiselessly for several seconds, until she glanced up past Aggy, towards the road.

Some number of yards away, the silhouettes of horseheads crested the nearest hill, backlit by a bloody sunrise at long last attaining itself.

"You'd do well to return to your kitchens," Martha called to Aggy, a tremor in her voice betraying nerves, "having hatched!"

Her anxiety, curiously enough, touched Aggy, and so infected her. She felt her calm dissolving slightly. Best to have it out, then: "You recall that evening, October most recently passed, when Jesse had you out of home on the charge of bedbugs?"

Martha said nothing. Betrayed nothing. She remained precisely as she was. Save the veins on her forehead, which flexed and quivered.

Aggy nodded towards Jesse. "Got you stuck in a rut, as I understand i-"

"I remember," Martha snapped.

"THAT HER?!" Drummond's voice carried from across the distance he had yet to close. "STILL HER TONGUE, JESSE!" It dripped with echo enough that all could imagine they had not understood him.

"Your husband took me on that evening," Aggy continued, her tone soft, but unyielding.

"Took you where?" Martha asked.

Aggy tilted her head as might a disapproving schoolmarm. "Drummond raped me in your own bed. Put two children inside of me, who I've just lately born."

"That was someone else put you in a family way," Martha whispered, the lie dying on her tongue.

"How I wish it was," Aggy replied.

"MARTHA!" Drummond cried, his voice quivering as the horse beneath him broke into a gallop. "SHUT YOUR EARS UP!"

"Sour though the truth may be," Aggy sighed, "my twins are his twins. Which, I gather, makes 'em your children-in-law."

Martha greeted this news as one receiving a diagnosis they had long ago deduced from their symptoms. Not with shock, or astonishment, or fury; with something more resembling disappointment.

Staring off towards the horizon, past her fast-approaching husband, she took the first step down towards the ground. Then another, then another.

Aggy wished she could have felt like smiling just then. She didn't. But it certainly occurred to her that, were circumstances other than they were…oh, but no thought with that clause was worth completing. Circumstances were precisely as they were. That was the end of the matter.

Drummond tried to dismount his horse before it had fully arrived at the foot of the Estate. No friend to inertia, it took him several feet of stumbling and bumbling to finally halt himself, by which point he was nearly cheek-to-jowl with Jesse. "What did she say?" he demanded of Martha. "Don't you believe a *word* of it, whatever it was!"

Martha turned towards her husband, fixing him with such a steely expression that the Master of the Estate seemed on the precipice of an apology, an extremity to which Aggy had never imagined Drummond could be pushed.

"Ah," Drummond blathered, "you're gonna listen to a girl black with lies? What did she tell you?"

"…" said Martha.

"Child of Cain, as Peter is so fond of saying? This is your font of wisdom? Tell me what she *told* you, damnit!"

"…"

Drummond shook his head, then grabbed Jesse firmly by the scruff of his neck and shoved the man to his knees. "Creatures of mischief they are, liable to spit whatever venom will cause the most trouble for honest God-fearing folks such as ourselves!"

"Master!" Jesse cried. "Please stop!"

Drummond shook Jesse until the belching and thrashing quieted. "You, tell me what has just transpired!"

"You swore to me," Martha hissed as she finished her descent from the porch, "that you would lay with no more of these filthy creatures."

Aggy shook her head – largely out of disappointment with herself, that she had expected Martha to experience disgust in accordance with a standard ethical worldview.

Oh, but of course not; Martha sized Aggy up. "What did you say to him, you damned harlot? Flashed your swarthy, drooping breast his way, hm?"

"Yeah," Drummond nodded, "she showed me her t-"

"Be *quiet,*" Martha demanded.

Drummond looked from Martha to Jesse, back to his wife, to Aggy. He growled something that could not possibly have corresponded to human speech. Which was not to say that it was meaningless.

The remainder of Drummond's posse trotted up behind him. Rotund white men all, and each armed in a manner bespeaking their insecurities.

There were seven of them – so her estimate had been short

by one, Aggy noted.

Yet seven was more than enough. In that moment, Aggy knew her fate was sealed. She found it a relief.

The only question was, how effectively could she keep Drummond's attentions here, right here, on her? And not on the children?

Fortuantely, Drummond seemed determined to make a spectacle of himself; "I would *never,*" he gasped, "in my *life,* lay with a beast such as this." He pointed to Aggy, naturally.

Martha leveled her contempt his way. "You were saying she showed you something of hers, were you not?"

"I was, but, uh, you told me to be quiet."

Here, at last, was a smile which Aggy had to work to suppress. She pointed to a space just above her waistline. "Your husband," she informed Martha, "wears a birthmark looks somethin' like the pawprint of a dog, right here."

Drummond cleared his throat. "Many men, *many* men have such a mark!"

"You…" Martha's mouth did a bit more flapping, occasionally peeling back into a snarl before huffing back down into a grimace.

Aggy glanced towards Drummond's posse. All eyes were on their ostensible leader. Quite a few of them looked more than a little bit amused.

"What is the point," Drummond demanded, "what is the *point* of a man owning a thing if he cannot use it in accordance with his whims?"

"You promised me!" Martha shouted.

"Do *not* raise your voice to me!" Drummond shouted, visibly delighted to be scrambling onto any sort of moral high ground.

"Oh, go kick rocks, you dishonest cad!" With that, Martha spun on her heel and stomped back up into the Estate.

"Martha!" Drummond clenched his fists at his side. "MAR-THA! COME BACK HERE!"

Martha stormed back into her home, pausing only to cry "get rid of the damned temptress!" before slamming the door behind her.

"Martha! Mar…ugh," Drummond sighed as he glanced to his grinning posse. He boggled his eyes at their giggling, then gestur-ed to Aggy. "You gonna run a rope around her neck or what?"

Jesse shot back to his feet; for a moment Aggy worried he might do something rash, something he would very quickly come to regret…then his eyes met hers. She watched his gaze soften, as though melting beneath her silent commandment.

She wondered what she must look like. For even as the men knocked her to her feet and fell upon her with blugeons and fists – for as undeniably painful as the experience was – Aggy felt strangely at peace. Which gave her a distance from which to witness, rather than experience, her ordeal.

She'd had a hope that had not immediately spun around and sunk its fangs back into her. She had hoped to keep all eyes here at the Estate, and she had; Drummond's men were fixated on her, and the man himself was galumphing his way up the stairs to placate his wife. This was success, in as much as Aggy would ever know it. These were her final thoughts, before a particularly well-placed blow knocked her mind loose.

Behold, success.

TWENTY-EIGHT

IT WAS WELL INTO THE MORNING WHEN SALLY REACHED Spoons Creek. Which, given what Jesse had told her, meant she was either quite a bit faster than she realized, or else horses were quite a bit slower; countless times, her had feet caught on stumps and low branches hidden by the dark, but not once did she lose her footing. This she ascribed to the simple expediency of remaining upright; now was not the time to fall, and so, she had not. Nor was now the time to shiver, to be cowed by fear, to evince the least hesitation at the edge of the abyssal creek, whose flow was, thank heavens, lively enough to announce itself.

Sally knelt on the bank of the waters and lay the basket beside her. Here, on the creek's edge, she couldn't help but wonder if the best thing for her to do might not be to take the babies back to the Estate. What chance did they stand in the current? Even if the basket should remain upright, a hearty splash of water scaling the lip of the wicker crib could soak the blankets, freeing the night to thread its sinister fingers through, freezing the covers and entombing the children in a swaddle of ice…

Oh, but it was morning in July. And Aggy had seemed so confident. And the children here, they seemed so…well, they seemed confident too.

Sally shook her head. No, no, now was decidedly not the time for second guessing. Whatever the kids' luck may be on the creek, it was orders of magnitude more agreeable than what awaited them on land. *This* land, at any rate.

Time was growing short – this Sally knew because she could

feel, but not quite see, her hands beginning to tremble. July though it may have been, there was nonetheless a chill.

She reached into the basket and drew the blankets tighter around the children, ensuring that the note bearing their names was well-hidden from the elements. Then she lifted the basket, taking an inexplicable amount of care to hold it steady (after that mad dash through the woods, she could have windmilled the damn thing around her head for all the kids cared), and placed it gently in the river. No plopping, no ma'am.

"Good luck," she wished the twins. And then she let go.

If she expected crying from the babies, even whimpering, some audible recognition of the fact that they were now being swept down a creek towards ever more truculent waterways, Sally was disappointed. Patience and Ambrose did little more than lay as they had, scarcely bothering to marvel at the way the scenery shifted. Within a minute, they were lost to Sally's vision behind a thick trunk, half uprooted and hanging over the water at a precarious angle.

Now was the time to tremble, then. Now was the time for second thoughts. But it was not yet the time to fall – that would come when she'd managed to find her way back to the Estate. For the sad truth was that, unlike the children, her chances for happiness were still greater there than they would be in the wilderness. So she turned, and she fought her way through the blindness of fear, and she did not fall.

TWENTY-NINE

BABY MOSES HAD IT EASY. HIS TRIP DOWN THE NILE WAS a gondola ride through a heart-shaped tunnel, little more than a lazy river lapping at the sides of his yacht-like nacelle – with its ample leg room and copious blanketing and complimentary champagne – until he drifted gently into his port of call, a reedy meander from which he was plucked to fulfill his destiny as a matinee idol.

If only, eh? What did Moses know of jagged rocks on the riverbed reaching up towards the surface, spanking the bottom of the southbound bassinet as it ripped along the ever-strengthening creek? Or what about those unwelcome visits from the current that came sloshing over the sides, just as Sally had predicted? Had Moses had those to contend with, hm? Certainly not. Nor was the world's worst tour guide (forty years in the same desert – one might call that a one-star experience, were it not for three wise men who would demonstrate that even *one* star should be enough to get one where one wanted to go) made to suffer the humiliations of soiled linens clinging to his thighs. Remember the verse about the befriender of blazing brambles marinating in his own stew? Didn't think so.

That baby had it easy.

What Moses didn't have, of course, was a maternal dispensation with whom to share the burdens of the river. Unpleasant though it was to be chucked and rattled by the current, Patience and Ambrose never once wept or shouted. Why should they? They had each other, they could feel each other even as the current tossed them apart. It gave their supernormal bond something to latch on to, something across which a deep peace and smoldering contentment could pass, warming them as embers breathing deep of a clear twilight.

Let the river turn, then. Let it run them, jostle them, splash them, rattle them, do its very best to drown them, let it do its very worst. They had only to reach for one another across the divide, a gulf bridged by a tether no element could touch, to find strength ready at hand from one another.

There was a fire in them, a fire their mother would recognize, if only she'd the chance to look upon it once more, to raise her palms against its radiance and be filled, be soothed, be emboldened.

Alas. It was a fire, Aggy's fire, that would sweep only further from its source, lighting a path through an era of moonless dusk, giving body to the hopes and fears of a mother who suddenly found the darkness an easy burden to bear. For she believed, *knew,* that the flames might one day spread, illuminating a day she herself would never see, from the endless midnight to which should would by then be consigned.

T H I R T Y

AGGY HAD KNOWN, WITHOUT A SHADOW OF A DOUBT, THAT this was where Drummond would take her. He liked his poetry blocky, obvious, easy to grasp. He liked nursery rhymes.

She smiled at him from her uneven footing atop the roots of the tree. Her good humor visibly unnerved him, which only deepened the swoop of her grin. This wasn't what happened in his favorite stories. People on the scaffold shouldn't smile, unless they were being martyred for some glorious cause. Aggy had no grand agenda to speak of. Knowing that she'd muddled up Pinchwife relations, driven a firm wedge between Drummond and Martha, and given her own children the chance to be together in whatever state the fates so decreed...this was enough. This was enough to make her smile.

Late that afternoon, Sally had snuck back in from her riverbound mission, quiet as sunrise. Made good time, she had; either Jesse had been mistaken in how long it would take to reach the creek, or...oh, who was she kidding, Jesse had been mistaken. In any event, Aggy had seen her babies' shephard shivering outside the door to the kitchens, wrapped in a blanket and embraced tightly by Ruth, as Drummond and his mob had secured the rope they had long-since cinched around Aggy's neck to the back of the carriage. Even as Aggy stumbled, hands bound behind her back, rope shredding the curve of her throat, doing her best to keep pace with the escort lest she fall to the ground and be dragged to Pleasance Square, she smiled. Sally was safe. Aggy would bring no one to the hanging with her.

At least, not to her ignominious spot atop the roots. For Jesse was here, brought by Drummond as half-hearted punishment. Aggy had, rather tragically, been right: neither Pinchwife had believed Jesse capable of consciously plotting against them, of deliberately assisting Aggy. They couldn't imagine an emotional life for the man, which left them incapable of imagining that Jesse might have been sweet on the ill-fated Aggy. *That* meant that Drummond had absolutely no conception of what torture it truly was, for his valet to be standing right behind him as he gloated up at the condemned woman.

Aggy watched Jesse over Drummond's shoulder and tried to send him a consoling look, an appreciative one, a caring one. Witnessing the hanging of a loved one had, in a tremenddously belated fashion, lit a fire in her. Might it do likewise for Jesse? He'd already demonstrated something approaching a seditious spirit. Perhaps there was hope for him yet.

Aggy cast her gaze towards the mob assembled in Pleasance Square. It had been less than twenty-four hours ago that she had committed the sin of revelation that earned her the place of honor at this public execution – how had such a crowd assembled so quickly? The vultures never stopped circling, she supposed.

Was her crowd (for this was how she thought of these people: as *hers*) larger than the one she had stood in not even one year ago, the one from which she had witnessed her father hung by the neck, the one that had instilled in her an untenable apathy (as all apathy was, at bottom)? She thought that it was. Why? Perhaps it was the novelty of seeing a young slave, sorry, ha, *indentured servant* of demonstrably childbearing stock being hanged, just as she reached her prime period of productivity.

Or, just as easily, perhaps not. Perhaps the crowd was the same size, or smaller. Perhaps any number of eagerly focused gazes would have seemed a crowd thousands deep, viewed from beneath that old hickory tree.

As the executioner slid the hanging rope around her neck, Aggy wondered what her surname was. If she'd ever had one. Had her father given her one? Or was she to have taken one for herself? Nobody had ever told her, and she'd never had cause to wonder. Even now, though, her curiosity was idle; she had no need of a surname. It wasn't as though she would be passing it on to anybody. It just seemed…fun. Yes. It was *fun* to think about.

One possibility was quickly dispatched; she had rather pointedly not included the name "Pinchwife" on the note bearing the children's names, a note she hoped whoever found Patience and Ambrose would read and adhere to. She hated the thought of her children being called by any names other than their own.

Still, to return to the issue of *her* own address: a surname seemed, upon further consideration, like a thing worth having. At least, it did just then. So why not choose her own? She was free to do so in this moment, free in a way Drummond could never keep her from being, free in a way he couldn't even begin to understand.

She scanned the area for inspiration. Hm…Aggy…Wagon? Aggy Wagon? No, that sounded ridiculous. Aggy…Greycloud? No. Aggy Sweatbrow? No. Something a *smidge* less literal, perhaps. Aggy Birdsmith? Aggy…ha, Aggy Wifewedge? Aggy Brickston? Brickston wasn't bad, but it still wasn't right. Ag-

She heard the groan of rope pulled taut, then the ground beneath her feet abandoned her.

She heard a crack, but her neck didn't break.

She heard the men and women and children who had come to watch her die, some clapping, some cheering, some hissing, some tutting, some sighing.

Her ears rang, but sight was the first sense to fail. The day was night, starless and warm, and she could taste her own tongue. Copper, blood, tongue.

They were jeering now. The people who had come to watch her die. Who were watching her die, who she could no longer see.

All she could taste was the ringing in her ears, was the air rushing past as her kicking feet swung the body. Her body.

She heard them lapse into silence, the people, then talk amongst themselves. The people.

She watched them turn around, almost as one, and shuffle out of the square. She watched them through the blind.

The people.

Show's over, she thought. A choked smile further warped her face, which she tasted, and heard. Nothing to see here, save silence. Silence and people. Look. Listen. Taste.

The blind contracted. Then it filled everything, all at once.

AS HER KICKING AND SWINGING FINALLY CEASED, THE bough from which Aggy hung snapped, dropping her to the ground in a heap.

Drummond shouted angrily and rushed, as best he could, to the pile that had once been Aggy's body. To his relief, he found her dead. The executioner reassured him that she had expired at the end of the rope. Good thing, too. If she hadn't, she'd have landed on her feet and been none the worse for wear. They had a little laugh about it, the hangman and Drummond did, then the latter called Jesse in to help clear the body.

As he obeyed, Jesse glanced up. It was a way to not look at Aggy's body, true, but to a lesser extent he was puzzling over how such a thick branch could simply *snap* as this one had. There was no breeze today, no dramatic inclemency that could have caused something like that. It was…disturbing. A miracle that had come a moment too late. Jesse shook his head, and did what he always did: he swallowed his grief and got to work.

Above his head, the old hickory at the southern end of Pleasance Square swayed of its own accord. It creaked and groaned, as though it had just been told the one about the tree that falls in the woods, with nobody around to hear it.

THIRTY-ONE

"WHAT'S GOING ON?" ONE LATE-ARRIVING FELLOW ASKED a more punctual man amongst the dispersing crowd.

The latter gave the former a sideways glance and mumbled "some poor nigger girl got strung up." The late-arriving man, who referred to himself as Praisegod (a name that often doubled as an explanation for his perpetual tardiness), was astonished at the note of genuine remorse in the other fellow's voice. Praisegod knew it wasn't because the fellow was sad about there being one less colored girl in the world – the fellow just didn't approve of the barbarism by which the subtraction had been accomplished. Such was the curious candor to be found passing between enlightened whites at a lynching. Shed of pretense and performance – the aggressive condescension or, at the other end of the spectrum, the self-congratulatory philosophizing – here was the scaffolding upon which so many those bearing the curse of Ham had been hanged. It was muscular indifference, disapproval without action, the back-of-the-crowd headshaking of hundreds, thousands, maybe millions of passive accomplices. Here was a man who seemed to wish the noose had been untied and put to more productive use, and yet here he was, shuffling away from the hanging, for which he had assembled with all the others, just another spectator.

A large part of Praisegod wanted nothing more than to curse the man, to recite to him some of the Bible verses that would have probably made him feel quite rotten about himself just then. But he didn't, partially because he didn't feel the fellow worth even the worst Praisegod had to offer, also partially because he was worried the man might know some of the verses that would have rendered his spectatorship A-OK, which would have started a whole big Bible Thing, which Praisegod didn't feel like getting in to just then.

Instead he sought higher ground. Literally, so he could get a better view of the corpse. Why not? The girl was dead already, and it was always fascinating to see a body of any hue sans the spirit. To witness a lifeless, human-shaped husk was like being told a great story, being thrilled and chilled all at once, without a word.

There was a tree a few yards into the departing crush that split into a V shape about seven feet up. Praisegod was hardly a physical specimen, indeed he had a paunch that was the most notable of his father's bequests, but he reckoned even he could climb such a tree as that. The hard part was shouldering through the mob, which was uniformly moving towards him, in the opposite direction as he was trying to go. Aside from a few sharp grumbles, though, nobody gave him much trouble. The tree was an even simpler matter, as it canted slightly forward in a way that made planting a foot and levering himself up onto it a manageable task. He may have been less than a specimen, after all, but he was still a relatively young man, not even thirty yet. A tree was not such an insurmountable task! Whoops. Well, second time was the charm!

Sat in his arboreal throne (nestled in boughs that would have been no good for hanging, he couldn't help but notice, no good at all), he gazed upon Pleasance Square, at the pale children cutting away strips of the dead girl's clothes, the most adventurous of whom saw fit to fondle the departed's breasts, much to the delight of his friends. The executioner and another man stood over the corpse, watching the kids carry on, perhaps finding similar mirth in the display. Praisegod couldn't be sure – their backs were turned to him. They certainly didn't shoo the children away. A burping, hangdog colored next to the man who wasn't the executioner made an effort, though, and got a shin-kick from the kids and a scolding from his Master for his troubles.

Praisegod looked upon this scene, a reflection across time he couldn't possibly have appreciated, and was disgusted. Not merely by the fondling drama immediately before him, though naturally he was angered by the desecration of this negro girl's temple, swarthy imitation of a holier body though it might have been. What kicked up the most soot from the darkest depths of his heart had been the casual, even jovial atmosphere of the crowd through which he'd pushed to reach this elevated station. They had all just been…watching, like that mumbling fool he'd spoken to. Being well acquainted with the latest local goings-on as he was – having indeed just emerged, rosy-cheeked, from a healthy quaffing of his savior's blood amongst likeminded friends, between whom many issues of national import had been discussed with all due solemnity – Praisegod knew that slavery was slowly, *so* slowly, losing some of the support it once enjoyed from the citizens of New York. How else could a gradual emancipation act have been passed? But that raised another question: how many people in this audience were here to cheer on the death of an uppity slave? How many were here to hang their heads and tut and then go to the pub and pat themselves on the back for having tutted? There was no way to know, because from up in this tree the departing heads all looked the same. They were going home after they'd stood and watched, instead of having *done something about it.*

Praisegod tried a few lines of reasoning that would exonerate himself from the same charge of voyeuristic apathy he was imputing to all the assembled, but each failed.

How could he call himself an intellectually serious person, then, if he should always be up in this tree (speaking metaphorically) and watching another poor black thrashing about at the end of a rope? Also metaphorically, as he'd not arrived in time to see the thrashing as such, a fact by which he was distantly disappointed. Not that he had to get here on time to be mortified by it. He knew what it looked like already. It was horrible. It was never *not* horrible. There was no new information to acquire, nothing to be learned from watching the life slip from yet another human body. Even if it was a rather fascinating process to behold, to see the spirit wrestle with the sin to which it had become acquainted, to witness its terror on the threshold of judgment, and even if the process ultimately terminated in a place of peace…it was not a pleasant process. Probably not to go through, but *definitely* not to watch.

So still actually also therefore it *was* a waste of time, to sit in this tree and shake his head at how unfair the world could be, when he could be out there doing something about it. He didn't know what that something was, but he knew it certainly wasn't to be discovered in Pleasance Square.

So Praisegod slid down the tree, returned to his slave Ezekiel and ordered him to "fetch my steed from whichever rail to which you hitched it," because Praisegod was nothing if not a stickler for torturous diction. As the slave, oops, the *indentured servant* (it could be so hard to keep the new terminology in mind), departed for the stables, Praisegod congratulated himself on his ethics. He only owned two slaves, and never once had he struck them. Not with a whip, anyway. He hoped they appreciated the tenderness with which their Master exercised his authority, knowing full well that they probably didn't, perhaps couldn't. They bore the curse of Ham, after all, sinful wretches belonging to a lesser species, possessed of humanity in passing resemblance only.

That didn't mean they didn't deserve to be treated decently, Praisegod reminded himself, ethically.

THIRTY-TWO

TO CALL PRAISEGOD'S FARM A "PIG FARM" WOULD BE AS reductive as it was accurate. The modest twenty-acre homestead had been, like his paunch, a gift from his father, bought cheaply by virtue of being flush against a swift river too aggressive and narrow to be of any use for trade or transport. This useless waterway ate up the entire western flank of the plot, cutting the terrestrial portion down to about fifteen acres and change. Praisegod was hardly about to violate commandment number five, even if he *did* suspect this 'gift' to be yet another passive-aggressive dig at his (attempted) faithful asceticism, from a father who found his son's piety unconvincing. So the son accepted the small largesse graciously, and set about arranging a life of comparable modesty. As such, he, in his bachelorhood, had two cows, six horses, five goats, an Irish gardener named Flann O'Nolan, only *two* sl...indentured servants, and eighty-five pigs.

So, yeah, it was a pig farm.

All of the above-mentioned lived in the stables, capacious and ill-organized, that stood between Praisegod's house and the ceaseless mockery of the river. As one might imagine, this live-stock box was an all-out assault on the senses, battering anyone unfortunate enough to enter with a dizzying arsenal of moos and whinneys and bleats and oinks and good god the *smells*, shit and piss and sweat and more shit. Well adept at acclimatizing to the smaller displeasures of life, Ezekiel and Mary, the other servant, had long since ceased to notice these sensory impositions any-more. Indeed, they relished them, the barnyard fetor being suffi-cient to keep Praisegod far, far away from the stables. Ezekiel, Mary's senior by a decade and then some, couldn't remember the last time Praisegod had even been in.

Nor did Ezekiel have much of an idea what Praisegod *did*. As in, ever. He had never seen his reluctant Master do anything that might be confused for work, and Praisegod only seldom bother-ed to directly monitor the quality of *Ezekiel's* work. The farm itself was undermanned and unfocused; while the majority of the labor revolved around the pigs (notching the newborns' ears, slaughtering in late autumn, fetching favored victuals from the nearby woods that were not actually a part of Praisegod's plot, collecting pork grease to send to market, or at least Praisegod's parents), Ezekiel and Mary would frequently find themselves distracted by errant tasks pertaining to the other livestock, to the detriment of the swine-centric scutwork. These essential tan-gents, though, went forever unnoticed by Praisegod. Most baffl-ing of all was the infrastructure: strapping though Ezekiel was, it was to the smaller, younger Mary whom the duties of domicile repair or construction often fell. Consequently Mary had become quite a bit larger and stronger than she might otherwise have been, filling out her petite frame with lean, striated musculature. Still, she couldn't match Ezekiel's hulking, six-three mass…so Ezekiel always told himself, at any rate.

Yet it was she whom Praisegod wanted to see digging the new latrines, and so it was she by the water, attacking the sun-baked earth with a flat-headed shovel ill-suited to the task, when the river giggled.

That it was Mary by the water was but the first of three coincidences that would define the lives of Patience and Ambrose. For had it been Ezekiel (a far less curious individual) by the river that day, the children would have rushed through Praisegod's property and seen naught but a wide set of shoulders hard at work.

And yet, it was Mary by the water, and it was her natural inquisitiveness which drove her nearer to the banks.

She saw the basket when she still was some thirty-odd yards from the river.

Naturally, toiling beneath the aegis of a man named Praisegod as she did, Mary's mind had been pounded into pious shape by a fleshbound Bible. That the basket baby…oh lord, babies *plural* babbling down the river were *classic* Moses entered her mind before she was wholly conscious of just what it was she was looking at. Two Moseses! Or were they Mos*es*, pronounced Mosies?

No time for moseying. Mary threw down the shovel so powerfully it plunged into the Earth and wobbled upright, not that she saw, not that she'd have cared just then. The river coursing through Praisegod's property was fast, and she wasn't sure she would be able to reach the Mosettes before they were swept beyond her reach, beyond her ability to help.

Enter coincidence two of three: the winter prior to Mary's

race to the river, a heavy snowfall had buried the world, laying so heavily upon all its wonders that the wonders were frankly more than a little overwhelmed. The snow melted slightly beneath the sun, but the moon, a heavenly body of a more generous disposition, i.e. the 'cool parent', allowed it to freeze again. One particular tree branch, stretching out across the river, already straining beneath its wintry load, found the late-night ice more than it could handle. So it snapped under the pressure, diving into the rushing waters below, into a sweep that never froze, never halted. Bad luck for the bough, though; its awkward, palsied crook-shape wedged tightly into the riverbed as it fell. Which rendered it helpless to do anything but reach a few plaintive sprigs above the aspiring rapids and hope it might one day be washed out to sea.

Flash forward some months, and one can perhaps see where the magic is about to happen, assuming one is not Mary. Mary, who couldn't see the mostly-submerged branch, who therefore didn't see it catch on some basket-weaving that had been ripped loose by the aforementioned bottom-spanking rocks.

Here, then, was what Mary saw, through the prism of Praisegod: a basket rushing down the river, soon to be beyond her reach…only for the basket to halt, seemingly of its own accord, and hold strong against the current.

"PRAISE GOD!" Mary shrieked as she plunged headlong into the waters, heedless of the cold.

"WHAT?!" Praisegod screamed from the house, as he always did when Mary was trying to gets God's attention instead of his.

"MOSES BABIES!" she sputtered as her feet slipped on the slick rocks of the riverbed, the waters reaching nearly to her shoulders now.

Even over the roar of the river driving itself directly into her ear, she heard the door to the house creak open. "WHAT?!"

"MOglurplrgurlp," she choked as she ducked beneath the basket, so dipping her mouth into the river, to dislodge it from the branch she now noticed but in no way considered might mitigate the miraculousness of the children's halted progress.

"...I DON'T KNOW WHAT THAT IS!"

By this point, Ezekiel had come near enough to see what was going on. He sprinted for the river, screaming "HOW CAN I HELP?!"

"GET PRAISEGOD!" Mary screamed at him.

"I'M PRESENTLY WITHIN EARSHOT!" Praisegod screamed at her, emerging onto his porch.

"THEN COME TO THE RIVER!"

"THE BUGS ARE OUT IN TOO GREAT A GAGGLE!"

"THERE'S BEEN A MIRACLE!"

"IT SHALL SURELY RETAIN ITS MIRACULOUSNESS BEHIND THESE BUG-BAFFLING DOORS!"

And so it did. Mary, wrapped in a towel, with Ezekiel rubbing his arms up and down her shoulders for a more dynamic drying, watched as Praisegod inspected the children in the basket as he might have horses at auction.

"Hm," he once again offered as he plucked up the sodden note bearing the children's names. He handed it, as he did all written words that came his way, to Ezekiel. Oh, Praisegod *used* to know how to read, had learned how on his mother's knee. Specifically, he'd learned how to read the Bible seven ways from yesterday. He'd crawl into the dusty space beneath the stairs of his childhood home to pore over its endless, eternal wisdoms, to relive its epic battles and suffer with Christ on the cross, over and over and over, until he had committed it to memory. Every chapter, every verse. At which point, he found himself needing to consult the book less and less. Why bother? It only ever served to vindicate his memory. So he stopped reading, because when one has the Good Book seared into one's mind, of what use would any other parochial little scribblings be? He had all of the answers he could ever need, right between his ears.

Years passed, and so too did a rather large subsection of what he'd been carrying between those ears. One can imagine a bubble in his brain labeled LITERACY, being threatened by another one that said THE BIBLE. The Bible bubble proceeds to pummel the former into bite-sized chunks, which it consumes until LITERACY vanishes. At which point, THE BIBLE's label becomes nothing but a series of indecipherable squiggles.

Basically, Praisegod forgot how to read.

So it was Ezekiel, whom Praisegod had acquired specifically to avail himself of the man's advertised literacy (and not for his field prowess, hence that so often falling to Mary) to whom he handed all written language. The pretense for Praisegod's not reading anything himself was his considering all non-Biblical scribbles to be unholy writ beneath his, well, consideration. Like most pretenses, it was easy to see through, and easier still to indulge.

So Ezekiel dutifully accepted the scribblings and read them aloud. "Just says *Patience* and *Amborse*."

Mary rattled an eyebrow skyward as she wrung riverwater from her hair. "Amborse?"

"Amborse," Ezekiel repeated.

"Sure it doesn't say *Ambrose?*"

Ezekiel squinted at the note, moved it further from his face, then nearer, then further. "I suppose you are right," he chuckled. "Does say Ambrose." He looked to Praisegod. "I do not see the intent."

"Those're names," Mary decided. "Patience and Ambrose."

"Ambrose, perhaps," Ezekiel allowed. "Patience, though, this is not a name."

"Could be."

"Patience is what you do. When you wait."

"Could be a name too."

Ezekiel thought about this, then shrugged. "I suppose you are right."

Praisegod ignored that last detail, opting instead to study the two children, mumbling the words that he decided were names to himself, as he looked from one baby to the other. "Patience. Ambrose. Patience. Ambrose." He leaned back to his two slaves, now indentured servants, whom he rather dangerously considered to be something like friends, his *only* friends, in moments such as these. I.e., when it was convenient. "Do they seem… different to you?"

"Compared to what?" Mary wondered.

"Each other." Praisegod leaned in again, sniffing as though the twinly divergence fell to smell. He pointed to Patience. "Galatians 5:22. Some translations list 'patience' as a fruit of the spirit. I myself prefer the King James edition, which has it as 'longsuffering,' but are they not in effect identical?" He brightened and turned towards Mary. "And my dear trembling drudge, this reminds me, I simply *must* show you the Thompson volumes I have lately acquired with the help of Ezekiel. Hot-pressed in Philadelphia only last year, he *sears* the King James Bible onto the page! He being Thompson, not our Ezekiel. It is a mighty tome, fit for a p-"

"I don't th-"

"Yes, yes, alright." Praisegod once again turned his attention to Patience. "My point is, this young thing called Patience – for no boy could be called Patience, that's absolutely a girl's name – bears an address of theological import. I know of no such worth to a thing called Ambrose, lest we be speaking of Saint Ambrose, patron saint of Milan over a millennium ago! And why, pray tell, would we be speaking of him?"

"Well, it c-"

"Precisely. Inspect the children further with their ecclesiastics in mind, and tell me what you see." Mary hardly had the chance to shift forward an inch before Praisegod provided the answer: "Our holy child is of a far lighter hue. She is white, while the infant who bears a name of Earthly provenance is of a muddier complexion, such as yourselves. Yet they have arrived together, in the same bushel. What is the game here, I wonder?"

"Maybe," Ezekiel offered, and that was as far as he got.

"Maybe," Praisegod interrupted, "the colored one was sent to attend the normal one, to be as a personal butler! Yes, that's it," he decided, likely persuaded by hearing the theory emerge from his own mouth. He studied the children now, shaking his head in that particular, softly-angled way that said *Ask me about my deep thoughts*. Ezekiel and Mary knew perfectly well that was what he wanted of them. So they held their tongues until Praisegod tired of his eternally unreturned sally and outed with it.

"In town," he finally continued, "I came upon the tail end of a lynching, which did cause the scales to fall from mine eyes as regards the conduct of a benevolent Master towards his sl… indentured servants. Having thus experience an epiphany, I cannot, in good conscience, take on another sl...unsalaried empl-oyee." Praisegod studied Ambrose some more, reaching out and pulling the child's tiny hand away from his sister's, much to the audible displeasure of both. "It would not be ethical, or Christian of me."

Having made a Christian decision, he heaved himself to his feet and fed the fire a few more logs he could never have split himself if he'd tried, which he never had. "That the white girl has a biblical name is a sign. She shall remain here, in my care, to be raised according to biblical precepts."

"And the boy?" Mary wondered.

Praisegod shrugged. "I shall have Ezekiel aid me in drawing up a bill of sale. Er, for his indenture. I can do that," he asked Ezekiel, "right?"

It was Ezekiel's turn to shrug.

Praisegod, not to be outdone, shrugged again, but even higher and harder. "Of course I can. I shall transfer the boy's indenture to one who will find more use for him, to one for whom the ethical treatment of the negro race is less a concern."

Mary and Ezekiel shot each other anxious looks.

"Surely you won't send him south," Mary mused aloud.

"I'll send him with whomsoever offers me the highest price," Praisegod replied coolly as he pulled Patience from the basket, lifting her from the blankets and hoisting her to eye-level. "There there," he scolded her as she began to wail. "You're in good hands, my child." His voice caught on the word *child* – celibacy had always been his lot in life, something forced upon him in his youth thanks to a lack of social grace and a slight but chronic case of halitosis. As with most men who came of age without ever having touched biblical (wink wink) knowledge, Praisegod turned his burden into a virtue, and so made it bearable. Consequently, he had ruled out the idea of ever having a child. Yet here one was, a girl brought to him by miraculous means, a blank slate upon which to write his name. Not *literally*.

He brought Patience nearer still to his face, which only intensified her displeasure. If Praisegod was bothered by this, indeed if he noticed it all, he gave no outward indication. "I shall raise you as mine own child," he informed her, "and you shall carry my name on, yea unto the next generation."

"But if she gets married," Mary started to point out, "she'll take her hus-"

"Hupup, shh." Praisegod glared at her, then splattered a smile on as he turned back to screaming Patience. "That's a bridge we shall cross as it arises. Isn't that right, Patience Pinchwife?"

Yes. And there you have it: the third and final coincidence that would set the timbre for Patience and Ambrose's lives. Washed down the river from Drummond's Estate, stopped by a winter-felled branch…and collected at their father's son's farm.

Seems like fate, doesn't it? Providence, perhaps? Could be. Could be. Or perhaps it's simple coincidence.

Given all that will follow from this…well, one must decide for oneself which is more unbearable.

So it was that Patience was not only her father's daughter, but her half-brother's adopted daughter, and so her father's adopted granddaughter. And what of Ambrose, then? Poor Ambrose? Why, he would be just another victim of the institution that would come to adopt all manner of curious euphemisms, sold down the river in quite a literal sense. But fear not: Praisegod would feel all kinds of sour about doing it, because he was enlightened now and it certainly didn't make him *happy* to be selling the boy at market the following day to a broker on his way to Louisiana. That said, he believed that a good or service was worth what someone was willing to pay for it, and if someone was willing to pay more for a newborn baby's indenture than Praisegod thought it was worth, than that was how much the newborn baby actually *was* worth. Such was the beauty of this, God's most favored nation. Value was determined by everyday folks like honest farmers and slave traders, and obviously also God. If that wasn't freedom, what was?

Still, Praisegod felt torn up about it for nearly a quarter of the ride back from town to his farm. Patience may have meant long-suffering, but what did she know of it? It was he, a worldly man of a more enlightened race, who bore the heaviest loads the world had to offer. Ambrose, Ezekiel, Mary, whoever else was dark enough to vanish beneath a moonless sky, they had it easy. All they had to do was what they were told. Praisegod had to do the telling, which was the greatest millstone of all. Longsuffering, indeed.

PART TWO

PINK MIST

1804

O N E

PRIOR TO THE ARRIVAL OF THE MIDNIGHT VISITOR, Patience had been a sullen child, gripped by a dismay she had neither the words nor the will to articulate. And even if she had, there would be no reason to suspect a supernormal explanation for her dreadfully normal depression. Praisegod was as good as his word: he raised Patience as his own daughter. He instructed her that she was of his issue, deflecting the maternal question in increasingly desperate ways (his personal lowpoint being an allusion to the virgin Mary as exemplifying the superfluity of *two* parents, which raised a whole host of questions about the nitty-gritty of the female reproductive system that Praisegod was ill-equipped to answer). Not once did he mention Ambrose to her, for Praisegod had wholly failed to consider that that long-gone baby and Patience could be related. Indeed, Praisegod had largely forgotten the boy before even the first anniversary of his sale. So Patience became an only child, and he became her only parent, and that was the way things were.

By the time she was learning to walk, Patience had grown accustomed to that supernormal depression of hers, ceasing to register it as anything but regularnormal. And not just for her. She assumed that everyone on Praisegod's farm and beyond (*beyond* being little more than myth to her at that age) lived in the same grey funk as she, that any outward signs of pleasure were pure mimicry as they were for her. Who or what everyone was mimicking, or to what end, these were questions that never occurred to her, which was to say they were questions. Patience was a singularly uncurious child – what use was knowledge or information in a world of such unceasing dullness? Praisegod told her what to do, and she did it, because he told her that was what she was supposed to do. She didn't much care why she was bound to heed his every command, or for what purpose she was to perform any given task. None of it mattered.

Perhaps this was an inheritance honestly received, this being near the state of mind into which her mother had forced herself more than once during the pregnancy. Perhaps it was hereditary apathy. Perhaps it was something more.

Whatever it was, it was Patience *before* the Midnight Visitor came to call.

T W O

THE THIRD OF JULY, A LONG, SWELTERING DAY THAT would end with that most unusual of nocturnal drop-ins, was odd from first light. It was the day Praisegod has chosen to introduce the concept of "birthdays" into Patience's life, the previous independence days having passed with far more attention to the anniversary of the nation.

"Say 'birthday'," he instructed her.

"Burfday," she returned flatly.

"*Birth*day. And tomorrow is yours."

"Ok."

"Do you know what a *birth*day is?"

She sighed at her feet, wrapped in burlap and tied off with string, as Praisegod had no intention of splashing out for footwear that would be outgrown in a matter of weeks. "It's a bad day."

"It's a *good* day," he corrected her, not unkindly. "It's a good day, upon which we celebrate the anniversary of your entering the world. Do you know what an anniversary is?"

"It's a burf…a birthday."

"Yes! So you know what a birthday is?"

"An addiversary."

"Very good! Tomorrow is also America's birthday. Do you know what America is?"

"No."

"It's where you live."

"Ok."

"It's God's most favored nation."

"Ok."

"Do you know who God is?"

"Daddy."

"In a way," Praisegod replied distantly, as though considering and then abandoning several addendums.

This ordeal completed, she followed her father on his rounds of the property, which were less rounds, more lines tracing the shortest distance from point A to point B. B being, in this case as in so many others, Mary.

"Addiversary," Patience repeated as a mantra while they walked. "Addiversary. Addi*ver*sary."

The more she said it, the more it began to sound like *adversary* to Praisegod's ears. "Shh," he grunted. "Stop. Listen. Listen to me, Patience. The coloreds are of a less favored species," he explained as he leaned against a fencepost outside the stables, "and appeals of a more rational sort will find little purchase in their minds. Better, I've found, to employ less direct means of coercion." He gestured to himself, leaning against the fencepost. "Mary shall awaken to find me here and wonder, 'how long has he been out there, awaiting my reveille?' It will impress upon her a brand of omnipresence on my part, even omniscience. It will frighten her away from ever doing less than her very best, for who *knows* where I should be at any given moment?"

"What's that?" Mary asked, emerging from the stables.

Praisegod blinked at her. "What? What's what? Nothing. How long were you standing there?"

"Where?"

"Nothing. Good morning."

"Good morning, Master," she replied with a curtsey, as she

had been instructed to do in Patience's presence.

Praisegod was never 'good morning' levels of solicitous like this unless he had a truly loathsome job that needed doing. Even the congenitally indifferent Patience had observed that, for example, the last time Praisegod had so favored Mary with a 'good morning,' she had spent the next several hours shoulder-deep in a cow's asshole. Patience couldn't imagine Mary had much appreciated the chore, but what Mary thought of her responsibilities was irrelevant. This was Mary's place, Praisegod never failed to remind his daughter; obeying was her purpose. It said so in his favorite book, which was something else he liked to remind Patience, Mary, really anybody unfortunate enough to fall within earshot when he really got a good steam up.

"I have a very important job for you," Praisegod informed her.

Mary nodded, and followed him and Patience to the necessary. That was what Praisegod insisted they call the brick-based octagon of bare wooden planks, anyway, but thanks to the loose lips of Ezekiel, Mary, and even the gardener Flann, Patience knew it had plenty of other names. The garden chapel. The cloaca. The bog shop. The temple of convenience. The house of office. The close stool. The privy. The latrine. The shithouse.

By any other name, it was a narrow booth over a deep pit that grew shallower every day. The shithouse had been placed about forty yards to the west of Praisegod's house, to keep the offal from seeping into the gardens. This put said offal rather nearer the stables than was conducive to a happy life for those who lived there, but given the stench endemic to those quarters, it made little real difference.

As they shouldered their way through the thick, buzzing fog

of horseflies and into the shithouse miasma which surrounded the structure, Praisegod doubled over and wretched as though he'd just been bopped in the balls. Mary and Patience, far more accustomed to noxious odors, got by with a slight crinkling of the nose.

"You see the problem?" he asked between heaves. "Our necessary has reached capacity." He waved his hand over the pit. "You must fill this in, bury it. Use soil drawn from nearer the river, I don't want any sod in here that might've borne crop." He gasped and stretched up to his full height. "When that's done, you're to take this damn thing apart, move it a ways away, and rebuild it atop another pit, which exists only for want of your digging it. Ezekiel will help with the heavy lifting, but you're to finish the bulk of this on your own. Understood?"

Mary stared impassively down into the shit pit. "Yes."

Praisegod shouted his own name, as was his wont, and all but dove from the outhouse's odorous orbit.

Staring after him for a moment, Mary let her shoulders slump, tilting her whole frame down with them. Patience watched her do this and wondered why anyone would subject themselves to such a direct bird's-eye view of that bog.

"Addiversary, Mary," Patience offered consolingly.

Mary replied with a few shallow nods.

"Patience!" Praisegod called from halfway to the house, the order to follow being implicit. Patience left Mary to her doodie duties, to deal with whatever shit Praisegod had in store for her.

T H R E E

BY SUNDOWN, MARY HAD NEARLY FINISHED COVERING
the pit enough for the flies to lose interest, their humming taking
on a disapproving tone as they took their buzziness elsewhere.
Taking their place by Mary's side was Patience, fresh from yet
another marathon session of listening to Praisegod recite his favorite Bible verses (a category which seemed to include the entire
dang Bible). She frowned at the thought that sooner or later, all
those flies would find the stables. Poor Mary, poor Ezekiel. She
often pitied them, from her bedroom in the house. But as always,
she shrugged that off. That was the way things were, and there
was no sense being upset about it.

"Girls!"

Patience looked up to see Ezekiel striding her way. Ezekiel
was what Praisegod called a 'first generation,' which was to say
he had been kidnapped from a place called Africa at a young age.
As such, he spoke differently than anybody else on the farm. His
punchy lilt and stilted phrasing were simultaneously endearing
and heartbreaking to Patience. His penchant for hailing her as
'girl' – when he absolutely, positively knew that wasn't her name
– was rather less charming, but as with all the other unpleasan-
tries of life, Patience had decided to take it in a stride almost as
loping as Ezekiel's. She wondered what Mary thought of being
called 'girl,' but not enough to make posing the requisite question seem worthwhile.

"Girls," he repeated now that he had just about reached her,
"how is the shit job?"

Mary smiled and looked down at herself, and the splotches of dirt and filth that covered her from head to toe. "I'm almost done with the filling. I didn't get to take the building apart yet."

"Ah, I can barely see your face under such shit!" As an aside, he informed Patience that "shit, this is a word you will have to learn soon enough."

"Shit," Patience replied. "Shit."

Ezekiel shot an uneasy look toward the house. "Maybe forget the word for now, eh?" To Mary he asked, "do you want a help, to finish?"

She shook her head. "Thank you, but I'm almost done."

"You will want a help unfilling tomorrow?"

"Unfilling?"

"No, digging, digging! The new pit."

Mary sighed, plunging the soiled shovelhead into the upturned Earth and leaning on the handle. "Ok," she allowed. "Thank you. But only on the digging, I can do the rest."

Ezekiel winked at her. "A deal, good girl. That is a deal!"

He turned and went striding back to whatever task he'd come from. Patience marveled at Mary slightly. Was she growing weaker in her old age? She must have been, like, a million years old – had she peaked already? Why was she letting other people pick up her slack? Why was she trailing slack in the first place?

Patience shook her head. It hardly mattered. Perhaps this was just another new wrinkle in the baffling patchwork of facts that comprised her life. Once-sturdy stalwarts would be lain low by the passage of time. Pillars crumbling, temples collapsing, that sort of thing. Ho hum. Call it lassitude or cooperation, it came to the same thing. Ezekiel would help Mary dig the new pit. There ended the investigation.

Patience, Ambrose

Taking its place, as surely as Patience had replaced the flies, was a more clear-cut examination.

"Shit," she chanted as she waddled to the unburied edge of the shit pit and nearly tipped straight in.

"Woah woah woah!" Mary shouted, lunging for the teetering toddler, only managing to snatch up the material at the back of her shirt after Patience's hands were wrist-deep in the offal. "The hell, Patience?"

More distraught at the snatch than the shit, Patience broke into a swift-onset variety of tears, peals between shallow breaths that, whether or not the girl knew it, invariably communicated their frivolousness. When she wept thusly, it was simply a matter of steeling one's ears and waiting for something else to distract Patience — Mary prayed for a colorful songbird to embellish the girl's peripheral vision, and so snap her into a fit of half-hearted giggles.

In the meantime, Mary scooped Patience up under her arm and carried the blubbering little bundle down to the river. Taking the girl's hands in her own (and why not, as Mary's had spent the whole day knuckling down into excreta) she plunged them into the cool, insistent current, ignoring the girl's cries of "too cold," watching the shit slide off of her hands and race downriver.

Patience observed this as well. There seemed to be a knot in the very back of her brain, a mystery as insistent as the waters but not at all cool, quite the opposite. It was a painless burn, a fire in waiting, wanting only timber.

A smile leavened her fugue as she watched the shit speed downstream. This was a smile of the sort that rarely brightened Patience's dour little visage, one born not of distraction but fascination. Thusly inspired, she unknowingly crafted a new mantra of her own, her very first creation:

"Shit goes down the river," she told Mary.

"Mhm," Mary replied as she scrubbed the filth from between Patience's fingers.

"Shit goes down the river."

"That's true. What else goes down the river, do you know?"

"Shit."

Mary chuckled. "Fish go down the river. So do tree branches that fall in. In fact, I found you floa…" she winced at her own near-miss indiscretion. Praisegod had forbade her and Ezekiel from ever, under any circumstance, so much as implying to Patience how she had arrived here. Praisegod had told Patience that she was *his* child. Rivers and baskets weren't to have played the least role in her having come to this miserable little pig farm in Gurewitch county. And needless to say, mention of Ambrose at all was strictly forbidden. "Gulp," Mary concluded.

"I was," Patience gasped, taking that awkward, deep inhale all four-year-olds take in the middle of sentences, "I was float on the river?"

Pausing in her finger-rinsing, Mary marveled at the question. Not for the content but for the form itself; it wasn't often that one heard Patience asking questions. Least of all about herself. "Metaphorically," Mary covered. "Life is, um, life is a big river and we're all on it."

"Oh. What's mebaphorically?"

"It means something that, uh…it means something that means something else."

"Oh." She tittered to herself. "Shit. Mary, is shit a bad word?"

"It is. I wouldn't let Master hear you using that if I were you."

"Mary, what if you were me? You'd be so little, and I'd be *this* big!" she shouted, throwing her arms up into a Y shape.

Flinching as shitwater speckled her face, Mary laughed. "Then I'd be the smallest girl in town!"

"Dad's not my Master, though. He bosses me around but I don't have to call him Master like you do."

"...that's true," Mary sighed. She gently withdrew Patience's hands from the water. "Look, all clean. No more doodoo."

"No more shit," Patience sang. "The shit went down the river!"

"That it did."

"Mary?"

So full of questions was the girl today, even names were becoming interrogatives! "Yes?" she asked as she reached out a hand for the little one to take.

Patience stared downstream, her piercing gaze relaxing into something a bit softer. Not vague; all-encompassing. "If shit goes down the river," she asked, "how come we don't just put our shit in the river instead of in a hole?"

Only able to stand to three-quarters of her full height, Mary rose and led Patience back towards the house, hand in tidy hand, savoring the cool water on her skin before the muggy summer sun slurped it away. "Because we'd have to lean over the river, and then we might fall in. Then *we'd* go down the river."

"But if the water goes down the river too, couldn't you just dig" (gasp) "a new little river from the old big river and build the fart house on that?"

Mary slowed her pace, picturing it in her mind. An outhouse with a small, hand-dug culvert beneath it, rushing the offal out to sea, or wherever the hell this river went, thus saving her the task of periodically burying their stored effluvium...

"You know," she finally said, "that's not a bad idea at all. Kind of brilliant, actually. If w-"

"Mary," Patience exclaimed, brandishing a pinecone she had scooped up from who knew where, "what if this was the key to your house?"

Mary smiled, but didn't reply. The question posited Mary's having a house, which was simply too fantastical a premise to indulge.

F   O   U   R

THAT TICKLE IN THE BACK OF PATIENCE'S HEAD SPREAD as the sun crawled nearer the horizon, until that heavenly body decided that this day, like all the others, wasn't worth illuminating any longer, and so fucked off westward to see what Lewis and Clark were up to.

(What they were up to was preparing the following day's fourth of July celebrations, the first of its kind west of the Mississippi. Patience wouldn't hear the expedition cannon they would fire, but she would most certainly feel its reverberations. Mebaphorically speaking.)

By nightfall proper, the ache that wasn't quite an ache began to throb. Its pulses occasioned not pain, however. It was like laying one's cheek on the ground and feeling a loyal heartbeat thump thump thumping in one's temples. A strange sensation, perhaps, but not a worrying one. Maybe even the opposite – there was something comforting about it. As though Patience had been searching for some sign of this cranial pitpat all her life.

What a joy it was, then, a relief beyond words, relief beyond belief, to finally find it.

"For what purpose do you grin so?" Praisegod wondered as he shooed her to bed, as though herding a turkey towards the chopping block.

"I'm just happy," she replied dreamily.

"Well, it's your good fortune to not be raised in a Quaker tradition, or you'd have earned quite a hiding from such an expression!" This was what passed, coming from Praisegod's perpetually drawn lips, for a joke.

"Ok," Patience replied, as she often did to Praisegod's comedy stylings.

Her half-brother/fake-father tucked her into bed, oblivious as always as to his true relationship to his half-sister/fake-daughter. "The time for evening prayer has arrived," he instructed her, which Patience would have called entrapment had she the word. Why, oh why did he insist on waiting until she was snug beneath her covers, cuddled into the Patience-shaped dimple in her mattress, to begin the prayers, during which she was under no circumstances to fall asleep lest she raise her father's ire? Why not begin the prayers earlier in the evening, before her energy went sweeping down the river with the rest of the day's shit? Was God a night owl who only liked to hear His praises sung at bedtime? Lunchtime prayers didn't work for His schedule? Such were the questions she could never ask of Praisegod. So she lay on her back, white-knuckling her blanket (a nice thick one, puffy and warm like a tall cloud on a sunny day, with just one sleepy sunbeam peeking through…), eyes bugged out and locked on a familiar knot in the ceiling beam above her, willing herself to remain awake, and so keep Praisegod from raising his voice. So much effort did the mere act of remaining awake demand, Patience never took part in the prayers, could devote only enough attention to her not-so-father's mandatory piety to indulge him in the audience participation sections, the call and response bits, those omnipresent 'amen's that snuck up on you when you least expected them.

At long last, the final prayer was said, Praisegod took his leave, and Patience was free to sleep. Free to dream, as well, though she'd never wholly seen the point. Probably because she'd never managed to have all that many.

The midnight visitor arrived at precisely the time his name would imply.

F   I   V   E

PATIENCE STARTED AWAKE, THOUGH SHE COULD NOT ACCount for why. She hadn't been having an especially bad dream – or any dream – and she wasn't aware of having heard any loud noises. But something had shocked her from sleep.

It was a boy. A young black boy, sitting on the floor across the room from Patience, legs splayed out in front of him, propped up with two arms stretched behind him.

He looked just as confused as Patience. Which put her strangely at peace with the intrusion.

Warmth bloomed from the back of Patience's head, outward in all directions. It splashed over her brain, poured down her torso, sluiced into her digits. Her whole body overflowed with it, this liquid amber tapped from her own skull. It was unlike anything she had ever felt before, and yet she knew exactly what it was. Something beyond fulfillment, and yet not at all similar to it. Contentment on a supernormal scale. A long-forgotten reminder of something she'd never known, brought swiftly and wholly back at one stroke.

And between them, one hundred people, one thousand people, one hundred thousand million billion or who knew how many people, caught in a tether pulled taut, flooded by an indefinable sense of comfort and completion for which none could account.

So there was a boy in her room, and somehow, there was a nation's worth of people in the empty space between them. It didn't make sense, yet Patience understood it effortlessly. Which confused her.

See, this was why she didn't like dreaming.

"Hi," Patience whispered.

"...hi?" came the reply. It was a voice from nowhere, from everywhere, from right inside her head, from that pulsing bit in the back. Did it pulse in time with the words, like a hand inside a sock puppet?

She looked around her room, unchanged from a moment ago. And yet, atop the usual furnishings, she saw the interior of a sparse brick hut, the floor packed tightly with sleeping bodies. The boy was one of these, sitting bolt upright, staring back at her through the funhouse mirror of twinly kinship.

She let the focus of her eyes soften. Her room was empty. There was the rocking chair, its paint still peeling on the armrests. There was the chamberpot, for when she couldn't make it to the shithouse. There was the mirror, giving her an unwelcome glimpse of her own bafflement.

Focus a bit harder, and her room was still empty. It just happened to have a small brick hut packed with black bodies plopped in the center of it. One of whom, despite his complexion, bore an expression that reminded Patience of her own, spotted in the mirror. The illusion was eerily, uncannily convincing.

Patience tilted her head to the side and clung to distinctions: "You're a lot taller than me."

Her new friend smiled and shrugged. "I can't tell." *Ah cain't tail.* His accent was different from hers, which Patience found inexplicably saddening. He almost sounded more like Ezekiel than her, except with unrulier vowels. "We both sittin'."

"You look like me."

"You look like *me.*"

"How old are you?"

"Four. Almost five."

"Me too. I'm turning five tomorrow."

The boy's expression brightened. "So'm I! Well, I turned five today. Since I'm five today my Master says I'm never gonna be free."

"Addiversary," Patience haughtily corrected him.

"Ooh. Addivers-fuh-ree?"

"Huh?"

"I never figured I'd be gettin' (gasp) learned by an imaginary friend!"

"Imaginary?"

"What's your name?"

Patience folded her arms and scowled. "Did you call me imaginary?"

"I'm tryin' to figure what should I call you!"

"I'm not imaginary." She pointed a finger at him. "*You're* imaginary."

Patience, Ambrose

"I'm Ambrose," the boy insisted. "What's your name?"

"I'm Patience, and I'm not made up, *you're* made up."

"Patience like the, the, the thing?" Ambrose grasped.

"I made *you* up," Patience groused.

"There's, um, there's a word I can't remember for what you are."

"Not made up!"

"Well *somebody* made the word up!"

Patience hefted her shoulders up and plunged them even further down towards her crossed arms. "Why are you in my room? You're not allowed in my room."

"This ain't your room," Ambrose insisted. "You're in our hut!"

"I'm not…" Patience gazed around her room, focusing on the familiar sights for reassurance. Chair, chamberpot, mirror. "No I'm not!"

"Are too!"

"Am not!"

"Are too are too!"

"Am not am not for infinity!"

"Are…" Ambrose's brow guillotined down onto the bridge of his nose. "What's infinity?"

"It's the biggest number there is."

"Nuh-uh. Fifty is the biggest number."

"Fifty-one's bigger than fifty."

Ambrose thought about that, then folded his arms, once again striking Patience as an inversion of herself. "No such number."

Eager to break the illusion, Patience uncrossed her arms. "Yes-huh there is! For infinity again!"

"Infinity ain't a real number!"

"I think *I* would know about numbers," Patience chirped. "*I* have an education because *I'm* a white."

At this, Ambrose appeared to actually deflate, as though whatever force had given him vitality and mass was seeping from his pores, maybe making a funny little squeak sound as it did.

"I'm sorry," Patience quickly added. "My dad says the blacks aren't as good as the whites, only" (gasp) "we gotta be nice to you since it's just how God made you."

"Father Daniel says blacks are just as good as whites, and the" (gasp) "way you treat us ain't right."

"Well, your dad has to read the Bible."

"He ain't my dad, and he knows the Bible front to back."

"You said he was your father."

"Father's what you call a guy's read the Bible."

Patience squinted. "Father's what you call somebody who loved a woman so very much that she built a baby."

Ambrose shook his head. "Fathers don't love ladies, only God."

"Then what's a man loves a lady til she builds a baby called?"

"That's a daddy."

"So you got a Father ain't a daddy," Patience clarified, "but my daddy's a Father on accounta he read the whole Bible."

"I don't know 'bout your daddy," Ambrose grumbled, "and you don't know nothin' 'bout my Father."

"I'm sorry," she repeated, then laughed. "Ah, I made you up so I don't know why I'm sorry!"

"No you *didn't*," Ambrose insisted. "I'm a real boy and I live in Louisiana and I pick cotton and I'm really good at it even though it hurts. I made *you* up as a birthday present to myself."

"Louisiana isn't a real place," Patience huffed, "and cotton isn't for picking, it's for knitting. And you talk like a fairy tale."

"Cotton is *too* for pickin', and if I weren't good at it then how come I don't hardly ever get whupped?"

"What's whupped?" As the question escaped her, she felt a chill dash down her spine. Why would she make something like that up for her imaginary friend? "Who's they? They…you say 'whup' or 'whip'?"

"I said 'whup', only they do both."

"How often you…how often do you get…"

"Which?"

"Whipped?"

"Only happened to me these four times now."

"FOUR!? They slashed you once for every year you've been a person!" So it was that Ambrose slipped unceremoniously from the realm of imagination, into the cruelty of the real.

"Not like it was for the birthday," Ambrose explained. "They only do it when you do something bad, like not" (gasp) "get enough work done or whatever."

"What'd you do?"

"Nothin'd make the whip fair."

Patience nodded. Dumb question. "Do you have ouchies? When I get in a prickler bush sometimes I get ouchies and sometimes they go away but I have a few that didn't."

Ambrose puzzled over this for a moment, as if he was unsure. Then, slowly, he rose to his feet and peeled the loosely-stitched sleeveless cotton shirt from his back. He paused again, shoulders slumped, staring at the ground.

In the hunched figure of her brother, Patience saw herself staring down into the shit pit earlier this very day. She only remembered a moment later that that had been Mary staring down

into the hole, not her. Patience's wildly misfiring empathy trig-
gered an even more horrifying transference when Ambrose
turned around and showed her a body that was, for a fleeting
moment, hers.

She gasped.

What she had expected were four neat slashes across his back
– gnarly, a little bit fascinating for their being grotesque, but
nothing truly stomach-turning. Even with a full two seconds of
hindsight, she realized how idiotic that expectation had been,
how soft her little life on Praisegod's farm had been.

Ambrose's back looked like the bottom of Patience's foot
once had, after she'd accidentally trod upon the shards of a brok-
en jar. A few tidy gashes, yes, but those were set in a scarred and
mortified landscape of welts, bruises, rotting skin, leaking sores.

Patience reached out a hand to touch her new friend's back.
Another gasp, this one smaller than the last, escaped her throat.
She withdrew her hand; absurd, that she should feel entitled to
touch him. Almost as absurd as assuming she *could*, through
whatever dreadful connection they shared.

If Ambrose wasn't imaginary, what the hell was he? Where?
Who?

Somehow, the part of her that recognized Ambrose as her
nearest and dearest kin, that supernormal knot in the back of her
brain that perfectly matched the one in his, down to the rhythm
of their synchrony, that little telepathic tussock recognized that
should she press her fingers against the thickest, knottiest scar
on his back, her brother would not recoil.

None of this was knowledge. Certainly not the *brother* bit. But
it was recognition, in a sense.

"Are the rest of these," she asked when she at last found her voice, "from whuppings?"

"Yeah. Whippin's and whuppin's."

"That…really stinks."

Ambrose lowered his shirt and turned back around. "I don't get 'em nearly as bad as others do. I just keep my mouth shut, make sure all the work gets did."

Patience's mouth flapped open and closed. She had absolutely no framework by which to understand this boy's life. Never once had Praisegod struck her. Heck, the one time he accidentally hit her with his walking stick, *she* had walked into it, and *he* had said sorry to *her*. Sorry to *her!* What kind of a… how could…

She blinked, and Ambrose was gone. Whatever he had been, imaginary or real or an angel or a devil or something else completely, now he was only one thing: gone.

S I X

EZEKIEL WENT TO FETCH THE BIG SHOVEL FROM THE TOOL loft and found it missing. Cursing forgetful Flann – and the extra hour or so it would take to help Mary dig the new shit pit with the small shovel – under his breath, he snapped up the nearly worthless little spade and headed to the intended site of the new necessary.

He was still a ways out when he saw Patience flailing in the river, fighting to keep her head above water.

"Girl!" he screamed as he threw down the shovel and rushed to her rescue.

With his adrenaline pumping as it was, he kept sprinting even after he'd realized his mistake. Patience wasn't drowning in the river. She was wielding the missing big shovel like a pole vault, ramming up clods of mud and hurling them into the rushing waters.

"What are you up to?" he shouted as he stumbled to a halt, running out of breath by the end of the question. He grabbed his knees and took deep gulps of air.

"I had an idea," she told him without looking up. Rearing back, she threw the spade of the shovel into the riverbank and jumped on the handle to drive it in. "I told it to Mary and she liked it. Hrng," Patience grunted as she dropped her weight to the Earth, driving a scoop of sludge up into the air. Arms trembling, she ferried this to the river and plopped it in. She turned and favored Ezekiel with a proud, beaming smile.

He shook his head. "That shovel is you times two, girl! Why not take the smaller one?"

She frowned and gestured grandly to the mud clot racing away in the current. "Shit goes downstream," she decreed, as though that answered his question. The brandished arm swung around in a long southern arc, pulling to the east and curving back to rejoin the unwieldy flow, as though *that* explained her dig-a-little-canal-that-loops-off-the-river-and-then-loops-back-into-it-and-build-the-privy-over-that-loop concept.

Which, for a wonder, it did. Ezekiel continued to shake his head, but the set of his mouth softened with each swing. "What about the folks live downstream?"

Patience looked at the river thoughtfully, as though it had volunteered a bright idea. It hadn't, of course. This had been her innovation, through and through. It had only transmogrified into a *plan* that urgently required her attention after Ambrose had taken his leave last night. Laying on her cheap straw cot, staring at the ceiling, Patience had felt the liquid amber receding, felt that familiar sense of incompletion reclaiming her. And yet, the resin remained below the surface, a reservoir that seeped into her bones, her heart, her mind. The change this brought about in her, from simply knowing what lay within her, was immediately apparent. Morning had dawned, and the moment Patience stepped outside and looked at the river, her only thought was: I'm the one. I'm the one to do this job.

Returning her gaze to Ezekiel, Patience shrugged and fixed her grip on the shovel. "Everybody's downstream from somebody."

"There must be one man at the top."

Patience plunged her shovel into the riverbank. "*He* shits in the river."

Ezekiel laughed and gestured for Patience to climb out of the river. "Alright girl, but you'd do best to start at the bottom of your little loop and dig up. Other way around, you'll be all wet!"

Leaning off the handle, Patience looked from Ezekiel, to the river, to the place where all shit flows. She turned back to him and said, with eerie maturity, "good point."

1806

O N E

MASTER BARRY INSISTED ON BEING THERE, EVERY NIGHT.
But never once was he courageous enough to draw a fistful of
pepper himself. This was a job he appointed to a slave. Every
night.

Nine days into this punishment, Ambrose had ceased to register who it was reluctantly rubbing the pepper, which no one on
the plantation could have known had been brought to this country along the same shipping channels as their grandparents had,
into Ambrose's eyes. Just as he'd ceased his struggling against
the wooden stocks that held his hands and feet out in front of
him, suspending his stooped body two inches above the ground,

bare back exposed to the climatic vagaries of Louisiana in late June.

Just a few weeks, he thought as a callused palm ground the spices into his eyes. In just a few weeks, he would be seven years old.

This evening's pepper-wielder scurried away the moment they had completed their loathsome task. Yet Master Barry lingered, gloating as he always did, exchanging snide comments with Hilditch the overseer. Tonight's asides were centered largely on the mucus dribbling from Ambrose's nose, into his mouth.

Nothing seemed to please Master Barry quite as much as seeing his property mistreated, on his terms.

After a minute or so, Master Barry went off to bed and sent Hilditch out on patrol, trusting that the pepper would dig itself deeper into Ambrose's eyes with each and every blink. As per usual, Master Barry got his wish.

In those rare snatches of insensibility that passed for slumber, Ambrose dreamed of his friend, of whose existence he remained skeptical. If she wasn't a figment of his imagination, perhaps some strange attempt to make sense of life, then what could she be? *Who* could she be? It had been ten-odd months since she had appeared to him a second time, once again on his birthday. She had seemed far happier that time than she had during their first encounter, possessed of a brightness that only served to deepen Ambrose's gloom by contrast. Perhaps recognizing how her cheeriness had a less-than-salubrious effect on him, the young girl had tempered her enthusiasm for the remainder of their conversation. Which largely centered on each questioning the existence of the other until their ghostly congress terminated, as it had the first time: arbitrarily and without fanfare.

It was after this second encounter on Ambrose's (and, according to her, Patience's) sixth birthday that his attitude changed. Or, he supposed, developed. The obsequiousness of which he had been so proud, which had thus far saved him from the worst of Hilditch's unpleasant paraphernalia, began to crack and peel, revealing something much harder beneath. Ambrose hadn't meant to grow combative, drew none of the martyr's pleasure as he suffered ever more tortures at the hands of his overseer and his Master. It was simply that, well, he had allowed himself to believe there could be more to life than this. That he could be unowned, be seen and treated as a person rather than a thing. True, it made little sense to draw this conclusion from speaking to Patience, a white girl who may or may not even have existed. But didn't there seem to be something…else to her? Didn't she strike Ambrose as entirely more than her diminutive, pale form? Wasn't it all too easy to imagine himself in her place? Almost impossible *not* to?

Really, these questions were beside the point. The seed had been planted, and it mattered not how. For now it was taking root, growing, reaching, budding, threatening to bloom.

How could he stop himself from sneaking a taste of that life, a life unowned and unbowed, here or there? From muttering a seditious comment under his breath, or stuffing fewer bolls into the gin than the machine could handle, just to make the spinning go a bit more smoothly? He felt he could no more control these impulses than not grimace as the dry bristles of a cotton plant scratched at his hands. Most times, these little rebellions went unnoticed.

Other times…

As usual, Ambrose only realized he'd been sleeping after he'd woken up. What roused him this time were two sharp, searching claws on his back.

The bird had returned. Ambrose imagined it was a crow, but it never cawed or squawked or made any noise that might clue him in. Nor did it ever pick at the whip-loosened flesh, as he'd once feared it might. Now as before, it simply landed on his back and paced, tracing a slow, silent, stabbing circuit. And now as before, Ambrose drifted into a punishing unrest, awakening to face the scorching vengeance of daylight while it was still just a pleasant splash on the horizon…with no bird on his back. No chance to see it, and so name it.

So began another day.

Ambrose knew how this punishment ended: when, and *only* when, he slipped beyond sleep into total unconsciousness. Master Barry would be satisfied by nothing less. He took these lapses into insentience as a surrender to his authority, to his race's supremacy. Many of the slaves discussed methods of succumbing to shock sooner, of facilitating that slip as quickly as possible. Ambrose understood that approach, but couldn't subscribe to it. That was giving Master Barry precisely what he sought; prostration to a way of life that Ambrose was increasingly loathe to accept. Neither authority nor supremacy did Ambrose find in Master Barry. That the adolescent slave boy would win, that he would somehow turn the tables on the whole Barry family simply by keeping cognizant in the stocks for weeks on end, was something about which even young Ambrose could not dream. But he would hold on for as long as he could, if for no other reason than it was something he could do.

Just as he allowed himself to be blinded by the lure of a life beyond these stocks, this cotton, this wretched, endless summer. Whether or not it made sense to, he consented to be devoured by hope, numbed by it.

He lasted another four days in the stocks before he lost consciousness. One day shy of two weeks. A personal best.

T   W   O

WHEN HE CAME BACK UP, ISABEL WAS SINGING TO HIM.

The bell, she sang, is a-ringing in the other bright world, and for a moment Ambrose thought she was talking about whatever spectral plane his friend Patience inhabited. Since their most recent spooky sit-and-visit, though, Ambrose had begun to believe that however mystical their means of communication, Patience herself was a real person who occupied space in the world as surely as Ambrose did. She insisted she lived in "New York," which sounded made up to his ears, but both Father Daniel and Doctor Mayhew assured him that it was, indeed, a real place, up to the north. That wasn't conclusive, but it was certainly compelling. Then, of course, there were the others, the hearts and minds between them, who somehow fell beneath the purview of whatever strange cord stretched across the country and conjoined the two of them in telepathic congress. Ambrose could feel, sometimes even *hear*, the souls between himself and his inexplicable interlocutor, and he could feel that those souls felt the two children, were in some way changed by their union. Were one to trace a straight line between himself and Patience, and subsequently interview any individual standing in that path, Ambrose was certain one would be inundated with reports of uncaused tummyaches, or soaring hearts for which the bearer could hardly account, in the moments those people passed beneath the shadow of that bond. Patience didn't seem to feel it as acutely as he did, but somehow this only strengthened Ambrose's conviction that the phenomenon was real, and precisely as he imagined it. He imagined, furthermore, that this affective tether had a sound, the sound of a far-off bell a-ringing, always a-ringing, never to be unrung.

Then he finished waking up and realized Isabel was just talking about heaven, boring old heaven.

She saw his eyes crack open and immediately fell upon him. "You're up!" she shouted in a twang even deeper than his. "Lord, what a fright you gave us! Thirteen days!" She snapped a rag off the floor next to Ambrose and dabbed forcefully at the moisture on his forehead.

"Wha…" He tried to push himself up to a sitting position, but couldn't manage to get his elbow firmly beneath him.

A sturdy pair of hands swooped down from behind and guided him back down to the ground. Tilting his head back, Ambrose followed the arms up up up to the face of Daniel, or Father Daniel when all the unfriendly ears were turned away. Daniel was something of a religious authority among the slaves, one of the few possessing the gift of literacy, and so one of the few who had read the Good Book for himself. In an unfathomable act of generosity, it was Master Barry himself who had taught Daniel to read. Ok, yes, that was overstating things – Master Barry had let Daniel sit in on his daughter's tutelage, though this was arguably more astonishing. In either case, the result was the same: Daniel could read, and so Daniel could lead. This he sometimes did, in his limited way, shepherding his fellow slaves through unfocused prayers and sermons, a distinction which earned him his nickname-cum-title. Amongst the slaves, at any rate; his self-appointed honorific was ecclesiastical contraband, carrying as it did a whiff of divine ordination that Master Barry would undoubtedly have interpreted, not entirely inaccurately, as a challenge to his own beloved authority.

However pedantic Ambrose could be about the distinction between biological and liturgical fatherhood, he did look up to Daniel as something more than a mere spiritual leader. So it was a mark of Ambrose's disorientation that he put his father figure at risk by uttering the words "Father Daniel" without first determining who was in the room with them.

Daniel and Isabel exchanged a look, one unreadable to Ambrose from his nasal-gazing prostration. But when they turned back down to him, their faces were warm, so he didn't imagine there'd been risk of someone overhearing his mistake. It was sobering to realize Master Barry might well have been standing just out of eyeshot, though. Sobering enough to get Ambrose sitting all the way up on his elbows.

"I'm ok," he insisted as he took Daniel's proffered hand. "I'm ok." He rubbed delicately around his eyes, feeling the cracked, irritated skin crunching beneath his fingertips. The world spun. A shiver raced through him, then took another lap to beat its own time. "There any water?"

Isabel glanced at Daniel. "I'll see if I can't fetch some," she began, looking back to Ambrose now, "but it might be a minute, if I have to sneak for it. Should Master Barry hear you're in a drinkin' way, he might figure you're once more fit for ploughin'."

"If you can hold out another hour or so," Daniel suggested, "Naomi should be back. She could fetch it with-"

"Hour's fine," Ambrose mumbled into his lap, hand waving without any real intent behind it.

"Here," croaked the unmistakable, tectonic voice of Doctor Mayhew. Ambrose felt the rim of a canteen pressed to his lips — despite the ceaseless heat of the day, the metal was cool to the touch. The water was even colder, so cold it was almost (but not quite) unpleasant.

Ambrose nodded his gratitude to Doctor Mayhew, but held his tongue from committing it to speech. Mayhew was a screwy old man who practiced a screwy old magic he called "voodoo." So said Father Daniel, at any rate, and Ambrose had never seen anything to counter the charge. Yes, Mayhew was a skilled muddler of poultices and salves, and he knew how to set broken bones, two facts among a host of others that made him far more useful to his fellow slaves than any of the so-called experts Master Barry fetched when the only alternative was the loss of a life (or as Barry preferred to phrase it, an investment). But Mayhew's utility was, as far as Ambrose could divine, just barely sufficient cause to overlook his devotional deviancies; cavorting around with unidentifiable bits of animal innards and smoldering shrubs, yodeling in languages either foreign or fictional, and dancing in ways that were, Daniel assured Ambrose, quite unbecoming a man of Mayhew's age.

If Daniel said the dancing was embarrassing, then Ambrose was happy to find it as such…but he had to admit, he was often impressed by how well Mayhew got around. Once upon a time, one of those white doctors Barry fetched to protect his investments had taken Mayhew's right leg from just above the knee. Ambrose had never learned precisely what had precipitated Mayhew's losing that limb, and the old man quite clearly disliked any discussion of the matter. All the same, Mayhew got along just fine without his leg, limping spryly on two self-constructed crutches.

Ambrose found it oddly poignant, to know that a man who saved others from similar misfortune had been unable to extend the same kindness to himself. But the poignancy was undercut by the knowledge that the means of salvation were voodoo. Shameful, uncivilized voodoo. So said Father Daniel.

Still…a moment ago there had been no water in the cabin. Now there was, and Ambrose was drinking of it greedily. When such wonders occurred at the hands of Doctor Mayhew, one did well not to press for too many details.

Father Daniel glared at Doctor Mayhew, as was his wont. The two had never quite gotten along. Ambrose often asked Daniel why, and received a litany against voodoo in response. And while he tried to avoid Mayhew when possible, the one time Ambrose had asked the Doctor to account for his antipathy towards the Father, Mayhew had simply responded with "I prefer a man who earns his title through his work, rather than the opposite." Whatever *that* meant.

"Amount of water you're giving him," Daniel said through a fake smile, "I'd wonder if you weren't hoping to drown the boy."

"Oh," Isabel sighed, hanging her head. Her usual response, when Daniel and Mayhew started in on one another.

"Plenty of water," Mayhew chuckled. "No sense givin' him less than he needs."

"Surplus is no virtue," Daniel replied.

"Surplus is more'n what's needed. You gotta *meet* a need to exceed it."

"Alright," Isabel said to both men at once.

"I meet needs," Daniel mumbled to himself.

Mayhew shrugged, then smiled down at the water Ambrose

was still drinking.

"Ambrose," Father Daniel intoned, "that is voodoo water. It will m-"

"Oh, leave off," Mayhew laughed.

"It will make you *sick.*"

"I have to 'fess up," Isabel sniffed to Ambrose, loudly enough to interrupt the bickering figureheads. "I'm the one rubbed pepper in your eyes."

That, at long last, got Ambrose to quit drinking. He handed the water back to Mayhew.

"On the seventh night," Isabel went on. "I'm so sorry."

"Don't matter," Ambrose shrugged. "Ain't like it was your idea," He mustered an unsteady grin. "Least, I hope not."

"No," Isabel smiled sadly. "But that don't make it right."

"Well, it certainly don't make it wrong."

She studied the preternaturally thoughtful boy as the smile melted off her face.

"You're a bright young man," Daniel boomed, casting a glance towards Mayhew, just waiting for the voodoo man to say something, anything, that the Father could interrupt.

Mayhew said nothing. He simply stared at Ambrose, his expression warm, maybe even…proud?

Ambrose, still too scrambled to charge back into that particular thicket just yet, returned his attentions to his lap. "Can I hear you sing some more?" he asked Isabel.

The bell, it turned out, was still a-ringing.

T H R E E

"YOU EVER WONDER WHAT'S LIFE?"

Herod, a slave only slightly older than Ambrose, slapped a sun-shading hand across his brow and squinted at Ambrose over a tuft of cotton. "What's life?"

Ambrose nodded, but didn't draw his eyes from the plant he was picking. "Yeah."

Herod frowned, then shook his head. "No. I ain't never wondered that." He returned to work. "What's that gonna do for me?"

Ambrose shrugged.

"Life's the thing ya live," Herod mumbled to himself, halfway to a laugh.

Ambrose smiled, but didn't fully share Herod's amusement. He managed a full five seconds of silent picking before returning to his furrow: "I'm sayin', if the point's we're gonna go to heaven forever, how come we gotta come here first? It ain't nice here."

Herod shook his head and favored Ambrose with his most sagacious sigh. "You gotta ask Daniel. He'll tell ya, prettier'n I can. But it's somethin'...it's about how it's so we can show God we're worth puttin' in heaven."

"But he made us, didn't he?"

At this, Herod's shoulders started to tighten. "Ask Daniel."

"Yeah, I know ask Daniel. But I'm askin' *you*."

"And I'm tellin' ya, ask Daniel. He'll tell ya, prettier'n I can."

"That's the thing," Ambrose replied, turning to face Herod head-on. "I don't want somebody to tell me pretty. I want 'em

187

to tell me clear."

"Ask Daniel, and tell him you want the clear."

Ambrose huffed quietly, then shifted to the next tangle over and plunged his hand into the bush. He felt, but did not react to, a bract slicing into the meat of his thumb. "I feel like I'd get somethin' clear straight off from Mayh-"

"Mayhew don't know what's he talkin' about," Herod snapped.

Ambrose said nothing to that.

"Trust me. I'm older'n you."

Ambrose was on the cusp of returning fire as he always did following Herod's inevitable recourse to age ("well, you're still dumber'n shit") when Hilditch the overseer thundered both of their names across the field.

That was a warning no one wanted to hear twice in one day. Because it was only a *warning* the first time.

Ambrose had only just begun to recover from his weeks on the stocks, not a fortnight behind him as it was. Exhaustion had a bridle on his more transgressive impulses. Today, in this particular moment, the only impulse he had was to heed Hilditch's warning while it remained so, to keep his head down and the furrow thrown towards the cotton.

For a few minutes, he managed to do just that. But eventually he couldn't resist turning his mind towards boring words that got interesting once capital letters were on the case. Words like Meaning, Purpose, Future. Words he'd never had time to consider as capitalized – which was to say, as concepts – before.

Ooh, Time, there was another one. Capital-T Time was ticking away towards the fourth of July, when he would get to see his strange friend Patience once again. Strange indeed, that he should so anticipate her coming. They'd seen each other only twice before, their conversations stilted, their meetings brief. Yet to find himself in her presence engendered a feeling of such immense calm, such overwhelming peace, it seemed to clarify so many of the questions raised by capital letters. He'd not have been able to articulate any of his insights, of course, but that didn't make them any less legitimate. So he told himself, anyway.

That night, he could hardly sleep for excitement. He lay sweating on the packed-earth floor of the slaves' cabin, staring at the ceiling, hoping Patience might put in an early appearance. No, it wasn't the fourth...but what was Time, huh? Before long, his hope calcified into an expectation. His excitement redoubled as he waited for something to happen. And, after countless impatient hours, something did happen: the sun came up, and Hilditch started shouting.

F O U R

DANIEL WAS, BY DINT OF HIS LOW COMPANY, CURRENTLY Father Daniel.

It was a small, quick sermon delivered around the side of the meathouse, precisely the sort of gathering to which Ambrose, despite his enthusiasm for both the message and the medium, was never invited. It was nothing personal, Father Daniel had informed Ambrose, but simply down to the boy's being too young to truly understand the lessons being imparted. No, these were homilies by, for, and about middle-aged men; Ambrose would only be granted audience by the calcareous, agonizingly unhurried hands of capital-T Time.

Ambrose didn't see what the big deal was. There were never more than five or six attendees, tops, and Saul was only fifteen. Heck, Daniel was by far the oldest of the group at forty-three. So what, Ambrose had to wait until he was fifteen to be in the group? That was almost…five…six…*nine* years away! Which was basically…what was Patience's word? *Fintinitty? Tinfinity?* It was never gonna come. And besides, if Ambrose was still hoping to join Daniel's special sermons in nine whole years from now, it would mean that Ambrose still lived here, that nothing had changed…

Frustrating though he found being boxed out, Ambrose did his best to respect Daniel's wishes by steering clear of these special sermons. Partially because Daniel's wishes weren't always tendered as *wishes*, but also because eavesdropping could only hurt his chances of being inducted into those selective ranks later on, when he was all grown up and fifteen. Better off playing hard to get.

On one temperate July evening, though, one that happened to be on the eve of his birthday, Ambrose was lugging a side of pork down to the meathouse, too busy imagining that it had been he who had tracked and felled the mighty swine with a well-thrown spear to notice the muttering clutch of penitents. It was not until he had circled the cubical structure and nearly walked right into Daniel's back that Ambrose realized what he'd unwittingly stumbled into.

For the remainder of his life, Ambrose would *what if* that exact moment to, well, death. Not so much for what came next…but for what came after that. And what came after *that*.

But return to the head of the landslide: what if he had simply turned on his heel and high-tailed it the moment he heard Daniel's voice? What if he had stumbled into the conversation at any point other than the one in which Daniel declared that the African slave trade had been ended? What if he hadn't had the temerity to drift right up to Daniel's side, dead pig still draped over his shoulders, and ask "did you say slavery's over?!"

It was ultimately pointless, wondering what *might* or *could* or *would* or *should* have happened. But given the consequences, however long in coming they might have been…it was just as impossible not to.

Daniel studied the young boy at his heel as though he were scripture. Which is to say, the Father sought, and so found precisely what he was looking for.

"Not…not quite. It's alright," he reassured the restive murmurers in the group.

"He ain't old enough," Saul groused.

Ambrose didn't have any particularly trenchant response to that, so he stuck his tongue out and made a fart noise.

Daniel sighed and placed a hand on Ambrose's shoulder, which the boy took to be as good as induction. How quickly he was growing up!

"I wanna know *everything*," Ambrose practically sang.

The Father smiled. He showed his teeth, at any rate. "The African slave trade is over. They p-"

"What's that mean?"

"It means, nobody can bring new slaves in from Africa. Which is where our ancestors came from."

"I got no clue where my ancestors come from."

"Don't ya?!" scoffed Jerry, second-oldest of the group after Daniel, but leading the pack in jackassery. "What color's your skin, you dumbass?"

Ambrose spat in Jerry's direction. "You ain't met my folks! You don't know nothin' I don't!"

"Alright," Daniel thundered.

"I know you got folks come from Africa at some point," Jerry pressed, "you're dark and owned as the rest of us!"

"Don't nobody own me!" Ambrose shouted, realizing his slight factual error only at the very end of the sentence. "Ah."

Such was the magnitude of the falsehood, however, that Jerry stopped to think about Ambrose's assertion. "Huh?"

"I don't know!"

Jerry smacked his lips and waved dismissively. "Go fuck a duck's butt, you bitch."

"You..." Ambrose waved a finger, only to discover profanity didn't come as naturally to him as it did to Jerry. "You...Jerry!"

"Enough," Daniel declared in his most ministerial timbre. With a strength Ambrose would not have imagined the Father possessing, he heaved the dead hog from off Ambrose's shoulder, hurled it into meathouse, and slapped his hand back onto Ambrose's shoulder – this time, with a force that was impossible to mistake for a welcome.

"Ah," Ambrose sighed once again, hanging his head. He suddenly saw why Daniel hadn't wanted him in the special group. "I'm real sorry," he whimpered. "Ain't the case, I wanted to kick up dust. I can listen."

"You would only have more questions," Daniel informed him gently.

"I can listen for the answers, in a way I ain't go-"

Daniel's hand tensed against Ambrose's shoulder, then shoved him gently but firmly back towards the fields. "There are no questions you can ask that would not be better off entrusted to me," he assured Ambrose.

"But ain't that what I'm doin' when I'm askin' ya?" Ambrose wondered over his shoulder as he stumbled along in front of Daniel.

The Father shook his head. "You simply needn't know the answers. I don't want you to get your little head all scrambled up with things that aren't your concern just yet."

"But what if it's a question you ain't thought of yet?"

The Father paused, then chuckled…in a way that struck Ambrose as mocking. "That won't happen."

"You don't know that," Ambrose replied, feeling himself growing unexpectedly frustrated with his surrogate father.

"Actually, I do," Daniel replied, his clipped diction implying precisely the same rising aggravation.

"How do you know?"

"Because I know all of the things that you know."

"You don't know that."

"Yes, I do."

"No, you *don't.*"

"Okay," Daniel snapped, slowing his pace as he visibly ratcheted himself into a more sagacious calm. "Alright. Tell me something I don't already know."

"Um…" Ambrose turned to look up at Daniel.

Daniel glowered down at him.

Ambrose shifted uncomfortably from one foot to the other. "Mmm…" He darted his eyes wildly around his surroundings, looking for something, *anything,* to get the juices flowing. "Birds, um…"

The Father nodded. "You see."

"I have an imaginary friend who's a real girl," Ambrose blurted out before having a chance to give it any thought. Upon reflection, though, that seemed a pretty solid candidate; there was no *way* Father Daniel could know that!

Ambrose chose to interpret the older man's slack features as a recognition of, if not defeat, then his having taken the first step towards it.

"Yeah!" he pressed on. "She's real and she lives in New York, and she's a white girl."

Daniel pinched the bridge of his nose. "Ambrose, you're a child. Of *course* you have an imaginary friend."

"She's not imaginary!"

"You just called her…" The Father sighed. "At any rate." Daniel squared his shoulders to Ambrose, and took a knee. "You don't know things yet, Ambrose. And you don't *know* that you don't know things."

"So," Ambrose frowned, "how do I get to know things?"

Daniel patted the top of his head. "Pray for guidance, and I'll provide you with what you need."

"So how do *you* get to know things?"

"I read. *But,*" Daniel practically interrupted himself, waving a scolding finger in Ambrose's face, "this is a rarified skill, best suited to holy purposes. This is why we have men such as myself, men of the book. To read, interpret, and spread the Word. We can't have everyone on the farm reading the Bible and creating their own interpretations, could we? It'd be, it'd be *chaos.*"

"Can I learn? Someday," Ambrose added, in the face of Daniel's evident disapproval.

Daniel shook his head and rose to standing. "Intelligence makes us dangerous, and they know it. So they will try to keep us stupid. The smartest thing you can do, then, is to let them believe you are. And as the truth is always simpler to maintain than a fiction, the *safest* thing you can do is to not let yourself get *too* smart." He smiled at Ambrose and tapped the side of his head.

Ambrose frowned. "Smartest thing is to stay stupid?"

"Look at it this way," Daniel explained, "if you only have to lie about one or two things, it'll be easier than having to lie about five or six. See what I mean?"

"…yeah," Ambrose lied.

Daniel smiled. "Smart boy."

"But not *too* smart," Ambrose replied, in a tone he hoped didn't sound as prickly as he felt, "right?"

Daniel chuckled in a way that made clear he didn't wholly get it. "Exactly right." He once more patted Ambrose on the head, then hustled back towards the meathouse.

Ambrose remained where he was for a moment, watching Father Daniel go, then aiming his gaze towards the sky.

There was a bird flying overhead, its massive pale wings locked out as it rode the wind. Flying a slow, silent circuit overhead. No doubt it had talons well-suited to pulling soft things apart, hidden flush against itself in a tuft of gentle feathers. Ambrose would go so far as to say he *knew* those talons were there. Even if couldn't see them, from down here.

F I V E

TIME, CAPITALIZED OR NOT, IS A CONSTRUCT, BUT MIDnight is eternal.

In a moonlit instant, an eleven-hundred mile slash across

North America, stretching northeast from Louisiana up to New York, came alive in the night. The thousands of people beneath its pall at that moment found themselves swept as one into surrealist dreams and troubling hallucinations.

Images of dismal flesh stretched to, yes, infinity.

Crackling voices, snapped taut along an umbilicus.

Warm embraces rending the twilight.

Interlocking crescents that limned a thing resembling hope.

In the morning, none of them would much recall what they'd experienced in the night. Not in any sense they could communicate, at least. But not a few would wake up feeling inexplicably optimistic about the coming day, regardless of what lay before them.

Alas, it was a feeling borrowed rather than kept. Quotidian abuses would reduce those morningrise idealists to their baser natures.

But that's for other people, for tomorrow. So let's put the sun back behind the horizon, because right now it's still *tonight*, and Ambrose is staring across the hut, across the country, at his sister Patience.

"Are you okay?" she asked him the instant she appeared.

"Yeah. You?"

She nodded. "I am." In what was quickly becoming the ritual of their reunion, initial pleasantries were followed by silence. With each passing year, the gulf between their experiences of life widened. What could they talk about? Patience was perpetually worried, should she discuss the minor trials of her life, that Ambrose would think she was grinding her good fortune into his eyes. Ambrose, for his part, had no intention of seeming to shame Patience for her happier lot by subjecting her to his travails.

But, of course, there was no discomfort in the silence. For it was not the absence of speech, nor the absence of meaning. It was silence entire, a whole kindness unto itself. If anything, the ease they each found in this quiet clarified that the words which broke it needed to be worthy.

And so, hoping to puncture the kindness in a way that might prove productive – as well as to exorcise the thought that was most haunting him at present – Ambrose asked her, "can you read?"

Patience hung her head, as though exhausted by being endlessly posed this question. "No."

Ambrose forced a smile. "I didn't figure. Me neither. We're little yet, though."

"Do you have a book?"

"Nah. Just a guy on my farm don't wanna teach me to read. He hogs all the stuff he knows like if he gives any of it away it ain't gonna be worth as much. I ju…ah, it's Father Daniel, you remember I told you 'bout him?"

Patience sat further up in bed, propped her pillow behind her back and crossed her legs. "Yeah. The Father ain't a daddy."

"Yeah. Father Daniel. I think he's kind of a jerk. He alw-"

"I thought you liked him."

"I guess I did. I guess I *do*. Only…he's irkin' me as of late." Ambrose recounted his collision with Father Daniel down by the meathouse, keeping it brief so as not to, ha, hog the entirety of their time together.

"So…" Patience frowned. "He's sayin' it's smart to be dumb?"

"Ah, yeah."

"That's dumb."

"I mean, it's actually smart, it's so because if you're smart, you're bound to get hided more'n a dumb fella, since a dumb fella ain't a danger to nobody. So if ya act dumb, people'll think you *are* dumb when actually you're smart."

"Ooh, okay. That's smart!"

"Yeah," Ambrose sighed, "but the thing is that Daniel don't actually *want* anybody gettin' smart. He wants 'em to be dumb as he tells 'em to pretend to be." *Since a dumb fella ain't a danger to nobody,* Ambrose's own voice taunted him.

"That's dumb."

"…maybe."

Patience ignored Ambrose's grave equivocation, instead shrugging and saying "I always thought the doovoo guy sounded cooler anyway."

"Voodoo," Ambrose corrected. A smile slowly stretched across his face. He snorted.

Patience tilted her head to one side. "Huh?"

"Doovoo sounds like doodoo," Ambrose observed.

"Yeah," Patience giggled.

"What if Mayhew was a doodoo man?"

"Stop!" Patience laughed. "Sounds like Daniel's the doodoo man, if anybody is!"

"Yeah," Ambrose replied, in a far more pensive cast than *Daniel's the doodoo man* probably deserved.

Patience stopped laughing pretty quickly.

"If you learn how to read," Ambrose asked, his eyes turned down to his lap, "you think you could teach me?"

"I'll teach you everything I ever learn," Patience replied at once, "long as you do the same."

The thought seemed to strike Ambrose in a literal sense, like a finger-flick between the eyes. He flinched accordingly.

The two children burned giddy fire to one another across the night, as a smile slowly spread across their face.

Face*s*. Oops.

S I X

HE SHOULD HAVE SEEN IT COMING, REALLY.

It was the beginning of picking season, only the third one Ambrose had fully participated in (that his being thrown into picking had coincided with the appearance of Patience was a fact that disturbed and frustrated him in equal measure). Last year, he had suffered quite a bit for what Hilditch referred to as his "creeping insolence." Ambrose couldn't wholly disagree with that assessment, even if it disregarded the catalyst for his apparent lassitude: hope, unmoored from reason.

Now, a year later, age-seven Ambrose swung the strap of his cotton sack around a stronger set of shoulders and a more refined sense of idealism. Hope now struck him as, ha ha, hopelessly naïve. It was, at least on its own, too passive, too accepting. Father Daniel had taught him that, even if he hadn't quite meant to.

Daniel was a man with a plan. What the plan was, Ambrose could not begin to speculate. Did the Father want to escape? Did he want to unite the slaves and rise up? Did he want to maneuver himself into a position of favor with Master Barry and flatter his way into a less onerous sort of servitude? Ambrose suspected that not even Daniel himself would have been able to say. But what was clear was that the man knew what step one in every single one of those pursuits would be: acquire knowledge, and hold it close. That was all, that was everything.

Was there still a hope-shaped hole in this? Without a doubt. Daniel was *hoping* his knowledge would benefit him in some way. But was that hole carved into a towering edifice of dastardly strategy? You bet your butt it was. Why else would Daniel preserve his monopoly on literacy, on information, on what little power men of his station could collect?

But hope was not the whole picture. No, it most certainly was not. There ended the lesson.

So out Ambrose went with his empty sack, plucking picking bleeding, astonished by how nimble his hands were becoming, how he found himself sucking blood from a scratched finger only half as often as last year, how the full baskets seemed half as heavy. All day he kept his head down and fingers busy, pausing only to wipe the stinging bullets of sweat from his eyes. Four times, Hilditch approached to observe the erstwhile problem child. Once, he stomped right up to Ambrose and shouted his name directly into his ear (a groundless warning). Not a single time could Hilditch even fabricate an infraction for which to pull Ambrose out of the field and toss him into the stocks.

This was the true face of creeping insolence: a mask of obedience. If Hilditch couldn't see that now, well, he would in time. Ambrose would make sure of it. How?

He hadn't the specifics down yet, but he knew enough to add his own corollary to that most important of Father Daniel's lessons: be sure to appear dumber, more docile, more obedient than you are…right up until you no longer have to.

S E V E N

TWO YEARS AGO, PRAISEGOD PINCHWIFE HAD BEEN RATH-
er astonished by little Patience's improvement to the privy situation. Needless to say, it was the work of but a few months for
the man to convince himself that it had been his idea all along.
How, after all, could a five-year-old girl have devised something
so ingenious?

"Proverbs, 21:1," Praisegod announced one day, apropos of
absolutely nothing, "states that 'the king's heart *is* in the hand of
the LORD, *as* the rivers of water: he turneth it whithersoever he
will.' And what am I, if not being the king of this land as I am?"
At this point he swept his arm along the firm current pouring
through the culvert that Mary and Ezekiel had painstakingly carved out of the earth, running beneath the new privy Patience had
not only single-handedly reconstructed, but improved by her
own initiative. "Is it not eminently, then, sensible, then," continued Praisegod, who had not even *watched* the privy's construction, "that I shall turneth the river whithersoever I will?"

Patience, Ezekiel, and Mary had all grumbled their assent, as
they were all eminently sensible themselves.

So much for brownie points. Patience's life had continued on
its trudging trajectory, her every attempt to prove herself in any
sense talented crashing upon her father's refusal to see her as a
fully realized human being. Though no Child of Cain, she was
born of the rib of Adam, which he saw as only a marginal improvement.

This inability to claw the least shred of respect from Praisegod's bible-clenching fists had, prior to Patience's latest spooky congress with her friend, been a source of unendurable frustration. But that was because, like Ambrose, hers had been a purely reactive existence. Now, however, she had received two very important things from her midnight visitor: an end and the means, however broadly sketched.

She would learn to read. Which was the means, not the end. The end, of course, was to teach Ambrose, and so to give him knowledge in return for that which he had given her.

His knowledge, of course, was that of hiding one's true light. Or, more prosaically; of seeming stupider than one actually was.

Unfortunately, being untried in even such bloodless forms of deception, Patience's appeal to Praisegod was "could you please teach me to read? Also, I'm stupider than I look." Hearing it from her own mouth, she winced and wondered if she wasn't accidentally on to something there.

"There's no call for it," Praisegod told her flatly. "How is it to aid you in stitching a garment, to understand the written word?"

Patience clasped her hands reverently at her hips and looked to her not-so-father's feet. "It wouldn't," she replied. "But I am a rib... I'm *from* the rib of Adam. I am afrai-"

(she imagined how the thought she was creeping up on might sound, coming from Praisegod's mouth)

"-*afeared* of the fires of hell, father. I just wan-...I want *only* to have a chance at asking for re...um...re-"

Praisegod's eyebrow rose nearer to its god. "Redemption?"

"Yeah." She racked her brain for all of the Bible verses she'd ever heard Praisegod recite, that she'd ever tuned out from a refusal to believe what they said about her without ever having met her. "For the sins of my father?"

Patience, Ambrose

The multifaceted irony was, tragically, lost on the both of them.

Nodding, turning his face towards the heavens, Praisegod took a deep breath in and held it. He swung his hands around behind his back, the right clasping the left just below the beltline.

Patience examined her own hands clutched in front of her crotch, and quickly relocated them around back to match Praisegod's. This felt a bit too presumptuous, so back around to the front they went.

"I…" He rocked on his feet, from the ball to the heel and back again. "It is true, God's forgiveness may extend to all who accept the divinity of his son. John 3:16 makes an allowance for this. Hm…" Still rocking, he pulled his right hand from behind his back and, with a finger-splaying flourish, brought it around to his chin. There commenced a stentorian stroking of stubble. *Scrtch scrtch.* "Well, here is my dilemma: I certainly have no wish to stand between a soul, such as yours may be, and salvation, such as may be achievable for you. But I can afford to short myself not a single helpful hand on the farm."

Rather than highlight how little she was permitted to do on the farm that might answer to the word *helpful*, Patience insisted "I can just learn here."

His lips curled like a worm withering in the sun. "You imagined *I* would teach you?"

"I, uh…"

"It would have to be Ezekiel. I've not the time to devote to a lost cause."

"Oh!" Patience brightened. "I think he'd do it!"

"But Ezekiel cannot read!"

"…yes," Patience reminded Praisegod, "he can."

"Well, of course, but I cannot spare him!"

Patience caught herself on the verge of saying something smart, and dialed it back. "I'm not saying to take Ezekiel away from the work," she pressed, casting aside the put-on piety, feeling herself so near her goal it had reached out and grabbed her heart, so heaven help her if it should pull away now. "I can learn to read right here! I can-"

"Learn to read *and* write here. Clearly we have need of locutional pedagogy as well!"

"That w…yeah, sure! I'll only ask Ezekiel to help if he's not busy, and I'll still keep making things even better like I did the priv-" She watched Praisegod's eyes narrow. "-vvvvery good ideas you have had, I will try to make things better like those. *And* I can learn, which will make me a more cultured lady and a better daughter!"

"What of the good work I have begun in *my* self, hm?"

She bit her tongue, hard, and kept from blinking until tears filled her eyes. "What?"

Praisegod cleared his throat. "What about me?"

A long-delayed blink sent a single tear screaming down Patience's cheek; she rubbed it away with the meat of her palm. Somehow, she had gotten it into her head that the man who withheld the world from her would hold her wants and needs in any kind of esteem.

Foolish, in hindsight, for gentle and lenient though Praisegod could be, there was a warmth lacking in his conduct towards her. Always had been. He sometimes made her feel a stranger, as though she were not his daughter, but merely a child who had wandered onto his property one day and never taken the hint to leave.

Patience, Ambrose

His unceasing reliance on scriptural support for his every thought and action was only recently beginning to give her pause. What kind of man would he be without that book? Were it not there to grant him divine sanction to own humans as chattel, would he? Or would he be like Mary's last owner, who had little regard for faith but for whom cruelty was nonetheless a natural endowment?

Patience imagined the answer to both was negative.

Her eyes burned now, through even the small liquid pearls blooming at the corners, trying vainly to extinguish her flame.

"I am afeared of hell," she repeated, working her throat to put a quiver into her voice. She considered cracking it on the word 'hell,' but decided that would have been laying it on a bit thick. Even without the crack though, this didn't sound real. She sounded exactly like what she was, a girl trying to fool a man. So she thought about that mighty hand wrapped around her heart, how this was the first step towards everything else, a step that would change not only her life but Ambrose's too, would change both of their lives, would change their *life*. She thought about the two *everything elses,* the one in which she learned how to read, learned how to *learn*, and the one in which she didn't.

She thought about the absurdity of it all, that the decisive factor dictating which of the *everything elses* came to pass should be the pious dunce standing before her.

"I long only for Christ's love," she concluded so persuasively that she very nearly believed it herself.

From the look on Praisegod's face, Patience knew at once: she had found the magic words.

"Ok, ok," he chuckled as he pumped his raised palms in the universal gesture for *relax*, "it occurs to me that there is a place to which I might send you to, with the dual advantage of granting you an opportunity to learn, and me a modicum of peace, until such time as you are literate, and mature enough to cease your whining."

"AH!" Patience shrieked, clapping her hands once. She immediately dropped them again, along with her eyes. "Sorry."

"No apologies necessary!" Praisegod laughed. "This is a rapturous occasion for us both."

Another shriek-and-clap threatened to emerge, but Patience managed to get in front of this one and turn it into a soft giggle. *Traveling!* She would be traveling off the farm, for the first time in her entire life! Physically, at least – she wasn't sure it made sense to count her conversations with Ambrose as travel.

"Where am I going?" she asked with unfeigned elation. "Where do I…where *shall* I be going to learn of God's love?"

"I'll be sending you to a very fine and intelligent woman who, as it happens, oversaw my own education." He smiled and clapped his hands, just as Patience had. "You'll be going to study with my mother, on my father's farm."

E I G H T

DILATORY THOUGH PRAISEGOD SEEMED IN MAKING good on his promise, around the slaughtering season in mid-September he gave Patience some supplies, a day's light rations and an Ezekiel-penned message for his parents.

The delay in Praisegod's getting his daughter on the road was largely down to this message; the young Pinchwife had up until now failed to mention to his parents, in their irregular communiques (for they had not met face-to-face since Praisegod had abandoned the name with which he had been born; father Drummond could not countenance Praisegod as he was now), that a miracle had entered his life. This was largely down to Praisegod's wanting to avoid the question of how he had acquired the child – which was to say, by whom, for "the river did it" would undoubtedly only raise more questions. So getting the phrasing of the letter *just right* was essential, and such perfection took time. From July to September, to be more precise, by which point Praisegod was perfectly satisfied introducing Patience as "my child, who is definitely mine, by female human issue."

Thusly satisfied, Praisegod sealed the letter (lacking a seal, he poured hot wax on the lip of the envelope and ground the knuckle of his right thumb into it, which taught him a valuable lesson about not doing that ever again), loaded his daughter up with supplies and a mount, patted the horse on the rear, said 'yip yip', and made everybody's lives a hell of a lot more complicated.

As the horse, whom she had never ridden before, waddled off the farm, Patience turned around and waved to her father. Doltish though he could be, Patience was going to miss him.

Praisegod waved back.

Patience frowned. She wasn't entirely certain why, but being sent off with nothing but a wave struck her as…underwhelming. Ah well. She waved a few more times, then turned around, took up the reins, and let her mount guide her off the only plot of land she had ever known.

Patience had ridden a horse plenty of times before, but never unsupervised. And confident though she was in her equestrianism, it was unnerving to be clopping along a poorly lain road, legs barely long enough to straddle an animal with whom she wasn't even on first-name terms, heading in a direction she was *pretty sure* was the right one.

"What's your name?" she asked the horse.

"Pblblbl," the horse snorted.

Patience leaned back and tried it out. "Pblblbl," she sputtered. "*Pb*lblbl." She leaned forward again. "I'm not gonna call you that."

Pblblbl flicked his tail. "F'ff."

So *that* was how it was gonna be.

And that was how it was, for the entirety of one largely uneventful day. She passed a few people on the road, most of whom paid her no mind. Each time she saw a stranger, she gripped the reins tighter, felt her shoulders hunching in anticipation of being accosted. *They will see you as a flower unplucked,* Praisegod had assured her, *and seek to deflower you.*

This imbued her with a head for defense and an eye for offense. Both were employed in vain; Patience's first leg of the journey exposed her to, at worst, complete indifference from her fellow travelers. This flummoxed her, until she came upon a section of the road bottlenecked by a fallen tree.

Just as she approached the obstacle, a silver-gilt carriage driven by a liveried slave drew nearer from the opposite side. The slave yanked the reins and called to her, "After you, miss!"

Thinking nothing of the courtesy, Patience shouted back her gratitude and availed herself of this stranger's generous disposition. She swung Pblblbl around the fallen log and past the carriage, taking care to observe where the horse put his hooves — to her right, the path dropped away to the creek-cut floor of the woods. A short drop, but steep enough to do damage, particularly if one should be entangled with one's mount mid-fall.

Pblblbl avoided disaster, though, and as he regained the full path on the other side of the log, Patience looked up to the kind servant who had given her the right of way.

He stared back at her as though Patience and Pblblbl had just switched places.

The smile fell from Patience's face. She dropped her eyes and gently spurred Pblblbl to pick up the pace. Negro men were a particularly dangerous sort, Praisegod had informed her. For nearly an hour's ride past the bottleneck she satisfied herself with this explanation for the man's expression, even as she found it nearly impossible to recall lechery in the man's features.

It was yet another hour's worth of riding before an alternative explanation occurred to Patience, one she only considered after brushing a lock of her gently-kinked hair from in front of her eyes: perhaps when they'd had the log and some distance between them, the sl…indentured servant had mistaken her for black. Upon drawing closer, he took her to be white.

Or maybe vice versa.

…that couldn't be it, could it?

Granted, her skin was more deeply tanned than usual, Patience having spent all summer providing as much support to Mary and Ezekiel in the field as she could, lest Praisegod cite a lax work ethic as grounds to not send her off for an education, or some such nonsense.

And granted, her hair was quite a bit curlier than Praisegod's. Looked more like Mary's, if it came to that. But…plenty of white kids had curly hair. Right?

The idea of even being *mistaken* for black disturbed her – yet that she felt this seemed some kind of betrayal. Betrayal of what, of whom? Patience couldn't put her finger on it. These were elusive abstractions she was as yet unable to grab hold of, but she could certainly make out their shapes as they went howling past. Some of them looked an awful lot like Ambrose. Most were far, far larger than that, formless and molten.

The rest of that first day's ride, she came no closer to understanding her reflexive revulsion, one that went far beyond the fear of looking like a runaway slave. And as the woods grew darker, as the trees seemed to loom a bit further down than before, a more immediate fear shouldered theory aside: was she lost? Had she taken a wrong turn? Praisegod had told her a day's brisk trot would see her to the inn by sundown. Had she not been trotting briskly enough? She had nothing, material or mental, that would prepare her to sleep alone in the woods. Worse still, she had specie on her to pay for a room at the inn. That made her a target, should she stumble upon any robbers in the night.

So fixated on fear was she, that she nearly trotted past the inn. She cursed the rather pitiful pool of light thrown by some unambitious lamps, hardly visible through boughs and leaves, and how the hell was a girl supposed to know oh I've gotta look to my left *now* or I'll miss it, seemed pretty ridiculous even just from a business perspective, grumble grumble grouse and so on.

With that almost but not quite out of her system, Patience guided Pblblbl towards the lively glow, hidden by a gloomy bushel.

N I N E

THE INNKEEPER WAS A PORTLY MAN, CLEAN-SHAVEN, YET with hair shooting out in a corona so perfectly unkempt Patience had to imagine he worked hard to kemp it that way.

"Where's your pa?" he snarled.

"At home," she replied as she imagined a confident girl might.

He leaned over the desk, meaty fists planted on the uneven, live-edged timber. "You a nigger girl or what?"

Ignoring the Ambrose-shadow in the corner of her eye, stunned by the innkeeper's articulation of her ethnic existential crisis, she hardened her face as best she could and asked, "what do you think?"

They stared at each other, silent and still. A second passed. Then another. Then another.

The innkeeper leaned his head back and roared, great heaving guffaws punctuated by his fat hands slapping his chest. He wiped a tear from his eye and ratcheted the laughter down to a more manageable volume. And it was *only* the volume that changed – the heaves were still just as big. It was like hearing someone cackling in another room as the door slowly closed. There was something preposterously inhuman about it that both amused and unnerved Patience.

"Alright kid," he finally managed, "how much money you got?"

As she handed him what Praisegod had allotted for the room, she noted uneasily that the innkeeper hadn't actually answered her question.

T E N

THE ESTATE WAS EXACTLY AS PRAISEGOD HAD DESCRIBED it. For Patience, cresting the hill at mid-day, it was an especially dramatic first impression. Its white bulk in the distance, perhaps greyed slightly since Praisegod had last seen it, looked like a poor stab at camouflage against the dreary, overcast sky. As though her father's childhood home had been sculpted from thunderheads.

Patience wondered if it had ever been struck by lightning. That would be have been pretty funny.

Winding along the path up the hill, she marveled at the terraces, majestic stepwise ascents that were somehow just as clumsy and awkward as Praisegod had promised. She couldn't help but be tickled by how subtly derisive her dad's descriptions of *his* father's (and so, all together now, *her* grandfather's) agricultural practices were, doubly so by how accurate they turned out to be.

Finally, she reached the Estate proper, the big white house at the center of it all. Here, viewed up close, was at last a discrepancy between Praisegod's account and reality. Yes, the Estate was precisely as gaudy and overblown as he'd led her to believe, even in its gentle disrepair, but what he had failed to mention was the strange grandeur of it. The entire property was so much more impressive than the pig farm, which rather contextualized the son's latent bitterness towards his father's possessions (a bitterness he still seemed incapable of extending towards the man himself, Patience had noticed). But the house, the *mansion*... good heavens, it was spectacular. Granted, Patience's architectural experience was limited to a shithouse and a crick, but even she could appreciate a well-built domicile.

And there on the porch, to let all the air out in a great big flatulent gust, was a man who was unmistakably Praisegod's father, Drummond Pinchwife. The soupy features, the set of his bulbous frame, the way he somehow slumped in his chair even as his snoring face tilted skywards…it was like a glimpse of Praisegod in his dotage.

Seeing no one to help stable the horse, Patience swung off Pblblbl and looped his reins around the railing of the porch steps. Oblivious to the solemnity with which certain *other* parties had once regarded those stairs, she mounted them eagerly and walked right up to Drummond, slumped and asleep.

This seemed in no way out of line to her.

Even she, however, recognized that poking Drummond on the forehead and shouting "WAKE UP!" might be crossing a line. So, not knowing what else to do, she sat crosslegged on the peeling white floorboards, back against the spindles, and waited.

"Psst!" hissed a voice from behind her. It added a small burp for emphasis.

Patience craned her neck and peered between the pillars. A slave with close-cropped salt-and-pepper hair glared at her from the bottom of the stairs. "Yeah?" she whispered back.

"You'd do best to get down from there, ma'am! He ain't gonna be happy, he wakes up and sees you on the porch!" Burp.

"Where am I supposed to wait?"

"Down here!" He whispered-shouted, just in case Patience misinterpreted his frenzied waving.

With a quick look at the slumbering Drummond, Patience shrugged and pushed herself to her feet. She took her time descending the steps.

"My name's Jesse," the man told her as he unthreaded Pblbl-bl's reins from the stairs.

Patience reached out and grabbed for them. "Hey, w-"

"It's okay." Jesse stroked Pblblbl's mane, and the horse leaned into his affection. "I'm the stableboy, among other things."

She lowered her arms, but not her guard.

The horse snuffled with satisfaction; Jesse smiled. "Who're you, then?" he asked Patience.

"My name's Patience. I'm h-"

Jesse gasped, choked, burped, and gulped, all at once.

Patience's blood didn't quite go cold, but it did cross its arms and reserve the right to plunge in temperature at a moment's notice. "What's wrong?"

"How're you here?"

"…horse," Patience informed him, pointing to Pblblbl.

"How'd you find your way? You follow a star?"

"…"

"You hear the voice of an angel?"

"Are you alright, mister?"

"Yeah! Who are you?"

Patience squinted at Jesse. "Patience, like I s-"

"Then how'd you wind up here?"

"Then…what? I came from my pa's farm!"

Jesse must have been using some sort of circular breathing, to be burping so steadily. "How's that?"

"My pa. Praisegod Pinchwife. You sure you're alright?"

"FINE!" Jesse sputtered and heaved.

"Who's this, Jesse?!"

They looked up to Drummond, neither fully awake nor upright, leaning heavily over the banister.

"What's that, Master?" Jesse whimpered.

"I asked you, who's this girl here? You understand what I said this time?"

"Yes, Master."

"Then I expect a goddamned answer."

Patience marveled: *goddamned?* Praisegod would have been *scandalized.*

Sniffling and sweating, Jesse sighed and looked at his bare feet as they ruffled the few blades of grass brave enough to grow on such well-trodden ground. "Um," he said as he lifted his gaze to about halfway up the stairs, "she's from your son's farm, sir. Says her name is…" he dropped his gaze to the lowest step. "Um… it's a fairly common name, no doubt all sorts of folks have it."

"Christ, you'll not want to hear me ask the question a third time!"

"Patience."

That certainly appeared to wake Drummond up. "Ex*cuse* me?!"

"Sorry, sir. That's the girl's name." Finally, Jesse brought his eyes back up to Drummond's. "Patience."

Patience's eyes, meanwhile, had never left the big man's fat face. Even had she not been observing it as carefully as she was, the change that came over it the instant he heard her name would have been impossible to miss. It was atmospheric, the way it charged the air. Drummond's eyes bulged, like two duck's eggs before the shit had been wiped off, his teeth clenched so hard Patience expected them to shatter and come tinkling out any second now. And ah, here was that bolt of lightning striking the Estate, though in a far less amusing fashion than Patience had imagined – a jagged, fulminant vein pulsing beneath the man's royal purple forehead.

He looked from Patience to Jesse to Patience to Jesse to Patience at Patience *through* Patience. Slowly, a trembling, ragged-nailed finger aimed itself straight between her eyes.

"You," he rumbled, tracking his finger from the space between her eyes to a spot on the porch just in front of him.

Patience glanced at Jesse and saw on his face a look of such terrible pity, she was more than half-tempted to snatch Pblblbl's reins back from him and make a break for it. But a break to where? After all, Drummond knew where she lived.

She was in some kind of trouble. That was clear. It was a kind Praisegod had either not anticipated, or…one he had decided not to warn her about.

Actually, she was in two kinds of trouble. The second trouble being that she didn't know what the first trouble was.

"*NOW.*" Drummond boomed.

Before she knew it, Patience was at the top of the steps, standing before Drummond, just where he'd indicated.

The moment she presented herself before him, he slapped his palms roughly on her cheeks, turning her head this way and that, boring into her with those poorly-set peepers of his. All the while, his grimace deepened. Whatever he was seeing, it brought him no pleasure.

Satisfied with his dissatisfaction, he released her head by shoving it a few inches backwards, sending her stumbling.

"Follow me," he ordered, as he spun around and opened the front door of the Estate.

Patience turned to glance back at Jesse, but Drummond caught her hard on the shoulder.

"Did you see me go that way? *Follow.*"

Patience, Ambrose

She had no choice but to trail her grandfather through the door. He slammed it shut behind her.

Alone at the foot of the porch steps, Jesse stared up at the closed door, struggling to make sense of the last few minutes of his life, struggling to make sense of how an orphan to his departed, would-be sweetheart should have found her way back to the Estate, *without* having been guided by the voice of an angel, or at least a devil.

It was impossible that this Patience lately arrived was the one who had been born here and borne away by Spoons Creek. And yet, it was beyond doubt. To gaze into her eyes was to see Aggy and Drummond staring back as one, such that seeing one or the other required only a minute focal adjustment. The illusion was as complete as it was discomfiting.

Jesse shifted his mind's focus ever so slightly, as though from the view through a window to his own reflection on the pane. He saw himself standing over a young Drummond, just as that man had loomed over Patience. He saw his lifelong master gazing plaintively from a face that was just as much Aggy's, up to him. To Jesse. To the owned one.

He imagined this chimera asking *are you alright, mister?*

Tears stung the corners of Jesse's eyes, but he refused to pull his gaze from the door. He would wait for it to open again, wait until he knew the daughter of the woman to whom he had professed his affections far too late was safe. He would watch the door until he knew Drummond wouldn't hurt her. And if Drummond *did* hurt her…Jesse didn't know what he would do.

As it happened, he would have three years to figure that out.

18⊙9

O N E

DRUMMOND HAD WANTED TO KILL HER AND BURY HER with the tomatoes.

He had expected this plan to be met with immediate approval from Martha, for whom the wounds of her husband's unfaithfulness *still* stung. Drummond could only chalk the sustained peal of that grievance up to a conscious commitment, daily made, to being a mule. After all, Agath…uh, Agra…oh hell, what had her name been? Aggy! Yes, Aggy had been the last slave he'd lain with, and that had been *years* ago. Why couldn't Martha just get over it? Move on, as it were? The moving on would be metaphorical, however, rather than literal: divorce was anathema to her, doubly so for the idiot son Peter whom she so adored. Peter had contracted a rather virulent strain of faith in his late teens, when most of his peers were being felled by influenza. On the day Peter insisted that his parents ever after refer to him as Praisegod (a request Drummond refused to grant, preferring to call him 'son' or 'boy' or 'hey you', *anything* but his chosen address), Drummond wished in a not-quite-idle way that P…his son has conformed to the prevailing epidemiological trends.

Martha, however, was as against Drummond pulling off a generational three-in-a-row in Pleasance Square as she had been the idea of divorce. Putting aside her inexplicable empathy for the girl ("it's not her fault you're a cad bastard," she was fond of saying), the root of Martha's opposition to both prospects was the same: Praisegod. Specifically, his faith. "You've done enough damage to this family," Martha snapped, "I won't let you drive my son from me as well."

Such were the stakes. After all, Peter's position on miscegenation was hardly a mystery to his parents: he found it utterly inconceivable, a backwards practice he struggled to understand as in the least ways distinct from bestiality, best relegated to the indiscrete tidewater aristocracy availing themselves of the more licentious verses of the Bible, assuming they consulted the book at all, before knowing their slaves biblically. Those horndogs.

"And whosoever lieth carnally with a woman," Peter had once berated the furniture in the sitting room, upon discovering that one of the men to whom Drummond regularly sold produce had fathered a child with one of his slaves, *"that is a bondmaid, betrothed to an husband, and not at all redeemed, nor freedom given her; she shall be scourged; they shall not be put to death, because she was not free.* Leviticus 19:20. Permission, no doubt, but doubtfully a recommendation,

hardly! *Exhort servants to be obedient unto their own masters, and to please them well in all things; not answering again.* Titus 2:9. Well, I grant that passage admits of some ambiguity. But it may just as easily apply to the topic of, of, um, all sorts of things. A lovely game of cribbage, for one. Or…well, that's one. There are, though, no attendant clauses that specifically extend its purview to matters carnal, though! What about *And Sarai said unto Abram, Behold now, the Lord hath restrained me from bearing: I pray thee, go in unto my maid; it may be that I may obtain children by her. And Abram hearkened to the voice of Sarai,* Genesis 16:2? What about *that?* Sarai only told Abram to fornicate with a bondmaid, *yuck,* because she was, *Sarai* was incapable of bearing children! It was merely a contingency, fornicating with a bondmaid, *yuck,* of which one is to make recourse only in the direst of circumstances, i.e. an incapacity to childbear!"

On and on he'd blathered, the upshot being that he expected his father to cease favoring this lascivious neighbor with Pinchwife produce (which Praisegod, in a fit of pique, referred to as "holy produce"). Drummond fired back a quip to the effect of having missed boy's ordination ceremony; it was but a few months after that that Peter requested a plot of land, that he might set out on his own. Martha had blamed Drummond for the boy's departure, and never entirely forgiven her husband for it. Hence her insistence: he would now do nothing to waylay the girl Praisegod had sent them, and so arouse ire or suspicion in their son. For should the girl that Peter claimed to be his daughter not return from the Estate, and should he come to investigate the disappearance himself, it would be a simple matter of one of those uppity slaves whispering venomous treason in his ear to complete the Pinchwife-rivening work that the girl's mother had begun. This, Martha refused to accept. More than once, she made ominous remarks that seemed to hint at a gruesome, not-at-all-metaphorical end for *Drummond*, should she be even further distanced from her boy.

And so it was written, and so it was done: Patience would stay, locked in the Estate but otherwise unmolested (Martha had fixed Drummond with a *very* hard stare about that), and the matriarch of the Pinchwife clan would personally see to the girl's education. That would accomplish the twofold goal of minimizing Drummond's chances to be alone with Patience, as well as having greater control over the information to which the girl was and was not exposed.

Drummond didn't approve of the arrangement. But that was doubtless a large part of why Martha so enjoyed it.

T   W   O

FOR THREE YEARS, PATIENCE RARELY LEFT THE SECOND floor of the Estate. The first floor was permitted only occasionally under strict Pinchwife supervision, and Drummond was *adamant* that the great outdoors were verboten (though Martha often allowed Patience to accompany her on strolls around the property, and of course Drummond seemed to have forgotten that the privy was *outside* the house). The reasons for this could be gleaned only indirectly, through the evident discomfort her arrival here had occasioned. Why such hostility to her presence? Even Martha, in the course of her lessons, was consistently more effusive in her castigations than her confirmations. This despite Praisegod having represented his mother as a depthless font of kindness! Patience suspected the hernia-inducing intensity with which Jesse had reacted to her name was a pretty big hint. Had he once known a woman called Patience? It seemed an uncommon enough name to make that unlikely…but the man's entire demeanor changed at hearing the word: *Patience*. And Drummond really had wasted no time in getting Patience away from Jesse…

Patience was often left to her own devices between lessons and meals, both of which were chaperoned by Martha. Poor Martha, upon whom the weight of pedagogy seemed to rest so heavily, who by the beginning of Patience's second full year on the Estate couldn't even muster up the energy to look put-upon. In all their time together, Patience never once managed to pry a personal detail from her instructor. How she met her husband, how long they had been married, what she thought of her life here. Those rare entreaties to engagement were waved away, as though she were an empress who'd had enough frond-fanning for the moment.

Martha certainly took no interest in the life of her young charge, only growing animated upon discovering Patience somewhere she oughtn't have been. Most explosive was the day she had come in from an afternoon constitutional to discover Patience snooping around the first floor sitting room, playing with the rolltop of the secretary. "OUT, you wretched beast!" was how Martha had banished the intrusive girl to her room, and so her lesson, which put a rather tense spin on that day's run at grammar.

The reason for Patience's being down there, of course, was not to investigate any Pinchwife paperwork. She had spotted Jesse lumping around the perimeter of the house, making a grand show of collecting sticks while peering intensely up at the second-floor windows of the Estate. Patience had hustled down to meet him at one of the first floor windows, only to hear Martha thumping up onto the porch. So Patience thought fast, and wound up rifling through the desk. Better she be thought an overenthusiastic learner with no sense of personal boundaries, than be caught trying to speak with Jesse.

Patience didn't know how she knew that…but she did.

That had happened a few weeks after Patience's ninth birthday, and so her latest cross-continental huddle with Ambrose, during which they exchanged much of import but little of substance.

"I'm gonna learn to read," she told Ambrose, her voice cracking with excitement.

"I heard tell coal's the way of the future," Ambrose told her. "They ain't gonna need slaves no more."

"Aren't," Patience corrected.

Ambrose smiled and rolled his eyes. And then they spoke of other things.

The longer she spent on the Estate, the more cautious she found herself becoming. It would have been so easy to creep downstairs late at night to find Jesse – the Pinchwifes were eminently predictable, and so avoidable – but Patience couldn't risk being surprised somewhere she shouldn't be again, for fear of being sent home illiterate, or not at all (the tireless menace of Drummond was not lost on her). Ambrose's newfound adage of concealing one's true intelligence only worked insofar as one had intelligence to conceal; after all, her thirst for literacy was no longer for the more abstract purpose of being able to teach Ambrose, and so maybe assuage whatever guilt or shame she felt at their situational disparities. No, she wanted to learn. That was the whole of it. She wanted to learn.

And over those three years, Patience *did* learn to read, thanks in no small part to the, yes, patient pedagogy of Martha Pinchwife. There were countless mistakes, frequent backtracking, and some skills Patience never came to wholly grasp (her penmanship would have been "cause for shame were it the scratch of an educated rooster," according to Martha). But in the end, Patience became literate, even refined enough to appreciate the difference between a well-turned phrase and, uh, a not one.

Patience and her inexhaustible (yet perpetually put-out) educator both discovered that the end had arrived when Drummond burst into the room in the middle of a lesson, pointed to Patience, and asked Martha "can she read yet or what?"

Martha gave Patience a quick glance out of the corner of her eye. "Yeeesss…" Martha drawled in a way she herself would ordinarily have been the first to upbraid as unbecoming, taking her time in sliding those glassy eyes back to her husband. "She's reading at a satisfactory level for her age. Quite remarkable for a negro," she observed, matter-of-factly.

Patience furrowed her brow. "A what?" she croaked.

"Well?!" Drummond exploded, his arms shooting upwards, eliciting a wheeze as he did. "Why the hell is she still here then?"

Martha smiled at him tolerantly. "It's not my place to decide when she stays and when she goes."

Patience turned her gaze from each to the other as they spoke, following the argument like a shuttlecock. But her attention was somewhere else entirely. On an entire life's worth of interactions. Praisegod…Mary…Ezekiel…Patience couldn't put her finger on it, but it seemed as though she could now only recall them through a prism which rendered their behavior towards her tentative and unnatural. As though they were perpetually on tiptoe, so as to not wake something old and fearful...

"Why didn't you tell me she could read, then?" Drummond demanded.

"Perhaps," Martha snapped, "for the same reason you might find it challenging to tell me the moment you become drunk on any given evening, hm?"

"Reading's not like drinking. Drinking's *fun*."

"Of course. And it is only the latter that you practice with any regularity."

Patience felt suddenly, hopelessly adrift. *Quite remarkable...*

With a herculean act of willpower, Patience tuned back into the argument happening before her. She's missed the last few sallies, but Martha must have landed a forceful blow; Drummond looked as though he'd have happily struck her as a servant. Instead, he scowled at his wife and once again asked, "can this little shit read the written language, or can't she?"

"She can," Martha allowed.

"Then she's gone." And with that, so was Drummond.

Patience looked to Martha, who stared at the lately-slammed door for several seconds. Slowly, she turned to Patience, forced a smile, and slowly closed the book in her lap.

The walk back to her own room was long and lonely. Patience found it a challenge to remember how one foot went before the other; her world had fully inverted itself, after having two facts suddenly, violently confirmed for her. First, that she was not the lily-white child she had been lead to believe.

Second...that there were quite a few people on this property who knew something about Patience, that she herself did not.

As she finally arrived back at her room, she paused as the wooden floorboard beneath her creaked at her footfall. She lifted the foot, then placed it back down. *Crrreaaakk…*

She lifted the foot once more, and placed it on the neighboring floorboard.

Silence, even as she applied her full weight.

A kindness.

T H R E E

PATIENCE SPENT HER LAST EVENING IN THE ESTATE AUDITION-ing floorboards. Specifically, the ones between her bedroom and the stairs down to the first floor. The pretense was some question or other for Martha that Patience simply *had* to ask, right this instant, which necessitated her trekking downstairs to ask her. The questions were beside the point, often inane, nothing worth committing to memory (though Patience had to admit, she was genuinely disappointed to discover Martha was unable to weigh in on whether or not bugs were ticklish) – the point of these excursions was to plant her feet on as many of those hall-way floorboards as she could, to determine which creaked, and which did not.

Most, it turned out, despaired of bearing weight, and weren't shy about letting their burdens know. But Patience nonetheless managed to find a smattering of stoic planks, and that night after Martha had seen herself to bed, Patience mentally rehearsed her footwork until courage finally rose to match her cunning.

The jig was very nearly up straight away: she'd forgotten about her bedroom door, which *gggggrrrrrrrreeeeeeeaaaaaaaakkkkkkked* as she slowly pulled it open. Wincing, she swung it the rest of the way, catching it just before the doorknob struck the bedroom wall. Patience kept one hand on the knob as she stared down the darkened corridor, moonlight spilling through those little square windows which lined just one of the walls, waiting for the door at the end of the hallway furthest from the stairs to fly open and spit out a fiery-eyed Drummond.

She waited, and waited. But the house remained silent.

So she called to mind the first of the stoic boards…then lifted her foot, swung it across the threshold of her bedroom door, and placed it down.

No creaking, no groaning. Even as she put her full weight down on the wood.

Patience smiled.

It was slow going to get to the stairs, but Patience scored a point for nominative determinism and successfully delivered a hand to the landing balustrade nearly a full ninety seconds after leaving her room. The stairs were surprisingly easy-going; Patience kept her feet to the outside of the steps, delegating some of her weight to the banister to lighten the load. That done, the final obstacle was the front door, which gave a bit of lip but ultimately lost its nerve by the time Patience had it cracked wide enough to slip through.

And then she was outside. Unchaperoned. Free.

Patience had no idea where on the property Jesse lived, but based on where Praisegod kept his servants, the stables seemed like a good place to…

"Oh," Patience grunted as her stomach lurched.

For the first time in her life, the gravity of other human beings left to sleep with livestock fully landed upon her.

True, she had felt pity for Ezekiel and Mary before. But it had been more abstract.

It had been impossible to imagine herself in that position, back then.

Patience grimaced — *quite remarkable for a negro* — then took a tentative step towards the porch steps.

The first board onto which she stepped groaned, then whispered "what are you doin'?"

Patience froze, squinting as hard as she could into the pocket of shadow at the bottom of the steps. "Jesse?" she called.

"Shhh!" Yes indeed, that was Jesse.

Moving quickly but carefully, Patience crossed the porch, descended the steps, and approached the looming silhouette quietly belching at her from just a few feet to the right.

"What are you doin' out?" Jesse demanded.

"Lookin' for you," Patience replied. "What are *you* doing out?"

"I'm quartered in a cabin off separate. I heard you slinkin' out, so I slunk out. Only I slunk out faster'n you slunk out."

"I slunk out slow."

"So I discovered, upon myself slinkin' out faster'n you slunk out."

Patience bit her lip, not wanting to overplay her hand. If for no other reason than she had absolutely no clue what sorts of cards she was holding. "Why'd you slink out, then?"

"I heard you slinkin' ou-"

"But why would my slinking out lead to your slinking out?"

Jesse thought about that, then burped.

Patience took a deep breath…then asked Jesse "what meaning do you take from the name Ambrose?"

It was impossible to clock the man's features in the cloud-smothered night, but based on the way his shadow folded over itself, and the noise it made, Patience was fairly certain Jesse had only just avoided sicking up on himself.

Tempting though it was to pose her question again…Patience held her peace. Waited for Jesse to regain his composure, such as it was.

"How…" Jesse finally gurgled, "…you…"

"So you take meanin' from the name."

"I do," he gulped as he wiped at his mouth with his sleeve. "Oh, Patience. Swept to Praisegod, so you were. It's hardly fair."

Hearing her own name from Jesse's lips electrified her entire body. No, it wasn't the name itself that bothered her; it was the emotion with which he said it. This man, whom she hardly knew.

"Hardly fair," Patience repeated. "Tell me why."

Jesse nodded. And then he did.

Starting with the day Drummond took Aggy to Pleasance Square. To see the old hickory tree.

F   O   U   R

PATIENCE DIDN'T BOTHER KEEPING QUIET ON THE WAY BACK IN. She swung open the front door as enthusiastically as if she was returning from an afternoon of play, not bothering to close it as she thumped her way to the stairs and took them one at a time, planting her foot smack in the creaky center of each step.

At the top, she turned to the door to Drummond and Martha's bedroom down at the other end of the hall, and waited. Waited for one of them to wake up, to poke their head out, to demand to know what was going on.

Patience, Ambrose

Oh, how Patience hoped it would be Drummond. She imagined clamping his monstrous face between her hands, yanking him out into the hall, hurling him down the steps.

And she imagined glancing into the room even as he was still crashing down towards the first story. Seeing the bed upon which Patience and her brother had been conceived.

Her brother. Her twin brother. A slave in Louisiana. While she, his twin sister, was free in New York.

Patience reached for the knob to the door before her with her right hand. Which was when she realized she had, without her own knowledge, traversed the second-story hall to arrive at the threshold of the Pinchwife's bedroom.

And she had her hand on the doorknob.

She trembled such that her hand slipped from the brass. With both hands together, she found the knob once again.

She was going to kill him. If she opened that door and stepped through, Patience would tear a hole in him with her bare hands. Abstractly, she knew this would bring her no comfort. It would balance no scales. But it was all she could think to do, because he had known. Just as Martha had known. Just as Praisegod, Ezekiel, Mary, even if they hadn't known the full extent, the sheer mind-scrambling punchline of Patience's parentage…they had known that she was not who they had taught her to believe she was.

They had lied to her. All of them. A torrent of dishonesty, the font of which slept peacefully on just the other side of this door. On the very same bed that he…

Tears rolling down her cheeks, Patience gripped the knob tighter and

AMBROSE HADN'T BEEN SLEEPING ESPECIALLY DEEPLY, BUT he nonetheless awoke as though catapulted through a rampart of gelatinous slumber.

"Guh," Ambrose opined. His ears rang, his teeth ached, and he felt a stabbing in his midsection, as though he'd swallowed a wasp. Yes, he felt terrible…except no, he didn't. He couldn't quite explain it, but he knew to a moral certainty that this terrible feeling he was feeling wasn't his.

He looked up and saw Patience, who wasn't there, standing at a door that most *definitely* wasn't there, her hand slowly cranking the knob.

For an instant, Ambrose wondered if it wasn't July already, if the summer hadn't snuck up on him. No; that was easily dismissed. So why was he seeing his sister?

His…what?

Ambrose opened his mouth to call to Patience, when the selfsame emotional extremity that had her in its jaws turned its attention to him.

Every sensation in his body, pleasant and otherwise, sharpened to a point and drew blood. And through the pain seeped knowledge, truth known from the outside in.

Yes, his sister. Patience was his Drummond was his Aggy was his *family*.

Ambrose had a family. They were all so far away. And most of them were either evil, or dead.

Here was his precious knowledge, then. It served no purpose save to flay his heart to ribbons and feed it to him.

And then Ambrose took a deep breath, and looked again.

Patience, her hand still on the knob, had turned to look at Ambrose. Across the chasm, down the hall, just a few feet away. They were together. In the only sense that mattered. They were

Patience, Ambrose

THE FIST IN PATIENCE'S HEART UNCLENCHED, LITTLE BY LITTLE. It wasn't so much that her rage diminished; more that the space it had to crash about in had expanded. The difference between keeping a wild dog in a lightless attic full of porcelain, and giving it one hundred and one untrammeled acres.

Patience knew that Ambrose knew. She knew he knew by precisely the same mechanism he had come to know. Which was to say, it was a mystery. Which was to say, it was a miracle. Which was to say, there was nothing at all to say.

What a relief that was. For Patience had no idea what to say to him. To her brother, who had been plucked from the river just as Patience had…only to be sold down it all the same.

By Praisegod. By that sanctimonious bastard.

The wild dog grew, to fill its acres.

She heard Ambrose sigh. Breathing space.

Patience looked to him. Glimpsed him in the moment of his disappearance. Continued to stare at the blank wall he had just a moment ago occupied.

Struggling to control her breathing, not bothering to attempt the same on her tears, Patience let her hand fall from the knob of Drummond's bedroom door. She turned and sauntered back to her own room.

Her feet only falling on silent boards, in this untested stretch of the hallway.

AMBROSE STARED AT THE WALL OF THE HUT FROM WHICH PATIENCE had only just vanished. Looked around the floor of the cabin, envying everyone whose self-conception had not been utterly upended in the last fifteen seconds.

No. It was crazy-making, to focus on that. Ambrose blinked hard, lowered himself back to the ground, and turned his mind to the most useful fact he had learned tonight:

It was possible to contact Patience on days other than...oh, god, on their shared birthday. Emotional extremity was a trigger, it seemed; hardly something that could be safely or reliably utilized.

But surely, there was more than one way to skin a squash. Which was a funny thought to fall asleep to. So Ambrose focused on that one, at the expense of all of the other ones clawing at his attention. Those were crazy-makers, after all.

F I V E

IT WOULDN'T HAVE BEEN ENTIRELY ACCURATE TO SAY THAT Patience was happy to be leaving the Estate. That she was *ready* to leave was indisputable; it took everything in her power not to lunge at Drummond and tear the flesh from his face each time he crossed her path that final morning. How satisfying that would have been! But no, if those stoic boards in the hall had taught her anything, it was that one only got anywhere worth going by being...discreet. In that, they concurred with Ambrose. Best to hide one's true brilliance, until the time was right.

But putting that admittedly rather colossal consideration to one side, Patience was ready to leave the Estate for the simple fact of being sick of the damn place. Three years primarily spent on a single floor of some rickety old mansion had made for no small amount of stir-craziness, and she was nearly beside herself at the prospect of experiencing the sky in more than fleeting sips.

What disturbed her, and held true happiness at her departure in abeyance, was how the previous night's revelations were beginning to put down roots in her mind. As she repacked the bags with which Praisegod had sent her to the Estate, albeit with the new clothes Martha had been forced to fetch her (for she had outgrown those garments with which she had arrived); as she raided the pantry for a few provisions she could take on the road (in the course of which, she had one of those impossibly rare interactions with one of the Estate's servants, this one an older woman still sprightly enough to flee the small dry store the instant Patience entered – based on Jesse's story, Patience would have put money she didn't have on that being Ruth); as she loaded up everything she had on dear Pblblbl, for whom Jesse had so clearly cared over these three years…

The truth of her lineage suddenly started to feel real. Which was to say, it started to feel prosaic. The initial shock of it all had provided a safe distance at which to hold the whole affair, but daylight burned off quite a lot of the intensity. Now it was nothing more than a series of facts, the cruelty of which fit all too neatly into the world as Patience understood it. She was a child of violence, several times over. Of course. Her father had executed her mother, and had been fully supported by both the social and legal infrastructure of which he was a luminary. Of course. The man she had believed to be her father was in fact her half-brother, and he had been the one to sell Patience's twin brother, which was to say Praisegod's own half-brother, to slaveowners in Louisiana.

Of course. Why not. The river along which she and Ambrose had been swept had a nasty sense of humor; that explained everything.

And, of course, it went some way to answering that question she had posed to Ezekiel, years before. About who it was that lived upstream, whence all the shit doth flow.

So close to amusing, to discover the answer. *So* close, but not quite.

As Patience finished saddling up Pblblbl, she glanced around once more for Jesse. Caretaker to the horse though he was, Patience had fetched the steed from the stables herself. All morning she kept her head on a swivel, but saw neither hide nor hair of the man. It wasn't difficult to imagine why he was avoiding her, but still…she would have liked to have said a proper goodbye. Last night, she had been so rattled, she'd just sort of…walked away from him. Hardly proper.

But he'd been nowhere to be found. Whereas Martha was almost impossible to avoid, yet somehow always met in passing. "Mind you don't track dirt back in," she chastened Patience as she made her first trip out to the stables. "I seem to recall having one just like that," she sneered from the door as Patience started to pack a blanket that, fair play, wasn't hers to pack. "You're slouching," she needled as Patience cinched her saddle to Pblblbl's back.

It helped to imagine Jesse watching her, from some unseen redoubt. The thought of someone who could appreciate her heroic self-control, marvel at the restraint it took to not whirl around on Martha and scream what she knew into the woman's face…it steadied Patience just as she needed steadying most.

What little equilibrium she'd managed to muster was fully cashed out when, as she was making her final descent of the Estate's front steps, she heard the porch creak behind her.

There was, of course, only one person on the property who weighed enough to elicit such a titanic groan from the carpentry.

"Do recall to Peter that this is not a boarding school," Drummond drawled from the top of the steps.

"He means Praisegod," was Martha's final word on the matter from beside him.

Patience halted at the bottom of the steps, chewing on her bottom lip until she tasted blood.

Slowly, she turned around, and glanced up the steps.

A familiar sight: Drummond grimacing down at her, tucking his thumbs into his beltline. Only no, that wasn't a grimace: it was a smile. A *smirk*, if it came to that.

Patience knew precisely how to wipe that unctuous little smear off of his face. She could call him "dad," and watch his chubby little cheeks collapse in on themselves. Nothing would have brought her greater pleasure in that moment.

Lucky for her, Ambrose's dictum asserted itself, and its wisdom was incontestable. So Patience hid her light. Her fire. For cathartic though it would have been so see Drummond suffer in real time…Patience didn't imagine he would let her leave the farm, if he knew what she knew.

More to the point, though…Patience knew there was more than one way to skin a squash. As surely as she didn't know what the hell that thought meant, or where it had come from.

Unless it was a gift from Ambrose. The sort he wouldn't have been aware of leaving. A coat forgotten after the weather turned warm.

That was enough to draw a sincere smile from Patience. She did her best to hold it as she waved to Drummond. To her father. To the man who had murdered her mother.

He wafted her away like a fart, then turned around and re-entered the Estate. Martha gave Patience one final look, then followed her husband inside.

Patience lowered her waving hand, but kept smiling. For the effort required to hold that stupid smirk was enough to keep her from storming back up those steps.

Getting up on to her horse was a challenge given how much her arms were trembling, but she managed it. "Yip yip," she told Pblblbl, who could not have been less enthusiastic about the instruction. But he went, and Patience did not look back.

She did, however, glance into the orchard as Pblblbl trotted along the road off the property. The trees all looked dead to her, but there were people out there working. They all stopped what they were doing to watch her go.

Because they knew. They all must have known.

Just as she was about to face forward, she saw Jesse peering out from behind the trunk of an especially hunched tree, watching her go, belches betraying his concealment.

Patience smiled at him. A far softer smile than she was used to feeling herself break into.

Jesse smiled back. And then he vanished into Patience's peripheral vision.

She managed to ride off the property before she *really* started crying.

S I X

ON HER WAY BACK HOME, SHE STOPPED AT THE SAME inn she had patronized on her way out to the Estate. Even after three years, it was the same innkeeper who greeted her. But that wasn't so strange. Three years wasn't long to an adult. Whereas for a little girl, it was enough time to become a young woman.

Patience, Ambrose

Maybe even a little bit longer. Depended on the girl.

Naturally, the innkeeper failed to recognize Patience, until she prompted him twice. "Came here on my own," she recounted, "you asked me if I was, um…"

"Ah!" he exclaimed. Such was the fullest extension of his enthusiasm, apparently, for he instantly regressed to salty indifference. "Same room?"

"Any room," Patience shrugged. She thought for a moment, imagining the improbable (but not impossible) scenario of Jesse belching his guts out to Drummond, then added, "as long as it has a heavy door and a lock."

The innkeeper's eye twitched. "You expecting trouble?"

Patience flashed yet another variation of a smile, this one more guarded than the others she had cycled through today. "A young woman alone on the road's always got to watch herself, right?"

"Mhm," the innkeeper grunted. "There are some true rascals hereabouts, you don't have to tell me twice. I'll put you in the safest room we got. Small window, heavy door."

"Thank you," she said with a shallow nod.

"Pah. You oughtn't be bowing before nobody save the Lord," he grunted as he reached under the desk and grabbed a key.

"I didn't bow," Patience informed him, staying rooted to the spot until the innkeeper acknowledged her with a nod of his own.

S   E   V   E   N

PRAISEGOD'S PIG FARM HADN'T CHANGED ONE IOTA SINCE PATIE-nce had left it. She considered this remarkable in some aspects, depressing in others. Yet from each of her reactions, she felt herself held at an uncrossable distance.

Which answered a question she had been asking herself the entire ride in. There would be no waiting, she knew. No savvy interim. However advisable such a spell would have been…it was beyond Patience. Ha, ha.

"Girl!" Ezekiel's voice boomed from nearer the house. He came thundering over a low swell of dirt, a touch greyer of mane but no worse for the three years since Patience had last seen him.

Mary came close behind, one of her arms hanging a bit more heavily than the other. "PRAISE GOD!" she cried.

"What?!" Praisegod called from the porch, lounging in a cushioned chair that looked to be a new acquisition.

"She's back!" Mary called.

Praisegod put down the stick he was whittling into a smaller stick and rose slowly to his feet.

Patience narrowed her eyes at him, but avoided a full-on grimace by reminding herself that Praisegod didn't know all that she did. He was not necessarily the enemy.

That remained to be seen, at any rate.

To her right, Flann the gardener grinned and waved a truly gargantuan pair of garden sheers at her from waist-deep in a bramble of some sort. Patience waved back.

Ezekiel and Mary reached Pblblbl and fell in line on either side of the horse, blathering to Patience as she crossed the property to the barn. Yes, they all missed each other. Oh, there was so very much Patience needed to hear about what had transpired in her absence. As a matter of fact, the privy *was* still standing over the river, and had required only a few spot repairs here or there.

Patience nodded at all of this, tried to match her friends' enthusiasm…all the while thinking of what they knew. Both had seen her come slicing down the river in a basket. With her brother. Both had watched Praisegod sell Ambrose off. Naturally, there was little either could have done to prevent that. But now that she was here with them again, their complicity, the dishonesty of their silence, stung Patience more than she had expected it to.

"I must speak with Praisegod," was how she banished them after making a good show of fellow-feeling in the stables. Mary offered to take Pblblbl and finish the de-saddling, and Patience was happy to let her.

She was starting to get anxious. A flutter in the stomach, that dizzy expansion of the skull.

Had she ever truly confronted anyone before? About *anything?* She couldn't think of any interaction in her life that would fit that bill.

After a final "thank you" to Mary, Patience left the stables and headed for the house. It felt as though her spine had gone hollow, was nothing more than a column of cold air running from her skull to her gut. *People confront each other all the time*, she sought to reassure herself.

But they do so confidently, hissed the part of her that was doubtlessly Drummond.

Just as she drew near enough the house to spot Praisegod stepping out of the house to wait for her on the porch, dressed in a spotless white suit that he hadn't been wearing just a few moments ago, Patience found her attention drifting more towards her privy than Praisegod. It seemed odd that the human body — hers, at least — had settled on the optimal response to nerves of this magnitude being an overwhelming urge to shit out every organ in her body. But there it was. Here she was.

There he was.

Patience took a deep breath and stopped just in front of the porch. She looked up to Praisegod, leaning on the railing, smiling at her.

Half-brother. Her half-brother Peter.

"You have grown larger," was his first observation.

We have the same nose, was what Patience noticed. But she held her tongue, instead gesturing to the front door of the house. "I wish to speak to you."

"And I, you!" Praisegod turned around and opened the door. Held it open for Patience.

So he had learned some manners in the intervening years.

Patience smiled. Her stomach lurched. Hot water shot up through her imagined spine cavity.

She took a deep breath. Stepped up onto the porch. One step, another step, another. Into the house she went, stiffly nodding at Praisegod as she passed through the open door.

E I G H T

"YOU PRESENT TO ME AS WEARY," PRAISEGOD MUSED as he stepped into the house behind Patience and let the door swing shut.

Patience, Ambrose

There was something to be said for waiting until they could both sit down, perhaps with some crackers, or coffee. But Patience wasn't hungry, and she didn't drink coffee.

There was also something to be said for getting this all over with, before she exploded.

Still standing in the small entryway to the house, Patience spun around and demanded "how did I come to be here?"

Praisegod blinked at her, once, twice. "May we take a seat before w-"

"No."

After a few more blinks, Praisegod cleared his throat, then coughed. "Ahem," he articulated as he recovered the power of speech, "well, when a man and a woman wish to explore the mysterious extremities of the Lord's glorious creation, the man sticks his d-"

"That's not what I mean."

Praisegod paused, left pointer finger threatening to pass through the loop of his right forefinger and thumb. He lowered the anatomical analogs and his shoulders in unison. "Oh, thank heavens."

"Who was my mother?"

Praisegod's eyes widened. He softened into a chuckle. "Ah, this again. As I have told you…" he cleared his throat and managed to stop smiling. "Your mother passed shortly after giving birth to you."

"And her name was Margaret," Patience recalled from the previous times she had asked Praisegod.

"Indeed it was," Praisegod smiled.

Patience nodded.

Praisegod's smile flickered. He glanced around the entryway.

"Might we abandon the atrium f-"

"He was my brother," Patience managed to choke out, even as emotion crushed her throat like a vice.

Praisegod's eyebrows fell unevenly, two dead leaves snapping off a tree. An old hickory, maybe. "What?"

"Ambrose. The boy in the basket with me. The one you *sold.*" Patience fought to keep a deep red from fully blinding her, thinking it a victory that she merely *shoved* Praisegod. "He's my brother."

Praisegod stumbled back a few steps. "What are you..." He glanced towards the front door, his features darkening. "Did Mary tell you this?"

"Was she the one who pulled us from the river?"

Without the aid of another push, Praisegod backpedaled further into the house. "Patience...I know not by what species of devil you are possessed, b-"

"Are you..." Patience took a step forward, not knowing what she would do if Praisegod didn't keep reversing, what she would do if he fell within arm's reach. "...are you *truly* going to stand there and tell me you don't know *exactly* what I'm talking about?"

"We didn't know he was your brother!" Praisegod babbled. "The note just said...it just had names, it had your names! Nothing else!"

Patience felt her upper lip twitching. She couldn't stop it. Didn't try terribly hard to. "And you didn't wonder?"

"About...what?"

"Who we were!" Another step forward. "Where we came from!"

"Naturally, I had occasion to wonder. Th-" Praisegod jerked as he backed into the banister of the staircase. "Uh, I...there was

no opportunity for such curiosity to bear fruit, you must understand. I…" Using the banister behind him as a backbone, Praisegod stood up straighter. "To be quite in earnest, I would have
anticipated some gratitude from you, that I so charitably raised
a riverbaby as my ow-"

Patience was astonished her eyes hadn't yet tumbled out of
their sockets. "YOU SOLD MY BROTHER!"

"This is a pig farm," Praisegod scolded her, snapping easily
into his patriarchal mold once again, "not an orphanage."

"Ambrose and I are not orphans, you poltroon!"

"Do not call me a poltroon! Y-"

Patience shoved Praisegod once more. Up against the banister
as he was, he bent awkwardly over the obstruction, his back
quietly cracking as he did.

"Ouch!" he yelped. "Don't push me anymore, there's a thing
behind me!"

"Did you never think about who lives upstream?"

"Lots of people live upstream!" Praisegod pointed out, which
was…fair.

Oh, but there was no graceful segue into this. So Patience
stepped closer to Praisegod, her face just a foot from his. "My
mother's name was Aggy. Drummond raped her. She set Ambrose and I on the river to save us from him, just before he had
her lynched."

Praisegod said nothing. Betrayed no reaction, save his eyes
darting wildly around Patience's face.

Patience stared right back at him. Struck by how pronounced
their shared features suddenly seemed. The nose, yes, but also
the softness of their jaw, the jut of the cheekbones, even the way
each of their hairlines squiggled a drunken path across each of

their brows.

The only plausible explanation for Praisegod's relative calm in the face of these revelations was that he was seeing precisely what she was, at precisely the same time.

"It is *supremely* improbable that you should have arrived here," Praisegod finally replied.

"Is it?" Patience asked. "You were downstream." *And the river has a sense of humor,* she thought but did not vocalize.

To this, Praisegod had nothing to say.

So Patience kept talking.

N   I   N   E

BY THE TIME PATIENCE FINISHED, SHE AND PRAISEGOD HAD drifted to the sitting room, which despite its name offered her half-brother-fake-father the most expansive space in which to pace. Which he did, periodically rubbing at the back of his head, sometimes cracking his knuckles, almost constantly making a low keening sound from the bottom of his throat.

Patience, meanwhile, sat on the loveseat, one leg crossed over the other, waiting for him to be done. She was not unsympathetic in her vigil; however selfish and dishonest he had been, his villainy was of a lesser magnitude than Drummond's. Which was a fact she trusted Praisegod to recognize, however sluggish his conscience may have been.

"Sister," he mumbled to himself, as he spun on his heel and started another lap.

This wasn't the first time Praisegod had blurted a lonely word into the living room; as with all the others, Patience let it stand.

Patience, Ambrose

Half-sister, she would correct him, when the time seemed right. This was less out of any pedantry than a desire to protect Aggy from him. Aggy was no Pinchwife. That mattered to Patience.

And, of course, to distinguish Praisegod from Ambrose. From her *full* brother.

Praisegod paused, then turned to look at Patience. He seemed on the verge of tears…then he shook his head, pinched his chin, and resumed pacing.

If the worst came to worst, Patience had decided here on this very loveseat not a moment ago, she would kill Praisegod. If he got it into his head that killing the messenger invalidated the message, she was ready to meet his action in kind. With her bare hands, if necessary.

But in truth, she didn't expect things to go that way. Praisegod cared for her, Patience had only come to realize after spending time with people who didn't. He cared in the smothering fashion of the times, yes, but affection was affection. And Patience belie-ved this was more than enough to stay him from violence.

Given the erratic fugue into which he'd descended, though… it reassured her to get clear on that contingency.

"My dad racemixed," Praisegod observed as he slowed to a halt. "My dad racemixed and you're my sister." He turned and looked plaintively to Patience, as though begging her to contra-dict him, to reassure him that he'd gotten it all wrong.

"Half-sister," Patience replied, her gaze fixed on his.

Praisegod sniffed, then wiped away the tears now spilling onto his cheeks. "You're a child of Cain with Pinchwife blood in your veins. I don't…I don't know what that means, in terms of…but, I'm…so sorry. I…" he sniffed and wiped at his nose with his sleeve.

Patience jerked slightly, only then noticing how tightly she was clenching the cushions of the loveseat in her fists. Violence, she had been prepared for. Indifference, of course. Contempt and mockery and all manner of spiteful responses, absolutely.

Fair play to Praisegod, then: she had absolutely not seen contrition coming.

"It's, uh…" Patience tried to think of something to say. It certainly wasn't *okay*; none of this was. And she was still fairly certain Praisegod was more bent out of shape over his father being a "race-mixer" than, ya know, a fucking rapist.

But this was, all things considered, a better reaction than she had expected.

"Can I…" Praisegod sniffed. "Can I…hug you…um…half-sister?"

Oh, scratch that.

Horrified though she was, Patience nodded her head, and allowed herself to be embraced by her half-brother, in an affectionate swaddle the man had never attempted when he had been her father.

He cried. That was definitely new.

Patience comforted him. At no point did she feel even the slightest temptation to join him. She simply waited for him to be done. She kept waiting, and waiting.

And in the middle of all that waiting…she had an idea.

"You could keep soaking my shirt about how sorry you are," she grumbled, having handily surpassed the considerable limits of her eponymous virtue, "or you could prove it."

Praisegod peeled his stupid, soggy face off of Patience's shoulder. "Huh?"

Patience smiled, doing her best to disguise how little she

believed her own words: "you can get Ambrose back."

Her half-brother thought about that. Patience took his not immediately dismissing the idea to be a good sign. "That…" he shook his head. "That is, at this stage, impossible."

Patience shook her head right back at him. "Not impossible, Praisegod. Just…*supremely* improbable."

Praisegod shook his head at that…but he didn't contradict her.

T E N

"SHE'S NOT IMAGINARY," AMBROSE GRUMBLED AT FATHER DANiel, getting more genuinely annoyed with the man than he ever had before.

Daniel shook his head and tore another piece of bread off the loaf in his hand. "Dreams can seem wholly real, I understand. Why, just the other n-"

"She's not a dream!"

Daniel threw the piece of bread towards the treeline and watched it for a moment. Ambrose held his tongue; the Father had somehow gotten it into his head that the birds he heard singing in the woods could be coaxed out with a loaf of fresh-baked rye. This was bread intended for the slaves, one of their few indulgences, but Daniel had intercepted it on the grounds that seeing the birds would prove more edifying than any morsel of bread.

Hearing the birds was quite enough, Ambrose maintained. But Daniel certainly wasn't about to listen to a child.

This much could be said for the Father: he didn't sneak any cheeky little bites for himself. He was a man of principle. Even if the principle to which he had committed himself was wasteful and ill-conceived.

Father Daniel's flock wasn't about to speak out against their spiritual leader's birdmongering, though, and for as long as Ambrose thought the man might be able to help find a path to Patience, through whatever connection to the spiritual he had... well, Ambrose could abide a bit of bread going to the birds.

"Plenty of Biblefolks had dreams weren't just dreams," Ambrose pressed. "And if anybody told 'em it was dreams, we'd know those people didn't know what they was talkin' about, since they didn't know they was gonna end up in the Bible when they said it."

"I do not understand what you're saying."

"Jacob didn't *dream* a ladder. That was the Lord talkin' to him, yeah?"

Daniel shook his head and tore off another piece of bread. "That *was* a dream."

"Alright, well, it was a dream that was real, since it was from the Lord."

"So you contend," Daniel clarified, throwing his latest scrap towards the trees, "that God Himself is speaking to you."

"No, no, that ain't wh-"

"You are treading the line of blasphemy, Ambrose."

"No! I ain't...I'm sayin' my *sister* is talkin' to me."

"Then why are you talking about the Bible?"

"Because I'm sayin', it ain't...you know, this ain't so far from the sorta stuff happens in the Good Book as a matter of course. Sense I gather from your lessons is, you couldn't hardly move for miracles back then."

"So you are being annually blessed by a *miracle.*" Daniel tore off a larger-than-usual chunk of bread.

"I got no idea. That's why I'm askin', though, if we could, I don't know, like…pray for it to get stronger."

"Pray for the miracle to get stronger."

"Would you quit sayin' what I said to you back at me? I'm just askin' for your help. Da-nah, uh…Father." Ambrose swallowed loudly. "Please."

Daniel paused, then threw his too-big chunk and cradled what remained of the loaf against his chest. Slowly, he turned to face Ambrose head-on. "Adolescence is making you insolent."

"I swear to you," Ambrose pressed, "I speak truly." He placed his hand on his heart. "I felt her. And when I did, I *seen* her at the same time. On a day wasn't my birthday. So…and by the way, yes I was indeed sleepin' at the time, but I can tell when'm I sleepin' and when'm I not, you know? So I'm s-"

"If any soul here were to be touched by the miraculous," the Father growled, "do you truly believe it would be yours?"

"I ain't sayin' it's a real miracle. I'm tryin' to help you get your head ar-"

"Oh, *you* are helping *me* get *my* head around it?" Daniel tilted forward, bending at the waist, hugging the loaf tightly enough to crunch its crust. "You were once such a pleasant boy. You listen-ed. *Now* look what has become of you."

"I'm…" Ambrose shook his head. "Why're you bein' like this? I ain't seekin' to maim ya. I'm here askin' for *help.*"

Daniel stared at Ambrose for a moment, blinking just a little bit too forcefully. "It's not uncommon, this…" he scratched at his cheek. "…sense of…hm. Sense of *purpose.* To believe oneself especially favored by God. It i-"

"I'm not sayin' I'm God-favored!" Ambrose replied. "I don't

care to put a name on it. I'm just askin', I'm *beggin'* you, I need some help ma-"

"The Lord has not chosen you."

Ambrose narrowed his eyes at Daniel. "…okay? That's fine."

Daniel narrowed his eyes right back at Ambrose. "I understand what seek to do. I *see* you, Ambrose."

"…I don't underst-"

"Okay. Here is how I help." Daniel stood back up, wincing slightly as he did. "I will pray that you come to understand your place. And that you treat your elders with greater respect."

Ambrose waved his hands in front of him – he was used to conversations with Daniel going very differently from how they seemed like they ought to, but even on that sliding scale, he had never found himself in an interaction that had so quickly rattled itself to pieces like this. "I ain't tryin' to disrespect! All I'm sayin' is, ah, I'm *askin'* if y-"

"Oh, I understand precisely what you are asking." Daniel scoffed, then clawed at his bread without taking his eyes from Ambrose. "And if you expect me to sanction your buffoonery, you are an even more ridiculous child than I had known you to be."

Ambrose frowned. In hindsight, he wasn't sure what he had expected from Daniel. Whatever the tether to Patience was, Ambrose was fairly certain it wasn't divine. At least, not in any sense Daniel would have recognized. Yet the phenomenon had struck Ambrose as being comfortably in the Father's wheelhouse.

Needless to say, he'd miscalculated. What was still unclear was precisely which variables he had most gravely misjudged.

"Well…sorry I bothered ya," Ambrose grunted as he turned and walked away.

"And I am sorry I cannot sanction your buffoonery!" Daniel called after him, picking up enthusiasm once he got past the words he clearly didn't mean.

Ambrose turned around to get one last word in, only to discover Daniel stuffing a chunk of bread into his face. And what a vacant, distracted face it was. Had Ambrose anything to wager, he would have lain it on the Father being entirely unaware of noshing at the expense of slaves and songbirds alike.

Which, of course, didn't change the fact that he was doing it.

E L E V E N

THE CRYING JAGS WERE NEW. THE FIRST ONE HAD FALLEN ON Ambrose the day after his non-birthday communion with Patience, when she had...not told him, but *taught* him. That seemed a better word for it. In the moment, Ambrose had been so stunned by Patience's appearance that the full import of what he had learned failed to penetrate. That moment came, rather inconveniently, when Ambrose had been engaged in the now-weekly task of rebuilding the chicken coop on a less shit-scorched patch of grass. He was nailing a fresh board just above the flap to the egg hutch when, all at once, it arrived.

All of Patience's privilege had been his. For however brief a time, he had been on that comfortable little farm in New York with her.

And then the man she called Praisegod had sold him off. Sold him down here. To a place where the greatest kindness was the absence of cruelty. A place with lashes and hooks and stocks and racks and guns, and men who took pleasure in the use of each in turn.

This was where Ambrose had been sold off to. While Patience sat in a mansion, and learned to read.

It was not her fault, and yet when Ambrose slipped into melancholy, it was impossible not to hate her. Just a little bit. Which he knew was irrational – part of the reason she had learned was to teach him, after all. But this was not a rational place. The only question was how all-encompassing the word *this* could be.

The crying was, of course, not welcome on the plantation. Most often it earned him the opprobrium of his fellow slaves; humiliating, that, but bearable. In a few instances, though, it called down the wrath of Hilditch. Even in this, Ambrose considered himself lucky; the worst he got was a hiding with the butt of Hilditch's rifle, a few good cracks across the face. He wasn't pulled from his labors for a formal punishment, which would inevitably have proven far more arduous, and drawn far more blood.

What a relief it would have been, to be able to make anyone else here understand his sudden, seemingly-inexplicable melancholy. Father Daniel had been his best hope of that, and, well, the less Ambrose dwelled on that the better. Surely, there was something the Father had read in one of his precious newspapers to so put him on edge...or perhaps youth had simply spared Ambrose from the full extent of Daniel's tyrannical impulses. The latter seemed more plausible by the day; the most faithful of the congregation seemed more disposed than usual to giving Ambrose the high-hat. The Father, it seemed had spoken to them.

After a few days of trial and error, though, Ambrose found a spot to which he could safely decamp when he felt the vapors wrapping their soggy little fingers around his throat. It was a conveniently growthless patch of ground surrounded by high reeds, on the hill overlooking the swampy side of Master Barry's land. In addition to hiding him away from prying eyes, Ambrose found the view oddly clarifying. The way the land melted into bog, then slithered off into the shadows cast by the moss-draped canopy of tightly-huddled cypress trees…there was something reassuring about that gloomy solitude, something Ambrose couldn't quite put his finger on.

He did begin to glimpse it in relief, though, on the day that solitude was punctured by the sight of a man emerging from the swamp.

Ambrose wiped his eyes and squinted at the figure. Yes, that was a man there. And yes, he had just emerged from a swamp that stretched, by every account, for miles and miles. And probably had gators in it.

The man looked up and, unmistakably, locked eyes with Ambrose.

"Oh shit, whoops," Ambrose heard the man cluck to himself, as he started to turn himself around.

On his crutches.

Ambrose wiped his eyes again. He considered flagging Doctor Mayhew down…but there was no percentage in Ambrose's starting a conversation before he'd fully stopped crying. Still, his interest was piqued: Ambrose couldn't imagine *what* Mayhew had been doing down there, but it was almost certainly something to do with his voodoo.

Which, since Daniel's spin on the numinous didn't seem poised to offer all the much, was probably worth learning more about.

So Ambrose kept his hands folded over his knees, and watched as Mayhew hobbled – or rather *skipped,* for even on his crutches he was a sprightly old codger– back into the swamp.

Not a day later, though, Ambrose spotted Mayhew rocketing from the privy towards the sewing cabin to which he had been relegated since the loss of his leg. However sprightly the older man may have been, Ambrose had no difficulty (alright, a *small* amount of difficulty) intercepting him. "What were you doin' in the swamp?" he demanded.

The instant the question left Ambrose's mouth, he foresaw Mayhew's response coming to deck him like a low-hanging branch: "what were you up to on that hill, that gave you such a fine view of the swamp?"

Ambrose pinched his lips together…then peeled them apart to answer Mayhew's question, in excrutiating detail.

It wasn't so much that he suddenly trusted the witch doctor. The man simply represented the antipodal pole to Father Daniel, a fact largely decided by the Father and his antipathy towards Mayhew. Which suddenly struck Ambrose as *deeply* curious, having found himself likewise reviled by Daniel.

That, however, was beside the point. What mattered was that Mayhew was the only other especially mystically-minded person on the property, and so the only other person to whom Ambrose could turn in his definitely-more-than-one-hour of need. Thus it was Mayhew who bore the full force of Ambrose's grief, his humiliation, his contempt for both himself and everything else besides. It had to be said, for a man largely agreed to be a goofy old one-legged nutjob, Mayhew was an attentive, empathetic listener.

After Ambrose was done with his unburdening (reduced to

tears, yes, though he managed to keep himself upright and more-or-less composed), Doctor Mayhew simply nodded, grunted as though in assent, then asked "where do you feel things?"

Ambrose's first impulse was to ask Mayhew what the hell he was talking about. He quickly slotted the question into context, though, and realized what Mayhew meant: he was asking where Ambrose felt the sensations he described when he was communing with his sister. Those feelings of the people living their lives in the shadow of their tether.

That was a logical question for someone who had taken Ambrose's account seriously to ask.

Ambrose slowly raised his hand and pointed to his chest.

Mayhew smiled. "The heart?"

Ambrose nodded.

The Doctor pointed to his right temple. "Never in the head?"

"Not never. Just not as much."

"But some."

"It's more like…" Ambrose sucked a sharp breath through his nostrils.

Mayhew let air out through his. "It's like the lines of your body melt off, and like *that*" – he snapped his fingers – "you're everything, and the whole world's appearing inside *you.*"

Ambrose's jaw physically dropped, accompanied by the gentle smack of his lips parting. Yes, he wanted to say, it was exactly like that. *Exactly.* But he couldn't say that. He couldn't say anything.

The Doctor bobbed his head up and down, up and down.

"How…" Ambrose managed to ask, "…did you know that?"

Mayhew betrayed the tiniest of grins. "Lucky guess." Before Ambrose had a chance to respond, Mayhew hobbled on his way to the sewing cabin, patting Ambrose on the shoulder and saying "come along. I wanna show ya something."

Ambrose followed without a second thought.

T   W   E   L   V   E

MAYHEW HELD THE DOOR TO THE SEWING CABIN OPEN AS THE boy stepped through. It took his eyes a moment to adjust to the gloom; there were, inexplicably, no windows, with the only illumination being the narrow blades of sunlight that managed to pry their way between the boards which formed the walls.

Except…that wasn't quite right. Because Ambrose could see two nimble-fingered women pounding away at their treadles as clearly as if they were under a spotlight. At yet, they were in the same instant nearly lost to the dusk of the cabin.

Very spooky.

Ambrose permitted himself a smile; if ever his strange affliction was going to be understood by someone other than Patience, it was here, in the gustless wind of looms hard at work.

Mayhew gently closed the door behind him as he padded happily into the cabin. Were it not for the strange lightless shine by which the room was illuminated, Ambrose might have convinced himself that he was imagining the ease of Mayhew's locomotion, that his seeming to carry his crutches more than lean on them was just an illusion, a misapprehension.

But Ambrose wasn't so sure anymore.

That uncertainty resolved into something more concrete when Ambrose took a closer look at the two unfamiliar women sat at the looms. The two women whose movements could not have been more perfectly choreographed to match one another. Whose dress was identical, down to the smudges and tears. Who matched even the pace of their breathing.

Who were, if Ambrose was not *very* much mistaken, the exact same woman twice over.

Ambrose had fully expected Mayhew's quarters would be strange or eccentric. Even if the one-legged, cross-eyed old goober had been a largely risible presence in Ambrose's life thus far – a pitiful man with whom Ambrose had held such scintillating discussions as 'biggest rocks found while digging a hole' and 'tallest hill I ever walked up' – there had always been a healthy respect for, and distrust of, Mayhew's voodoo bona fides.

Which was probably why Ambrose felt so…underwhelmed? Yes, underwhelmed. He had expected metaphysical astonishments of a more dramatic sort in Mayhew's quarters; the old man crouched before a fire, liveried in human bones, igniting funny herbs that would induce all manner of wild times. Perhaps there would be some chickens bleeding out into a copper pot shaped like a scythe-blade moon, or a goat bleating as a machete cracked into its neck (a blow that would be struck the moment Ambrose entered the hut, naturally).

What he had not expected were the more modest astonishments of lightless light, or a lady twice over. Those were certainly astonishments, of course, but they were, well…

"Medium potatoes," Mayhew chuckled, "I know." He nodded to the woman at the loom. The manifestation on the left, specifically. "Such were her words."

"Not small potatoes," both of the women…er, both of the *woman* said at once. "Not big potatoes. Just medium potatoes." Their…*her* treadle-pumping rhythm dipped not a whit as she

259

spoke.

Ambrose cleared his throat. "So," he asked the version of the woman on the left, "you're not twins like me?"

"Nope," they both replied. "Just an only child twice over."

Heh heh heh heh, the version of her on the right giggled. And *only* the version on the right.

Ambrose frowned, first at the doubling act, then at Mayhew.

The Doctor lowered himself to a tilting bench in the corner and slapped his extant knee. "If it helps ya, I don't fully understand it either."

"Is it voodoo?" Ambrose asked.

Mayhew shrugged. "Don't believe so, no. Folks'll call it as much, since it's somethin' they don't understand, but voodoo's got history. Somethin' came with the folks got brought over here from away. That…" he pointed to the women. "This…" he gestured around the entire cabin. "This comes from the swamp." He leaned back and giggled to himself. "All-American."

"And you're sayin' you don't wholly understand it?"

"Not hardly at all. Not a whit more'n I understand moonshine, but that's yet to let me down."

"What's moonshine?"

"What's…" Mayhew threw his head back and laughed. "Boy, I got so much to teach ya!"

Heh heh heh heh, the woman on the right cackled.

Ambrose frowned at her, then turned back to Mayhew. "I wanna learn to reach out better." He jabbed a finger into the center of his own forehead. "I wanna control it."

"So…" Mayhew rubbed at his forehead. "Boy wants to control a sidereal fiber, eh?"

"Sidereal fiber?" Ambrose all but sang. "Is that what my te…"

my thing to my sister's called?"

Mayhew shrugged. "No idea. But I liked the sound of it. So I said it!"

Ambrose frowned.

Mayhew laughed. "First score's teachable," Mayhew granted. "Score of learnin' to reach out better. That's a muscle, and work'll make that stronger." He grimaced at the floor between himself and Ambrose. "Second score's not."

Ambrose cleared his throat. "I forgot what the second score was."

Mayhew smiled up at Ambrose. "Forgot your own score, eh?"

"Sorry."

"Control," Mayhew reminded him. "You said you wanted to control it. When no such thing can be done." He waved a finger. "But I'll help you on that first score, certainly I will."

Ambrose turned around and scoped another seat, flush against the wall behind him, set exactly opposite the bench Mayhew had sat on. Ambrose padded over to it and sat. Slowly, as though he expected the seat to be yanked out from under him. "I'm waitin' to see how the jaws snap shut," he grumbled.

"The what?"

Holding his hands out and pressing his wrists together, Ambrose pantomimed the jaws of a trap snapping shut. He provided a *"thck"* sound for emphasis.

Mayhew's eyebrows sloped down to his temples, a look of genuine disappointment.

Ambrose said nothing to that.

Slowly, Mayhew's disappointment calcified into something more appreciative. "Smart boy."

Ambrose flinched slightly. The compliment was more stunning to hear than it was validating. Because he already knew he was smart. Not in the knowledge-and-facts sense like Daniel, or the reading-and-writing sense like Patience, no. But Ambrose was smart in ways neither of them were.

And Mayhew was the first person to recognize it.

"Smart Doctor," Ambrose replied.

Heh heh heh heh, the woman on the right laughed. Only this time, she didn't laugh alone.

1812

O N E

"OK," PATIENCE SAID, STEELING HERSELF FOR THE THIRD annual *try to teach Ambrose to read in forty-five minutes* extravaganza. "So. Um. First thing I guess is, uh, you see this squiggle here?"

Ambrose squinted through the midnight river at the paper Patience held up. He saw it as though standing several yards away. In poor light. And the font was tiny, to boot. Still, he saw it. "The one above your finger or to the side of it?"

Patience glanced at her finger on the page. Shifting the digit slightly, she clarified: "to the side. The left."

"My left?"

"Your right."

"Ok."

"See it?"

"I do."

"Ok. That's the letter 'A'."

"Ok."

"Draw it in the air for me."

Ambrose lifted his hand and traced a perfect letter 'M.'

Patience sighed. "That's an 'M'!"

"That's the one you was pointin' to!"

"No," she huffed, slamming her finger down on the page again, "I pointed to *this* one!"

"That's the one I just drew!"

"No, the one you drew is *this* one."

"*Ok*, but that's only 'cause you told me to draw the one on the left!"

"No I didn't! I said your right!"

Ambrose threw his arms up. "*Thank you.*"

"No! Your right, not *you are right!* I was telling you to look at the one to the side of my finger on *your* right!"

"Ooooooooh." Ambrose squinted at the page again and quickly traced the letter 'A' in the air.

Patience nodded, satisfied. "Ok."

"That's a 'K'?"

"That's an '*A*'."

"Ok."

Patience closed her eyes and took a long, deep breath.

"Don't huff," Ambrose snapped, wiping sweat from his brow. Bad sign – Mayhew had helped sharpen his focus enough to sustain these spooky birthday pow-wows for longer than they had lasted on their own. But it took effort, which rather distracted from the educational experience on both sides. For the first half of their time together, Patience would try to teach Ambrose to read. For the latter half, he would attempt to guide her through some of the exercises Mayhew had taught him, in hopes of holding the tether open from both ends.

At no point would either meet with any success, in either role.

"Ok," Patience finally agreed. "Moving on."

"Yeah," Ambrose agreed. And after a few more minutes of squinting at squiggles, it was Ambrose's turn to educate his sister.

"Look at my face," he told her, "but see how it's appearin' in your mind. Don't see it through your eyes."

Patience did that growl she always did when she got frustrated. "I still don't know what that means."

"It's like, listen to my voice. You ain't gotta *listen* for it, rather. I mean, you don't gotta do any work to hear it. Ya just *hear* it. It's easy."

"Right."

"You wanna focus on the feelin' of how it feels to not have to work for it. That easy feelin'."

"It doesn't feel like anything!"

"It does. You just gotta learn to feel it."

"All I feel is…fucking frustrated!"

"Okay," Ambrose nodded, wiping another runlet of sweat from his eyes and doing his best to ignore the molten knot throbbing between his eyes. "Feel how your frustrated feelin's just *happenin'*, and you ain't gotta work to f-"

"I can't *try* to feel something that doesn't feel like trying!"

"You can," Ambrose told her. "You gotta."

"There," was Patience's final word on the matter; Ambrose

265

felt the tether slip from his grasp. It was the sensation of dropping something heavy over one's bare foot.

He jerked hard, rolling onto his back like a startled beetle. By the time he came back up to a seat, Patience was gone. It was, once more, just Ambrose and the wall of the cabin.

And it would, once more, be another interminable year before they would have the chance to try again.

Composed though Ambrose had remained during his conversations with Patience, he was just as frustrated as she was. Almost certainly more so, in fact; for one, he couldn't help but feel the onus was on him to pump up whatever eldritch muscle it was that would allow him to connect with her on days other than their birthday.

For another, he was *still* waiting to be bought back by Praisegod.

Wheels were in motion, Patience had assured him. Praisegod was sufficiently mortified by what he had done – and/or had been sufficiently browbeaten by Patience – that he had set about tracking Ambrose down. Which ought to have been a short hunt, Ambrose felt, as he was able to tell Patience precisely where he was – down to the county, at least. But Praisegod had either disbelieved her or been too stupid to make use of that information; instead, he had taken to querying the brokers he had used in the sale to see if they remembered one particular slave infant they had sold off nearly a decade and a half ago. They, in turn, would send letters off to other middlemen, who would send letters back, and so the broker would send another letter to Praisegod (all of which Patience read for him, naturally) with apologies and no useful information. Three years of this, and Ambrose was still here, still on Master Barry's plantation.

Patience, Ambrose

What stung him most of all about this – besides the obvious cruelties of the plantation – was that Patience seemed satisfied by their half-brother's efforts. She had never said as much – since her first informing Ambrose of this development, the two had dedicated so much time to their educational sallies that the matter of Ambrose's rescue had fallen to the wayside. But Ambrose couldn't help taking as a development unto itself.

This squiggle was an A, that one was a K. Or was *that* one a K? No, that was an A. Here, it seemed, were the matters at the forefront of Patience's mind.

Maybe that wasn't fair. With only a little over an hour together each year, it was impossible for them to talk about everything they wanted to. Particularly when they were so dead-set on edifying one other with the fruits of their respective studies.

…but this was Ambrose's life they were talking about. Or, rather, *not* talking about.

All the more reason to redouble his efforts with Mayhew, then. Which he did.

Many were the hours Ambrose spent sitting in the sewing cabin with the Doctor and that nameless, twice-over weave-woman whom Ambrose was about sixty percent certain didn't exist in any traditional sense.

"You just have to focus *really* carefully," Mayhew would tell Ambrose, "on the ease of the enterprise."

"I'm *trying*," Ambrose would reply.

"Well," Mayhew would scold him, "don't."

Such were the frustrations. After two years of this, Ambrose periodically took to secretly following Mayhew out into the swamp, on his semi-regular expeditions into that soggy wild. No matter how many times Ambrose followed him, though, and no

matter the distance he covered, the younger soul invariably turned around and left the older to his business. It wasn't entirely
fear that kept Ambrose from finishing the journey…just mostly.
But there was some measure of respect in it, too. For Mayhew
had made clear that Ambrose was "not yet ready for the swamp,"
and frustrating though that was, Ambrose believed that the Doctor would not withhold a resource from Ambrose for no good
reason. He wasn't Father Daniel, after all.

Oh, Father Daniel. Ambrose crossed paths with him quite oft-
en – it would have been difficult not to, given how popular the
man of God was on the plantation – but it had been quite some
time since they had spoken. The Father no doubt saw Ambrose
as a lost soul at best, more likely a traitor to the faith. Which
stung Ambrose. For as controlling as Daniel had proven himself
to be, it was impossible for Ambrose to fully wrest his affections
back from a man who had commanded them for so many years.
Who had, until the last few years, proven an able steward of
them. So Ambrose kept his distance, careful not to precipitate a
conflict. Lucky for him, Daniel did the same.

"It's just like water flowing through," Mayhew would note in
the middle of a lesson. "Don't ride it."

"So where am I standin' here?" Ambrose would snap.

"Oh, that's just a metaphor."

"I know it's a metaphor, where am I standin' *in the metaphor?*"

"You shouldn't be standin' in the metaphor. It's just water."

Which was not the sort of comment that revealed the ease of
the enterprise, as a rule.

Naturally, Ambrose running off to flex his mental muscles
came at the expense of his productivity on the plantation proper,
a lapse that did not go unnoticed by Hilditch. Whatever patience

that bastard possessed ran out the day Ambrose threw a ham-hock into the meathouse a touch too carelessly (Ambrose, of course, had been doing his best to put up a tough front for Daniel and his coterie, so often huddled in their usual meeting place). The slab of pork caught a loose nail in the threshold as it flew, and tore wide open; upon discovering this, Hilditch was nearly beside himself with glee as he ordered Ambrose to the stocks. For old times' sake, he called on poor Isabel to fetch some spice.

Neither the pain nor the humiliation of that or any other punishment affected Ambrose in quite the same way it used to. Precisely why that should be the case – how it *could* be – he could not say. Hilditch's passions remained as agonizing as ever, and if anything, both the pain and humiliation seemed to have increased as Ambrose grew older. Yet what mattered was one's capacity to feel the pain…and Ambrose had, it seemed, cauterized a few of those nerve endings through sheer force of will.

Perhaps what had changed was Ambrose's endurance in the stocks. He was far better at slipping into a liminal state, remaining just conscious enough to see how his fortitude infuriated Hilditch and Barry. For there was, ultimately, only so much pain they could inflict. Even when Hilditch had, in a fit of pique, fetched a pair of pliers and peeled one of Ambrose's fingernails off – the pinky nail of the left hand – that was one tenth of a finite measure. And having borne that portion, Ambrose knew he could handle the rest.

All that *truly* bothered him, in these fugues, was when he awoke in the middle of the night to feel two sharp, searching claws on his back.

The bird. That fucking bird. The one he had never seen, the one that meant to shred his flesh to the spine and nest in the hollow. It was still alive, it was still *here*. Perhaps it had been waiting for him. Perhaps it would outlive him, outlive everyone on the farm. Perhaps it wasn't a bird at all.

Dawn brought resolve, bleeding color back into Ambrose's heart as surely as it painted the horizon. Many sunrises after, Ambrose would succumb to unconsciousness. And he would awake from that to news of a bell a-ringing in another bright world – Isabel had apparently yet to find a song she liked quite so much as that one.

Then it would be back to the field, on best behavior for a time. Until Ambrose felt comfortable once more plowing through his tasks and fucking off to the sewing cabin. This he would do until Hilditch noticed. Once more with the tortures, and the best behavior, and the fucking off. Over, and over, and over.

All the while, Ambrose ticked off the days in his mind. Charting the passage of interminable years, until the day when he might try again with Patience. Try to divine the difference between an A and a K, try to notice the ease of the enterprise.

T   W   O

THAT AMBROSE POSED THE QUESTION AT ALL WAS A MEASURE of his respect for Mayhew. That Ambrose had decided on his plan of action before he heard the answer traced the limits of that respect.

"You aren't ready for what's in the swamp," was Mayhew's answer, tossed out as the old man peeled worn-down cowhide from the thick beam at the top of his crutches.

Ambrose's heart leapt; that there was a *what* in the swamp was more information than the Doctor had let slip before. That struck Ambrose as an invitation for the narrow end of a wedge.

"You said to me that's what I'm workin' for," Ambrose pressed, keeping his voice as calm as possible. "The swamp. Some power in the swamp's gonna push me over what little humps I got in my m-"

"Won't push you *over*," Mayhew tutted. He held the grey, frayed slice of cowflesh out in front of him, then flicked his wrist.

The bolt of leather *whapped* at the air, then once more hung at rest in Mayhew's hand…as a fresh, deep-brown bolt of spongy padding.

The Doctor nodded at his little magic act, then wrapped the cowhide around the support beam of his crutch.

"See," Ambrose whined, pointing to Mayhew's refreshed leather, "I ain't even tryin' to do that. I just wanna t-"

"Swamp won't push you over anything," Mayhew resumed as he reached for a pin to secure the crutch padding. "What I've been tellin' ya is that you have to get over that yourself. Because he…" Mayhew sighed. "*It*…the thing in the swamp…it'll only push you, and fast. Push you whichever way you were already headed. So if you're headed into some kinda hump…" Mayhew balanced his crutch against his thigh and punched his right fist into his open left palm. "You'll hit it hard as if you got launched out of a cannon."

"I reckon I'm over. Serious, I reckon I'm just about over whatever humps I got."

"Oh, yeah?" Mayhew planted his hands on the crutch pad and leaned. "When was the last time you talked to your sister? Birthday?"

"I'm almost there," Ambrose insisted. "I can feel it. I just need a push."

"Ah," Mayhew tutted, as he pushed himself to his feet. "I oughtn't have used that word. *Push* doesn't capture it. Recall the cannon I invoked."

Though the conversation continued beyond that, it was effectively over, and Ambrose knew it. He knew it as surely as he knew that he would be trying his luck with the swamp first chance he got.

After giving it some thought, Ambrose decided the best course of action would be to follow Mayhew into the swamp the next time he went, hide, and wait for him to leave. That would save Ambrose having to work out where and how to summon whatever entity (a fella, if the pronoun Mayhew had let slip was any indication) it was that lived out there.

So not two days later, after Ambrose had sworn up and down to the Doctor that he would be a good little pupil and keep to the plantation grounds for now, he followed Mayhew down to the swamp. Rather booking it, Mayhew was, which made it difficult to keep a low profile while pursuing him. That lack of discretion was mostly amusing to begin with, but became quite a bit less so as Ambrose rocketed out from behind one of the lonely brick pillars of what would one day be a sugar mill, and all but collided with Father Daniel.

"Excuse...*oh,*" Daniel grunted as he recognized Ambrose. "In a hurry, I see."

"I am, yeah," Ambrose mumbled as he moved to get back on his way.

"Off to the swamp again?"

Ambrose tripped to a halt, then turned to face the Father. "What?"

Daniel grinned, lifted his chin, and enunciated: *"Off to the swamp again?"*

Patience, Ambrose

"Are you..." Ambrose took a step towards Daniel, then shook his head. "Course you're watchin' me. Freak."

Daniel frowned. "I am not a *freak*. I am a community lea-"

"Sure thing, *freak.*"

"I'm not a freak!"

"How 'bout you mind your own goddamned business," Ambrose shouted as he turned and resumed his pursuit.

"I will pray for you!" Daniel called after Ambrose.

"Fuck you, freak!" Ambrose laughed to himself about that for a good two minutes, until Daniel's voice began echoing in his mind.

It had sounded sincere. Fearful. *I will pray for you.*

"Freak," Ambrose reassured himself as he reached the edge of the property.

He paused on the swampy banks, listening for the metronomic *thud-STEP-thud-STEP* of Mayhew's crutched gait. Lost to the swamp, it was. Good. Ambrose pressed onwards, his feet slipping and sticking in turn. The sawgrass slashed at his bare ankles, leaving tiny wounds for duckweed to punish.

As with each time he had ventured out into the swamp, all Ambrose could think as the thick canopy blotted out the sun, and his every step sank to the top of the ankle, was how the hell Mayhew managed such a treacherous journey. On one leg and two crutches! Either the man had made this trek so often he knew precisely where to plant his props, or there was something spooky about his progress.

Or, who was Ambrose kidding, both.

T H R E E

Scratch that: Mayhew was one hundred percent using the spooky route through the swamp. After what must have been an hour, Ambrose had followed Mayhew in further than he had ever gone before. Were it not for the periodic glimpses of the man stolen between the ever-thickening crush of natural wonder, Ambrose might well have believed he'd gone too far. And even with those glimpses, Ambrose considered that he had rather overshot the mark, as related to his own capabilities. The swamp must have offered some invisible platform for those it deemed worthy, and not counted Ambrose among that esteemed number; he was reduced to leaping from trunk to trunk, getting slapped with trumpet vines and tangled in Spanish moss all the while, just to keep out of the mire that was, last time he'd fallen in, up to chest height.

Frustrating though it was, he did his best to silence his grunts of displeasure and keep going. He'd come too far to turn around; if he quit now, he didn't believe he'd be able to motivate himself to fight his way back out here again, knowing all the trek entailed as he now did. Surrender here meant another full year of psychic isolation, of vexation and pain.

"Gah!" he shouted as a sheaf of loose bark slimed out from under his feet, just as he had switched to a new complex of roots. Cursing himself for being so vocal, he clung motionless to the trunk and glared into the gloom ahead of him.

He neither saw nor heard any indication of Mayhew. Which could just as easily have been good or bad. Which made it emphatically neutral, Ambrose supposed.

He took a deep breath, carefully lifted the foot that had most recently slipped, and swung it out towards what looked to be a fairly sturdy log sticking out of the water.

"Mind the mire!" chirruped a voice from the bog.

It was, Ambrose was absolutely certain, not Mayhew's voice.

Withdrawing his foot, Ambrose clung tightly to the tree and tossed his gaze every which way through the swamp. Suddenly, each and every dapple of sunlight seemed a pair of eyes, each shifting shadow a hunched and watchful form.

These were sinister visions slightly at odds with the sing-song voice he'd heard, Ambrose realized. But on second thought, it didn't get much more sinister than singing in a swamp like this.

"M…" Ambrose bobbed his head down, trying to wipe sweat from his forehead without releasing the trunk of the tree. "Mayhew? That you?"

His voice seemed to echo around the swamp more enthusiastically than it ought to have, before diving headfirst into the sickly green waters. A few bugs resumed buzzing; Ambrose hadn't even realized they'd stopped. How considerate of them.

In a flash, he imagined himself dying out here. He imagined those bugs tearing him apart, nibble by nibble by nibble.

Assuming the sing-song monster didn't get to him first.

Ambrose cleared his throat, and tried to dredge up a deeper octave: "who's out there?!" he demanded.

"Mostly bugs!" that sing-song voice called back. "Turtles, birds, toads. Bog-standard list of critters here, and I assure you, I've hit that pun blindly."

Ambrose jerked, nearly slipping from the tree once again. "Who said that?!"

"Ah, he narrows the field considerably!"

From just a few yards in front of Ambrose, great orb of darkness slid out from behind a copse of cypress trees.

The entire swamp froze. Or maybe that was just Ambrose. He was definitely still sweating. But his teeth had set to chattering as well.

The bulk drew closer, drifting lazily through the waters, a perfect half-moon of hungry shadow.

Ambrose expected its formless girth to coalesce into recognizable features as it approached. Arms, legs, a head, a standard-issue human body.

What he recognized it to be instead was the biggest, roundest, blackest hog in the history of the universe. Only it wasn't a pig. Pigs weren't three feet tall and just as wide. Nor was it black. This pig-shaped planetoid was the color of *absence*, a hole punched in the night through which one might glimpse the truth of mysteries best left unsolved.

Ambrose hugged the tree tighter, and felt his feet kicking at it in a vain attempt to climb.

"Hello!" the pig chirruped in a sing-song accent.

Ambrose blinked once. Twice. Three times. *Jesus please us*, Ambrose thought, *the swine speaks!*

The pig wriggled from side to side. "And he listens too, old squirt!"

More blinking. Ambrose pointed to himself and raised his eyebrows inquiringly.

"Yes, you, and what a blinding din of a noodle you've got! Our mutual acquaintance Mayhew spoke so fondly of you, but he rather understated your case!" The pig cocked his head, but lacking a neck, had to cock his entire body to achieve the effect.

Those beady little eyes set in the starless night brightened. "My, you've a *blinder* of a north-south grapevine! Twinners! Heavens, I've not seen one of your lot in quite a spell. Though it'd be more apt to say *two*, instead of just the one, eh? Two of your lot? Being twinners as you are? Ha!"

"I, uh…" Ambrose set his jaw towards the swine. "You can hear my thoughts?"

"Surely as I can your speech, yes indeed."

"So…" Ambrose nodded at the pig.

"Yes, yes, of course, no ill-intentions, mean you no harm, all that and more besides. Would you like to come off the tree?"

Ambrose glanced down at his feet. There…wasn't anywhere else to go. There was tree, and then there was water.

"Step on off," the hog encouraged him. "I vouchsafe your little piggies against any splashing."

"My…little piggies?"

"As in the popular nursery rhyme. As in, the little piggies, which is to say tootsies, protagonists of the prattling verse which follows them as they indulge their disparate passions. One has a grand old time at the market, raising a host of questions regarding the economy of this universe, while another just sobs quite a lot. Never saw the point of the whole thing, but human children are so easily amused."

"…"

"The piggies are toes."

"The fuck are you talkin' about?"

"Off the tree you come, now. We are building trust!"

Eyeing the hog skeptically, Ambrose took a deep breath, then held it as he lowered one foot from the tree's roots and swung it over the water.

"Splendid! Trust!"

Bracing for wet, Ambrose put weight on the sacrificial foot.

It came to rest on what felt like solid Earth.

The sheer dissonance of standing confidently on water nearly knocked Ambrose out. He took a moment to collect himself, then peeled his body fully from the tree, brought his other foot to meet the courageous one…and stood on the water.

He stared down at his feet, scratched his nose, then looked up to the half-submerged pig. "This how Mayhew gets around out here so easy?"

"I can, of course, have a cheeky little peek into your noggin, you'll recall. So no need to ask a question when you've already got the answer, Ambrose! I may call you Ambrose."

"…sure," Ambrose allowed.

"Wasn't asking, chappie, but cheers for being such a good sport. Imagine now I am pointing to myself, for my piggy little limbs are incapable of self-reference."

"…"

"Are you imagining?"

"Oh, you can't see?" Ambrose grumbled. It was remarkable, how quickly astonishment could dribble itself into frustration.

"Chuffed though I am by a spirited youth, I shall not hesitate to dunk you."

Ambrose rolled his eyes, then tried to imagine the black pig growing a human arm out of its back and pointing to itself.

"Quite horrific, that image," the hog mumbled, "but it shall do. In any event! Greetings, formally tendered! I am Bulstrode! No-Good Bulstrode's the *full* kit and caboodle, only most friends call me simply Bulstrode. And I'm quite a friendly little bastard, as you've no doubt discovered. This ties a bow on your first question."

Ambrose furrowed his brow. "I didn't ask any..." he sighed.

"Once you're accustomed to it," Bulstrode assured him, "it does save ever so much time."

"Can you just get outta my head, let me talk for myself?"

"Would that I could, chump. You're just too fascinating a specimen!

Ambrose sighed and thought something pointed.

"Oh, come right off that, lest I make good on the dunking!"

"You're seriously the thing in the swamp Mayhew's been talkin' up all these years?" Ambrose asked; unnecessary though it may have been to articulate, it made him feel better. He felt more in control of what came out of his mouth than what popped into his head.

"Indeed I am, for it is I!"

"You just float around the swamp, waitin' for folks to come wanderin' in?"

"Oh...you're both quite a ways off the mark and, in another sense, bang on."

"..."

"Right," Bulstrode continued. "Sharing engenders trust. Yes...well. Too complicated to delve into my business at length, and to be entirely honest not in the least rewarding to you. Suffice it to say, and you must surely know this as well as the next fellow, everyone has their own little schemes and dreams. Those of myself and my ilk are quite a bit bigger, though we get some lovely bumps from helping you lot out. At present my chosen associate is our dear mutual acquaintance Doctor Mayhew, though he's rather *pro* at the *quid* without the *quo*, the mash without the bangers, if you see my meaning."

"...I don't."

The pig smiled. Hell's bells, it *smiled*. Pig faces not having been designed to express mirth, it was a bit like watching somebody trying to squeeze their head through a sweater they'd long ago outgrown.

"...you know damn well," Ambrose continued, "I don't see the meanin' to half the shit you're sayin'."

The half-moon of smiling swine glided towards Ambrose. No ripples in its wake, far as he could see.

An image occurred to him of there being nothing to this pig beneath the water, that Bulstrode was just a perfect semi-circle floating on its flat edge, little legs paddling furiously.

Bulstrode chuckled, his snout a mere foot from Ambrose's nose. "Terrific imagination. Muscular, full of piss, a splash of vinegar." The hog's beady little eyes flashed. Ambrose didn't bother trying to work out what sunlight they were reflecting; he knew a dead-end when he saw one. "I suppose we've exhausted the pleasantries, and then some; you seek more reliable connection to your friend across the country, yes?"

"My *sister*," Ambrose corrected.

Bulstrode sat with that for a moment. "Ah, I see just where I've erred. Human relationships. Sticky. Very sticky, those are."

Ambrose felt as though something was expected of him here. Yet nothing worth saying occurred to him. And once it did, of course, the pig would know of it before Ambrose himself. So he said nothing.

That seemed to satisfy Bulstrode. "Yes. You wish for me to help *you* to un-thumb the dike, as it were. That you may have a lovely old natter with your kin."

"Y-"

Patience, Ambrose

"This wished in spite of the less-lovely natter lately had with Mayhew, who therein did communicate to you the perils of engaging my services from a position of insufficient readiness."

"...th-"

"A position you recognize yourself to be occupying, though you will call this tosh even as you thrill to my apparent omniscience."

"..."

The pig inched closer. "Bang-on, I've gotten that."

Ambrose nodded.

"Once more: not an interrogative, dear sir." Bulstrode drifted closer, closer, ever closer to Ambrose.

Instinct drove Ambrose away from the approaching pig, but conviction held him fast. "So you know I want...whatever it is you do out here. I want that."

"You've a mighty fine gift," Bulstrode mused. "Bum luck I didn't come upon you before Mayhew, what? Ah, I jest, for you were yet unborn! Alas," it continued, "you're to hear me attest to a limitation, a rather uncommon occurrence you'd do well to note in passing! The testimony proceeds thusly, and you will find it fully traces the nature of our dilemma as regards *whatever it is I do out here,* and your insufficient readiness: your endowment, such as links your coconut to that of your relation's, is a finicky biscuit, delicately baked, and covered in flaky, breaky bits besides. I wield a scalpel — and here I have abandoned the convectionary imagery — on a scale well-suited to human-sized affairs, but I'm afraid it would be as a bison in a pottery barn, were I to get to shuffling onions in your tomato soup."

Ambrose considered this with all due solemnity, nodding his head with his finger on his chin. Finally, he asked, "huh?"

Bulstrode sighed. "Right. A picture for your predicament: a dike, as mentioned, only let us call it a dam. That's dam without the 'n', not malediction but millpond. This levee is a psychic prophylactic, to keep your noggin from being raw-dogged by its own extrasensory tumescence."

"I d-"

"*Le sigh*, I simplify: in your mind is a grand dam, which holds back the flood. The flood, in this metaphor, is y-?"

"Is it my magic powers or whatever?"

"Indeed. You've heard this one before."

"Seems everybody goes for the water mebaphor, is all."

"Metaphor."

"S'what I said."

"You didn't."

Ambrose shrugged. "Doesn't matter."

"I dare say it does. It's m-"

"I don't think it does."

"It *does*. It's me-*TA*-phor. Ta, ta. With a 'T'."

"And what'd I say?"

"You said *mebaphor.*"

"Before what?" Ambrose goaded.

"I return to the discourse," Bulstrode continued briskly. "The flood is your gift. Once a year, upon the anniversary of your birth as it happens, your mind squeaks open a stopgate, rendering your abilities briefly accessible. And here I am, a wrecking ball in this imagining. You see the dilemma?"

"I g-"

"It's well wi-"

"God *damn*," Ambrose shouted, "would you let me fuckin' talk for myself?!"

Patience, Ambrose

"Ah." Bulstrode nodded as best his spherical body would allow, more an aborted forward roll than anything. "Very well. Do speak."

Ambrose nodded. "Well...I got no clue about half the words you just said."

"Which half flummoxed you? *Of course* or *do speak?*"

"You know that ain't what I mean."

"So I do. May I charge onward, having been subjected to your limitations?"

"Long as you wanna speak sense."

Bulstrode sighed again. "Very well. Rejoining my alluvial analogy, it's well within my grasp to punch a hole in what holds back the flood of your mental potential, or *potemential*, apologies. But done bun can't be undone, so will say one of your lot's more worthwhile royals well after you're gone. Once the hole is punched, the waters rush as they will. Consequently, if you're not careful – egads, even if you are! – their force could well tear the hole still wider, why not, and wider still, until the whole edifice falls down goes boom, and you're left holding the pail at the bottom of an ocean."

"You're sayin'..." Ambrose scratched at his chin. "You open up that river between me and Patience, I'd drown in it likely as I ride it."

"Got it not quite in one, but late's better than never!"

"It ain't like you make it easy to figure what're ya sayin'."

"Pot to kettle, if you ask me." Bulstrode's leaking, seeking schnoz drifted closer to Ambrose's. Whether Bulstrode planted the idea or Ambrose was just quick on the uptake, he understood the pig's design at once: whatever deed there was to do would be accomplished by their bonking honkers.

And however equivocal a front he presented...Bulstrode wanted to do it.

Yet just before the noses touched, Bulstrode pulled away. "Here, then, is your moment of decision: my proboscis is my brush, your mug my canvas. Say the word and I shall paint you into a beautiful corner, from which extrication falls to you and you alone. But consider the decision carefully, for reasons elucidated by the aforementioned pastry-based watch-it."

Ambrose studied the pig's dull little peepers, searching for some kind of emotion he might recognize. He sought but did not find. It was like staring at a pair of closed eyes. Except they were open. They were staring right back at him.

"Do *you* reckon I'm ready for the flood?" Ambrose asked.

"My *goodness* no. You are quite some distance from ready."

"How far?"

"Far."

Ambrose swallowed. His mouth was suddenly as dry as he could ever remember it being. And that included his time on the stocks. "So I try my luck in the rapids now, or swim in smoother waters a few years from now?"

"More than a few. But yes. Here is the dilemma, plainly stated."

"...gimme one reason why I sh-"

"Reasons why you ought to trust me number at precisely naught. I am a multiloquent swine you have met in a marshland, who answers to the name No-Good, and desires a sweet little eskimo kiss. All good sense counsels distrust."

"I don't see what you get outta this."

"You could not possibly, nor is it your concern. But," Bulstrode added in the face of Ambrose's evident skepticism, "Rest assured, there will be no debts incurred on your part."

Ambrose swung his arms stiffly at his sides. "...have I made up my mind already, and I just don't know it yet?"

"Would you genuinely like to know?"

"...no."

"Ah. Mum's the w-"

"Yes! I changed my mind. Tell me."

"You have."

Ambrose looked down at his feet, floating over the surface of the water. He lifted his gaze to Bulstrode once more. "What'd I pick?"

For a wonder, Bulstrode had nothing to say to this. He simply fixed his eyes on Ambrose. His dull, fleshy little eyes.

Nodding, wishing in a distant way that Bulstrode *wouldn't* make him carve his fear into words, Ambrose finally said "I want you to do it."

"Suit yourself!" the pig squealed, which wasn't the most reassuring thing it could have shouted as it lunged forward to bop Ambrose on the nose with its own slab of a schnoz.

The hog's wet honker made a funny little *smush* sound as it bonked the boy's. Then Ambrose was hurtling through a void.

F O U R

IT WAS LIKE BEING SUCKED THROUGH A TINY HOLE POKED into a pickle. Inside, inside, inside where? Inside *here* was wet and smelly and cramped and looooooooong. One moment Ambrose was peering in from an edge, presaging the centuries-hence dawn of children nervous at the mouths of waterslides. The next he was not merely inside, he *was* the inside, stretched to encompass the entirety of the passage, half-boy half-pickle.

He felt her at the far end. She wasn't stretching – Patience's part of the pickle remained unpunctured. Only it wasn't the far end. It was precisely where he was, even as his own vacant body could be described likewise.

And who did he feel in between, inside of him, a part of him? Countless minds and hearts, wants and needs, loves and hates, hundreds and thousands, all oblivious to the mystical pickleboy and the spectral tether in which he brined. They weren't the point, though. They were a distraction. Frenchy Bates was teaching her daughter how to swim, but that wasn't the point. Gregory Jefferson was concerned about the blood in his stool, but that wasn't the point. Marie de la Baum wanted to find the stray cat that meowed outside her window *every fucking morning* and kick it in the head, but that wasn't the point.

The point was that his tether now no longer simply passed over these people as it connected him to Patience – it had grown seeking tendrils, tendrils that had sought and found, oh, how they had found!

Ambrose was in an instant open to everyone in the space between himself and Patience.

He screamed, feeling his hands slamming into his temples as one might in a half-stirred memory, haunted by the sound of his voice crying out from a great depth.

The production collapsed into a single point, which expanded into a star, a heavenly body with two titanic parallel wounds slashed into it. Day inverted, the sun became a nose, and Ambrose was in a swamp staring down the nostrils of a magical pig-shaped monster.

Patience, Ambrose

"Ta-da!" Bulstrode sang. "Congratulations! Though you'll find a great challenge in controlling the blasted thing, once you funnel out the riffraff and hullaballoo, you'll be nattering the days and nights to bits with your dear Patience, as easy as picking up the phone and saying halloo!"

Ambrose shook his head gently, then with a bit more vigor. "The what?"

"Halloo!"

"No, the other thing."

"The phone? Ah, yes, 1812, when *is* my mind at. Let's just strike that comment. Anything else I might do to be of service?"

"Um…" Ambrose wasn't quite sure what he had expected to happen…but he had definitely expected more. In both the process itself, as well as the result. Putting that mortifying light show to one side (which was surprisingly simple; it was already vanishing as a dream). He felt much the same as he had before; anxious, achy, impatient. As far as being endowed with what was essentially a magical power went, this was very nearly underwhelming.

Except, of course, for the voices in his head, the faces sweeping past him, all insubstantial as tricks of light. Hard to be certain if they were even *there,* in any meaningful sense.

"They're there," Bulstrode clarified. "And take to go the homophone, for *there there* may serve as an evergreen condolence, for the many unlovely nights through which you will soon be suffering!"

Ambrose thought he felt a bit light-headed. Was that how it felt to be fully exposed to, uh, the metaphorical floodwaters? Would it take them time to come rushing down? Or was he just getting anxious and imagining things? He felt his heart beating faster, his breath growing quicker and shallower. Oh god, was this it? Was it happening? No. That was what fear felt like. Right?

"There there," Bulstrode reassured him.

"Can you take it away?" Ambrose wondered, not-so-idly. "Not sayin' I want you to, but, like, say I'm thinkin' twice and maybe feelin' like I ain't th-"

"Oh, color me bummered. Must we take our wild, wet metaphor from the top?"

"No. I'm just askin'."

"Yes, I see you are. But would that I could grant you anything you now lack, it would be ears with which to listen. I have giv-"

"I am listenin'!"

"*I have given* you nothing to take from this place that you did not drag in with you. Those floodwaters have always been sloshing around that colossal noggin of yours."

Ambrose nodded. "Okay. Okay." His fingers and toes burned, tingled, and somehow felt as though they'd gone numb, all at the same time. Was this…it? No. That was nervousness. It was why his guts had gone all watery.

Or was that the floodwater? No. That wasn't literal. This was…

"So I can do this," Ambrose mumbled to himself. "If this ain't nothin' I ain't been carryin' around my whole life…I can do it. I'm gonna be okay."

"I certainly hope so. I would love to pop in on you some years hence, once Mayhew has sodded off to the great Rascal factory in the sky. And ah, what an earful I will get from him if you should perish. Oh well!" With that, Bulstrode turned, lingering on Ambrose's face for just a moment. "Best of luck, you damn fool! With the 'n', in this instance!"

Ambrose wanted to tell him to wait, wanted to ask him more

questions…but, of course, he already knew the answer to each of them. Oh, how he feared he was going to regret this.

No, he reassured himself as he stood a little straighter. He was strong enough to do this. He had not spent the last three years sharpening his mind to have it turned on him by a swamp hog.

Bulstrode completed his soundless revolution and skirred back into the sickly gloom, crude-black tail corkscrewing straight towards the sky. Ambrose watched the spot he had lately occupied, as though divining meaning from ripples left in the pig's wake, as they settled into stillness.

But of course, the pig had stirred no ripples, left no wake. It was a perfectly meaningless departure. So Ambrose stood silently and watched the swamp, unchanging save the verdure tossed by what little breeze crept through the mire.

At which point, he received his first lesson on the limits of power: the magical platform Bulstrode had put beneath his feet vanished. Ambrose fell straight down into the swamp water, sinking deep enough to swallow a mouthful.

F I V E

FOCUS.

It was hard to do because there was so much *chatter*, so much human clutter in his way. Each time he reached out for Patience, reached out by opening up and letting her appear as might any sound or sensation, a hundred strangers thrilled to his embrace, a nation's worth of thoughts pouring in like, yes, a flood. And each time, his labors were rewarded with little more than with a brief overcoming, an unmooring from himself. It was like being knocked off balance by an unexpectedly powerful gale. Not the end of the world, easy enough to keep one's feet on the ground. But the stumble was nonetheless embarrassing; who the hell can't stand up to wind?

Or was it water, rushing from the pig-shaped hole in the dam?

But that was neither here nor there. Er, actually it was *here*, and that was the problem. Ambrose wanted his mind to reach up and out, to *there*.

So focus.

He once more plunged into the mystical pickle sphincter Bulstrode had opened (making a mental note to devise a more poetic descriptor for the aperture as he did). As before, he felt himself stretching, filling the entire space at once. His challenge now was to compress whatever curious vessel his mind boarded to take this journey. For even if he thought of *himself* as being stretched and kneaded like a blob of surly dough, he knew full well that *he* was lying flat on his back on the floor of his hut, staring at the darkened ceiling and trying to *focus*. Whatever this was voyaging along the supernatural highways and byways of America, it wasn't entirely *him*.

Or maybe it was. Maybe it was more him than the body was. In which case…no. Later. For now?

Focus.

There was a little girl in Flat Lick, Kentucky who was afraid of the well. Her parents had sent her to fetch water, as they always did. But this girl, who was pale and blonde and definitely not Patience, found that the bottomless rock-rimmed hole in the world never ceased to terrify her, it seemed in fact to find *new* ways to scare the bejesus out of her each time she met it. Today it was making a noise, what was that noise? A low, satisfied rumble. What had made it so happy? As she tiptoed closer, clutching the pail nearer her chin, she could hear the water at the bottom, because yes alright the well was *not* bottomless, it had a bottom full of water, but maybe underneath *that* there was no bottom, she had never had the courage to look straight down into it because if she did she knew something would reach up and grab her, something slimy and sticky would splat onto her face and yank her into the depths that she could hear now were churning, bubbling, laughing. She gripped the handle of the pail so tightly her knuckles cracked, deafening pops and snaps that sent reverberations through Ambrose's entire body. He pulled himself back into his flesh, seizing hard at the moment of return.

He sat up and felt his forehead. Damp. His hands were clammy. He was sucking air like he'd just run twice to the bog and back. His desperate gasping made him a little bit dizzy, even. Ok. Ok. Through a more efficacious act of willpower, he slowed his breathing and settled his nerves. That little girl would have to conquer the well, day in and day out, and he felt for her terror, had *felt* it. But she would have to face her fears alone. As would Patience, if Ambrose got too caught up in the goings-on of Flat Lick, Kentucky to pursue mastery of his newly granted skill. And come to think of it, he was having to face his fears right now too. So, sorry little girl. Ambrose needed to

Focus.

The man wanted to paint something that represented the plight of the everyday schmuck. Not metaphorical representation, but *literal*. A genre painting of quotidian living, a glimpse into the lives of not the wealthy but the *not*-wealthy. So noble a pursuit, was his current engagement! The man delighted at his own humble ambition. Last year he'd made quite a splash when he had taken mere oils and canvas, and created a wholecloth universe in which some black broad ladled out slop to all kinds of white folks. He also put a dog in it, something for the women and children. What a majestic vision it was! How representative of what men of less-than-elevated station might see on the street! Pepper-pot, smoking hot. Yes indeedy! But this new piece was going to top that. Yes indeedily dee. What he needed was to catalogue the sorts of objects regular old losers, who were the lifeblood of their nation and a powerful demographic to have on the hook so to speak and so on, might have in their homes. He did this not by speaking to anyone who belonged to that demographic, for such people could only serve to muddle the clarity of his vision with their dust and dirt, yuck, no thanks. No, far better to simply stare at his own possessions and imagine what it would be like to have the things he had, just worse. So these urchins should have a china cabinet in their home, yes, no doubt. But they would *not* have a truly fine set of China, er, china, made in Dresden, fashioned in the style of fifteenth century chinaman's pottery, white with the musulman's cobalt blue scribblings on it, the sort of thing you'd know right away what it was when you saw it, or at least in this case you'd know right away what it was designed to look like, and frankly they did such a good job you might well expect it was the real deal unless somebody told you otherwise, and he rather wished his great grandparents had kept that particular factoid to themselves but oh well the cat was out of the bag, the crab was out of the sack, the animal was out of the receptacle. Point was, here was the point, poor fuckers won't have nice pottery. So he would paint them an early classical revival cabinet – all hard angles and unadorned wood, though *his* cabinet had glass doors that slid from side to side so he might as well paint those on, even if flat panes of glass might be out of this family's price range, there was no sense slumming it *too* hard – and fill it with blue and white china that nope no he would fill it with…just white china. Brilliant! Satisfied with his day's labor, the painter retired to his bedroom, where he would manipulate his genitals until he fell asleep. What did he hope to accomplish by doing this, Ambrose wondered as he himself snapped back into his body?

He pushed himself up to a seated position and stretched his neck from side to side, as though that descent into artistic indulgence had filled his ears with a foreign liquid that he hoped to dislodge. Feeling free of that tremendous pretention, Ambrose considered what jumped out as the most important detail of that entire vignette: the manipulation of genitals. Recognizing this intention in the man, even if the intention *behind* the intention was a bit less clear, stirred something in the scaly bits of Ambrose's brain. That seemed like a thing that a man might do, should he find himself in a certain mood, late at night, in isolation.

This would require further investigation. But for now…

Focus.

S   I   X

"WHAT THE HELL WERE YOU THINKING," MAYHEW MUMBLED, AS he had taken to doing periodically. It had long since stopped being a question; it had become, really, just about the only thing the old man said to Ambrose anymore. The Doctor continued to bring Ambrose into the sewing cabin to help him train his mind, but gone were the warmth and kindness of years past.

What stung Ambrose most, he supposed, was the speed and apparent ease with which Mayhew had rescinded his friendship. Either the man had been faking the entire time…or Ambrose's jaunt into the swamp had just offended him that deeply. Being torn between those two possibilities was deeply frustrating, as it left Ambrose uncertain of whether he should be angry at Mayhew in return, or begging for his forgiveness.

Perhaps a little of each, Ambrose conceded on those unhappy nights when sleep came easily. His dreams had more than likely ceased to be just dreams; they brought him sights seen from behind the eyes of strangers, often tortures of the most tedious sort. Someone bending to tie the laces of their shoes, someone brushing their hair behind their ear, someone opening and closing the door of a cupboard trying to figure out where it was catching.

What made these visions so oddly unbearable to Ambrose was those glimpses he got of the people he was, for want of a better word, inhabiting. The hand reaching down for the laces was palest white; the hair falling in his face was long, stringy, auburn; the cupboard door he was fiddling with was one in a colossal room full of them, the kitchens of a mansion. In each of these not-so-dreams, he carried within him a fundamental knowledge of who *he* was, which did little but create friction each time that self-conception came into contact with a compelling fiction. For each time, Ambrose believed that he *was* the person on whom he was eavesdropping, while in the very same moment he knew for a fact that he was *not*.

More disturbing was that, when he awoke, the feeling would modulate and liger. He would know for a fact that he had once more become himself…yet he would find it impossible to *believe* this.

Patience, Ambrose

He needed help. But he was not yet strong enough to reach Patience and ask it of her, and he was either too proud or too embarrassed (a fine line, that) to ask it of Mayhew.

"I can do this," he insisted to Mayhew one day, apropos of absolutely nothing save his own crippling self-doubt.

"Quiet," Mayhew replied. "Focus."

So much for reassurance, then.

Such was his desperation that as summer yielded to autumn, Ambrose found himself lurking by the meathouse, arms folded against the first chill of the year. This would earn him a hiding, he knew; he was meant to be harvesting. But he needed to speak to someone, and he had a feeling the conversation would go easier if he could wax mystical a bit. *Without* needing to explain that there was a talking pig puttering around the swamp.

Sure enough, the man he hoped to see showed his face in time: Father Daniel came loping along, and without his usual coterie at that. "I had heard from several quarters that you were down here," Daniel grumbled, "in lieu of at your labors."

Ambrose flushed with an anger he had promised himself he would keep in check. "And you're worried about my labors, huh?"

Daniel sighed and shook his head. "What do you want, Ambrose?"

"Oh, so you're assumin' I'm here waitin' for *you?!*" With that, Ambrose stormed off towards his damned labors, cursing himself once again. He wished that recognizing foolishness in oneself led naturally to extinguishing it. In Ambrose's experience, recognition wasn't good for much of anything. Except making one feel worse.

He wished he had never gone out into that swamp. That was

far easier to wish than that he had walked away from Bulstrode; Ambrose knew himself well enough to know that the moment the hog had made its offer, Ambrose was doomed to accept. Oh, but if he had only listened to Mayhew!

No. No, he could do this. He would not be swept away. Really, he hadn't yet felt in danger of being overwhelmed by those intrusions into his mind. He felt fully in control of them. Well, mostly. Except maybe at night, in his sleep. Otherwise, though, he felt quite confident about his progress.

It was the frustration that felt out of control. The anger. The humiliation. All of the things that had been there before. Things that didn't have anything to do with Bulstrode punching a hole in the mental dam. Because all that did was allow the outside world *in,* psychically speaking. That had nothing to do with… that other stuff.

He missed Patience. It felt strange to say – unless one wanted to count their infancy, he and his sister had probably spent not even twelve hours together at the very beginning of their lives. Yet there it was, as powerful a feeling as any of the many currently besieging him.

There was at least something actionable about that, though. Mayhew's obstinancy confused and frightened Ambrose, while Daniel's presumption and general dickheadery never ceased to enrage him. While he hoped to one day crack the shell the Doctor had thrown up around himself (the Father could fuck right off, *oh, what do you want Ambrose,* like the whole world revolved around him, it was ridiculous), Ambrose wasn't entirely sure how to begin that project. Well, come to think of it, an apology was probably the first step. But Ambrose wasn't there yet.

He knew exactly how to get through to Patience, though.

Reach, focus, try, relax. The *how* wasn't the issue. It was only a question of building the brute strength to make the connection, and developing the control to do so gently.

So Ambrose kept at it. And hoped Patience was doing, if not the same, then something similar.

Because on those increasingly rare nights when Ambrose remained entirely himself…he wondered if his sister hadn't forgotten him.

S E V E N

PRAISEGOD'S FAVORITE NEWSPAPER WAS *THE STRING-fellow Advertiser*, a rag local to the Estate on which he had been raised. Still in publication, as it happened, and consequently one of the few secular publications with which Patience had been educated during her time with the woman who had turned out to be a kind of mother-in-not-so-law.

The Stringfellow Advertiser wasn't exactly at the vanguard of journalism, to put it politely – and knowing this first-hand only deepened what would have been Patience's bog-standard confusion, at Praisegod insisting he get his news from a paper printed by and for his native Stringfellow county. Despite, and Patience could not square this for herself, Praisegod's farm being very emphatically *not* located in Stringfellow county.

Yes, Praisegod paid quite handsomely to have a witless bit of toss printed in a neighboring county specially delievered to him (by a young boy who was quite clearly doing his daily best to hurl the paper through one of the second story windows – a loud *thnk* on the wall let Patience know when it was time to fetch the paper). Which meant he was regularly receiving his news a day or two later than his neighbors. Which meant he was often angrily disputing his friends on their facts, only to marvel as Patience read these facts to him just a score and some hours later.

Patience couldn't understand what about this particular publication warranted the extra cost and inconvenience – as the name suggested, over half of the content was advertising – but she also granted that she wasn't old enough to have experienced nostalgia yet. To hear Praisegod speak of his childhood, one would think he'd been birthed in the Garden and cast out for the sin of pubescence.

My, but the frequency with which biblical allusions occurred to Patience certainly had increased – exponentially – in the three years since she had returned to Praisegod's farm. In all the excitement about having her entire self-conception flipped like the table of a money-lender, and her increasingly frustrating efforts to hold Praisegod's feet to the fire as concerned the liberation of Ambrose via the very marketplace that had doomed him, Patience had plum forgotten the entire pretense by which she had sold Praisegod on this whole literary excursion: saving her everlasting soul through regular studies of the Bible.

Her father-brother certainly hadn't forgotten though, and so even as Patience berated him for his complacency, for not sending off another letter, not hiring another retired lawman to track Ambrose's precise whereabouts (or even send them directly to the county in Louisiana that Patience had countless times named for him, which he refused to believe was anything more than a word that had come to her in a dream)…even in the thick of this, Bible studies claimed an hour of Patience's day, twice a day. In them, Praisegod would pace the room, genuinely astounding her with his word-perfect memorization of the whole tome, lecturing and hectoring, but never actually instructing. It was enough to make her wish, from time to time, she'd just stuck with illiteracy.

But then there was that other duty, the one she was now discharging. Praisegod had never been one to read newspapers, and had, prior to Patience's trip to the Estate, insisted that he had no need of being informed of terrestrial goings-on. The tune had always changed slightly whenever Ezekiel was near at hand, and modulated into a whole different key now that Patience had returned; suddenly, rather than shunning all updates of earthly concern, Praisegod demanded he be read every single word in every single not-so-new issue of *The Stringfellow Advertiser*, no matter how trivial.

It was, Patience had to admit, a rather deft dodge of his own rule: Praisegod refused to read the news himself. To have it read *to* him, though, was apparently a satisfactory loophole, certainly large enough to slip the strange shackles of piety in which he had locked himself.

On some days, Patience suspected this was all because Praisegod had forgotten how to read. She dismissed the thought as ridiculous each time; how could a grown man *forget* how to read?

Whatever the reason, Patience often found herself in Praisegod's living room, sitting upright in a hard-backed wooden chair that had apparently been upholstered sarcastically, with a thick blanket draped over the seat and buttoned with what appeared to be iron nails painted rusty. The man of the house always sprawled across a more competently assembled couch, staring at the ceiling as though the words Patience read him were scrolling along above his head.

Thusly arranged, Patience and Praisegod together learned of the United States' annexing the Republic of Florida, the rout of the Indians at Tippencanoe, and the declaration of war against England. Each time she read, Patience felt herself, for lack of a better word, expanding. Converting the squiggles into substantive symbols became easier and easier. The tiny circle of her understanding spread ever outward, gradually welcoming a tidbit about local government here, a nugget of international diplomacy there. That naïve know-it-all arrogance of youth and the more mature acknowledgment of one's impossible smallness in an endlessly complex world somehow found a way to coexist and, yes, engorge in tandem. The cause for the latter was self-explanatory – Patience was almost daily learning of battles fought over a land she had never heard of, or reading descriptions of inventions that sounded indistinguishable from magic to her ears (or eyes, as the case may have been). The former, though, was borne of Praisegod's seeming inability to keep track of what Patience read to him. It was perplexing, that a man who knew every single chapter, verse, *word* of the Bible should be unable to recall, say, who had led the American forces at Tippencanoe, when he had been read the name no fewer than a dozen times. But it was undoubtedly the case that he had forgotten, as Praisegod was often interrupting Patience's recitations with "who?" or "wait, what was that?" or "that's a state now?" And almost without fail, Patience would be able to answer Praisegod's questions without recourse to the text. She found it impossible, humbling though the rest of the readings often were, to keep her head from inflating in those moments. Just a bit.

Where Praisegod had no apparent recollective difficulties, though, was in the advertisements, with which he also insisted on being regaled, in full, every single day. Once, Patience read him an ad for:

SHELLSTROP MALTHOUSE

KILMARNOCK STREET

PITHY SHELLSTROP

PROPRIETOR OF THE ABOVE ESTABLISHMENT

HUMBLY RETURNS HIS VERY BEST THANKS TO HIS NUMEROUS
FRIENDS AND THE PUBLIC, FOR THE GENEROUS SUPPORT
GIVEN HIM IN HIS BUSINESS, THESE NUMBER OF YEARS, AND
BEGS TO INFORM THEM THAT HE HAS AT PRESENT AN
EXTENSIVE ASSORTMENT OF

DELICIOUS MALTS

OF EVERY DESCRIPTION, OF ALL MANNER OF CEREALS THAT
ARE BARLEY, REQUISITE IN THE FORMULATION OF ALL SORTS
OF

ALCOHOLIC DRINKABLES

OF SIMILARLY NUMEROUS VARIETY, THAT CAN BE CONSUMED
TO INDUCE A PLEASURABLE STATE.

Being a teetotaler (save those cases in which the alcohol in question had once coursed through the veins of a savior, in which case, *look out)*, this ad ought have been absolutely irrelevant to Praisegod. It certainly ought not have rated as more deserving of cortical real estate than William Henry Harrison's name. And yet, upon hearing the ad, Praisegod mused at the slightly amended verbiage, as compared to the construction of the same ad in last Wednesday's *Advertiser.* "It had been 'good malts' last week," Praisegod marveled. "Yet they remained in the man's possession. And thus, they have become 'delicious malts"!" He giggled, and Patience thrilled at the chance to prove him wrong. Alas, upon digging up last Wednesday's paper, she discovered that he had been right. Another point for the pedant.

On one notable mid-July day, not long after Patience's ill-fated attempt at educating Ambrose on the difference between, A, K, and OK, Patience opened the paper to a story that encompassed both the smallness of human thought, of which her half-brother was becoming quite an exemplar, and the bigness of the world by which her would-be vainglory was daily kept in check.

Too astonished to read it out loud, she pored over it as quickly as she could, punctuating the piece with a loud, braying laugh.

Praisegod, lost in some ceiling-set reverie, started upright. "God's wounds, what was that?"

Patience giggled, "I just read something that was funny."

"And you'd keep it to yourself? I love a good joke!" insisted the most austere man Patience had ever met. "Let's have it!"

"Um..." she looked back down at the paper. Praisegod probably wouldn't understand what she'd found so funny about the fact that, just after the United States had officially declared war on England, a brig called the HMS Colibri was already en route from Halifax (the one in England, naturally), bearing news that the Orders in Council – one of the main catalysts for the current conflict – had been repealed. All very political and official, that, but the upshot was simple: England had made a decision that America didn't like, and so America decided to go to war over it...just as England was coming to announce a change of heart.

Which meant the entire war currently underway could well have been averted, if only the Americans had set the vote for declaration a few weeks later, or the English had repealed the Orders in Council a few weeks earlier.

True, it wasn't *funny*, in any traditional sense. But there was just something so heartbreakingly, idiotically elegant about the missed communication, here reported in a typeface smaller than that which peddled Shellstrop's malts. Hundreds, maybe thousands of people were going to die in a war fought, in no small part, over convictions that no longer tracked to reality.

So, yes, not quite funny. It was more like…the experience of looking at Praisegod now and thinking, *there's my dad*.

That wasn't the sort of thing Patience imagined being able to explain to her half-brother. So she scanned the paper for something else that might plausibly have prompted the laughter. "Ah," she announced, "what was funny was, there's an advertisement here seeking volunteers to join the infantry, and the ages they've p-"

"I see nothing funny about that," Praisegod mumbled, lying back down on the couch.

"What was funny was, the ages they've put for 'able bodied men of patriotism, courage and enterprise' is eighteen to forty-five. Can you imagine a forty-five year old man fighting in a war?" She forced some more laughter, hoping it didn't sound as artificial to him as it did to her.

Thirty-three year old Praisegod shook his head and again mumbled "I don't see what's funny about that," this time in a tone that said *and neither should you*.

Patience hated that tone. Even years out from learning the truth, Praisegod sometimes seemed to forget that he wasn't her father. So, as per usual, she decided to remind him. "Hey, Peter?"

"Praisegod," he corrected her.

"Peter," Patience corrected him.

He had the decency to look pre-emptively browbeaten. "Uh oh."

"Shut up while I'm reading."

Praisegod nodded wisely, as though silence had been his idea.

Patience shook her head slightly, cleared her throat, and resumed her reading with the article about the HMS Colibri. It was, she had to admit, substantially harder to see the humor, reading it right after that call to arms.

E I G H T

THAT NIGHT, PATIENCE DREAMT OF A SHIP ON THE OCEAN. IT WAS the HMS Colibri, no doubt, that futile tub puttering across the expanse of the Atlantic Ocean towards a nation already on the war path.

Of course, the ship was simply a shape, the ocean a roiling dark, for Patience had never seen a boat fit for more than two people at once, had never seen a body of water wide enough to hide its far bank. So she dreamt of shape and shadow, the head of an axe parting fog, waves breaking against a star-filled sky.

Yet it was the ship, she knew. The message coming too late to mean anything. And so, a message without meaning. Words to no purpose. Just a ship on a shape.

Patience awoke in tears. She could not have said why. There was meaning there, but no message fit to convey it. A shape, a great lightless shape, and no ship fit to sail upon it.

She wondered if the men in England who had dispatched the Colibri felt as she did. Content to shoot off a letter. Uncertain of what else they could do.

Patience yanked the thin linen sheet resting on her belly up to her face. She'd tucked it in tightly enough at the base of the bed that it took a few good pulls to free it, each of which occasioned still greater sobs from Patience.

Here she was, then, in that familiar midnight cul-de-sac. She knew she ought to be doing more to help Ambrose…but she couldn't begin to imagine what that more could be. Letters could only travel so fast, and moving through what Praisegod liked to call "the proper channels," however unsatisfying it was, seemed much more promising than Patience setting off on her own.

But three years had yielded nothing. Brokers and middlemen, middlemen and brokers. It was proving more intractable than it had any right to be.

What else could she do, though?

Nothing, that was the conclusion at which Patience always arrived. She was doing the best she could. It wasn't fair, but that was life.

Such a thought was normally enough to console Patience. But as she swaddled her lamentations in linen, she found herself on this night thoroughly unconsoled. For each time she closed her eyes, there was that shape, that shifting carrion black over which no far bank could be seen.

N I N E

AMBROSE FELT HER.

It took him until the winter, by which time he'd almost entirely lost interest in what was happening on the plantation. He still broke his back at the labors to which Master Barry and Hilditch ordered him, of course, but he could no longer be bothered by the pain. Even the bird which alighted upon him as he was punished for his increasingly unsatisfactory efforts was met with mounting indifference.

For the things happening on the property here were small. His suffering was nothing. It bored him. And how could it not?

For at the ass-end of 1812, Ambrose lay flat on his back, as he had every night since his marshland encounter with the pig-shaped creature from a world beyond human comprehension. Ever outwards he reached, making himself small even as he traversed a gargantuan path. Over the months he had felt more lives, more hearts, more minds than it seemed possible could exist at one moment. From time to time he had been sucked into their heads, as though they were eager to show him, show him what they saw not for the sight but for the seeing itself. That happened less and less now – more common was a detached observer's perspective from which Ambrose had little trouble disengaging, as opposed to the hungry first-person perspectives that reminded Ambrose of nothing so much as the way Bulstrode's bog had swallowed his every footfall, sucking his leg down to the knee and clutching him tight as he fought to extricate himself. Worse still was how seductive such glimpses through another's eyes could be. Even when Ambrose felt it a simple matter to pull his mind from the mental muck, there were times when he was loathe to do so. Sometimes it was fascinating to just sit, or stand, or *be*, and watch someone live their life, from their perspective, yet with a perspective they themselves could never hope to attain. It gave their lives a clarity that Ambrose had never been able to achieve in his own. Would not have wanted to, even had he been able.

Patience, Ambrose

Because goodness, there was such an astounding number of people doing an astounding number of things across the country! He'd encountered ex-slaves, freed by legal means or their own cunning, founding a seminary. He'd seen a woman clipping the hedges in front of her house, fretting over the dullness of her shears. He'd heard a children's choir that were either being torn limb from limb by alligators, or else were performing a song called 'pitchfork vs. shovel,' and he'd felt the instructor who had neither the heart to stop them nor the talent to improve them. He'd seen windows washed, bourbon distilled, guns fired, trees felled, beards trimmed, books sold, love made, love made again just so he could be sure how it worked, bread baked, chamberpots emptied, booboos kissed, cattle herded, laws passed, hopes dashed, corn hulled, doors opened, yo-yos yoed, blessings offered, cloth dyed, rounds made, glass glazed, gifts given, milk spoiled, rabbits shot, knuckles cracked, jackets tailored, flowers planted, die thrown, scotches hopped, dominos toppled, love made a third time just because it was a lot to remember and he wanted to be *really* sure he got how it worked, puddles jumped, hearts broken, dogs pet, wheels spun, curtains hung, barns raised, fires started, views admired, weight gained, furs traded, babies born, crosses borne, liars winning, songs composed, tables waited, iron forged, skies watched, signals missed, machines fitted, hands shaken, prayers offered, plans cancelled, criminals sentenced, stores opened, memories scrambled, jokes told, choices regretted, monocles polished, beauty wasted, horses shod, children abandoned, candles lit, hills climbed, promises made, oaths recanted, blood shed, wine spilled, kindness tendered, snowballs thrown, friends ignored, fingers burned, bricks lain, heroes cheated, barrels hooped, carriages drawn, divorces considered, talents exploited, tragedies overcome, ankles twisted, nails clipped, stars named, maps redrawn, widows scammed, holes dug, money wasted, faith affirmed, grievances aired, futures imagined, pasts denied, prices haggled, vows said, letters sent, trades learned, jars opened, crowds assembled, fiddles tuned, habits adopted, furniture moved, baths taken, heights feared, truths resisted, lies embraced, smiles forced, horizons broadened, journeys begun, lips puckered, parties thrown, hips hooray'd, rules enforced, backs stooped, axes swung, expectations met, romances pursued, tempers flared, impulses indulged, crises averted, carriages overturned, teeth pulled, beds made, boats sunk, groceries bought, balls thrown, kilns fired, dust collected, bugs squashed, duties shirked, breath wasted, losers bullied, muscles strained, moods swung, heirlooms stolen, traditions begun, lovers parted, wigs powdered, bags filled, cheaters caught, birthdays celebrated, love made but this time not because it was fun to watch but because Ambrose needed to see something that affirmed life to counteract the death, all of the death, the death from which his mind could find no reprieve.

Everyone, everywhere, at all times, seemed to be dying, be it the actual moment of expiration or the plodding, inexorable descent. With every new experience Ambrose encountered, he grew more inured to the inexhaustible abundance of possible lives, thoughts, and feelings, which in turn made it easier for him to tune them out, to control for their novelty in his search for Patience. Death was the one thing to which he couldn't seem to build a tolerance, though. It hounded him, buffeted his mind from one necrosis to the next, battered him with its endless endings. How could he possibly chart a new beginning of his own, with his consciousness held hostage by conclusion? And oh, how dreadfully unsatisfying these conclusions were! Did any man, woman, or child ever pass with a settled heart? Feeling their affairs in order? Was there anything in the world that was not someone else's unfinished business?

Numerous times, he considered going to Mayhew for help. But no; as disconnected from his own life as Ambrose was coming to feel, he couldn't bear to make that appeal. It wasn't so much the personal humiliation he feared anymore, so much as it was the position into he would be putting the Doctor. For Mayhew would be unable to help. And that would tear him up, for the Doctor was bigger-hearted than he liked to let on. So Ambrose continued to join him in the sewing cabin, no longer practicing according to Mayhew's prompts, but simply trying to hold himself together until it was time to leave.

It occurred to Ambrose that he might appeal directly to No-Good Bulstrode. The pig had loosed the flood, after all; perhaps, despite its demurral, it might have some valuable insight on the means by which the resultant flow might be directed? But after two fruitless treks into the swamp, one of which was only fifteen minutes of searching and several hours of being completely, horrifyingly lost, Ambrose deduced that the pig had no interest in being found.

Never once did he seriously consider asking Daniel for help. Because the Father was the sort of man who believed that people who asked for help were weak, and people who asked for loyalty were leaders. Ambrose didn't believe that…at least, not entirely. He believed it just enough to want to avoid getting trapped in such a dynamic. For he feared he might find it a touch too comfortable.

It was a challenge to keep all of this in mind — all of the

avenues of help he had closed off to himself – on those long, sleepless nights when he found it impossible to keep the rest of the world *out* of his mind.

And it was at his lowest ebb, it seemed, that he would catch a glimpse of her. Patience. It was unmistakable, that sense of completion, the warmth of her presence even across the miles.

Yet there was something impossibly content about her warmth, a broadening that shone like a beacon through fog. She was…happy. Happy without him. Which made him happy for her, yet sad for himself.

He called to her, knowing that she was too far to hear. Or perhaps she could hear him perfectly well, but didn't yet know how to respond to him in kind. But probably not. She seemed diffuse, as though comprised of dust swirling in a gust of wind. Like the ones that swept across the field, got stuck behind the barn, and spun around and around, looking for the way out. Sometimes the mites collected into a Patience-shaped blob. More often, they were just a billion individual particles, twirling on an invisible current.

That feeling though, that sensation. It was her. He was close.

He felt his face warp into an unfamiliar shape, a contortion that he quickly identified as a grin. A great, big, genuine smile of the sort he'd not worn in…he wasn't sure how long. Quite a while, that was as close as he could get.

Letting the smile calcify, trying to commit the feel of it to memory, Ambrose closed his eyes and let himself sleep, was *allowed* to sleep by a nation that had so very much that it wanted to show him.

Tomorrow night, he would try again. He'd been making progress, and instinct told him he was nearing a tipping point. It was

Patience, Ambrose

a trembling in the ear, the feeling one gets when approaching a cliff's edge, stepping closer and closer to the precipice, just to see how far down it really goes.

1813

O N E

IT WAS ALWAYS HARD TO SAY PRECISELY HOW PRAISE-god would react to any of the things Patience read him. For every scoff over Shellstrop bigging up his malts from one week to the next, there was something closer to indifference on the man's face as Patience broke wartime updates of retreats in Canada, or surrender in Detroit.

So what a surprise it was, when Patience reached and recited a headline regarding the fall of a city called Ogdensburg, that Praisegod all but rocketed through the ceiling.

Patience paused and glanced over the paper just in time to see her half-brother crash back down into his seat. She asked a question with her eyebrows.

"Ogdensburg?!" he shouted.

Patience nodded. "Funny name, I know."

"Ogdensburg *New York?!*"

"Uh…" she scanned the article. "Looks like it."

Praisegod slumped down into himself, his chin coming to rest on his chest. "Ogdensburg has fallen," he mumbled.

"Should I read the rest?"

"There's *more?!*"

"…yeah, I just read the headline. There's a whole article after that."

"Goodness Gracious, Power on High…" Praisegod clapped his hands together and commenced a silent prayer so forceful that it beaded his brow with sweat.

Patience nodded, folded up the paper, and took it out to the sun room. There she learned of everything else the state of New York was up to as February slugged its way to a close. Mostly war stuff, which was fair, though there were some deaths and marriages to read about. Obituaries always had much more information about their subjects, which made them more enjoyable to read. Morbid, that, but Patience considered that the fault of the editors and writers. She was but a humble reader.

That sense of passivity reared back and bit her the following morning, when Praisegod gathered all hands (i.e. Patience, Mary, Ezekiel, and Flann) together for "a dismal disquisition."

"O woeful day!" Praisegod exclaimed from his porch, unknowingly adopting his father's preferred mount from which to sermonize. In the early days after her return, Patience had tried to talk Praisegod down from the porch whenever he installed himself there, but one could only meet failure so many times before surrender seemed prudent. "O piteous flight, to which the consideration of which we are propelled...to...?...!"

Patience frowned up at him from the foot of the steps, shoulder-to-shoulder with Mary, Ezekiel, and Flann. Praisegod, for his part, had tried quite a few times to talk her up to his level. Too bad for both, the parent they shared was the one who fully embodied the bullheaded gene.

Praisegod glanced at Patience and turned his palms up. "What am I saying?"

"I feel like I know where you're going," Patience called back to him, "but I've not clue how you mean to get there from the sentence you just started."

Praisegod waved that away. "As Adam and Eve were forced from the Garden," he continued on surer ground, "as Abram was called to 'get thee out of thy country,' as the Israelites were driven from Egypt, and the Christ family secreted themselves from the cruel King Herod's gaze, as Lot and his, uh, lot...well, that's a bad example in this case. But you get the idea."

They did not get the idea. Patience certainly didn't – unless, of course, she *did*, and his message was simply not the one she had expected to hear.

"We have to leave the farm," he translated.

Oh. So it was the latter.

"What?" Patience shouted.

Mary wondered "why?!"

Ezekiel demanded "for how long?!"

Flann asked "where will we go?!"

"Alright," Praisegod droned with his palms outstretched. "Let's keep our heads about us. And our wits. Ours heads *and* our wits."

Patience considered reminding him of his reaction upon hearing the news out of Ogdensburg…but she was too stunned to be needling him just now. They were *leaving?* What did that mean for…

"Where will our letters be delivered?" she demanded.

Praisegod shushed her.

"You shush, and answer me!"

Her half-brother rolled his eyes and lowered his arms, leaving them to dangle awkwardly at his sides. "As you all know, there's a war on at the moment. And I've just received word…" he raised a single finger towards the heavens. "…that Ogdensburg has been taken by the British!"

He did not receive whatever reaction he was expecting to get, unless the reaction he was expecting was "where? Who? So?" in counterpoint.

"Ogdensburg!" Praisegod traced his hands through the air, outlining the town on an imaginary map. He glanced at Patience for backup, but she simply boggled at him as though not understanding that he was a drowning man asking nicely for a life preserver.

"Answer me," she growled.

"Shh," Mary encouraged her, placing a gentle hand on Patience's shoulder.

Patience frowned, but complied.

Praisegod did not fail to notice. "Oh," he grumbled, "so you shush when *Mary* tells you to sh-"

"Say what you were to say," Ezekiel snapped.

Praisegod cleared his throat. "Ogdensburg. It is a small village in the northern climes of the state. Our forces have been chased from this very Ogdensburg, simultaneously eliminating our opportunity to disrupt the Yank's supply lines in th-"

"I thought *we* were the Yanks," Flann whispered.

"Ah," Praisegod nodded, "disrupt the *Brit's* supply lines in this particular region, as well as clearing the path for them, who are the Brits, to sweep through the rest of New York. Which, it seems essential I remind you, includes our humble Yankee pork farm!"

"So how will we continue to receive our mail?" Patience demanded.

Praisegod made a high-pitched groaning sound. "What is your fascination with the mail, dear sister of mine?"

Patience darkened. "Ambrose!"

"...*oooh,*" Praisegod nodded. "Right. No, I'm afraid we shall be putting a stop to that diversion at once. As we all of us head sou-"

"What?!" Patience sputtered.

"Who's Ambrose?" Flann wondered.

"Oop," Mary gulped softly. "Flann, there's a whole passel of chaos we forgot to tell you about." She gestured for him to lean in, and began whispering in his ear.

"As all of us head south and west," Praisegod continued, making a point of ignoring Patience as she stepped forward, towards the porch steps. "All of us save Ezekiel and Flann, who will be required to remain here and tend the farm, w-"

"I must stay?" Ezekiel asked, throwing his arms out, "as war approaches?"

"Should the grounds be left *un*attended," Praisegod replied, "we shall find ourselves divested of our livelihoods whether or not the British ever arrive."

Ezekiel took a step forward. "And what if they kill me and

Flann, hm?"

"Wait…" Flann pouted at Mary and Ezekiel in turn. "What?"

"That would be bad!" Praisegod gestured between himself and Ezekiel. "We are on the same page there! But what it is that I am now saying to you, is th-"

"Peter," Patience said, soft as a secret.

Praisegod silenced himself mid-sentence, and stared down at her.

Patience planted her foot on the first step up to the porch. "You're abandoning Ambrose?"

"I…*we,* are momentarily halting the search. To be resumed at a la-"

Without another word, Patience ducked her head and march-ed up the stairs towards Praisegod.

Her half-brother took a step back, half-raising his hands into a defensive position.

Patience powered straight past him, into the house, letting the door slam shut behind her.

Flann folded his arms and glowered at Mary. "First off…how long you known they were half-kin?"

"Years," Mary replied.

"About three," Ezekiel clarified.

Flann threw his hands up. "No one told *me,* so they didn't!" He directed his visible displeasure up towards Praisegod.

The man of the property stood on the porch and sputtered down at the people who ran his land.

"Frankly," Flann finally insisted to break the silence, "I am *terrifically* confused!" He turned toward Ezekiel. "And who means to kill me, you were saying?"

"I'm not going anywhere without them," Mary announced

uneasily, gesturing towards Ezekiel and Flann.

Praisegod shook his head at her, sometimes cranking it far enough to glance at the door behind him. "Now wait just a second! We must keep our attention fixed on the *greater good!*"

"What is this greater good, then?" Ezekiel demanded.

Praisegod raised a confident finger, which he waved exactly twice in Ezekiel's direction before pausing.

"You do not know?!"

"Yes, of *course* I know!" Praisegod insisted. "I'm just, uh, *distracted.*" He cocked a thumb over his shoulder, to the door through which Patience had disappeared.

"Doesn't sound to me," Mary teased, "like your attention is fixed!"

"Well…" Praisegod shrugged. "I don't know what to tell you. I was not expecting such resistance! The ponderous pachyderm of war is heading directly for us and you…question my wisdom!"

"Your wisdom," Ezekiel shouted, "says to us, please stand under the foot of this creature, let it crush you!"

"Not necessarily! Perhaps you will simply, ah, wave to it as it passes by!"

Flann folded his arms and shook his head.

Praisegod zeroed in on his gardener. "Listen, Flann, you would stand idly by as your beloved shrubberies run to r-"

"He would not be standing!" Ezekiel roared. "We would be running with you!"

"I do not *run,*" Praisegod snapped. "I am executing a *tactical retr-*ah!" he jumped as the door to the house behind him swung open, belching out a Patience burdened by luggage. Two bags, to be precise. "Ah," he beamed, "you see, my dear daugh…my dear half-sister leads us by silent example!"

Which was partially right. Patience remained completely silent as she trotted down the porch steps, dragging a steel-framed leatherette case with her left hand, lugging a more modest canvas valise in her right. The former was full of the most strictly utilitarian clothing she owned; the latter, of provisions fit to last her at least a few weeks. Which she hoped would give her enough time to find her way to more.

She also remained silent as she embraced Mary, and Ezekiel, and Flann, one by one by one, finally summoning them together for one final hug. It was a measure of their affection for one another that none felt the need to minimize the moment with language.

Praisegod, naturally, had quite a lot to say. "Alright, that is more than enough. A baker's dozen of physical contact, if we were to portion it out. Into, um, twelve. There would be extra, for there is too much, by one. One portion. Alright!" He clapped his hands. "That is enough!"

Patience only squeezed her friends tighter. How, she wondered, could Praisegod be so naïve as to trust *anybody* here to keep the farm running in his absence? Somebody had signed a paper a few years back that turned all slaves in the state, abracadabra, into 'indentured servants' (a distinction upon which Praisegod leaned as though it were a load-bearing column for the edifice of civilized society), but this was nothing more than a euphemism to disguise the survival of the status quo. His servants were slaves, and Praisegod was leaving them in charge of his non-human property, unsupervised, under the assumption that they would keep everything precisely as it was until his return.

It disturbed Patience, to only now realize that Prasiegod was perhaps genuinely uncertain of what distinguished a servant from a friend. Daughter and sister had a firm line between them, after all, and he struggled enough with that one.

Perhaps he was banking on the British threat to keep his laborers in line…but couldn't that just as easily be an enticement to leave? What could be more satisfying than running north the moment Praisegod vanished over the horizon, defecting to the British and taking up arms against the nation that had institutionalized their enslavement? Oh, how Patience wished they would. For too long, they had been forced to endure the shit that rushed downstream to them. What would they find in the headwaters?

She wondered, she imagined, and she envied them even the chance to discover. Because it was her lot to be swept up in the shit, to be washed down the river, nearer her brother, true, but very likely further from the means of finding him.

Patience broke the embrace, then smiled at each of them. Ezekiel and Flann returned the mournful grin. Mary seemed far more displeased, a fact which Patience chose to attribute to something other than herself.

What that something was, she would have plenty of time to decide.

She nodded and, without another look back to her half-brother, she headed towards the stables. The one in which her friends slept. Along with the animals.

Patience held off wiping away her tears for as long as she could. She didn't want Praisegod to see, and if his screaming to her was any indication, he was certainly watching her leave.

"PATIENCE!" he shouted, his voice cracking. "THERE'S A GOOD GIRL, BRINGING THE CARRIAGE ROUND, YES?"

She wished she could have held off longer. Alas. The tears

came, and she could not abide them on her face. So up came the hands.

"PATIENCE! BRINGING IT ROUND, YOU ARE!"

She tried to savor the simplicity of it all. Bringing Pblblbl out of his pen, hooking him up to a carriage that Patience had no faith would truly protect her from the cold, tossing her bags into the back, climbing up onto the bench, taking up the reins.

There ended the certainties. She had known how to do all of those things. What came next, though…she couldn't say.

Only that she was going to try her best. And that she should have done this long, long ago.

Oh, but where was her head; there was one final certainty to savor, one last action she knew perfectly well how to do.

She snapped the reins, and guided Pblblbl, and so the carriage, out of the stables.

Praisegod shouted something to her as she and her trusty steed clopped off the property. Impossible to hear what he was saying, over all the clopping. That and her snuffling, which quickly graduated to sobbing.

Not sadness, those tears. No. They were terror. Much worse.

This was a mistake. This was impulsive, and stupid, and she was going to regret it.

But the one thing she would regret more than what she was doing now would be stopping, turning around, and going back to Praisegod.

Patience shut her eyes once she got Pblblbl on an especially straight road, and she reached for Ambrose. But she didn't know how.

It was such a long road.

T W O

IT WOULDN'T HAVE BEEN ENTIRELY ACCURATE TO SAY that tears yielded to resolve; there was quite a bit of overlap between the two, a lengthy interval in which Patience took heart in her decision to find Ambrose on her own, even as she continued to paw periodically at her eyes.

She kept the setting sun to her right as much as possible, moving southward along roads with which she was unfamiliar. There would be no tree-obscured inn with its churlish keeper tonight, no. But that was fine by Patience. She was setting off into a nation at war. There would be some nights on the road, she knew. More than a few. But that was what the carriage was for.

As clouds choked the sun and night fell early, Patience once more closed her eyes and thought of Ambrose. She tried to remember his lessons. Trying without trying. The ease of the enterprise. Effort without force. All easier said than done, particularly when one was performing the exercise atop a moving carriage. Much as Patience trusted Pblblbl...her horse remained a horse, and she didn't *entirely* trust the beast to not clop them both straight off the road and into a ravine.

Still, on those especially wide and curveless stretches of the path, Patience would close her eyes and try again. Without trying. She would fix Ambrose in her mind, then recognize the effort with which she did. So she would try to relax, and either chastise herself for failing to relax, or become so relaxed that she grew distracted and thought about something completely different, everything from the frightening (how would she get more food when she exhausted her provisions, how would she defend her-self as she had neglected to bring any weapons) to the frivolous (did horses ever wake up in bad moods or were they just always in a horsey mood). Eventually, she would recognize her distrac-tion, and chastise herself for *that* on her way to once more calling Ambrose to mind. Which she would invariably try too hard to do.

So it went.

What a relief, then, when night fully draped itself across the path and forced Patience into parking her carriage in a clearing just a few yards off the beaten soil. There was even a decently-clean-looking puddle for Pblblbl to drink from, as Patience tied his reins to a thick sugar maple trunk, wished him good night, and climbed into the back of the carriage.

It took a bit of maneuvering, but she managed to wrestle the thick blanket she'd packed from the bottom of the heavier case. She bundled herself in it as tightly as she could…and found it wanting. Shivering, she glanced out the window just in time to see the first flakes of a storm lilting down from the heavens.

Patience felt her chin quiver. Oh dear – that was usually the first sign of a big old cry on the way.

Grunting, she unbundled herself and pulled as many other heavy garments as she could from the case, doing her best to wrap herself in them, bunching up a dress that in hindsight was perhaps not a *purely* functional garment and propping it between her head and the carriage window.

It had seemed the right choice at the time. Praisegod wasn't going to do anything to help Ambrose anymore, so Patience nee-ded to step up. Simple as that. But the truth of it, she whimpered to herself from within a phalanx of fibers, was so much harder.

This was all going to be so much harder than she'd imagined it, in the five seconds she'd taken to think the choice over before throwing herself at it.

Four quality sobs escaped her before she clamped the lid down. Yes, this was going to be hard. Yes, it was going to get even more uncomfortable than this. More dangerous, too. Yes. But she was doing it for Ambrose. She was doing what she ought to have done, long ago.

If that thought didn't quite warm her, it opened her to a fire she'd never fully touched before. Yet one that had been waiting within her, for longer than she knew.

It took some time, and quite a bit of fidgeting and fussing. But by the time a half an inch of snow had fallen across the carriage, Patience finally drifted off. Not all the way into sleep, no, but into a twilight of shape and shadow. Some of which came to resemble the face of her brother, lit by a familiar light.

T H R E E

BUT QUICKLY, AS SHE'S DRIFTING OFF TO SLEEP, THERE'S something you ought to see! No two snowflakes are alike, this is one of those lovely chestnuts that one hears quite a lot, despite one's best efforts. But why begrudge the phrase its ubiquity? For it is perfectly suited to nearly any topic by virtue of communicating almost nothing of substance. It's really little more than a semantic receptacle one can cram and jam full of just about any emotional baggage one wishes.

It also happens to be largely *true*, at least when one is constrained by a human timescale. The likelihood of two snowflakes being identical is about one in one million trillion (1,000,000,000, 000,000,000). This further works out to there being about one trillion trillion trillion (1,000,000,000,000,000,000,000,000,000, 000,000,000) different possible snowflake variations. And when one considers the construction of a snowflake, doesn't that seem a bit conservative? You get a bit of dust, any old dust you've got, be it pollen, volcanic ash, meteor burnoff in the upper atmosphere, whatever you want. Just something miniscule, teeny-tiny, itsy-bitsy, with which water vapor might become intimate. At which point, like so many marriages, they freeze together and begin a long descent. Along the way they pick up more water, which in our familial metaphor might be children, pets, a mortgage, anything that might help elucidate the signified process. The ice thickens, its form dictated by the cloud and the fall (here we lose hold of our domestic metaphor, and good riddance); moisture levels, temperature, wind conditions, all that good stuff. The flake takes a hexagonal shape – that's about the only aesthetic consistency among all the trillion trillion trillion variatons – and upon that six-sided canvas, paints itself into unique being. Rather tragic, then, that it must all end in homogenous oblivion, the flakes dropping anticlimactically to the ground to be buried, tromped through, peed upon, and otherwise less-than-appreciated.

So what, huh? Who gives a shit about snowflakes? Well, it's worth considering the chaos and unpredictability that shapes each flake, and the statistical near-impossibility of any two flakes being alike, or the outrageous unlikelihood that someone might glimpse, in the chaos of a storm, a single snowflake of a shape that might be recognized as corresponding to some object in the world, let alone that the shape would bear any relevance to any given situation…for what comes next.

What comes next, just in case it seems obvious where this is going, is *not* that two identical flakes float down, tethered to one another, and land right on the window of the carriage in which Patience sleeps, even as Ambrose was doing his damndest to reach out to her. And the two flakes *certainly* didn't have the twins' names or heaven forfend *faces* carved into them. That would be absurd.

Not that what comes next isn't absurd in its own way. Nor is it indicative of anything other than a staggering but nonetheless entirely plausible statistical anomaly. What comes next is, simply enough, that just as Patience was nearing the threshold of slumber, she glanced one final time at the moon through the carriage window, at precisely the moment a particular snowflake kissed the glass. Backlit by the moon, she could make out its shape, its unique form: a hexagonally-framed, perfectly articulated human fist with a raised middle finger.

Patience stared at it, watching as it seemed to melt into the moon itself. She looked up at the heavenly body, imagined the finger stamped on its surface, and laughed. Oh, if only she could fathom the impossibility of what she'd just witnessed! Would she forebear from laughing, perhaps descend fully into the emotional morass she had been fighting to stay above? Or would she be even more deeply engulfed by laughter?

It would be reckless to speculate. Best stick to certainties, then: Patience saw the snowflake, recognized what it looked like, even dimly appreciated the improbability of its formation, of its landing on her window, of her looking up just in time to see it. She didn't take it for any sort of sign. She simply smiled at it, and it drew her mind from the thankless task of devouring itself. It was not, however, distraction enough to fully redirect her attention from what it was she had been focused on. Which was to say, her brother, and the fire, the shape and the shadow.

Which was to say, it introduced some ease to the enterprise.

F O U R

THE EXPERIENCE WAS THAT OF HEARING HIS NAME CALLED across a crowded room. Not that Ambrose had ever been in an especially crowded room, unless one counted this cabin in which he slept. Not that he was the sort of person whose name would be called across a crowded room.

He had simply experienced enough through the eyes of others to identify what this experience was like. The name across the room. Yes indeed. For there was the chatter, the endless babbling inside his skull that he was finding more and more difficult to tune out.

And there was the bid for his attention. Whether or not she knew it. She'd called for him. Finally.

Ambrose pushed himself up to a seat, closed his eyes, and paid unwavering attention to the points where he felt his body as something distinct from the rest of the nation. The distinction did not survive scrutiny.

He opened his eyes and saw her, curled up in more clothing than Ambrose had worn in his entire life, eyelids fluttering.

This wasn't her room, either the one on the Estate, or the one on the pig farm. This wasn't anywhere Ambrose had ever seen before. It was…the inside of a carriage. This, too, was something he had seen, through the eyes of others. And only through the eyes of others.

He blinked, and saw only the far wall of his cabin.

A gasp escaped him, as he suddenly felt himself run through, gored by panic-tipped malaise. He reached up and clutched at his chest.

No. No, he'd finally found her. He wasn't going to let this go.

Ambrose focused not on the pain, or the exhaustion, not on what this connection was costing him, not on the rising chorus of voices all calling for him, the entire room screaming his name, no, no, he did not focus on these.

He focused on the warmth he had felt. It was a fragile little flame, liable to be snuffed out by the slightest gust. But it was warm, and it could grow if only it found its way to kindling. Or vice versa.

Ambrose knuckled down on that feeling…and then let everything go, opened himself to the warmth, let it come to him.

He opened his eyes.

F I V E

"PSST."

Patience stirred, the world around her but a fluttering slash of light as she and her eyelids wrestled for control. "Hrn?" she grunted.

"Psst. Patience."

She peeled her face from the drool-soaked dress she'd balled up beneath her head. It took prying her eyes open with her thumbs, but Patience finally managed to get a glimpse of her bedroom. Much to her surprise, it turned out to be the inside of a…oh, right.

"Ugh," Patience grunted. She creaked upright, then turned and faced her brother sitting across from her in the cabin that was on the other side of the…oh, right.

Huh?

Blink, blink. Patience glanced back out the window and determined that, yes, the world was still smothered beneath pillowy snow. She was, indeed, almost perfectly certain that it was February.

"*Patience,*" he snapped.

She jumped. "Ambrose! My god!" She rubbed furiously at her eyes, damning her exhaustion. "What's…are you…?"

"I found ya," he hissed, and it was only then that she noticed the signs of strain on his face, the vein bulging in his forehead, the sweat glazing his neck. "I'm doin' it!"

"Wuh! You're doing it!"

"Yeah, I know! I'm doin' it!"

"That's…amazing!"

"Yeah, I know!"

"…how?"

"I don't know! It was like…I heard ya sayin' my name!"

Patience smiled. "I was trying! I was, um, I was thinking at you, I guess!"

"Well…" Ambrose grimaced. A bead of sweat sliced down the side of his face. "I reckon it worked!"

Frowning at her brother's struggle, Patience gestured between them and asked "is there…anything I can do?"

Ambrose shook his head. "I think it's just…it's hard when I'm thinkin' about it. I just have to not think about how ha…how hard it is."

"Oh, okay."

"…"

"…" Patience cleared her throat.

Ambrose grit his teeth. "…so say somethin' to me!"

"Ah! Okay! Um, hello!"

"Say somethin' to distract me!"

"Oh, um…uh…how are you?"

Ambrose let out a sharp breath.

"Um…" Patience glanced around her. "I'm in a carriage."

"Mhm," Ambrose nodded. "How come?"

"Some stupid village upstate got overrun by the British. So Praisegod wanted us all to pack up and run away. South then west."

"So…" Ambrose glanced around the carriage. "Where's… him?"

Patience knew precisely who he meant. Ambrose hated Praisegod, often refusing to address him by that or any other name. She couldn't blame him.

Particularly after what she was about to tell him.

"He's not here. I just took a carriage and left," Patience sighed. "By myself."

Ambrose said nothing. Just stared at Patience, listening. Struggling.

"He…Praisegod just wanted us to just, *leave*. So I guess he wasn't worried at all about claiming his post."

"The mail," Ambrose clarified, in a tone that made clear he knew *precisely* what Patience meant in bringing that up.

Patience nodded.

On the positive side, Ambrose now seemed *fully* distracted from the effort required to hold open the tether. "So he's got us both when we're kids…"

"Yeah."

"Then he figures I'm too black to keep, so he sells me off…"

"Mhm."

"Only he finds out we're kin," Ambrose continued, visibly trembling with rage, "and the most he's willin' to do is send some letters…"

Patience said nothing to that, recognizing her own complicity in that complacency.

"Only *now* he don't wanna stick around long enough for them letters to get back to him."

Patience glanced at the cabin around the fist-clenching, tooth-grinding Ambrose. It was more sharply defined than she had ever seen it – prompting the absurd but undeniable fear that he was somehow going to will it into being in the carriage here…or that he would will her through, to Louisiana.

"It's terrible," was all she could think to whisper to him.

Ambrose didn't respond to that. To judge by the look on his face, it wasn't for a lack of things to say.

Patience cleared her throat. "What I was thinking, um, was, uh, I read this thing about how they needed soldiers. I was gonna mention it in July, but…ah, they need soldiers. The army, I guess. And I'd bet you Louisiana is gonna need troops pretty soon, or whenever the war gets there. So if you can…" she sighed. "If you can join the war I guess, and maybe sneak off during a battle and go north, I can meet you. And we c-"

"You want I join up and fight?" Ambrose squawked. "For *this* country?!"

"You wouldn't actually be fighting *for* it! You could run away as soon as you can!"

Ambrose shook his head. "Runnin' away for me ain't simple like it is for you."

"I know. I'm s-"

"You *don't* know.

Patience shrugged. "Whatever."

"*Not* whatever. You don't know the first goddamned thing about my life."

"...you're right," Patience granted him, more to close out that line of conversation than anything else. "Sorry."

All at once, Ambrose seemed to recall the effort it took to maintain this dialogue: veins trembled on his forehead, the thick cords of muscle in his neck flexed, sweat drenched the whole kit. "Kind of you to wanna help," he grunted. "Plan is you wanna meet me somewhere after I run off from the war?"

"Yeah," Patience nodded.

"Well, fine. I got somethin' you can help with 'til then."

Patience brightened. "Yeah? Great! What is it?"

"Go kill Praisegod."

Patience shook her head. "I'm not going to do that, Ambrose."

"Why not? After what he done to us?"

To you, Patience nearly replied. Instead, she said "I'm not a killer."

"Happy to send me to war, though."

"I'm not...I don't want you to fight in the war! It's s-"

"You reckon I'll have any chance to run off prior to I've gotta fire a single shot?"

"Just pretend to fight! It's just so you can run away!"

"To what? You?"

"...well, yes!"

Ambrose scratched at his neck and ducked his head. "That ain't gonna solve any of the problems we got."

"What are you talking about? You wouldn't be a slave anymore!"

"People see me with you," Ambrose replied, lifting his gaze to meet Patience's, "that's all anybody's gonna take me for. Your property." He took a deep breath. "And we'd probably have to pretend as much."

Patience studied her brother, feeling her chin start to quiver. It was at once familiar, that tic, despite her not recalling ever feeling her face move like that before. "We'd know, though. We'd know it wasn't true."

Ambrose said nothing to that. He just smiled. It wasn't the sort of smile anyone ever hoped to see on the face of a loved one.

"Just…" Patience sighed. "Just think about it. About trying for the north. I'll keep heading south either way."

"Oh, sure," Ambrose replied. "And you keep thinkin' about what *I* said."

"About Praisegod?"

Ambrose nodded.

"*That* won't fix anything," Patience mumbled. "If you want to talk about things that won't fix anything, th-"

"Yeah," Ambrose replied. "I fuckin' know."

And then he vanished with a gasp.

Patience stared at the empty half of the carriage across from her. At the snow falling outside, lit only by the moon overhead.

It was impossible to question that feeling of deep, profound completion she felt each time she and her brother reached each other. Their material reunion would be an undeniable positive.

It was something worth struggling for. Worth making sacrifices for. All of this, Patience knew to a certainty.

But if that conversation lately concluded had convinced her of anything...it was that she didn't actually know Ambrose in any meaningful sense.

Which had been his point.

Go kill Praisegod.

Impossible. She could never do that. However much she understood...or could at least make sense of Ambrose's hatred for the man...Patience had lived with him for too long. She knew him too well. So however much he deserved it...however responsible he was for all of the suffering Patience and Ambrose – especially Ambrose – had incurred for their separation...

And however easy it would have been for her to do it...for he trusted her so, would have happily allowed her within throat-slashing distance...

...she couldn't do it. She couldn't hurt Praisegod. For no better reason than she knew him too well.

Which, she supposed, had also been Ambrose's point.

Patience shivered, wrapping herself tighter in her garments, and watched the snow fall through the window.

S   I   X

IT WAS A DISMAL COUPLE OF WEEKS THAT FOLLOWED PATIENCE'S unhappy conversation with Ambrose, during which she wondered whether her brother's failure to rematerialize before her was a necessity or a preference. She was certainly doing all she could to reach out for him, but days on the road took a toll that could only be paid with sleep, which fell heavily upon Patience each time she lay her head to rest on her bunched-up dress. Oh, but this whole 'running away' business was proving quite a bit more challenging than she'd imagined. It was a cross between spells of deep tedium, shivering on the carriage bench as she marched Pblblbl this way and that across the state, and intervals of deep anxiety as she summoned every ounce of assertiveness she poss-essed to clomp onto other people's property in search of a hot meal or bale of hay (for herself and Pblblb, respectively) they might be willing to trade for having a newspaper read to them. There were, surprisingly, more takers than not. It was not lost on Patience that their kindness was, in no small part, down to their mistaking her for white.

It wasn't so much that either of these emotional extremes exhausted her – they weren't even extremes, save in relation to each other – as much as the uncertainty built in to the entire ent-erprise did. Patience was accustomed to knowing what was going to happen on any given day, and when. Which made the unpre-dictability of the road deeply, deeply frustrating.

She couldn't help but hear Ambrose's voice in her head, whenever she caught herself fretting over things like that. No doubt, he would have…well, yes, he definitely *would* kill to be in her position. To be out and about on his own, with even the *chance* of a hot meal, and a case full of chilly provisions as a back-up. He would have killed, and she heard him saying as much in her mind. She quite often wondered if that was her imagination or not.

Her journey wasn't strictly southbound; abstract though the war in which America was engaged felt to her, she was aware that battles were being fought not too far from her. On quiet, windless days, she could sometimes hear cracks and pops echoing to her through the woods, their direction and distance impossible to divine. In those instances when she could identify a skirmish as being in her path, though, she would double back, find a new road, and venture north, often hunkering down in a lonely hollow off the road for a night or two, just to be safe.

It was in just such a clearing amongst the trees that Patience awoke one night to find Ambrose sitting across from her. The intensity of his expression, the way his heartbeat throbbed in his throat, at once banished the fear that he had been deliberately abandoning her. At least, that wasn't *entirely* the reason for his weeks of absence.

"That looks like it hurts," she observed sympathetically.

Ambrose nodded. "Feels like it, too." He managed a smile.

Patience returned it. And then she asked him the sort of question she would never have asked, were they still relegated to just a single conversation per year: "do you have a favorite noise?"

Her brother looked at her as though her tongue had launched from her mouth, sprouted wings, and soared out the window of the carriage. "Do I what?"

"Do you have a noise that you like hearing more than all the other noises?"

"…" Ambrose's gaze slid off of Patience and out into the middle distance for a moment. He returned his attention to his sister. "The hell's that got to do with *anything?*"

Patience shrugged.

Ambrose rubbed at his nose and shrugged. "I mean…I suppose, I do like…" he raised a finger and waved it over his right shoulder. "There's a bunch of trees on both side of the main road leads up to Mas…to the house." He opened his hand and waved it gently in front of his face. "There's somethin' about the way they all sound when the wind gets goin'..." he smiled. "Almost like you can hear every leaf on its own, but all together. I ain't wholly sure how to explain it. But..." he nodded and smiled at Patience. "I reckon that's my favorite noise."

"That's a good one," Patience told him.

"You got one?"

She did, as it happened; the sound of Pblblbl crunching through snow, when the day was still and just a few birds were braving the cold to shout about whatever bright ideas they'd had that night before.

And then Patience and Ambrose were off, recounting the stories of their lives in greater detail than the once-yearly pow-wows had ever allowed. Neither spoke of their grand plans, their schemes to accomplish this goal or acquire that skill. Those were all well and good, but Patience found it a balm to set that to one side for the time being.

As did Ambrose, if the increasing frequency and ease of his appearances were any indication. As winter clawed its way to a close, the twins dove further into those piddling little anecdotes that serve no real purpose but to amuse, the ones that are often the most freighted with meaning. Patience told Ambrose about how, in her childhood, she'd briefly convinced Praisegod that 'boner' meant 'a deep happiness born of faith,' a jig that was up when Praisegod wished Flann a great many boners, to the evident elation of the gardener (who had been the one to teach Patience the word in the first place). Ambrose told Patience about the time that, in his many astral projections across the country, he once found himself behind the eyes of the president himself, James Madison. He attempted to exert a bit of control, hoping to compel the man to draft *some* kind of document condemning slavery, but managed to do little more than cause the esteemed personage to suffer a sneezing fit.

"Have you managed that before?" Patience asked.

"What? Makin' a man sneeze?"

"Not necessarily that. But…making them do stuff. Controlling them."

"Oh." Ambrose shook his head. "Ain't never done that before, no. But long as I was in there, seemed worth a jump."

"What's the craziest thing you ever saw through somebody else?"

"I mean…it's kinda crazy to see *anything* through somebody else."

"Right," Patience granted, "but there's gotta be a spectrum."

"A what?"

"A range. Some stuff that's crazier than other stuff."

"Oh, sure." Ambrose dipped his chin slightly as he thought that over. "I was inside a guy who choked one time."

Patience's eyes shot wide open. "To *death?*"

"No. He coughed it out. But that was still pretty damn crazy."

"Eh," Patience opined, waving her hand out in front of her.

"The hell you mean, *eh?*" Ambrose laughed. "You'd rather he died when I was in there?"

"It would have been crazier if he did."

"Well, you ain't wrong there," Ambrose mumbled, in a way that made Patience suspect he had quite a few much crazier stories he wasn't sharing.

On and on these stories went, night after night. It was, in an odd way, all they had in common; their lives were so different, as were the climates in which they lived, the food to which they had access, the social environs in which they had grown up…all different. But both had pointless stories to tell.

Without them, Patience was certain she would have long since lost her wits in the lonely wilds of New York. She could only hope she provided Ambrose with any comparable kind of comfort.

An indirect answer came one night as they lapsed into one of those increasingly rare bouts of silence, when one or the other of them had grabbed the bolt of lightning that cracked along the margins of their every interaction. That night it was Ambrose snatching the handful of chaos, wincing as his shoulders fell as far as they could go. His right shoulder drooped a touch more than his left, which Patience somehow knew was a consequence of the way his scars had healed.

"You think if I cut a path north," he whispered, "we'd find our way to meetin'?"

"I know it," Patience replied at once.

Ambrose nodded. Once, twice, then a third time like he meant it. "Okay," he said.

And then they spoke of other things.

S E V E N

AMBROSE HAD LIVED LONG ENOUGH TO KNOW THAT WHEN MASter Barry locked eyes with you, the safest thing to do was *look away*.

Yet he held the gaze of the man who held legal title to him, like a piece of land, like a beast of burden. Ambrose held his gaze, and kept his shoulders squared.

Patience, Ambrose

In the periphery of his vision, he saw Hilditch take a thudding step forward. Just waiting for an excuse.

Ambrose drew a long, slow breath through his nostrils. Tried his best to control the intensity of his blinks; they did tend to get quite forceful when he was nervous.

Master Barry's shallow, dry little eyes jerked and jittered around Ambrose's face. When they'd had their fill, they whipped their way over each of Ambrose's shoulders. Checking for any witnesses, and finding none.

Though he would never know for certain, Ambrose would have wagered his life that this lack of an audience was the deciding factor. In a way, he supposed he had made that wager by asking the question at all. Which was why he'd been careful to catch Barry in the place no slave dared tread; the patch of boot-packed soil just outside the plantation's front door.

Barry leaned back on his heels and folded his arms. "Where the hell you heard about a war, boy?"

Ambrose's bones went cold; this was a hurdle he hadn't foreseen. He'd prepared any number of arguments touching on why he, as an only intermittently cooperatively slave, should be requesting his Maser's permission to take up arms against the British...in defense of the nation that had enslaved him. *Better the devil I know* was the throughline of these arguments, and in truth, Ambrose found none of them all that persuasive. Yet he trusted that Master Barry's was a racism of low expectations. Ambrose didn't need to convince Barry with his reasoning; all that mattered was that Ambrose convince Barry that *he* believed these specious lines of reasoning.

But then, Ambrose hadn't thought to account for how he'd come by the premise. Because Master Barry had grabbed hold of the one loose thread; at no point had he briefed his slaves on the war. Which meant there was no good reason for Ambrose to be aware of the conflict for which he was volunteering.

All he had going for him at that point was that there weren't necessarily any *bad* reasons either. The only bad thing was his knowing something he wasn't supposed to know.

Ambrose shrugged. "I heard it. I guess...ah, you know. Ah. Is it, ah, true?"

"Nobody signs up for a war they ain't sure on," Barry growled. "Where'd you hear it?"

"Ah..." Ambrose waved a finger loosely beside his head. "Raisin' the new shed over on the west side. Heard somebody say somethin' about it."

Barry nodded, then turned to Hilditch. "Who's workin' on that shed over on the west side?"

"This one," Hilditch replied, nodding towards Ambrose. "Saul, Nathaniel...some other..." Hilditch stepped forward and jabbed Ambrose hard on the shoulder. "Who else is workin' there on that shed?"

Ambrose shrugged. "Um...I ain't totally certain who it was I heard sayin' about the war. Far away, you know, everybody's voices kinda turn to the same soup. I w-"

"That's a different question from the one you was asked," Barry spat. "One more crack at answerin' the right one, before I visit regret upon ya."

Go on then, Ambrose was tempted to say, followed by any of the many seditious thoughts swirling around his head. He managed to hold tight to his purpose though, recognizing fleeting obedience as the surest path to his ultimate liberation.

He did nothing to endanger anyone else by naming those who

had worked on the shed with him. That was nothing more than a fact, one Hilditch could extract from nearly anyone else on the property even if Ambrose held his tongue.

So he bopped himself lightly on the forehead and said "oh, yeah, it was Saul and Nathaniel, then there was David and Abraham too."

Hilditch nodded at Barry.

"Mhm," Barry grunted as he returned his Overseer's nod. "So...which of those four told you about the war?"

"I swear," Ambrose replied as meekly as he could manage, "it's just as I said, that I can't put a name to the voice, as I heard it whispered over a gr-"

"You managed to pull two more names outta your ass. Why don't we just wait and see what rattles one more name loose, hm?"

"Shall I fetch the lash?" Hilditch practically sang.

Barry grimaced at him. "No. No, my mind was leanin' more on *wait* than *rattle*." He turned back to Ambrose. "You wanna go to war to protect this land, I say that's somethin' approachin' a laudible quality of a sort don't align with your kind's nature. But nonetheless, bully for you. Only cost to me shippin' you off is, I wanna hear the name of the fella what told you there was a war on in the first place." He reached out, pinched Ambrose's cheek in one soft, fat hand, and rattled the boy's head in every direction. "No name, no glory."

Ambrose sighed as Barry pulled his hand away. "I swear, Master, I couldn't make out one man's voice from another's, 'cross that kinda distance."

Barry shrugged and chuckled. "As it pleases you." He turned around and waved for Hilditch to follow. The Overseer lingered to glare at Ambrose for a few more seconds, before doing as his boss beckoned.

"I couldn't make out the man what said it," Ambrose called after them, "but I made out what he said, clear as day."

Barry and Hilditch kept walking away.

Ambrose tried to do a bit of risk assessment in his mind. If he said what had just occurred to him to say here…it might cause a bit of disruption in the short term, sure. But there would be no longterm consequences. Certainly not. Barry seemed to like him too. Which would protect him, Ambrose hoped. *Knew.* Well, both. Knew and hoped. Because frustrated though Ambrose was by him, he wanted no genuine misfortune visited upon the man…

If Ambrose didn't arrive at a feeling of full resolution, he'd at least made up his mind. Close enough. "I heard what was said about the war," Ambrose called after Barry, "and I heard it said that the man doin' the sayin' had heard of the war from Fath… from Daniel!"

That stopped Barry in his tracks. It didn't quite land the same way with Hilditch, so the Master stopped the Overseer with a swift hand on the shoulder.

Slowly, both turned around to Ambrose. Their expressions jittering somewhere between a loom and a leer.

Knowing suddenly got quite a bit more difficult for Ambrose to keep hold of. *Hoping* would have to take up its slack. So, he *hoped* there would be no longer-term consequences for Daniel.

What an unsatisfactory substitution that was.

E I G H T

AFTER WEEKS AND WEEKS OF CREEPING PROGRESS THROUGH the woods, Patience was all but certain she must have covered half the distance to Louisiana. Needless to say, she was anything but delighted to discover that those long, lonely wilds had, at some point that passed without her recognition, yielded to the largely indistinguishable woods of…Pennsylvania.

Fortunately, there was pleasure to be had in the revelation, when, one day in April, she crested a hill and came upon a sign of such tremendous irony, as pertained to her personal journey at least, that her overwhelming eagerness to tell Ambrose nearly opened a connection with him from her end. The sign, a surprisingly sturdy iron rectangle with scarcely any embellishments, welcomed her to Reading, Pennsylvania. Granted, she would come to discover the city's name was pronounced 'redding,' rather than 'reeding,' but nonetheless…come *on* with that shit.

She giggled all the way into the city, though the laughter grew more and more anxious the further she rode. Reading was the largest city Patience had ever seen…by virtue of being the first, yes, but even putting that to one side, she had to imagine the metropolitan hellscape wheezing before her was massive by any standard. Taking in the number of shingles boasting of smithies and forges she saw (mostly graphic, just a picture of an anvil or a hammer), as well as the absolutely bonkers quantity of ass-drawn carts laden with beams she passed, Patience deduced that this was a city that produced a tremendous amount of iron. And, of course, there was the suffocating pall of charcoal smoke in

345

which the entire city drowned. On a single block, Patience passed two separate homeowners doing their best to smear the black schmutz on their windows to the corners of the pane. She'd long since lost count of the number of people she'd passed coughing into filthy kerchiefs, thanks in no small part to her doing the same into her elbow.

To put it as politely as possible…this didn't strike Patience as a place deserving a literary name, however mispronounced it may be. It'd have been much better suited by something reflecting its chief industry, like Iron Town, or Coalstench, or…well, Patience wasn't a professional place-namer, but she certainly knew an ill-fitting appellation when she saw one.

But alas. Reading it was, and Reading it would be.

The upshot of all this iron production, of course, was that the city was terrifically well organized (from a management standpoint – the roads were little more than wheel ruts that hadn't yet refilled with mud) and had a history as a military supply depot stretching back nearly sixty years. It was, in short, a city with a functioning hierarchy and a hell of a lot of firepower. A much safer place to pass through than the effete Philadelphia, that was for certain.

These were just some of the facts Patience heard as she tied Pblblbl off to a hitching post, and descended the carriage to have a go at guilting someone into buying her a meal. Her ear was naturally drawn to the single voice reciting all of those facts because of its familiarity. Yet her mind refused to accept the familiarity of that voice, because of the sheer improbability of Patience's hearing it. Improbability itself grew two muscular arms to throttle Patience's disbelieving mind, emphatically reminding it that this was a logical waypoint for someone heading south, yet hoping to avoid the effeteness of Philadelphia. Intuition rolled up its sleeves and leapt into the fray, putting improbability in a headlock, only to discover a faith in one's sense data dropkicking it in the back.

Unsteady from the battle royale in her brain, Patience planted a hand against the carriage and stared across the long, open thoroughfare. To Praisegod Pinchwife sitting on the stoop of a laundromat and extemporizing with grand waves of the hand, to the visible displeasure of Mary, who was sat cross-legged on the ground before him, her head heavy in her hands.

In Reading.

It wasn't ironic. It was *meaningless*. On this, all of the many combatants in Patience's brain could agree.

She began to laugh, starting at a soundless titter, ratcheting up through a breathy cackle, all the way to a well-supported chortle.

Just as Patience was reaching deep-bellied guffaw territory, Praisegod looked up and saw her. A far more varied sequence of emotions flashed across his face.

As Praisegod fell silent, Mary stirred from her fugue to look up at him. She followed his gaze to Patience, and exploded into a smile Patience would have sworn she could *hear*.

"Patience!" Praisegod shouted, as he heaved himself to his feet. Using Mary's shoulder as a support, not that Mary had offered it. "There you are!"

Go kill Praisegod. Patience heard the words as though Ambrose had spoken them directly into her ear.

The thought had several seconds to reign unchallenged in her mind before, at long last, some anonymous faction within her offered a forceless "nooo…?"

Her heart plummeted to her feet as Praisegod came jogging

towards her, Mary hot on his heels (which was to say, deliberately slowing her pace).

Patience shifted uneasily from one foot to the other. Was she…was she about to commit a murder? She had no intention of doing so…but she also apparently didn't have any intention of *not* doing so. Some period of separation from Praisegod had left her ambivalent to the concept of making him pay with his life for what he had done to, and then failed to do for, Ambrose.

On the subject of murder, ambivalence seemed like it was already further to the far extreme than one really ought to be.

"There you are!" Praisegod wheezed as he finally drew to within killing distance. He planted his hands on his knees to catch his breath. "Heavens."

Mary glanced at Patience over Praisegod's bent back. It was a warm, sympathetic look; Patience wondered if she would help her murder the man who owned her, or if she would intervene on his behalf. Or if she would remain neutral. Ambivalent. Because inaction would be a choice for Mary. Yes it would.

Patience consoled herself with the lack of weaponry she had on her. No knives, no firearms. And she certainly didn't believe herself capable of killing a man with her bare hands.

Relaxing slightly, she made the conscious decision to further soften the pinch of her lips, as Praisegod rose to his full height and sighed. "It is the air here," he announced, still gasping and spinning a hand through the smog in front of him, "that poses such difficulty for respiration." He planted his hands on his hips and took another deep breath. "I do not typically struggle in this fashion. You know." He turned to Mary. "You know this."

Mary simply shrugged.

"This struggling is unusual for me," Praisegod grumbled as he turned back to Patience.

Patience simply stared at him, doing her very best to not mentally catalogue the most vulnerable parts of Praisegod's physiology. It did seem kind of crazy, to have so many critical veins just sort of...*there,* an inch or so under the skin.

"Well?" he demanded. "Are you going to ask me for what is the reason I am here? In lieu of perhaps sheltering at the Estate belonging to my race-mixing father?"

"Our," Patience corrected him.

One word, *any* word, it seemed, was all Praisegod had been waiting for: he folded his arms tightly across his chest and cried "how *dare* you?! Under pretense of bringing around the carriage, you *abandoned* me! When there w-"

"I never said I was getting the carriage," Patience reminded him.

"Do not you *dare* to interrupt me! Don't you...ah...*don't* dare!" It was only then that Patience caught wind of the booze on his breath. Not wine, no, certainly nothing Christ would ever have bled.

Teetotal no more, then. She almost felt sorry for him, to be feeling all of that pain and fear without the strength to face it directly.

Patience smiled.

Praisegod's face turned a distressing shade of purple. "Are you *laughing?!*"

More laughter was Patience's response. No, she wasn't going to kill Praisegod. It suddenly seemed absurd that she'd ever considered it.

She glanced over his shoulder to Mary. "You want to come with me?"

Mary blinked. And then glanced at Praisegod. Which was an answer. One confirmed in words not a moment later.

Patience nodded. "See to yourself," she counseled Mary.

"Ex-*cuse* me," Praisegod groused, "I have asked of you a *question!* Did you laughing? Were you laugh? Were…did y-"

Patience reached out and slapped Praisegod twice on the cheek. Not a mortified matron slap, nor a duel-challenging slap. No, this was the soft, patronizing *get a load of this kid* whap still rarely seen outside of Italian families.

It was, consequently, not the sort of gesture Praisegod knew how to interpret. So he stood, perfectly still, eyes swimming slow laps around his sockets, as Patience turned around and walked away.

She vowed now to pass the night here; she'd be goddamned if she let Praisegod chase her out of Reading. Although, she realized with a smile, he very probably didn't realize the humor in how the name of this city was spelled. Nor how that humor came at his expense.

N   I   N   E

PERHAPS IT WAS THE GRAVITY OF KNOWING HE WOULD BE OFF to war before he knew it, or maybe it was all down to Ambrose struggling to share his sister's satisfaction in her having spared the life of their "illiterate, dumb son of a bitch" (her words, delivered in last night's moonlit palaver) half-brother.

Whatever the cause, the result was the same: Ambrose found it difficult to touch anything resembling guilt when Father Daniel wound up in the stocks. Which struck him as strange; there was absolutely no doubt that Daniel was there because of the lie Ambrose had told.

The Overseer shouted about the dangers of getting uppity as he locked an acquiescent Daniel into the wooden shackles. He shouted about listening when it was not one's place (bolting the wrists into place), of applying the sweet gift of literacy to unholy texts (locking Daniel's ankles in, hardly more than a foot below his wrists).

Ambrose watched the Father struggle to minimize the agony of being bent into a pin-shape, and all the while asked himself one thing: did Daniel know what it was that had landed him in the stocks? *Who* it was? Nothing Hilditch was hollering outed Ambrose as the one who had set this horrible farce in motion. And it was all but guaranteed that Daniel *did* know about the war, given his penchant for reading the newspapers Master Barry left around his house.

It was wrong to be so consumed with self-concern, Ambrose knew. But all the same…it seemed fair. It seemed *earned*, at any rate. Which was probably not the same thing.

He watched from across the clearing as Daniel struggled to hold his back straight. Ah, of course…it was probably the Father's first time in the stocks.

Good, Ambrose caught himself thinking.

Oh, but what was getting in to him? He wished he hadn't spoken to his sister the night prior. Something about that had thrown him off. Except it wasn't entirely that. Except it wasn't *not* entirely, or mostly, that. Except it w-

Mayhew thudded up behind him. Ambrose heard a crutch groaning beneath the Doctor's arm as he lifted his hand and slapped it across Ambrose's shoulder. "Terrible to see," he opined.

Ambrose glanced up at the Doctor. "I thought you and him hated each other?"

The Doctor shook his head. "We come from two different directions. But we've always been headin' for the same thing."

"And it's a race to see who gets there first," Ambrose agreed.

Doctor Mayhew sighed. "Never been a race."

Ambrose wanted to respond to that. Bum luck that he had nothing to say just then. So he crossed his arms and looked back to Daniel, squirming in the stocks.

And to Master Barry, crossing the clearing, heading right for Ambrose. With a smile on his face.

And a jar of pepper in his hands.

That brought it all home for Ambrose. All of those horrible things he felt he ought to have been feeling, but wasn't…they all arrived, tangled like roots. He couldn't fully parse one from the other, but he knew damn well they were all there. All? Yes. *All.*

"Oh," he whispered, "no."

Mayhew squeezed his shoulder. He probably meant it to be reassuring, but it registered as vaguely menacing. "First time rubbin' the spice?" he asked.

"I ain't gonna," Ambrose insisted.

As Barry drew closer, Mayhew dropped his voice. "There's no choice to it," he murmured.

Which Ambrose already knew was true. Though he tried to convince himself it wasn't, right up until Master Barry stepped far too close for comfort, and shoved the jar of angry red spice into his hands.

Barry didn't need to say anything. He just smiled. And Ambrose obeyed. He stepped forward, despairing as he felt Mayhew's hand slide off of his shoulder.

Patience, Ambrose

Each step he took across the clearing rang through his body like a gunshot in an empty barn. He felt the pressure of his foot touching Earth thrum up his thigh, into his hips. He felt the strain of muscles yanking bones up and onward, footfall after tectonic footfall.

He saw Isabel. She wasn't singing. No bells were a-ringing. She was standing beside the near well, hands clasped at her waist.

Ambrose bowed his head, and kept it bowed until he reached Father Daniel. Locked in the stocks. Bent in a way no body was meant to bend. But that was the idea, of course. That was the point.

Daniel craned his neck to meet Ambrose's eye.

Ambrose fought the urge to turn away.

"It's okay," Daniel told him.

Ambrose subsequently fought the urge to cry. That was a battle he lost. Didn't bode well for his future in warfare, that. "I am so sorry," he forced himself to say.

Daniel just nodded. A shallow nod. All he could manage. "It's okay," he repeated. "Do it."

Grimacing, Ambrose reached into the jar and gave his fingers the lightest possible dusting of sp-

"That ain't enough," Master Barry snapped from right beside Ambrose. "You gotta get a whole handful." He pantomimed scooping spice with a hooked hand.

Ambrose thrust the pepper at Barry. "You wanna do it?"

Master Barry's brow fell so heavily over his eyes, Ambrose was fairly certain he heard it make a *clonk* noise.

"I mean," Ambrose recovered, "I just don't know if I got the knack."

"You gotta get a whole handful," Barry repeated, an octave

lower.

Ambrose swallowed hard, then got a whole handful.

Father Daniel kept his eyes open. Even as Ambrose started grinding the spice in, Daniel kept his eyes open.

Ambrose kept it together until the second time he felt the Father's eyeballs against the meat of his fingers. Like grapes, withering to his touch.

At that point, he threw up. Away from Daniel, fortunately. Which was indeed what passed for fortune here.

IT WOULD HAVE BEEN OVERSTATING THINGS BY QUITE A LOT TO say Ambrose cleaned up his sick. But he did hang around, after the rest of the plantation had lost interest in Father Daniel's plight, to kick some dirt over his eruption. It seemed the least he could do, to not leave Daniel with the stench of that.

Still, as he finished covering it, he found himself frustrated that he hadn't needed to field any protest from the Father. *Oh, you don't have to do that. No need. How kind of you.* That sort of thing.

Ambrose would have kept a-kicking no matter how much Daniel fought him on it...it just would have been nice, to be fought on it a little bit. Would have made him feel more appreciated, certainly.

Which was an insane thing to think. Ambrose hated himself for thinking it. But there it was. There was the thought. It had come without invitation. As did everything else in the world.

Ambrose kicked one final cloud of dirt over his offal, and turned back to Daniel. Fully prepared to tutt over the Father's ingratitude.

Daniel was unconscious.

And there was a bird on his back.

Instantly, the scars on Ambrose's own back ignited in sympathy. Yet his mind failed to fully connect the horrible creature tracing slow, silent, stabbing circuits around Daniel's shoulders with the one that had so terrorized him on the stocks. Because the one that had visited him had been something massive, something dark and sinister, with blood-red eyes and a splash of crimson across its ten-foot wingspan. Such was the beast he had always imagined.

Not a sparrow. He certainly hadn't imagined a chubby little chipping sparrow, hardly larger than a grown man's thumb. With its fat, fuzzy neck, and sprightly little beak. Its stupid, vacant pin-head eyes. No, Ambrose certainly hadn't imagined that.

Yet there across Daniel's back bopped a chipping sparrow, alternately marching and bouncing, its head cocking this way and that. As though it had alighted on a log. Or a splash of moss. As though the surface beneath its feet were not the back of a human being.

But the sparrow didn't care, of course. The world was nothing more than that thing upon which its talons could find purchase. Nothing more.

"Fear not," Daniel mumbled from his stupor.

Ambrose took a small step forward. "What?"

Daniel craned his neck upwards, flinching as it *cracked*, and smiled. "Fear not, therefore. Ye are of more value than many sparrows."

Ambrose didn't sleep that night. Nor did he speak with Patience.

Both of which would become a habit.

1815

O N E

"HOLD!" ANDREW JACKSON SHOUTED, WHICH WAS EASY for him to say. He was safe and sound behind the parapet. Him and the militia, a group for whom he hadn't the least affection or appreciation, yet whom he coddled nearest his bony bosom simply because they were his favorite color. Ambrose and the rest of the artillery crew, a far more tactically useful subsection of Old Hickory's command, were bade to stand tall beside their cannon, in front of everybody else, ready to fire just as soon as Jackson had decided they'd held quite long enough.

The masters of the heavy ordinance were, almost to a man, darker hued than their not-so-brothers in the militia. Black, brown, and red, they had been tucked behind cannons by Jackson and friends as a kind of wartime marginalization, to safely preserve the more adventurous and dramatic posts for the white men. How much it rankled all the officers, then, that the artillery proved the more decisive force in nearly every battle! How despised they were for their utility!

Ambrose regretted having ever conscripted himself into this mess. The antipathy directed towards the artillery brought with it, naturally, a vengeful white vigilance, the pale militiamen forever on the lookout for the least punishable infraction. Ambrose saw one artillery gunner fold a tatty blanket in a fashion not to the liking of a militiaman, for which the latter thrashed the former with a riding crop. In another instance, an older palsied Native American canoneer found himself incapable of standing fully upright, no matter how many white militiamen yelled at him to do so; this older man subsequently found himself hanging from a tree by his ankles, until Ambrose and several of the other gunners managed to bring him safely down.

The consequence of all that unwelcome attention was – atop the low-level paranoia of knowing oneself to be perpetually marked – that Ambrose hadn't had a single opportunity to defect as he had planned, hadn't had the chance to break ranks and run to the North, towards his sister. He was trapped, then, all but stitched right into his uniform.

Which left him no choice but to fight for this country. Not *his* country, as the militiamen were so fond of saying. No, Ambrose had no illusion about America being his. The truth ran in precisely the other direction. With no chance to escape and the very real threat of violence should he fail to discharge his expected duties, Ambrose was a hostage to Washington.

Patience, Ambrose

Or, more specifically, Jackson. Ambrose had first come under Jackson's command when he had been sent to Pensacola late last year, and had since learned to loathe the man's peremptory nature off the field of battle as much as on. Even ostensibly positive qualities came with far less likable riders attached; Jackson was the sort of man who polished his own boots when he could have easily conscripted someone else for the task, true, but Ambrose knew this because Jackson was fond of looking up from his boot-polishing labors and shouting "look! I am the sort of man who polishes his own boots, when I could have easily conscripted someone else to the task!" at passersby. "I will polish no other man's boots!" he sometimes added, though no one could determine what it was that prompted the occasional addendum.

Ambrose supposed, if he really thought about it, he could imagine a Major General he would have willingly followed into battle. The cause would have been twice as important as the man, of course, and this hypothetical General would look quite a bit different from any the United States would ever see fit to engage…but Ambrose could imagine it, in the same way he could imagine a cow with wagon wheels instead of legs.

What he couldn't imagine, in this or any other reality, was a Major General he would happily *precede* into battle.

Yet here he was, crouched beside a cannon, several yards in front of the sort of man who polished his own boots, and so on and so forth.

Before them, fog choked the grounds of a plantation, which belonged to some twit called Chalmette, some five miles outside of New Orleans. Shrouded beneath the milky pall, the advancing British were invisible but far from inaudible; the rhythmic *clomp clomp clomp* of their marching, the jangling of their weaponry, the bellowed commands…if anything, the vapor in the air seemed to amplify the symphony of their approach, filing the sounds into sticks and drilling a vicious paradiddle on Ambrose's ear drums.

What a pointless war. What did Ambrose care about a reheated conflict between two nations that could scarcely have held him in lower esteem if they tried? Patience, with whom Ambrose had been trying and failing to connect in multiple senses of the term, had done her best to keep his spirits high. But as his anxieties intensified, he found it increasingly difficult to reach out to his sister, to inform her where he was. Which left her no choice but to make her way to the last place she had known Ambrose and his batallion to be bivouacked. Naturally, by the time she arrived, they were invariably gone.

Not that it would have done either of them much good if she'd finally managed to reach him. That vengeful white vigilance was a many-headed beast, and it never rested.

To wit: Ambrose felt something small and hard *thwack* him on the back of the head. He turned around to see a little knot of white faces giggling at him from behind the parapet. "Hey!" one of them cackled. "Look front, soldier!"

Ambrose sighed and glanced back at the gangly Andrew Jackson, nearly invisible in his deep crouch, peeking heroically over the lip of the parapet. There was no doubt in Ambrose's mind that the Major General would one day soon be depicted as mounted astride the bulwark, a rapier clutched in one raised hand, that surprised-porcupine shock of grey hair standing at attention atop his potato-shaped head. No doubt there'd be a tattered American flag flying over his shoulder, just to alleviate any lingering confusion as to this man's mythic bravery. Such was the nature of wartime hagiography.

Ambrose wondered if he would be included in such a painting at all. Probably not. Far more likely, Ambrose and his fellow artillerymen would be scrubbed from the record at the nation's earliest convenience. A slave at war wasn't courageous, after all: he was just doing what he was told. Nevermind that Ambrose had volunteered to be here. Nevermind that he had fallen all over himself requesting the most dangerous postings available (under the misapprehension that this would make for a more overstressed, and so distracted, and so *escapable*, fellow soldiery. Oops). Nevermind all of that, because Ambrose was a slave, and as far as anybody knew or cared, he was just doing as he was told. And where was the nobility in that? Far better to be the one doing the telling, it seemed.

"HOLD!" Jackson screamed as loudly as he could, because that was easier than shouting "HERE WE ARE! GET READY TO SHOOT US!"

"Dickhead," the rammer-wielding man next to Ambrose mumbled. Emphasis on *man*: where almost all of the slaves who had been thrust into the ranks of the artillery were no older than seventeen or eighteen, Rammerman must have been about thirty. There had been little opportunity for Ambrose to bond with his fellow fodder since their drafting, and even less inclination to – much easier to watch a stranger die than a friend, after all – but even during those less-than-ideal fraternization opportunities, Rammerman had held himself aloof from the younger recruits' social sallies.

This just-uttered oath of solidarity, then, was perhaps the first word Rammerman had ever addressed directly to his fellow artillerymen. It touched Ambrose that the man should seek some kind of community in the moment before his possible (read: probable) demise…and in touching Ambrose, the gesture enraged him. Goddamnit, now he was going to be sad if Rammerman died!

Jackson shouted his favorite command once more.

And then, quick as a startled cat, the fog lifted.

It didn't dissipate, melting beneath the unforgiving sun. That would have been both more easily comprehensible, as well as aesthetically of a piece with the day's dreadful mood. No, this mist *lifted*, like a chubby little chipping sparrow had alighted upon it, thought *this would be a* perfect *statement piece for my nest*, and made off with it.

What remained was a razor-straight little row of redcoats, blinking into the face of a far less disciplined pile of Americans. Though, to their credit, the Yanks were just disciplined enough to wait for Jackson's command to "FIRE!"

For some reason, Ambrose imagined there would be a second or two of lagtime between the order and the effect. There wasn't. The cannon next to him *roared*, belching its load into the enemy's ranks. Ambrose watched the six pound cannonball that he had stuffed into the mouth of the cannon, the gunstone globe he had moments ago cradled against his chest, one that was identical to the orb he immediately heaved off the pile to his right and was now once again cradling, connect with a human man's bellybutton and rip said man clean in half. Oh, but that was a poor choice of words; clean had nothing to do with it. The man's torso went flipping backwards, managing at least two or three yards, arms flailing and tongue flapping the whole way. His legs kept walking for another few steps before they unceremoniously toppled forwards.

Patience, Ambrose

And that was just one cannon's handiwork; there were seven others behind the parapet, all thundering their disapproval. Among them, including Jesus Christ there was a musket resting on Ambrose's shoulder, *directly* on his shoulder, "FUCK!" he screamed to register his own unhappiness at the arrangement as the musket fired, puncturing his left eardrum and sending him staggering into the cannon, dropping the cannonball onto his own right foot and crushing the three smallest toes, and now someone was screaming at *him,* which seemed unfair, he wasn't allowed to be pissed that there was a militiaman using him as a human shield, "STOP YELLING AT ME!" Ambrose screamed again before he realized that he was being ordered to pick up the cannonball he'd just dropped and slide it into the mouth of the cannon so that it could rip another man clean in half, *messy* in half, so he slid around the front of the cannon, becoming momentarily lost in the sulfurous depths of its maw, until the militiaman who had been firing over his shoulder's eye popped, pierced by a well-placed bullet, and he collapsed to the ground, the militiaman did, and now someone was yelling at Ambrose again but he could barely hear it over the cacophony of the battlefield, crash boom roar bang squish clunk ching click boom crash bang bang COME ON so Ambrose stuffed the ball into the cannon and leapt out of the way as Rammerman swung his eponymous tool around to drive the powder and ball deeper into the breech, and this time Ambrose screwed his eyes shut and clapped his hands over his ears but he felt two firm hands wrap around his wrists and yank them away, and a voice attached to the hands shouted NO, and Ambrose opened his eyes and it was Rammerman staring straight at him, straight not down because Ambrose might have been just fifteen years old but he was tall enough to be a target, and Rammerman yelled the words "Eyes open!" at him, and then the cannon went off and Rammerman flinched, which Ambrose thought was so funny he started to laugh, he couldn't help it, even after Rammerman slapped him hard on the cheek and stormed back to his rammer, even as Ambrose was being once again yelled at to load the cannon, he couldn't stop laughing, the world had made a joke and it had gone over everyone's heads, and just then a cannonball went haha soaring *over his head*, close enough to tousle his hair like it thought he was a scamp but it loved him anyway, and by god wasn't *that* the funniest thing that had ever happened to him, that he had ever heard of, that he had ever seen, this was the funniest battle that had ever been fought in the history of warfare and he had a front row seat, it was all too much, and for a while the people who didn't get it told him to stop laughing but he found that as long as he kept sticking cannonballs into the cannon people stopped yelling at him, they left him alone, they just let him laugh, because it was just objectively fucking funny, god-damnit, holy shit, even as Rammerman didn't get out of the way of the cannon in time and was standing right in front of it as it went off, hitting him with such point-blank force it all but vapor-ized him, ground him into a pink mist that spread and hung like the whiter kind, the disappearance of which had inaugurated the battle, this most hilarious of all battles, the mist was back and this time it was personal, it was a friend, it was Rammerman, he will be mist, haha, tee hee, ho ho.

T W O

THEY WON THE BATTLE. OR, TO DISCARD HUMILITY FOR A moment, the American *artillery* won the battle. Not singlehandedly of course. But maybe…three-fourths-handedly. At least half-handedly, without a doubt.

Even the most slapdash survey of the carnage made clear that the heavy weaponry team had done the heavy lifting, as far as thinning the numerically superior British ranks went. But, of course, it was not the way of the world to acknowledge that the numerically inferior – i.e. Team Minorities – had proven a more decisive force than the brave, noble, honorable, *white* militia.

Which was to say: the slaves, freemen, Native Americans and foreigners who comprised the artillery, who should by rights have been the lauded and laureled saviors of the day, were immediately denied even a footnote testifying to their merit. Ambrose had expected to be written out of the historical record; it hadn't occurred to him that the hypothetical scribes could just refuse to write him in to begin with. That he had failed to consider this struck him as naïve. Thus deepened his already benthic cynicism.

After the battle Major General Jackson made a tremendous show of thanking everyone and everything that wasn't an artilleryman.

Straight out of the gate, he thanked the Kentucky Militia, which was galling for a whole host of reasons. Foremost among these was that Louisiana had contributed nearly half as many free black men – *free* black men, which meant that didn't even count Ambrose and just about everyone else on artillery he had ever interacted with — as Kentucky had contributed *anybody*. And, of course, Jackson had been volubly dismissive of his militias prior the battle. Yet somehow his appreciation for them only flowered upon watching them be absolutely outfought by the artillery.

So, yeah, that was enraging, but Jackson wasn't done sprinkling gratitude to the furthest corners of white superfluity; he thanked the gunsmoke-obscured heavens, he thanked the gracious plantation owners who had supplied provisions (three guesses to whom *those* went), he thanked the inferior quality of the British leadership, he even thanked nuns at a local convent for kneeling before/mumbling at a statue no doubt inscribed as Our Lady of Slipshod Victories or something.

All insult heaped upon considerable injury. If there had been any miracles on the battlefield that day, they had been worked by the artillery.

Ambrose tried to console himself by thinking about the grand old laugh he'd had at the absurdity of it all, perhaps the most unrelenting fit of mania he'd ever experienced. Yet, try as he might, he couldn't recall the feeling that had prompted those mirthful peals. Had it even *been* mirth? It didn't seem possible now. It didn't seem possible he would ever feel something so warm and carefree again. No, it had been mania in a darker, truer sense of the word.

His hands trembled as he sat with the rest of his non-white gunnery crew and took a silent meal. His fingers refused to grip the boiled salt beef ration long enough to bring it to his mouth. Granted, that could have just been his taste buds commandeering the hands in self-defense, but he was certain he was hungry enough to eat *anything* just then. He tried to will his hands to steady, ordered them to *hold* the beef. They proved insubordinate.

Patience, Ambrose

"Hold," he mumbled to his hands, and okay, *that* was pretty funny. He started chuckling into his provisions. But it never quite exploded into full-blown guffaws the way it had on the battlefield. His mouth, he was convinced, was making the noise purely to satisfy his ears. As long as they could hear it, no further escalation was required.

His right ear could hear it, but his left ear could not. All it knew was a shrill ringing. A present from the militiaman with the poppable eye.

Ambrose studied the feeling that was lifting his shoulders, pumping his diaphragm. It wasn't humor or cheer. Nor was it despair. It was…insubstantial. He couldn't pin it down. It was like the silhouette of a real, full-bodied feeling cast on a piece of canvas. He could study it all he liked, but he would discover no further details. Just as easy, if not easier, to crumple it up and stuff it in his pocket. Huh?

"I said," Rammerman rumbled, "what's so funny?"

"Oh. I can't hold my food. See?" He held his hand up to Rammerman, who was slouched in the empty seat next to Ambrose. "So I was just tellin' my hand to 'hold' it. Get it?"

Rammerman considered this joke for a moment. "Like the General told us to hold."

"Right," Ambrose replied.

After further consideration, Rammerman decided to laugh. It was a deep, resonant sound, short staccato bursts of four that rose chromatically, yet somehow started from and ended on the same pitch. *Huh huh huh huh, huh huh huh huh.* It reminded Ambrose of the spooky duplicate weavewoman in Doctor Mayhew's sewing cabin, albeit a more musical rendition. And perhaps, something more: the man's laughter seemed to echo within his cavernous chest, growing at once portentous and meditative, like a clumsy bishop dropping four tomes in an empty cathedral, over and over again.

Ambrose felt the first thrill of something like joy. A kindred spirit! A man over whose head jokes could not soar! He extended his hand to Rammerman and said "my name's Ambrose."

Rammerman shook the proffered hand and grumbled "charmed" like a sarcastic earthquake.

"...what's your name?"

"Not your problem." With that, Rammerman evaporated, back into pink battlefield mist.

Whether this was intended as a snub, or to save him the grief of being parted from a friend, Ambrose saw no upside in calling for the man's return. In both cases, it would be best to let the conversation lie. Besides, he was getting funny looks from his fellow diners.

But it chilled Ambrose that Rammerman had been able to stop laughing, just like *that*. It chilled him and filled him with envy at the same time. Ditto for his vanishing trick, though Ambrose found less to envy in this than in his dead friend's firm grip on his giggles. Because Ambrose didn't have any grip at all. His grip-to-giggle ratio was off. He couldn't stop. He bit his tongue until he tasted blood, and yet his shoulders kept bouncing. Which was wonderful, because as long as his whole body was shaking, it didn't really seem like any individual parts of it were.

T H R E E

REACHING PATIENCE THAT NIGHT WAS ALMOST IMPOSSIBLE.
Between them stretched an unbroken theater of suffering, as had
increasingly been the case over the three years of continued conflict. This elevation of the nation's baseline suffering pushed
Ambrose to become ever more dexterous with his techniques
for filtering out the noise. Still, barring a few hiccups (or, in President Madison's case, sneezes), he found ways to adapt, if not on
the timetable he would have liked.

"We ain't where I told you were were anymore," was how
Ambrose had taken to greeting his sister on those increasingly
infrequent nights that he found her.

Now, however, something had changed. It was as though the
firmament in Ambrose's mind had shifted, no longer rising but
falling, plummeting away, leaving him suspended over a reservoir of the very agonies he had been seeking to ignore. Or maybe
it would be more apt to say, there was a pain-shaped hole in his
heart, and the people of this great nation were eager to fill it.

Every attempt to open and extend himself after the Battle of
New Orleans was met with a torrent of woe and despair that was
impossible to ford. Brute force having failed, he was lately
endeavoring to welcome these emotions as old friends. The
shellshocked soldier who accidentally throws his dog across the
room, breaking its leg on a desk, because it had leapt on the bed
as its master was deep in a nightmare? Yes, Ambrose understood
that fear. The girl who can't make sense of the hunched and surly
brother-shaped monster that has returned from battle? He

understood that all too well. A wounded slave, down a leg and unable to sleep, so unable to work, so unable to justify his continued existence to the man who owns him (yet who had not put his own life on the line to protect his country), so waiting for the noose now being tied for him? This, with the pernicious cannonball limp in his right foot, Ambrose understood best of all.

And how could one possibly ignore what one understood? How could one unlearn a skill that had been acquired at such cost, through such a sustained application of effort? Could Patience unlearn to read? Not forget, but actively *unlearn* what she already knew? Could someone unlearn to play an instrument, or unlearn a second language?

Perhaps if Ambrose waited long enough, he would stop feeling the way he did now. Either he would forget his troubles, or they would simply fade into the emotional background (*the mists*, his mind hissed on sleepless nights, *the pink mists*). It was easy to imagine something similar happening to many of the people on whose misfortunes he was unintentionally eavesdropping. But did that mean he would be unable to speak to Patience until then? Until the country's traumas diminished, or at least modified into something he could no longer understand?

No. That wasn't an option. If ever there was a time he needed to speak to Patience, to find sense in her presence, it was now.

He stared hard at the insides of his eyelids and charged. Charged through the noise, the electric wall of all things awful, past depressive spirals and angry drunks and self-destructive behaviors and horrified children and shattered families and concerned spouses and insufficient tributes and humiliating generosities and bleak futures and bleak futures and so many bleak futures, until he found his sister.

Patience, Ambrose

"Hey," he whispered. She flickered before him like a candle, whatever room in which she now found herself glittering like a mirage. She'd taken to squatting in properties abandoned by those fleeing the war, doing her best to thread the needle of heading towards the last place she'd known Ambrose to be, and simultaneously keeping from wandering into theaters of battle of which Ambrose was entirely unaware.

She must have had to flee some little pocket of warfare – Ambrose didn't recognize this lodging, and Patience rarely moved unless she needed to.

His sister rubbed her eyes and stared at him. "There you are," she mumbled. A lazy smile came to her face, but vanished as her eyes opened wider. "Is something wrong? You're all...wavy."

"Just having a hard time..."

When he failed to finish the thought, Patience offered another smile. Ambrose recognized this one – it was the one his sister put up when she was afraid her real expression might shatter her brother in front of her. "I'm sorry," she told him.

Ambrose just nodded. His head felt like some colossal hand was kneading it, testing to see if it was ripe yet. "I was in another ba-"

"But look!" Patience giggled. She twisted away from Ambrose and grabbed a sheet of paper off the ground. "Look...oh, sorry, what were you saying?"

"No, you go."

"You were saying something already. I interrupted you."

Ambrose shrugged, wincing as he felt the line between them threatening to twist itself into a knot. "Might be best you go, give me a minute to pull together."

"Okay," Patience said with a nod. "Well..." she brandished

the periodical she'd grabbed once more. "Look at this! From today's paper! And I'm in Louisiana, you know, so it's news that's just about to reach ya!"

Ambrose looked at the page, back to his sister. She always did this when she was excited. Forgot that he couldn't read. There was certainly no malice intended in these futile gestures, but they nonetheless stung Ambrose, as would a glancing blow after it had bruised. As always, he sulked silently until Patience realized her mistake.

"Right! Sorry!" Patience looked at the page, as though checking to make sure Ambrose hadn't blasted the words off of the page with his stupidity. "Right. Well, what it says is, a peace treaty has been agreed to, by both England and the United States! It's called the Treaty of Ghent, and once it…what's wrong?"

"Nothing." Ambrose grunted as a full-body spasm ripped through him. "Did I go wavy again?"

"Well, that," Patience told him. "But you're groaning too."

Ambrose put his hand to his mouth, and only then did he hear it. Yes, he was groaning. "I just…"

"They have a treaty!" Patience chirruped. "The war's over! It still has to be ratified, but that's just a formality. This is basically done! You don't have to fight!"

"Ain't…" his head spun, the bridge of his nose tightened. "Ain't this what happened at the start of this? They were sending over some papers would've meant we didn't gotta fight at all?"

Patience laughed, because she didn't understand. "Yes, but this time they got here before…" And then she understood. "Oh, no. What happened?"

"There was a battle," Ambrose mumbled. His voice wavered. So too did the image of his sister before him.

Patience, Ambrose

"Oh. Oh no. Ok. It's ok," she cooed. "Just take a deep breath." She looked up and around, presumably at the vanishing likeness of her brother. "Ambrose. Look at me. We can talk about it if you want, or we can talk about something else. Or we can just sit here together. But we should be together right now. Ambrose. *Ambrose*. Look at m-"

And then she vanished. He didn't mean for her to. But he couldn't hold the tether anymore.

"NO!" he screamed, and because whatever web of silence these spooky unions weaved had lifted like mist off the battle-field, a pink fucking mist, the men and boys sleeping around him stirred, mumbling variations on the theme of *shut up*. Someone threw a rock at him and missed. Missed Ambrose, at least, if the distant "ouch" was anything to go by. *Mist Me!* Ambrose thought. Hahaha. Haha. Ha.

Where had he heard that before?

Everything was hazy and opaque. It was all mist.

An entire war fought for naught, concluding with a battle fought for naught. In both cases, peace could have endured if only the two sides could have communicated with one another as immediately as could Patience and Ambrose. Three years of war, caused by missed communication. Fought for naught. How many people had died in that time? How many lives had been torn apart, brutalized beyond the threshold of endurability? And how many other times throughout history had this kind of shit happened?

The sheer magnitude of what he was trying to consider dwarfed his abilities to consider it. His mind hadn't space enough for all the unspeakable, idiotic miseries of the world, because the last three years were just the latest in a long legacy of pitiful, pointless tortures the human race had inflicted upon itself. And if it kept happening, over and over and over and over again, then maybe, just maybe…

"We deserve it," Ambrose whispered.

This time, only the kid next to him told him to shut up.

F O U R

FOR ONCE, IT WASN'T HARD FOR PATIENCE TO WORK OUT WHICH way she was going. Asking anyone heading north on the road would get her a glassy, dead-eyed answer, and once she made it to St. Bernard's Parish, all she had to do was follow the smoke, the stench.

The battlefield had, at one point, been a plantation. Such was Patience's understanding. But as she stood upon the hill, frozen to the spot from which she had gotten her very first glimpse of what one of the northbound refugees had referred to as "Chalmette's battlefield," she struggled to imagine any kind of life as having ever taken root here. Chalmette plantation had not always looked like this, of course. But it seemed impossible that a place that would *ever* look like this could suffer a root to take. Unconscionable, at the very least.

The land before her smoldered even all this time after the battle had ended, a flat, blasted expanse, like naked flesh caramelized in a housefire. It was as the Earth might have looked, Patience considered with a shiver, had it only sky enough for fire. All the while small, squat bodies patrolled the ashes, sometimes pausing in controlled collapse, presumably to rescue something from the ruins. But Patience was too far to make out who these people were, or what they were searching for on these seething barrens.

This was where Ambrose had been. And he had seen this not in decay, as Patience now did, but at the moment of its undoing. Been party to it, in fact. Mere days, perhaps hours, before the last time he had managed to reach her. At least a week back.

It was a curious sensation, to feel one's legs buckle, yet hold them steady all the same. For to fall to her knees here would be to lose sight of the carnage. It would vanish beneath the top of this pleasant little hill. A bit worn by footfall, perhaps, the green scalped to dry soil, but otherwise quite alright to look at.

Which was why Patience refused to fall. Because this was what Ambrose had gone through, was only a small portion of the misfortune he had been forced to endure. Either by Praisegod's idiocy…or by Patience's reckless encouragement. For it was she who had urged him to war. Assuming he could escape it, as easily as she had Praisegod's farm.

She glanced behind her, to Pblblbl, and the carriage. Both where she had left them, the latter cinched to the former, the former to a hearty trunk near the road. The road, worn by footfall.

She closed her eyes as the roar of soldiery filled her ears, the horrible quiet of a victorious force beginning their weary trek off the field of battle, dragging cannons, and carts full of provisions, and wagons laden with men whose names they had only just learned…

A deep breath banished the spirits. Yet another mark of her stupid, unearned fortune.

She would find Ambrose. She wished she could tell him that. She wished she could make him know. And believe.

Patience took one more deep breath, committing the fetor of the battlefield to memory. As long as it burned in him, she would carry it too.

It seemed, quite literally, the least she could do.

She dug the knuckle of her thumb into her forehead as she stared at her horse, her carriage. Both of which were still up, still hanging in…but clearly the worse for wear. Years of hard living had taken their toll.

For the first time in as long as she could remember, Patience wondered what she looked like. Tried to recall the last time she'd made a point of glimpsing at anything that threw a reflection.

Irrelevant.

She looked to Pblblbl and wondered where she would go. Ordinarily, she would head wherever Ambrose told her he was, each time receiving a new location from him before she had reached his previous one. Yet now, for the first time in years, Patience had no idea where Ambrose was. Where he might be. And, consequently, where she ought to go.

She stared at her horse. And her horse stared back at her, cloudy eyes still as sharp as ever between his charming little cream combover.

"Pblblbl," he told her.

Patience told herself it was fine to fall to her knees now; her back was to the battlefield.

F   I   V   E

FOR A TIME, AMBROSE FELT IT WAS SATISFACTORY TO stop reaching out. It was merely a matter of getting his head right, he repeatedly assured himself. The Battle of New Orleans had rattled him, rattled him *hard,* and a few things had shaken loose. One had been the clarity of mind required to make any kind of bid for freedom; Ambrose had watched himself be dragooned back to Master Barry's plantation after the war, unable to raise so much as a disapproving finger. That wasn't the only thing that had been shaken loose, though. There were other things, harder to articulate or examine in any detail. But they were big, important things.

Ah, well. Simple matter of giving them time to settle again, and then he would be back on his feet. Metaphorically speaking. He would actually be on his back, staring at the ceiling, reaching reaching reaching. Once he was better. Which would happen. Eventually. It had to.

This withholding seemed robust enough to stay the roar of other lives for 'a time,' that safely indiscriminate metric that can encompass *all* time, if one so desires it. To put a more concrete date on it, to tell himself *by* this *month you have to be ready to contact Patience for* this *amount of time*, was too daunting, too terrifying to countenance. Deep down, deep *deep* down whatever hole his mind had been thrown into, he knew any deadlines he set would go zooming by, leaving him without the tiniest mite of progress to show for their passage.

'A time' was precisely right for him, because it tacitly granted the possibility that he would never get better, never unscramble himself, never want to reach out again, until the day he died.

But, as it happened, that 'time' came to a premature end, revealing that complete withdrawal was no longer an option. The pig had punched a hole in the dam, a hole Ambrose had personally – and rather indiscriminately, it now seemed – spent years prying to ever greater diameters. In so doing he had torn a hole in himself, from and through which he stretched across the country, touched by countless minds and hearts. And, unbeknownst to him, touched them in return.

The first voice that found *him* did so in the middle of a long afternoon, as he was chipping old paint off Master Barry's house, in preparation for applying a new coat. Standing with his legs two rungs apart near the top of the ladder, his right foot still aching and divoted from where he'd dropped the cannonball onto it (alas, the damage was not enough to get him assigned to the sewing cabin like Mayhew), he was scraping at the dead flakes with a trowel when a strange voice said, from directly behind his head, "Please God, I need strength now."

Forgetting he was two stories off the ground, on a rickety old workman's ladder that likely predated the colonies themselves, Ambrose swung around and demanded to know who was there. His inertia tipped the ladder away from the house, at which point he swung his arms in a great big circle not because he thought this would help, but because this is what the human body does when it loses balance atop a great big ladder.

In the instant he came unmoored from the house, the ladder teetering at an almost perfect vertical, Ambrose was taken back to the moment during the bombardment of Fort McHenry when he'd been thrown from a parapet by the force of a mortar landing. His tumble was of the headfirst variety, which gave him a perfect view of the ground rushing to meet him, and he'd made his peace and said his prayers when his spin spun him just enough to land him on his heels. His legs cracked into the hard Earth. He felt them *shatter*, saw shards of bone punching through his flesh, piercing what tatters remained of his trousers. He'd gone into shock then, at which point the memory became flat and colorless, but an indeterminate time later (or, simpler still, *a time* later) he came to in an ersatz hospital in Baltimore to find himself in the care of an ogre who was also a nurse. He would never be able to walk again, she brusquely informed him, and what turned out to be the hardest part of this was that his wife was unconditionally accepting of this lifelong limitation. Alas, he could not be. Self-loathing ate away at him, and pride kept him from recognizing that. So he took it out on his beloved, and after a year of trying her hardest to get through to him, she'd taken the kids and disappeared. So now here he was, sitting alone at home, the crutches resting across the chair's armrests now the only things left between the gun in his lap and the hollow under his chin. That and the presence he had felt, intermittently, over the past few weeks. It was comforting. It was understanding. It was *there*. It was God. It was his last hope. So he prayed, he was worried he had forgotten how but it came to him as naturally as if he'd been doing it every day of his life. Please God, he begged, I need strength now. Please.

And then the ladder rebalanced and smacked hard into the side of the house, nearly bucking Ambrose.

He clung hard to the sides, trying to catch his breath and make sense of what had just happened. He'd seen…he'd *felt*…

Someone had entered his mind.

Uninvited.

Someone had been reaching for *him*.

Suddenly he felt so foolish, so childish, to think he could send his mind soaring across the country and not lay a trail for someone to follow, whether they meant to or not.

That man, that poor man, was at this very instant sitting in that chair, with those crutches on his lap. A far from sufficient disincentive to his placing the gun into that hollow under his chin, those crutches were.

In his extremity, he had prayed to his God. Yet somehow, as though it were a simple clerical error, the prayer had wound up being forwarded to Ambrose.

This was happening. That man, in that chair, with that gun in his lap…that was happening, and it was happening *right now*. Ambrose had suffered a few minor hallucinations since the Battle, as well as two more major ones. The first of the latter sort had been a redcoated corpse sprawled in the snow, the top half of his head splattered five feet beyond his body…yet there had been two holes in the snow above the jaw where his eyes would have been, and somehow those holes had been staring straight at Ambrose. The second had been a cannon sticking from the window of Master Barry's house – the very house he was now painting – that had stayed trained on him no matter where on the property he went, without any gunner in evidence to turn the cursed artillery.

What had just happened was not a third foundling for that ignominious brood. He didn't know how he knew – the other two times had seemed pretty fucking real to him – but all the same he did. That was a real person in real distress, just…

Just like him.

What if…

Ambrose climbed down the ladder, put his feet on solid ground, and tried to organize his thoughts.

What if the severity of his own trauma had left a mark on the people who had fallen beneath his reach, as he'd strained and struggled to reach Patience? What if, as he was feeling them and dismissing their pains, his own distress was so great that they felt him too? Felt him as a benign…what had the man felt…a force of sorts, as comforting, as understanding, as *there*? And what if they mistook that sense of spiritual companionship for something more than a scared, confused kid in Louisiana trying to make sense of the world, just like they were? What if they mistook it for…

Uh oh.

Ambrose had never tried reaching during the day, while on his feet. The first instance of connection on that long-ago fourth of July had happened in bed, at night, which had led Ambrose to believe that setting to be an essential part of the process. But there was no time to wait for the sun to set. Those crutches were a poor safety.

Setting his feet shoulder-width apart, gripping hard to the sides of the ladder for balance, Ambrose closed his eyes and reached.

As before, a universe of misfortune flooded into him, nearly drowned him. The difference was, this time he didn't fight the current. He dove deeper, seeking the riptide that would carry him away from shore.

He felt his body, the thing clinging to the ladder, trembling, weeping, pissing itself. But he couldn't worry about that. And so, did not. He needed to find the man, the man with the gun in his lap.

Where was he? Ambrose couldn't sniff him out, could barely identify individual minds in the great soup of anguish. There were glimpses, but nothing so complete as what he'd seen atop the ladder. A hand missing every finger but the thumb and the ring finger, a wedding band on the latter digit. Lopsided shoulders that made someone dizzy whenever they tried to shrug, which was a problem because this was a *very* indecisive person. A tooth, knocked out by the butt of a musket, found by a scavenging orphan. Little vignettes but nothing useful, no man with a whole life and two crutches and a gun and a hollow.

How long had it been? How long could that man hold on without an answer? Unsure of the first and unwilling to countenance an answer to the second beyond 'a time,' Ambrose did the only thing he could think to do: he broadened his reach, as wide as he could possibly take it, encompassing as many hearts and minds as he could, recognizing the commonality of their pain but failing to make any greater connections, now was not the time to ponder, now was the time to *act*, there was a man with a gun that might not be in his lap anymore and Ambrose needed to do something about it, which in this case was telling every unhappy heart he could reach "I'm here. It's okay."

He felt the tether shudder, felt Patience, *saw* her for the most fleeting of moments, knew that she had heard him, and knew that everyone between the two of them had heard as well, even if they wouldn't understand who or what he was the way Patience did, they had *felt* him, as he had felt them, felt a massive spasm wrack a hundred a thousand a hundred thousand oh who knew how many minds at the same time. It was fear and confusion and anger and comfort and understanding and *there*.

Then Ambrose slammed back into his body, hard enough to knock it backwards. He heard the wet snap of his skull hitting the ground, but mercifully enough he was out before the pain got to him.

S I X

HE AWOKE IN THE BRICK HUT, STARING AT THE CEILING.
Had that all been some sort of dream? No. He dismissed the
possibility at once: there was no way he had imagined his time
atop, and at the base of, the ladder. Not given the way his head
was throbbing, for one thing.

He blinked, bringing the two worlds before him into one.

Sunlight stabbed its way in through the window, bathing the
horseshoe of angry faces arrayed before him in fire. Each of
them belonged to his fellow slaves, save one pasty exception:
that of Hilditch the overseer.

The question of how long they had been standing there and
observing his unconsciousness seemed equal parts valid and ill-
advised to pose. Instead Ambrose rubbed the back of his head,
which radiated a hollow gonging ache as far down as his shoul-
derblades. He winced, sucked air, and looked up at Hilditch.
"What happened?"

Veins popped on Hilditch's neck, spread like tines on a pitchfork.

Remembering himself and his station, Ambrose added, "sir?"

"I was gonna ask you the same thing," the overseer snarled.
"You got your head on enough to get down the ladder, yet you're
so fucking stupid you crack it from two feet off the ground! How
the fuck's that happen, boy? How'm I gonna look upon that
happening?"

Hilditch doubled for a moment, then regained singularity.
Ambrose let his jaw drop and stretched it from side to side. His

ears popped as he did so. "I can't say, sir. I'm really sorry."

The overseer glared at him for an entire wordless minute. Finally, he sighed and shook his head. "You ain't been nearly so much trouble as you used to be, and I'm feeling downright Christian today. So I'll call that blow you took punishment enough and leave you to endure that. But next time you got a mind to sleep on the job..." he wagged his finger from side to side. "Uh, don't." Perhaps recognizing that leniency was off-brand, Hilditch hocked and spat on the floor before turning and shouldering through the assembled slaves, favoring them with a colorful reminder that they all had work to do.

Still, Ambrose's amphitheater remained where they were, watching the boy shuffle back up on his butt until he could wrap his arms around his knees.

At the head of the contingent stood Daniel and Isabel. Ambrose flashed back to his regaining himself after a long stretch in the stocks, Isabel leading him back with her singing. He wondered if the bell was still a-ringing in that other bright world, and if it was, whether anybody was left to hear it. If, indeed, that bright world still existed.

Over their shoulders, he saw Mayhew and those mysterious weave-working women...now just the one woman. And there were Herod and Grace, and...hell, who *wasn't* here? And how was Hilditch not ripshit about such plantation-wide lassitude? Things must have changed during Ambrose's time in the war...

For an instant, he realized that the war had just been a dream. And then he remembered that, no, it hadn't been.

"What's going on?" he inquired.

"We were going to ask you the same thing," Daniel monotoned.

Patience, Ambrose

Ambrose worked his jaw a bit more. He looked forward to a time when he could ask a question of someone who wasn't waiting to turn it right back around on him. "I think I fell."

"No shit," came a voice from the back of the group. Sounded like Paul. Ambrose didn't know who Paul was. He didn't think there had ever been a Paul that he had met.

"We were all thoroughly engaged in our labors," Daniel began, clasping his hands behind his back, "when what do we hear but *your* voice, directly behind us, assuring us that you are here, and it's okay. Wasn't that the message? 'I'm here? It's okay?'" He took a step forward and crouched in front of Ambrose. "Naturally many minds first turned towards disturbing prognoses. Some of us, myself included, pondered a divine explanation. But as we conferred – it was impossible, for those of us amongst company, not to recognize the commonality of the experience – each of us determined that it was unmistakably *your* voice which had claimed, and so attempted to calm, our minds."

"Um," Ambrose replied. This didn't make any sense. He had thought, by sending that out to everyone within his reach, he was addressing people who had experienced the trauma of war. Veterans like himself. But Daniel hadn't fought in…ooooh, ok, right. Quite obvious in hindsight: trauma had many faces, and perhaps by broadening the scope of his reach further than usual, he'd accidentally held mystical congress with the wearers of each and every mask at once. Naturally, this would include slaves, for what group of people was more reliably exposed to the cruelest, basest tortures as a matter of course? War was destructive, but it could also be productive. Cathartic, might have been a better word. An exorcism. What of the bloc who suffered violence with no hope of a peace treaty, no expectation of redress, no honor to their sacrifices?

A man who had willingly entered the theatre of combat and been broken by it, now sitting in a chair with a gun in his lap. Such a man might find succor in a friendly voice assuring him that it was here, that it was okay. But what of those whose every waking moment was spent under observation, in fear of the arbitrary authority that exercised itself as such? How might a disembodied voice declaring that it was *here*, inside their heads, sound to them? Might it be more sinister than soothing?

"I'm trying to make the right decision," somebody in the group said.

Ambrose's jaw hung slack. "What?"

Daniel's face did that spooky droop again. "You weren't listening to me?"

"No, I heard you."

"Then about what are you asking 'what'?"

"Who said they're tryin' to make the right decision?"

"…a lot of people? Most people," Daniel observed in a way that threatened to become a sermon. "You see, th-"

"Ok," Ambrose allowed, "but I was talkin' about who *just* said it."

Daniel paused, finger raised in the air. He turned and surveyed his flock, turned back to Ambrose, and finally lowered his finger. "Nobody just said it."

Oh. Uh oh.

"Guide me," another voice implored. "Please Lord, I beseech thee for guidance."

Now it was Ambrose's turn to raise a finger. "So ain't nobody else heard that, right?"

"Heard what?"

Patience, Ambrose

Ambrose grimaced. "Ah, shit."

"I just want daddy to be better," another voice demanded.

"If you help me now," another offered, "I will believe in you for the rest of my life."

"Help me sleep," came yet another. "It's been too damn long, sorry for my lang-"

"There's this girl," interrupted another, "I just want to know, does sh-"

"Lord, please remind me where I left that blasted key, I kn-"

Ambrose clapped his hands to his ears, which only seemed to amplify the voices.

"-good harvest this year, we-"

"-quit the drink, it's making me-"

"-out of town, otherwise the-"

"-get that feeling back-"

"-so many of them were-"

"-have to be my fault if-"

"-please, I-"

"-help, it's-"

"-make them-"

"-trying to-"

"-over the-"

"-soon-"

"-and ever-"

"ALRIGHT!" Ambrose screamed. He wasn't sure if he'd only screamed it with his mouth, or if he'd done it with his mind as well. At the moment, he didn't really care. All that mattered was it bought him a bit of cognitive quiet time. 'A time.' Hee, hee.

It wasn't until he placed a hand to his forehead that he realized he was sweating. He lifted his gaze to Daniel, who was still crouched in front of him, a *very* thoughtful look on his face.

"What the hell has gotten in to you?" the Father asked, his concern either genuine or not genuine. Hard to say. Impossible to say.

The boy gave a weak smile. "Bulstrode's hole's too open."

"Gurp," Mayhew gurped.

Both Ambrose and Daniel directed their attention to Doctor Mayhew. The rest of the group followed suit.

Mayhew blanched. His crutches clattered to the floor, and he quickly bent over and snapped them up, not even bothering to pretend his one visible leg was all he had to balance on.

Daniel glanced from Mayhew back to Ambrose. He took a deep breath, then rose and approached the Doctor.

Ambrose couldn't quite make out what they were saying to each other, but they spoke for quite a while. And looked back at Ambrose quite a lot.

That was nice, Ambrose mused to himself. The Father and the Doctor, getting along. That was nice.

Not nice enough to placate the voices, though.

S E V E N

THE SWAMP WAS TOO FAR TO TREK OUT TO, YET AMBROSE OPEN-ed his eyes from a dead sleep to discover himself in the deep and dark once again.

He glanced to either side of himself. Father Daniel on the right, Doctor Mayhew on the left. They had carried him out here. No, no, Ambrose had walked on his own. They had simply walked with him. Yet they had their hands under his arms. No, no.

Patience, Ambrose

No, no.

Beneath his feet was solid earth. Not water. They were in the swamp, but they were not *in* the swamp. They were *at* the swamp. Ha, ha. No, no.

"So do you sneak him provisions?" Daniel quietly wondered.

"Huh?" Ambrose asked.

The Father gave him a strictly-corner-of-the-eye glance. "I am speaking to Mayhew."

"Oh," Ambrose replied, "oh."

Daniel studied Ambrose for another moment, then lifted his gaze to Mayhew. His grip was loose on Ambrose's arm. But it palpated. Like he was ready to tear the boy's arm off, just as soon as he got the high-sign.

Made sense, that. Ambrose had found the plantation's populace engaging with him differently in the days after his telepathic broadcast. At first, he took their eagerness to include him into conversation, the no-after-you deference with which he was favored, as a show of respect. *Here*, he imagined them thinking, *is a boy of true power and intellect, and as a sidebar he's also quite handsome and probably very good at sexual intercourse, whatever that is*. But as the luster wore from this new social order, Ambrose began to notice behaviors at odds with admiration. The gazes diverted. The breaths held. The mumbling in his wake. It was a familiar attitude that Ambrose recognized, to his horror, as precisely the sort he and the others adopted around Hilditch.

"Fella out here," Mayhew was telling Daniel, "he's not the sort's gotta eat."

"What does that mean? Everyone needs to eat."

"Yeah...but this fella, he ain't exactly part of *everyone*."

Daniel sighed. "You're mad on bog fumes."

"How 'bout if I say you're a bout to meet a fella who's his own daddy, and I heard as much from a burning bush?"

"Those are different testaments."

"Same book."

"That's…anyway, that's completely different from…magical swamp friends."

"Right up until my guy starts crankin' fish 'n loaves outta thin out air. Then i-"

"That's *completely different*," Daniel snapped, turning on Mayhew, wagging a finger over Ambrose's head.

It was fear, Ambrose realized. His friends were afraid of him, and why wouldn't they be? He'd demonstrated to them a dreadful ability to claw his way into their minds and carve his own thoughts over top of theirs. They had no sense of the nature of this mysterious power, or its limitations. Neither did Ambrose, of course, but how easy it must have been for them to convince themselves that the boy was more competent than he let on. Was that not a hallmark of fear, that projection of omniscience – or omnipotence – onto the feared party?

Ambrose felt sick at the realization. He hadn't wanted this! He'd just wanted to comfort the man with the gun in his lap. His aims were, on the sliding scale of aims achieved with mental mumbo-jumbery, modest. Yet he'd cast himself as a telepathic tyrant, ready and willing to barge into unsuspecting minds on a whim and start rearranging the furniture. He wanted to let them all know they had nothing to fear from him, but even people he had once considered dear confidants, like Herod and Isabel, had been too quick concur. Oh, yes, yes, nothing to fear, we know, nothing to fear at all! Spineless blathering, nothing more. It broke Ambrose's heart.

Patience, Ambrose

Just before Mayhew and Daniel had jointly pitched this trek into the swamp…that was right, they had come to Ambrose, yes, now it was coming back…just before that, Ambrose had genuinely considered reaching out and cramming the words "stop being afraid of me" directly into people's minds. A rather self-defeating gesture, that would have been, but one that might have brought him some kind of relief from the serpentine pressure that had slithered itself around his chest and squeezed wrung crunched.

Good thing they were out in the swamp, then. Ha. Huh?

"The water into wine wasn't *magic*," Daniel whined at Mayhew, "it was a miracle!"

"So," Mayhew wondered, shrugging Ambrose's arm higher over his shoulder, "what's the difference between miracles and magic, then?"

"God and Faith create miracles! Magic is just *tricks!*"

"No, lemme tell you the difference. Miracles is just magic you think you got an explanation for. They're just Bible Magic."

"That's sacreligious."

Mayhew gestured around the swamp, then to himself. "Yeah, no shit. Th-"

"BOO!" trilled No-Good Bulstrode, as he peeled himself out from the shadow of a fallen log.

"AAH!" Father Daniel cried. He leapt backwards a step, releasing Ambrose fully to Mayhew as he stumbled into a shallow puddle. He glanced back at his foot, then returned his gaze to the colossal demon pig and crossed himself.

"There's a good sport!" Bulstrode yodeled. "So sorry, but you're *such* a good sport."

"He's in a bad way," Mayhew informed Bulstrode, shifting

Ambrose forward slightly with a nudge of the arm.

"Oh, make no mistake," Bulstrode clucked as he waddled up from the waters, "I and all those others possessed of similar psychic sensitivities have been *quite* aware." He paused. "*Ss-ss-ss,* such sibilance! And from a swine, no less! *Ss!*"

"What…" Father Daniel held his hand over his heart. "What are you?"

"I told you on the way in," Mayhew tutted.

"I was not listening," Daniel whispered matter-of-factly.

Bulstrode ignored the two men, and focused on the boy between them. "That last battle rather tore you open, hm?"

Ambrose nodded. As he tilted his head up and down, up and down, he stole glimpses from the eyes of others. A flash of bread pulled fresh from the oven, a flicker of a cat knocking a cup of charcoal pens from a desk.

He stopped nodding, and he was back in the swamp. Mostly.

"I'm in trouble," he told Bulstrode.

"I should say so," the pig replied.

And then said nothing.

Mayhew glanced nervously at Daniel, who was still too transfixed by the swine to respond in kind. "So," the Doctor ventured, turning back to Bulstrode, "you'll help h-"

"Gutted, chum, so I am. But no. No help from me."

That, Ambrose knew, would be the final word on the matter. As surely as he knew Mayhew and Daniel would try to press the issue on his behalf. Yet Ambrose couldn't find his way to feeling disappointed. For that, he would have to have gotten his hopes up.

And the truth was…he was having a hard enough time keeping track of where he was. *Who* he was.

Patience, Ambrose

"Why not?!" Father Daniel demanded, no doubt setting some sort of record for the speed with which a man made peace with having his mental model of the universe half-nelsoned by a hog in a swamp.

"I simply shan't. There ends th-"

"Shan't? Or *can't?*"

Bulstrode rolled backwards to flash his horrifying little grin up at Daniel. "Shan't, can't, these are differenceless distinctions with which you ought be well-versed, Father."

"What does *that* mean?"

"Oh, it shall strike you as a blue-borne bolt soon enough." Bulstrode turned to Mayhew. "I was clear with the boy. No peeps through panes darkly, I assure you. Gave the glass a grand old scrub before passing it off." The hog glanced sympathetically to Ambrose. "Did I not?"

Ambrose blinked, then shook his head and focused on the pig. It had him pinned by those porky little eyes...

"Afraid I did," Bulstrode whispered.

Which was either an answer to Bulstrode's own hypothetical question...or an answer to the one that Ambrose had thought, but not had the courage to vocalize.

So Ambrose didn't ask for clarification. He truly, absolutely did not want to know. Nor did he want his final question answered.

Fortunately, Daniel and Mayhew saw fit to bicker with the swamp demon, and each other. Which left Ambrose to sink into the despair he had long been too numb to fully experience.

Why? That was his final question, one he knew Bulstrode could hear, and one he was ever-so-glad the pig was neglecting to answer. For had Bulstrode wanted, he could have plucked the thought from Ambrose's head as easily as he had the boy's last question:

Did you know what was gonna happen to me? Did you know this was gonna happen?

Afraid I did, Bulstrode had whispered. Though that hadn't sounded like fear in his voice.

Such was the mill into which one million and one lives had been thrown, and ground to dust.

E I G H T

THERE WERE TIMES WHEN THEY SEEMED NEARLY MATER-ial, when Ambrose was sure he could feel them on his skin, warm and breathing. Each time one brushed against him, it uncoiled itself and threaded around his heart, his lungs, his brain, twisting and squeezing, splattering its motives and ambitions across his mind, then slithering off to make room for another. Things people wanted, things people were afraid of, things people needs hopes dreams loves hates sorrows, the entire spectrum, the impossible everything. A few times Ambrose tried to reach for someone specific, someone suffering in a way he felt he could ameliorate, but his ability to focus was deteriorating. The narrower a channel he attempted to carve, the more interference he picked up.

Other times were quiet. The misguided petitioners fell silent, or were silenced, and Ambrose was alone with his thoughts. At first this constituted a precious reprieve, but as the days became weeks each hiatus inaugurated a new, deepening loneliness. In the absence of his sister, he realized, the prayerful mob was company. Imposing though they could be, they were nonetheless grateful for him. He could feel that from them, feel them feeling him, drawing strength from him each time he reached out. There were moments when he considered confessing to them what he was, *who* he was, of correcting the misapprehensions by which they were all happily engaged. But what would that accomplish, telling them the presence they imagined to be holy was anything but, just some fifteen-year-old slave boy from Louisiana who gotten some latent abilities goosed by a pig? Nothing, that was what, unless one counted raising the floor of national misery as 'something.' Worst of all, setting them straight could well mean they would stop calling for him, stop asking him for help. Powerless though he often was to provide assistance, it was a wonderful feeling to have someone reach for *you*, one he was loathe to surrender.

Yes, ok, that was not all: these people were not afraid of him. Not entirely, anyway. They had a kind of respect for him. Respect of a kind. Or perhaps it was something else. But it wasn't fear, of this Ambrose was certain.

This diffuse appreciation grew in importance to Ambrose as he became more and more isolated in his bodied life. His friends were frightened of him, or maybe they weren't. Father Daniel and Doctor Mayhew seemed to be collaborating as closely as they ever had, united in keeping Ambrose as healthy as they could – which increasingly meant little more than ensuring the labors that the boy was unable to complete himself were accomplished by someone, be it one of them or one of their acolytes. It was difficult for anyone to believe Ambrose could survive even a single night in the stocks, or an afternoon of Hilditch's more sustained attentions.

Or maybe they weren't. Daniel and Mayhew seemed to argue as much as they got on. Always about nothing. Which was to say, always about Ambrose's future.

The boy himself saw nothing of the sort for himself. Each moment of presence was so colossal, swelling to fill the inside of his skull, pressing so hard against the bone Ambrose could feel it cracking from the inside. There was no room for future in there. None at all.

At night, always at night but sometimes during the day, during the day, Ambrose felt little fingers pawing at the cracks in his skull, digging for purchase and pulling their way in prying their way in at night, during the day. He wasn't reaching, and neither were they. They didn't need to reach. They were all right there. They were all just right where he was. During the day, at night.

Daniel and Mayhew and Ambrose were so much further away. And he knew he was one of those three.

N   I   N   E

JULY FOURTH CAME AND WENT. PATIENCE WAS AS GOOD as her name, scanning the abandoned barn in which she sheltered, rain pouring in through a cratered roof. Why was she scanning the barn like this? It wasn't as though Ambrose would be hiding in one of the cobwebbed troughs. His image would superimpose itself upon her surroundings, if it were to appear to her at all. But the day came and went, and at no point during it was she anything other than alone.

So she stayed in the barn, waiting for the rain to stop. It wasn't as though she had anywhere to go, anywhere to be. The idea was to find her brother, and she had lost him.

The thought struck her like a bolt. What if she had...*lost* him? What if he had...

No. He was alive. If he had died, Patience would know. She didn't know how. But she would feel it. It was inconceivable that she wouldn't.

She pushed herself to her feet and grabbed some more hay for Pblblbl. He didn't react to the offering until Patience pushed the bounty directly against his nose, at which point he tried to eat it directly out of her hand.

Having been bitten once (she considered it a minor miracle she hadn't lost a finger), Patience made sure he saw it, then placed the hay on the floor.

Pblblbl drooped his head slightly, but made no effort to retrieve it. He just let his noggin dangle, a little runlet of drool stretching down from his lips.

Patience swallowed hard, and placed her hand on Pblblbl's nose. Her poor, loyal mount was getting old. It was, sadly, all too conceivable that she might lose him.

At which point, she would be all alone. With neither home nor direction. Patience chewed on her upper lip as she stroked Pblblbl, and did her best not to think about it.

As always, she made an attempt to reach for Ambrose, not knowing if he could hear her, not knowing if she was doing it right, not for a second believing the answer to either was positive.

But she would not be discouraged, no. She had her will, and the fire to see it done. That had to be enough. She had to believe it was enough.

T E N

THEY DIDN'T REALIZE HOW MUCH THEY NEEDED HIM.
They didn't understand that it was his presence, his reaching for
them, their reaching for *him*, that soothed them so. Otherwise,
and he could tell this from the glimpses he received just prior to
arrival and just after departure, they were shredded. How tattered can a flag get before it ceases to signify? Before it becomes
just a bunch of rags flapping about on a long stick?

Huh?

Shit, he'd done it again. Ambrose curled his toes, rolled his
neck and tried to come back. Tried to get back in. It was strange
to think of himself as outside, and maybe that wasn't even the
right way to frame it. But it sounded right, right? Right-ish, no
doubt, right. No, that wasn't right. It should be *double* right, because it was right twice over, right because he'd been left alone
outside on the plantation, left to sit inside himself and his body
which felt wrong. Right. It wasn't the place to be anymore, this
body. There were others out there who wanted him, needed him,
weren't jealous of him the way Father Daniel was, they were
jealous of his attentions, they wanted more and more of him,
even if they didn't realize it, even if they didn't have the first clue.
Somewhere inside they knew, knew he was outside, open up all
the doors and windows and call for him, that's what they were
doing without even knowing, without well you know, maybe
they weren't being too attentive or oh haha sorry I didn't see you
there, mind's wandering a bit and I reckon my feet are taking
notes, oh come on, well I guess she's not gonna talk to me either,

Patience, Ambrose

I wonder what Daniel said, I wonder if there was any part of him that felt bad about it. Don't think so, doesn't seem likely. Would he be impressed if he knew I could read? Would that turn him around, make him think gosh this kid's an asset here, this kid's got drive and determination, this kid's a real get-up-and-go type who won't take no for an answer, this kid's a self-starter and he's always getting smarter, this kid's not the kind of kid just wants to play around, this kid's not afraid to roll up his sleeves and get his hands dirty, obviously literally but and also otherwise, too. Well too bad pal, I never learned. I never learned.

Ambrose blinked and he was standing on the bank of a raging river, grasping for some insight as to how the hell he was going to ford it, when was the last time he'd seen the water this high, no way his horses could (blink) be serious, but well he was the doctor, and if he thought draining some blood out would do the trick then best have it done swiftly, after all it wasn't easy sitting in the happy place when the doc had a very pointy stick in his (blink) drawer, where else could it have gone, had she absent-mindedly thrown it, what, into a different chest or what, because there were only two places socks should be, the drawer or the basket, and he had one sock in the drawer but the other was where, it was gone, and what the hell was he supposed to do with just the one (blink) storm, it was definitely a fool me once and so forth situation, last time he'd brought his umbrella but it hadn't rained and then there he was just carrying around his umbrella which made him look quite the doofus, all day he was just this doofus with the umbrella, but then what if it actually rains today and he doesn't have it, he'll be the soaked-through doofus, he'll just (blink) be back inside himself, sitting against the side of the barn, trembling and sweating, trying to hold on this time, trying to stay Ambrose, to remember himself, to (blink) keep on squeezing, cow ain't gonna milk hisself, that's what she would say and just how she would say it too, it's such a put-on voice it turned her stomach, like please, like come on, like ugh she was just being crabby because her fingers hurt, oh boy did they ever, but oh well the cow ain't gonna (blink) listen to reason, he just had to stay strong because of course he was gonna try to make a better offer, say oh please stay I'll pay you more you're the best employee I've ever had, well guess what buster that's because you're a rotten boss and a rat man, and that's why I'm (blink) colorblind, Jesus Christ, how had he never noticed this before, and why oh why did it have to be now on their first date when she said she liked the yellow flowers and he picked some for her but she just giggled and said oh you do tease me, and he was like I mean if you want but why are you laughing and good god how embarrassing that that's how (blink) to stand, legs apart, then as you bring the blade down you have to kind of sit with it, are you listening to me, hey, *listen*, look at this, see what I'm doing, you have to actually *look*, good golly quit being so (blink) nervous, it had felt slick as hell when she'd asked but now she just felt sick, because there was an air of finality to it, she didn't understand what it was or where it came from but all of a sudden it felt like she was standing on the edge of a very high (blink) tragedy, she could only imagine what had befallen him, what horrors he was (blink) daily living, and if he'd died, would she know, would she feel it or would things (blink) be precisely as they were now, their birthday passing like it was any other day, no contact, no conn-ection, no nothing, no (blink) way to explain why Ambrose couldn't shake this one, or maybe this one wouldn't let him go, which curled up as he was on a patch of ground that had been shadowed a moment ago but now it was much later in the day and (blink) he was back in her eyes, behind a face he only recognized from the outside, trying to find her brother, to meet him, missing him and fearing him not fearing him but fearing *for* him but now she knew he was there, she felt him and he could feel her feeling, it was that warm completion again, it would be enough to carry them through, through what, through anything, for a while, for a while this would be enough, enough for both of them, at least for a little while, for long enough, for just a bit.

E L E V E N

By September, most of the farmers who had been put to flight by the war had found their way back. Great for them, maybe, but bad news for Patience. Generosity seemed to have been yet another casualty of the conflict; now, when Patience dared her way onto someone else's property asking for scraps, she was peppered with questions too quickly for her to imagine the answers. Because no, she wasn't actually going to tell people who she was, where she was from, what she was doing wandering around Louisiana farmland all by herself.

The most frightening demonstration of The Way Things Were Now came one stormy night when Patience had found what she believed to be an abandoned barn large enough to house both Pblblbl and the carriage. Sure enough, the barn was abandoned, but the house just next door wasn't. Patience was awoken by three men armed with long rifles. One of them announced precisely what he wanted to do with the young girl they had found in their barn; the other two, fortunately, talked him down, and hurried Patience on her way. All fine in the end…but that was down to more good fortune, and nothing else.

So Patience returned to nights in the wilderness, days on the periphery, keeping her head down on the road whenever she passed another traveler. Her food she once more sourced from scavenging, sneaking into unfenced fields and taking all she could before the frosts came in.

She was on her hands and knees in a field of rotten-in-the-earth garlic when she was struck by something familiar. Like remembering the lyric to a song one hadn't thought of in years.

Only it hadn't been years. Not quite one year, even.

Patience shot to her feet. "Ambrose," she whispered aloud.

As quickly as the feeling had come, it was gone again.

Despite knowing there would be nothing to see, Patience glanced around her. Lo and behold: nothing to see. Nothing but weather-tossed furrows and sickly, drooping scapes.

Patience closed her eyes and tried to focus. Tried to focus on the ease of the enterprise. Just like Ambrose had told her. Trying without the effort. Trying…

From some impossible distance, she heard a long, rolling *crash*. Like thunder tripping on its own shoelace.

She opened her eyes.

Nothing. Just a field of rotten-in-the-earth garlic.

Patience sighed, threw down the squishy head of garlic she still held in her hand, and walked back towards the road.

She passed through the row of trees between the field and the path, then stopped.

Here was the source of that spectacular crashing sound: Pblbl-bl lay dead on the ground, having taken the carriage down with him. One of the wheels was either being turned slowly by the wind…or it was still spinning from the fall.

Pblblbl, on the other hand, was perfectly still.

Patience stood on the slight rise, watching the wheel spin. Listening to it *screek…screek…screek* with each revolution.

She decided that it was wholly her choice, to collapse down into a seat just where she was, in the shadow of the magnolia trees. She determined it *would* be her choice, to refuse to let herself cry.

That same gust that was spinning the wheel of the carriage – for it *had* to be the wind, Patience decided, as somehow the idea that she was witnessing the inertia of her horse's demise was too horrible to fully countenance – tossed the boughs of the magnolias above her.

She recalled Ambrose naming that as his favorite noise. Wind through treetops. *Almost like you can hear every leaf on its own,* he'd said, *but all together. I don't really know how to explain it.*

Neither did Patience. But she suddenly understood what he meant.

The wind continued to whisper through the trees, even as the wagon wheel slowly *screeked* to a stop.

T W E L V E

AMBROSE WAS LOSING TOUCH, LOSING THE *ABILITY* TO touch. In its place arose a superlative touchability, his mind an exposed nerve for the nation's most distraught to pluck and pick like a fiddle string. How had it happened, then? Had he lost any semblance of psychic proprioception, and so lost his ability to locate the boundaries of his reach? Or had his mind kenned that the world yet possessed few things worth grasping, and so amputated his sixth sense, leaving it to wither away from disuse? Who knew. Who cared. It brought him to the same place. Reaching, and not finding.

But, except, having said that, at some times he was confronted by the opposite problem, the exact opposite problem. Not reaching, but finding nonetheless. Like opening up your cupboards to find that your dishware's been replaced by one thousand and one little towels, useful in moderation but not in these quantities, and not when what you're after is a bowl. Like that. All the people, all their pain. For an instant, one of them had been Patience. For a few instants, non-consecutive though they were. He would find her, but more often he would lose her. Was that possible? To lose someone more than one found them? Apparently. That was what happened. Patience would be here but not most times, most times she'd be gone. Lost in the mists. The pink mists. Or maybe he was. Hard to say. Say?

What?

Ambrose blinked and he was on the ground and he blinked and he was in a tree and he blinked and he was sitting at a desk and he blinked and he was playing a game of kick-the-ball and he blinked and he was heaving a massive pack over his shoulders and he blinked and he was watching the sunrise and he blinked and he was sanding down a table and he blinked and he was scowling at the paunch that had snuck up on him and he blinked and he was cleaning up his son's mess and he blinked and he was still asleep and he blinked and he was still drunk from the night before and he blinked and he had a secret he couldn't tell her and he blinked and he blinked and how many eyes there were from which to see, in which to be entombed. What had he focused, how had he done, it seemed like he once, didn't him?

Huh?

Huh. Nest, no, *how*. Nest how tricked could opal he grabbing possibly scarf focus plinth when repeat what tickle felt jar like confess the bulb entire elated fucking scratch population ignore of dizzy the smoke fucking gamble country teach was hidden battering barrel him thoughts with dray whatever swim objects fashion or sweep feelings loaded or splat thoughts generous they instrument happened credible to running have gruel ready useless at head hand heart blink?

Blink??

Blink?!

Blink!!

Blink

b l i n k

AND HE WAS STAGGERING THROUGH THE CREAKING, TEETER-ing clapboard box that Father Daniel ambitiously liked to refer to as a church. Where was he? Not the Father but the Daniel. Daniel would know, Daniel what do, Daniel to. Too. Also. Daniel as well.

In addition!

Blink fishing not right now blink *back* in the church Daniel in back the back of the church why here why him for help did he ask who cared he was back Ambrose and in back and Ambrose was back.

"Help me," Ambrose sputtered.

The flat, affectless tone shot Daniel to his feet. "Good God,

Ambrose, what's wrong?!"

"Blink," blink blinked. Blinkingly, he blinked. "Not, don't know."

Daniel wrapped a hand around Ambrose's back and cupped the other behind his head. "Lay back," he advised.

"Back!" Ambrose cried.

"I've got you, just lay back."

"NOT," Ambrose blinkingly reiterated. "DON'T KNOW!"

"What don't you know?"

"*Blink*," blink replied like Daniel was an idiot blinky, *child* failing to understand the most blinkingly basic blink. Concept. "Where?"

"You're on the lawn outside the church," Daniel explained, because now they were. Inside to out in the back of a blink. "Do you recognize it?"

"No," was all Ambrose could blink, because there was a roof over his head.

"What did you do to him?" someone was yelling at Daniel.

Daniel threw his hands up. "I didn't do an-"

Blink.

Voices.

Trying to help him.

Hated him.

Not like.

Just a boy.

Gone too far.

No shit.

Never would.

How did.

How dare.

Patience, Ambrose

You dare.

Blink Ambrose was awake, sitting upright, staring at Master Barry and Hilditch and Mayhew and Daniel and Blink and Herod and Salmy and Medla and Prtrt and Wzklop and Blink shapes and other such.

"Hell, let's ask the boy!" Hilditch exclaimed. He nearly leapt across the room, crouching alongside…um…oh, right. Ambrose. He, Heditch, Hil*ditch* shot a finger at Daniel and yelled at at at Ambrose. "This here fella poison you?"

"Blink?" Ambrose croaked.

"Talk sense, boy!"

"Tell them," Daniel implored. "I was only trying to help you! You came to *me!*"

"You shut your fucking mouth," Hilditch suggested, "before I stick something in it used to be attached to your body!"

Daniel appealed to Master Barry. "You would let him, then?"

"You kill a strong young nigger's might got a score left of pickin' left in him," Hilditch replied on Barry's behalf, "ain't no 'mount of bootlickin's gonna keep you from swingin'."

Barry simply shrugged his assent.

Daniel turned back to Ambrose. "TELL THEM! PLEASE!"

He was trying to help me, Ambrose said. I went to him… Ambrose said.

He was trying to help me, "Ambrose" said.

Hilditch slapped Ambrose's face. "Your own name ain't sense, you shit! I said SENSE!"

Ambrose said, he was just trying to help me.

"Daniel" was just trying to help "me," Ambrose said.

"Hell," Hilditch said to Barry as he pulled the hat off of his head. "I reckon that's close as we're gonna get."

Barry raised an eyebrow. "To what?"

"WHY IN GOD'S NAME WOULD I HURT HIM?" Daniel shrieked, shattering in an instant that pious shell he had spent years constructing around himself.

The gravity of that was not lost on anyone in the room. Even Ambrose felt himself more rooted to the moment than he had in…since. Sometime. Whoops.

Hilditch thought on Daniel's outburst for a moment. "You're bitter," he finally replied.

"He ain't the bitter type," Doctor Mayhew insisted.

"Shut up," Barry warned.

Mayhew pinched his lips together, rocking back and forth on his feet. "He ain't the type."

"Shut up."

"He's bitter," Hilditch continued, cocking a thumb at Ambrose, "because this little bastard got him thrown in the stocks."

Daniel sputtered for a moment, then shook his head. "I haven't been in the stocks in years!"

"Yeah!" Hilditch switched to a full-on pointer finger in Ambrose's direction. "That was him!"

"I don't *care* about that!"

"He ain't the bitter type," Mayhew insisted to Hilditch.

Master Barry took a threatening step towards Mayhew.

Listen to me, Ambrose said. Daniel was trying to help me ",", Ambrose said. I already "said," Ambrose said.

Master Barry tilted the raised eyebrow towards Ambrose. "What did he just say?"

"Sounded like 'dead' to me," Hilditch fibbed.

"He said 'said!'" Daniel exclaimed.

"One more word outta you, I swear to whatever fuckin' God

you like, I'll send you to him 'fore you can slap your grubby little hands together!"

Mayhew crouched beside Ambrose. "You've gotta tell 'em," he implored.

"Tell," Ambrose insisted. "Don't."

Blink.

Black.

Nothing.

THIRTEEN

GLIMPSES OF ANOTHER WORLD. GLOOMY YET EXPANSIVE. The mood was festive, almost recklessly so. A few souls, well maybe not *souls* but, hm, a few minds, they meant business. Boisterous business, yes, but they took their fun seriously. There were all the usual jeers and catcalls one expects in such a hall of iniquity. All in good fun, though. It was ultimately all just a bit of fun, and if one might taunt another, it was all but guaranteed the current would reverse. The shit-talking would flow the other way, before too long. Or after too long. It didn't matter. They had all the time in the world, all the time in any world. The hall never closed, had always been open. It was all good fun, good enough for eternity and then some. Great music, too. The food? Forget about it. Like actually forget about it, they didn't need food here. Or drink. Which wasn't to say you couldn't get them, but…oh, goodness, the things one could have here, for which you had no need! Imagine it and discover it yours; and for those doing well this go-round, find imagination dwarfed by the gift. It was hard to process anything beyond snippets, little gasps of informational overload, but before long a patchwork overview could be cobbled together.

This made it no easier to process, but it did clarify just how impossible to appreciate the whole thing was.

Oh, what gorgeous, horrible music.

PATIENCE AWOKE IN NEW ORLEANS PROPER, STANDING on a dock and watching slaves unload a cotton shipment from east Texas (why Louisiana should need to import cotton, she couldn't begin to imagine). She had walked here. Had walked everywhere since her horse had died. Because what the hell else was she gonna do. Only she didn't remember walking onto this dock. Watching these ships. Watching the slaves unload them. She simply awoke here, standing, watching, with the knowledge.

It was the feeling of turning your home upside-down in search of some beloved heirloom, only to blink and realize you've spent the last several hours sifting through the ashes of the inferno that consumed your home and everything in it weeks ago. It was like remembering a tragedy from years passed, one with which no peace had ever been truly made.

In an instant, an old scar appeared on her heart, something brand new that had long since scabbed and healed.

The river between them was open. Wide open. Because there was nothing at the other end. It was cold, reaching for her. Arms of cold and empty.

She felt it creeping from the feet. Rising waters. Ice on her ankles. A still tide dancing to that gorgeous, horrible music.

Hadn't she always known it would be for naught? Hadn't she known that, one way or another, it was not her lot to see her brother again? What had been her plan, really? Honestly? She hadn't had one. She'd set off with hope, nothing more. This was how it was always going to end, one way or another.

Patience didn't realize how tightly she was clenching her fists until her shoulders started to ache. Until her vision went blurry at the edges.

She watched the dozen-odd slaves bustling about the ship, all under the watchful eye of a single white man clutching a rather fiendish-looking lash.

The world, she recognized from a great distance, is a terrible place.

And, a fact seen from still further away...

There was no way to be certain, of course. That was no more possible than was denying what she knew to be true. The cold, the empty, oh Christ, the *music*...

He was gone. He was gone because she had failed to save him.

Patience didn't believe that for a second, but, again, it was somehow easier to think in those terms than in more realistic ones. The truth, which she glimpsed as a predator through the brush, was that Ambrose had died because that was what slaves did in this country. They died.

Yet they remained connected. Patience and Ambrose did.

Patience stared at the Mississippi, the open vein through which New Orleans' commercial lifeblood flowed. How much actual blood the river must have seen, yet how goreless it appeared! Of course it would be so; blood, like shit, flows downstream. Ambrose had been even further downstream than this, near the point at which the shit flows to sea, to seek out foreign shores.

"What about the folks live downstream?" Ezekiel had once asked Patience, a billion years ago, when Ambrose had been just an imaginary friend.

What had she said then? What, in her idiot youth, had she

deemed an acceptable response to that? "Everybody lives down-stream from somebody." That was what she had said. Out of the mouths of babes.

Patience watched the timidity with which the Mississippi slithered past the docks, onto its final few miles to the sea. It was just these waters upon which she and her brother had been set in 1799. Here they were. Here was the bottom, where all the upstream shit did flow.

The waters were brown, choked and clouded. Mud, silt, the alluvial effluvium of a nation forever purging itself. Yet it would never be rid of that which poisoned it. It would never be free.

Patience dropped the little bag she had fetched from the over-turned carriage, and set off against the current. Leaving the docks to wander upstream. Why not. She had nothing else to do. Nowhere else to go. And she never would. For her brother was gone…yet he lingered. Which was perhaps the worst part.

Ambrose was dead, but his absence remained. It was all that burdened Patience as she staggered against the flow of these awful waters, fighting back tears for no other reason than she felt she had given this land enough of those already.

F O U R T E E N

AMBROSE STIRRED WITHIN THE DEATHWELL. IF FOCUSING ON the boundaries of his living body had revealed the expanse of all things appearing within him…this was precisely the opposite. That which existed clung to him like damp satin, outlining a form Ambrose did not recognize as his own.

He clenched his fist and found it missing. He opened his jaw and lost his entire head in the realization that followed. He could find no body belonging to him. Yet he felt its form, its implication. The way the world clung to it. If one could call this a world.

If there remained a *one* to do the calling.

There had to be. Ambrose was having thoughts, which must logically mean he was still…something. Perhaps not alive. But he existed. No, perhaps not that either. Perhaps he was now nothing more than a collection of thoughts unthunk. Perhaps it was best to stop using *logically* as a guide to conclusions.

Ambrose softened himself. Focused on that which came to him. Without effort.

There was some definition to this place, enough to call it a *place*. Gloomy, yet expansive. The distance shimmered, and so betrayed itself. Closed-eye sight. That was what it reminded Ambrose of. That, at the very least, was the thought which arose. *Closed-eye sight.*

He heard voices. Or perhaps he merely had the idea of voices. They spoke in pure concept. Not to him. To each other. Those which did not speak, sang. To the tune of the music.

They were here, those voices. Whereever this was, they were. Yet recognizing the placehood of this world implied the existence of another. Not logically. But simply. And so it was. Here in this closed-eye kingdom of the simple.

He did not turn his thoughts to that other world. For he was only thoughts now, only thoughts. And thoughts could not turn. They could only be turned.

So Ambrose let himself be turned, focused without effort, until he felt pressure and pull. He felt them. This was more than thought, he was certain. It was pressure, it was pull. It was holding one end of a long rope and feeling someone adjust their grip on the other. Not pulling, nor letting out slack…just shifting.

A baby shifting at the other end of an umbilicus.

There was grief. Ambrose could not pinpoint where it was, whether it was coming from him, from the living infant on the far side of this cord, or if it was a property of the union itself… but no, he could. He could say. He could not speak, but he could say.

This was a line between worlds. And he was in this one. But Patience remained in the other. And she grieved him. But she did not know that he was not wholly gone. And he did not know how to tell her that he was not.

But they had been here before. This was not the first time he had preceded her into a new world. He did not know how he knew that, or precisely how it was meant. But it was true. Simple. And so, true.

This knowledge taught him more than it could ever contain within itself. It was not simple. And so, it was untrue. But it was useful.

Ambrose poured himself into the cord.

He did not pull, he released no slack.

He simply was. Simply.

FOR THE LIFE OF HER, PATIENCE COULD NOT WORK OUT HOW she was still alive. Though she would have been the first to admit she knew little of how the human body worked, or what its limitations were, she nonetheless found it difficult to understand how she had managed to keep moving with so little food, so little water, so little rest or warmth or protection or company or any of the hallmarks that had up until the past few months seemed so essential. She wasn't entirely certain where she was (beyond *upstream*, for she had yet to find anything diverting enough to peel her from this aimless trek to the headwaters), nor what time of year it was (though she did know it had begun to snow, that had been pretty hard to miss even for a half-catatonic headcase like Patience). Nor was she much better at keeping track of things like how much she was eating, precisely how much water she was scooping from the river, how many nights she spent squatting beneath a roof instead of lying out in the elements.

So, she granted, it was entirely possible that she was leading an altogether healthier lifestyle than she realized. It was possible in the same way that a baby spontaneously doing a cartwheel was possible.

Patience giggled at the thought just as she had it, squatting in a barn that was either abandoned or just far enough from any other property to make it impractical to access during the wintermonths. She glanced out the open door to the snow falling beyond, then back down to the project she was unaware of having begun.

Using a flat wedge of rock, she'd peeled bark off a birch tree and scraped thin shavings from the interior side. These she'd stuck beneath a loose pile of small dry twigs, which were themselves loaded into the wooden hand drill she'd taught herself to construct after a marathon month of trial and error.

Behold: a dry little pile of sticks and such.

Patience planted two flat palms on either side of the vertical hand drill, a prayer to the fire gods. She rubbed her hands against one another, cranking the stick between them.

The drill belched a ringlet of smoke.

"Ah!" Patience grunted. She rubbed faster.

Another little eruption of smoke.

No vocalizations from Patience this time. Just a setting of the jaw, and a quickening of the rub.

The tinder caught. Nothing dramatic at first, just a gentle glow and crackle. Patience nurtured it with breath and hope until it was ready to be transferred to a larger timber teepee she'd assembled inside a ring of rocks. Where the *real* magic would happen.

WHOOMPH, her gentle glow and crackle announced as they claimed the wooden pyramid in their own name.

Patience stared at the humble little fire in disbelief for several seconds. She'd done it. After weeks and weeks of failed attempts...she'd done it.

The crackle of the fire sounded quite a bit like applause to Patience's ears.

She'd done it!

Patience shot to her feet and let out a victorious "WHAAA!" Her delight bounded around the empty barn, somehow seeming to grow more and more excited as it did. Patience giggled at the enthusiastic echo. She looked up, as if hoping to witness it.

Through a window in the hay loft, she saw the moon.

On its face, she saw what the frozen night had once painted upon it, to melt into its features forever.

Patience's smile was slow to fade. Which she counted as a blessing, as she did any long-tailed pleasures she chanced upon out here in the wilderness.

Slowly, she turned her gaze back down to the fire.

It was warm, this fire. It felt good. But that was all. *Good.* Not exactly the reaction Patience imagined was typical of someone alone in the woods, in the middle of winter, finally summoning their first flames. But it was all she could muster in the moment.

It was possible she was too numb for anything more ecstatic, be that numbness emotional or phyiscal. Yes. It was also possible that she was overthinking her own responses. Also yes.

But…somehow Patience didn't think it was either of those. It was almost as though…

For an instant, several thoughts all got stuck in the same metaphorical doorframe, and Patience's mind was a perfect blank.

In that instant, she felt pressure and pull. And from them, warmth. Power. Love, enough to keep her going.

She felt what had kept her going.

And then the thoughts came through the door, and Patience knew that all of them were wrong.

That night, she let herself cry. But she kept the fire burning.

FIFTEEN

OH, AND SPEAKING OF FIRE: LET'S LEAVE THE TWINS TO THEIR limbos of space and time for the moment, that we may fly up up and away, back to the April most lately passed in the year of somebody's Lord 1815, way over in the Dutch East Indies, to the island of Sumbawa. Later generations would know this landmass as Indonesia, but for today, in the past, now, which is *then*, it's the Dutch East Indies. Sumbawa's still Sumbawa though. And unfortunately for the residents of Sumbawa, and eventually the entire globe, Tambora is still Tambora. What is this tautological Tambora? O, you've only another moment or two before you find out; there's a rather dramatic demonstration in the offing.

As we wait though, take in what the landscape has to offer, for there are not a few clues to be found. Mount Tambora, upon which we have come to rest, is a perfectly symmetrical cone of earth jutting fourteen thousand feet straight up from its base. The mouth of the mountain (and one can perhaps imagine what sort of mountain has a maw) gapes with a diameter of just under twenty thousand feet. And, as it has since the year of 1812, poor Tambora (which also answers to 'the entirety of the Sanggar Peninsula') has been developing a rather lethal case of halitosis. What sulfurous belches with which it rattles the island, what appalling lack of decorum that leaves all pardons unbegged! Yes, we're dealing with a nasty piece of geology here, a real rotten stratovolcano just about to blow its top. Why? What did the ten thousand people who are about to die (and that's just from the initial eruption, of course) ever do to the volcano? Did they forget to toss in a virgin or two? Did somebody miss a prayer, or magma forfend, take Tambora's name in vain?

Of course not. Don't be silly. It's just the Earth, still a bit keyed up from its creation 4.6 billion years ago, letting off a bit of steam. Pressure and relative densities, that's what it comes down to. Tectonic flatulence to relieve the bloat. Nothing personal, the planet might do well to remind the families pinned between the hundred foot drop to the crag-shattered ocean and a wide, creeping slug of liquid fire. Nothing personal!

Whoops, here we go! Hear that bubbling, rumbling, grumbling sound? The denizens of Sumbawa sure do!

NOTHING PERSONAL! Tambora insists as three pillars of flame launch into the sky, like spotlights at the premiere of the latest multimillion dollar disaster film. To enhance the 4-D experience, ash, aerosol, and sulfur all blast out of the ever-widening hole, the caldera draining its molten load down all sides of the mountain at once. Before long, eight-inch fists of pumice smash into the island. *Nothing personal!* each one might well declare as it punches through someone's chest. *Nothing personal!* Oops, there goes a head! Good thing Ambrose wasn't here to see *that*, eh? *Nothing personal!* as the pumice stones join forces with whole trees ripped up by the root to form landscape-shredding rafts three miles across, that stampede their way out to sea.

In addition to its fiery enema, Tambora also gave itself one hell of a high-and-tight during what would remain, well into the twenty-first century, the largest volcanic eruption in recorded history; the mountain divested itself of sixty megatons of sulfur, twenty-four cubic miles of pumice and ash that were, in the process of being quite quickly divested, launched into a cloud that towered as high as twenty-seven miles above the volcano itself. When all of that cleared – and make no mistake, it took a *very* long time for that to happen – what remained was a still-active volcano just over nine thousand feet tall. Which, for those keeping track, meant that about a full third of Tambora said sayonara that April…and yet, the mountain remained active. Tambora will one day have more to say to the planet, but in as much as it is the concern of this story, it will now take its bow.

Of interest to us is that missing third of Tambora, all that smoke and rock and so forth. Where did it all go?

Well, why not follow it? After the thicker, less refined ash particles fell back to Earth – as well they *should*, the scoundrels – what remained was the real cream of the crop, the finest-grain offal a volcano could hope to offer. Having taken in the local sights – of which there weren't a whole lot left – wanderlust set in amongst the dust. There was a whole wide world to see! And so it was that, across the miles and the months, Tambora's eructative motherload rode the wild longitudinal winds to exciting new climes, importing their own foreign culture to the people who lived therein. Extra-dazzling sunsets for England! Super-neato twilights for China! For the States, dry fog which shone red at dusk and could not be dispersed by rain nor wind! A permanent pink mist! Plunging temperatures! Snow in June! Blotted suns! Harvest failures! Typhus outbreaks! Monsoons! Dying livestock! Famine! Protests! Civil unrest! Riots! Arson! Looting!

Nothing personal!

Yes, it was the so-called…oops, hang on…

1816

O N E

YES, IT WAS THE SO-CALLED 'YEAR WITHOUT SUMMER', A year in which Tambora's eruption would indirectly multiply its initial body count by at least eight. 80,000 lives snuffed out, as freezing temperatures from June through August killed crops across the eastern United States and western Europe, as the shift in climate spun up natural disasters of unparalleled severity in China and India. Increased rainfall would lead to droughts in the coming years, particularly in Europe. The devastation answered to a different name all over the planet, but the fact of it was universal. As was the fact that not nobody but nobody had ever heard of Tambora.

So naturally, as far as most anybody in the darkened portions of those god-fearing United States knew, it was the end times. A frostier apocalypse than they'd been led to expect, sure, but only slightly less dramatic than the more standard fire-and-brimstone affair. Figures, if one's gonna die, it's always preferable to get the drama of the eruption. A whole lot quicker and sexier than freezing to death, those eruptions are.

In any event, fear was an understandable reaction to the precipitous drop in temperatures. Anger was acceptable, if one had that sort of relationship with one's favored diety. Arousal would have been a bit more left-field, but there's no way to predict how one will react under pressure.

But imagine being alone in the woods as the winter carried on, and on, and on, the frost returning just as spring seemed to be gathering steam. Imagine following a familiar, narrow, unnavigable river upstream, sometimes venturing inland in search of food or other amenities – but always being stunned at the infrequency with which one felt the need to do so. Imagine how loose one's grasp on the passage of time might become. Feel the endless cold burrowing in at your hips, climbing up your ribcage one rung at a time. Thrill to that tender warmth from another world, chasing off the chill. See the first time your breath fogs as it leaves your body. Marvel at the steadiness of the hand which banishes that mist. Hear that dreadful hush, the auditory advance party of snowfall. Hear the music.

Imagine what it would be like to experience all of this in a grief-sticken stupor, alone, over what seemed a single, endless month.

But was, in fact, seven.

Imagine. Focus. Just not too much effort, now.

Patience, Ambrose

And there she is. We've found Patience.

T W O

PATIENCE KNEW SOMETHING WAS WRONG WHEN SHE REACHED
the lake. Well, not quite. She arrived at the lake thinking this just
one more pleasant place to stop among many, on this long, endless trek through the winter. She spared a thought, as she lowered herself into a Patience-sized crook in the roots of a tree high
on a beautiful hill, for where she was now. Missouri territory,
perhaps? She didn't think this was quite the right landscape for
that; these low, rolling green hills struck her as more of a north-
eastern phenomenon. But she had never been to the Missouri
territory. Furthermore, she couldn't recall how in the hell she'd
come by a conception of *any* area's topography.

She lay back against the bark and tempted fate with a smile.
The weather was warming up a touch, finally. It was in that perplexing period of indecision, where it was warm enough to rain
during the day, but got cold enough to turn to snow at night.
Somehow, Patience found this deeply frustrating; she suspected
it was because such a modest change scarcely registered for her.
She had this warmth within her…something mysterious she believed had to be Ambrose, protecting her from some great beyond…yet at the same time, she knew it couldn't possibly be him.
That was grief whispering lies into her ear. She had merely been
wandering for a week, maybe two. Her survival was surprising,
to be certain, but there was nothing supernormal about it.

Still…as she often did in quiet moments, she let that warmth
flood her mind. Felt it not as a single sensation, but as an

423

unbroken flood of thought. Not thoughts, plural. Thought *itself*.

It was pressure, it was pull.

As always, Patience couldn't be certain how much of all this was just her mind playing tricks on her. So she steadied herself in certainties, gazing out at the colossal lake and admiring the way its eerily still surface so flattered the deep azure above. It was inconceivable to her, that water as glassy and pure as this could be fed by that useless sluice of silt and shit alongside which she had grown up. But she had yet to pass Praisegod's pig farm by, which meant the farm was yet upstream.

She thought about that. Racked her brain for what little she knew about the geography of the nation. Missouri territory, in relation to New York…they weren't anywhere near…and how long *had* she been walking, anyway?

Clunk.

A horrible creature, blood-red and the size of a fist, fell upon Patience from above, a small proboscis jutting from the top of the apple, it was just an apple. She had been sitting under an apple tree.

Laughing at her own stupidity, she snatched up the fruit, brought it to her waiting mouth and took a mighty chomp. She could hardly chew it, laughing as she was. After giggling through her first bite, she looked up into the crown of the tree.

Apples, crisp apples everywhere!

She turned and surveyed the scene around her. Natural splendor, and nothing more. Nobody to disturb her, nobody to chase her from the generous tree and its Patience-sized cradle of roots.

Patience had time enough to throw her head back for one lonely "HA!" before her brain tapped itself on the shoulder.

Apples. Apples in the apple tree.

Which, though she hadn't gotten out a *whole* lot to explore the orchard at Drummond's Estate, she knew damn well didn't happen in the winter. She remembered looking longingly out the window between lessons with Martha, and smiling at those little red buttons tucked amongst the green.

In the summer. She remembered doing that in the summer.

Rather than attempt a full mental review of what she had believed to be just the last few weeks of her life, which would no doubt have proven grueling and embarrassing and more than a little traumatic, Patience simply took another bite of the apple.

Not bad. Sweet, but a little on the mushy side. Not perfect, in other words.

Which unfortunately convinced Patience in an instant that a.) the apple was real, which meant that b.) it was the summer, which logically lead to c.) madness, because d.) it had snowed last night, and e.) it looked likely to tonight.

So what the f.) was going on?

She glanced down at the apple in terror, momentarily convinced it was drawing breath to answer her. Fortunately for the both of them, it kept quiet.

T   H   R   E   E

THIS WAS NOT A PLACE WITHOUT TEMPTATION. THERE was, after all, another life. One to which he was no longer connected, one no longer occupied. It was a life that had once held so many things. Ambitions, concerns, favorites, grudges. To name but a few. To name but four. These things and more all shriveled to dust and blew away, once the life was left to rot, carried off on the same slow wind that shuttled all things towards the dark. It was the work of a life to forever draw these things back into oneself, as they slowly blew away. Yet the life here considered was forfeit. Blinked to black. So they blew away. The four things that made the life.

Yet the temptation remained. What a curious thing. It was the temptation to see what had become of the space around the life. An idle curiosity. What ever became of that rake that went missing last autumn. Where did that stray dog who marched around the property each day go at sundown. How did Father Daniel escape the ordeal in which Ambrose had left him. All equally weighted. None more important than the other.

So Ambrose went to see. Because he could go. And to go would be to have went, at some point in the future. And so he did. To find the rake had been set against a post near the outside edge of Barry's fencing, and lost to indistinguishability from said post after a layer of soil covered the tines. To find that the stray dog gallumphed each evening to the nearest neighbors, of whom Ambrose had not known, for that was where the dog lived. To find that Father Daniel had been partially skinned (his back), partially dismembered (his left arm), and then hanged for the crime of Ambrose's murder.

There was injustice in that last fact. But then, there was injustice everywhere. That was the fact. That was the only fact.

And so Ambrose returned to the point in time he had last come to know. Of his sister beneath the apple tree. Yet he discovered that time was neither linear nor consistent in its passage. He returned some time later than he had left, to discover that backward glances could be nothing more than that. Glances.

He could not find her. Could not reach her. He could only

observe, from impossible distance.

Without meaning to…he had abandoned her.

Yet more injustice. Alas. This was the fact.

MERE DAYS LATER, THE APPLES HAD FALLEN FROM THE tree, shriveled and sour, as the surface of the lake locked up in tremendous floes of ice. Winter was closing back in, before it had fully departed for the summer. For it was summer, Patience had determined. It wasn't simply the apples; there were biological markers of time, reliable reminders of each month's passage, and it was only as Patience's personal flow began anew that she thought to take stock of how many of these she had experienced since she'd left Louisiana. A precise count eluded her – years in the wild had rather innurred her to the discomforts of the process, rendering them unremarkable – but it had been more than three or four, that she could say for certain. Add the apples to that, and Patience fixed it for June, maybe July.

Which conclusion was immediately contradicted by the freezing waters of the lake, which she circled in search of any place she might shelter. For as the temperatures dropped once more, Patience felt the unfamiliar discomfort of the cold settling into her bones. Whatever had been keeping her warm through the previous months – *months*, she still struggled to make sense of how she could have been wandering in a fugue for *months* – seemed to have abandoned her all at once.

Ambrose had gone. Left her. She still felt an eldritch draft from the tether left open…but her brother seemed to have vacated the other end. Taking his half of the fire with him.

She would mourn this fact, perhaps despair of it, at her earliest convenience. But this was neither the time nor the place. The nights out here were oh so punishing, each worse than the last.

She needed to find the nearest town. She'd no idea where that might be, or how to find it, but lounging on the edge of the lake as she had been was no longer an option. Where to go, then, in search of civilization? Well, following the river had served her quite well thus far. It only stood to reason she might find similar success by tracing the lake. After all, weren't navigable bodies of water considered ideal spots to plunk down a town? Granted, a lake fed by whitecap runoff as Patience was beginning to suspect this one was (for she was surely further north than she had expected, and on clear days she could see a truly breathtaking range of mountains further still in that direction) would probably only be accessible by land. Which would rather cut down on the commercial opportunities. But there might be a fishing town somewhere around here, right?

After two days limning the eastern edge of the lake, the harsh winds slicing off the water forced Patience inland with little to keep her warm save her mounting frustration. It was unacceptable, that this should be how she died. After all she had been through, all she had done! Yes, she spared a thought for Ambrose, who had likely found the nature of his demise to be similarly underwhelming. It was surely not often someone's final thought was *terrific, this is a suitable end for me!* Nonetheless…freezing to death beside some anonymous lake was just, well, not okay. Patience couldn't allow it.

If for no other reason than that, she would survive.

"This is such b-b-bullshit," she chattered to a squirrel (who looked just as baffled as she felt) as the sun slid ever nearer the horizon, and the winds off the water ran scales to warm up for a long night of howling. "Winter in s-s-summer!" She growled. "Wh-where are y-y-y-you, Amb-bro-s-s-s-se? It's l-like, sh-

sh…!" Patience froze. Not to death, though. At least, not yet.

Two men stood in her path, reduced to purple silhouettes by the setting sun.

Patience could tell they were well-bundled white men, though. And she could see that they had rifles.

Patience felt like a fool, just standing there and shivering. But she wasn't in any condition to run away. Short of burying herself in the snow and waiting for a thaw, she had no choice but to throw herself at the mercy of these two.

Still…she would fight if she had to. She w-

"Ooh!" one of them squawked. "You're not dressed for this, eh?"

"You need a coat?" the other asked.

Patience nodded furiously, her survival instinct overriding the skepticism with which she viewed eagerly offered generosities. "Y-y-y-"

The second man unclasped his coat, which looked to have belonged to a very large animal that had surely not yielded the fur willingly, and swung it off his shoulders. "Here ya go!" he yodeled as he tromped over to Patience. He moved to swing the garment over her shoulders.

Instinctively, she flinched and pulled back.

"Ah jeez," the man groaned, "I'm real sorry about that! I oughta have asked if ya mind if I'm gonna briefly enter your personal space!"

She shook her head. "No," she offered, much to her great surprise. "*I'm* s-s-s-sorry." Waving her hand, she gestured for the man to briefly enter her personal space.

He did so with surprising delicacy, as though she were royalty, and he but a serf. As he smoothed the fur across her shoulders, the first man stepped forward, hat in hand. "You can have my cap too, if ya like!" he offered.

Already warming up in the flesh of some unknown, unlucky beast (against whom Patience bore no ill will, but all the same was immensely grateful had been murdered and flayed), she looked at the man's headgear. That had most *certainly* once belonged to an animal – it still had a tail attached to prove it. "It's not, uh…" she looked up into the first man's eyes. "…alive, is it?"

The first man jumped a bit, eyes goggling up to his hat, as though Patience's asking that question was liable to make the answer 'yes.' He gave her a remarkably subtext-free smile and said "not lately, ma'am!"

"Don't you want to keep it on?" she asked him.

"This here hat?"

"Yeah."

"Oh, I've been wearing it all day. Might do me good to air out the old head hair, eh?" He took a step towards Patience. "Permission to briefly enter your personal space?"

She nodded, and so had a *very* warm hat placed upon her head. "Thank you," she said to the first man, as the second was pulling the tall, shin-loving moccasins off of his feet. "Oh!" Patience exclaimed. "That's alright, I'm f-"

"Freezing cold, I'll bet! Pah, look at me, interrupting you like some kind of, ah…"

"Woodpecker!" the second man offered.

"Ah…"

"Compliment!"

"Ah…"

"Familiar smell!"

"Actually, now that I've had time to think on the matter,

woodpecker seems to have aged the best of those examples! Seein' as it's kinda timeless, ya know?"

"I appreciate you saying as much."

"Is it alright with you if I use your example of woodpecker?"

"Ah heck, I'd take it as a sort of compliment, if it comes to that!"

"Ha ha! A *Compliment!*"

"Familiar smell!"

"Ha ha!" The first man turned back to Patience. "I interrupted you like a woodpecker, it's been decided, and to clarify it was *I* who was the woodpecker, which was downright rude of me. I hope ya can forgive me, but all the same it ain't right for a man in the wrong to go around begging the wronged party to make him feel alright about the nasty thing he did. As a way of letting ya know how I feel so downright cruddy about the whole affair though, I'd love for ya to take my brother's mocassins – you don't mind if I offer those, do you?"

"Certainly not, for you're o-"

"Excellent! Oh, sor-"

"What's that?"

"Sorry!"

"Not at all!"

"Please continue."

"My mocassins are yours, to become hers!"

"For a walk with us just back to our place!"

"It's a heck of a cozy spot," the second man explained to Patience as he removed his mocassins, "just what the doctor ordered, in the sense of a metaphor, given how darn unseasonable the weather's been of late!"

"Neither of us are doctors."

"Ah, forgot to mention. No doctors here."

"She could be a doctor."

"So she could!"

"In which case, she could make her own orders!"

"Ah, so she could!"

"So, what do ya say, doc?"

The two men looked to her expectantly.

"Uh…" Patience considered the situation. As a general principle, it seemed ill-advised to accept invitations from strange men met in the woods whose most salient personality trait was *an eagerness to undress.* Particularly when those men were holding guns. It *also* seemed a lapse in judgment to accept such ferocious generosity at face value. In Patience's experience, the amount an individual was willing to give you was commensurate to, or perhaps just south of, what they hoped to take from you in return.

True and true. But, well, she had no idea how much colder this cold snap could, uh, snap, or for how long it could snap, or indeed why it was snapping in the first place. And having lost whatever it was that had kept her warm, to remain out here alone would likely mean freezing, her death mask a grimace of idiot disappointment. Even putting that to one side… these two guys just seemed *swell.* They seemed like swell fellas, which…Patience had read enough papers to know was a red flag in and of itself, but, well, she didn't have a rejoinder to that, except to say that these fellas seemed swollen with their swellness, in a way that left precious little space for even the most well-hidden of sinister bits. Besides, it made sense that it was 'swell fellas who turned out to be not-so-swell' who racked up the column inches. That was notable. Less notable were 'swell fellas who actually *were* swell.' Why would anybody write about them? How would

Patience have ever heard of them? Swell didn't sell. Did that mean swell didn't actually exist? Of course not. She'd also never read about freed black men and women living productive lives, contributing to their communities or raising happy families. That didn't mean that never happened. Right?

Come to think of it, why *didn't* anybody write about stuff like that?

She shivered.

"Ok," she told them. "Thank you. I would really appreciate a chance to get out of the cold for a bit."

The two men cheered, pumping their rifles above their heads and hopping up and down.

"Yahoo!"

"Yippie!"

"Yoohoo!"

Patience laughed, unsure if it was with them or at them. Or, she remained skeptical enough to posit, at her own near-future expense.

ONE VOICE PEELED ITSELF APART FROM THE OTHERS. It didn't so much drift to Ambrose as it did curl itself around the shape he might once have recognized as his own, and squeeze.

"Fancy a run-in such as this," No-Good Bulstrode tittered through mist, his sing-song natter condensing into a viscous, phlegmy starburst, his thought more substantive than all those of which Ambrose was composed, "in a placeless place such as this one!"

Ambrose said nothing, for his were fragile thoughts now. He *was* fragile thoughts. He could be wafted away, like smoke from the mouth of a cannon.

Just as Bulstrode wished it, no doubt; the hog had much to

say. "Peregrinate through the passage of memory, ye ding-dong, and in due course you shall come upon a promise I once tendered you. Regarding my cracking open your n-less dam being a gift given *gratis*. No debts incurred, you will no doubt recall my having said. You recall?"

Ambrose embodied assent. Yes, he remembered.

"Doubtless, doubtless." The form of the hog shimmered before Ambrose. Around him. But no…it was not the hog. It was no shape at all. No design a human mind could hold without buckling beneath its immensity. "Well," Bulstrode continued, "that was all true enough. Only…we do delight in our norms of reciprocity, don't we?"

We do was the thought Ambrose became. This he managed, for it allowed Bulstrode's *we* to mean the demon and Ambrose. Before the demon had the chance to clarify what other creatures such as himself might have been included in that *we*. For down that way, Ambrose knew, lay a deathless dark from which he would never be free.

Whereas if he did as Bulstrode asked…he hoped he might one day be free. If only in earning the privilege of a proper death.

This was hardly his desire, though. For even as he did what the demon asked of him, Ambrose found the strength to keep the tether open. With the hope that one day, perhaps, Patience might find the way through to him from her end.

F O U R

THE FIRST MAN, IT EMERGED, WAS NAMED KIRK. THE SECond was called Dirk. They were brothers of the surname Serkis, which meant their parents had either been very cruel or had a terrific sense of humor. Considering how relentlessly these two smiled...actually, it was still a toss-up.

They hailed from a town called Hungry Neck in Canada, and as far as they knew had never left it. Patience, clueless as to where most any geopolitical boundary lay, could only take them at their word. And was happy to do so, for if the Serkis brothers were correct, then Patience was now in Canada. Which made her an international traveler. The thought tickled her just enough to allay the less pleasant associations evoked by the mention of brothers.

Each time her delight in these two curious Canadians warmed her overmuch, she found herself turning to the tether. It was reflexive, the simple wish to share an experience. Yet all she felt for each glance was the cool sigh of that horrible place beyond all others. Beyond her understanding.

It made for an unpleasant counterpoint. Particularly when Hungry Neck was such a terrifically pleasant place; it was a small community spread over a very large distance, with the Serkis tract's nearest neighbors about as far as Praisegod's farm had been from the Estate, it seemed. This displacement wasn't unusual – what *was* unusual was that people living so far from one another should consider themselves a single community. "Well, it *is* Canada," was Kirk's theory. Dirk agreed. It was, indeed, Canada.

Whatever Patience had expected of the Serkis property, she was disappointed. They owned quite a bit of land – which Kirk assured her had come cheap – but were utilizing none of it. Patience was hardly an agricultural adept, but even she could recognize deep, fecund soil when she saw it; the dusting of snow couldn't hide that rich chocolate hue, and Patience could only imagine how pleasant it would smell when — if — the warm months ever returned.

Arable land laying fallow to one side, what the brothers had to their name was a single small cottage, which could fit either two rooms or four closets, and that was it.

"How much land do you guys own?" she asked incredulously.

"Ah…" Kirk and Dirk ticked off their fingers, counted on each other's fingers, shook their heads, started over. Simultaneously, they answered with two different numbers.

"What?"

"I'd thought it was six hundred," Kirk said to Dirk.

Dirk shrugged. "I bet you're right. I don't know where I got eight hundred."

"Well, now that you mention it, eight hundred is a familiar number."

"Six hundred's not exactly a stranger either, I'll say that much!"

"How's this, why don't we call it seven hundred and I'll throw in fishing rights on the lake."

Dirk stuck out his hand. "You've got a deal!"

Kirk shook Dirk's hand. "You drive a hard bargain, brother!"

"You're a savvy negotiator yourself, I'll say that much!"

"That's quite a lot!"

"Thank you!"

They continued to shake hands, pump after pump after pump.

Patience cleared her throat. "Um…you two live alone here?"

"Sure do!" they replied in unison.

Here they were: Kirk and Dirk Serkis, the men who shit in the headwater.

Who were, by quite a large margin, the nicest people Patience had ever met.

It wasn't fair. None of this was fair. These two had simply been born up here. They hadn't done anything to deserve it. And they clearly didn't appreciate how fortunate they were. They had no idea how many people lived downstream.

And goddamnit, their kindness made it very, very difficult to dislike them.

It wasn't fair, Patience groused to herself even as she smiled at the brothers' hospitality. It wasn't fair that the world should be so unfair as a matter of course.

She shivered as a lonely chill sloughed through the tether. It could, she tentatively granted herself, be said that there was more than one way to live upstream from someone else.

F I V E

THEY SERVED PATIENCE SALT PORK, FISH VENISON, POTA-toes, and beaver-tail soup. It had been ages since she'd eaten this well. Had she ever? Before she could answer that for herself, they brought her Indian corn, buffalo hump, smoked trout, boil-ed mutton, peas and dried onions. She told the Serkis brothers she was quite full, but thank you. Recognizing they'd gone too far, they only made her some rubbaboo, their favorite treat com-prised of flour, water, maple sugar, and pemmican. Patience ma-naged a few bites — it was quite good, but she was truly stuffed. Forgetting she'd said that, the Serkis brothers assumed she hadn't liked the rubbaboo, and instead rustled up some wild rice, berries, rutabagas, and high wine they'd picked up on their last trip to market. Patience reminded them that she was absolutely packed to the gills, but thank you so much. Chastened, they brought her chocolate. Which, alright, maybe Patience wasn't *totally* full after all.

Naturally, it occurred to her that they were fattening her up to eat her later. Good luck to them; if they tried to stick her with a fork, she was liable to explode with force enough to demolish this cabin and half their tract besides.

The more she learned about them, though, the more she came to recognize that the truth was both simple and impossible to accept: Kirk and Dirk were truly swell, because sometimes, people could just be swell. If only they were given the chance.

If they were fortunate to be able to give it to themselves.

"How do you guys have so much food here?" she asked them as they all lounged around a fire nearly as well-fed as herself.

The Serkis brothers looked at each other, then back to Patience. "We don't have so much food, I wouldn't have said," Dirk replied.

Patience meant to gesture back towards the table, still strewn with the wreckage of her feast, but couldn't manage to swing her arm around. "I just ate so much, though!"

Kirk nodded. "That checks out, then!"

"...huh?"

"The reason we don't *have* so much food is because you *ate* so much food!"

Dirk nodded. "Your reasoning is sound, Kirk!"

"I appreciate you saying as much!"

Patience managed to push herself up onto her elbow. "Did I...did I just eat all of your food?"

Dirk shrugged. "Only so much of it."

"Oh my god!" She made to sit all the way up, but her belly got stuck against her thighs, so she rolled back down to the ground. "I'm so sorry!"

The brothers gawped at her, possessed of a terror wildly incommensurate to the situation. "What?"

"Whatever for?"

"You've done nothing wrong!"

Patience came to rest and clapped her hands to her forehead. "I ate all your food!"

"Only so much!"

"I'm so sorry, I..." she shook her head. "I had no idea!"

"How could you have?" Kirk asked.

"I don't know!" Patience nearly sobbed. "I just kept ea-"

"No," Dirk interrupted, "and I am *so* sorry for interrupting you like a familiar smell, but what I think my brother meant by asking how could you have, and brother please let me know if I do you wrong by trying to speak on your behalf..."

"I will indeed," Kirk nodded, "but I trust you and love you with all of my heart."

"That's how I feel!"

"Hoorah!"

"At any rate," Dirk reassured Patience, "my dear brother meant to ask you how could you have known the quantity of food we did or did not possess." He turned to his brother. "Is that fair to say?"

"It is indeed," Kirk agreed, "and it was well said at that."

"Oh, that's kind of you!"

"I would have said it was *very* me, eh?"

"Ha ha!"

"Ha ha!"

Patience pulled her hands away from her face. "You're not mad?" Hearing it posed aloud, she realized that even if the answer to the question as intended was 'no,' there were other meanings that might have a more affirmative response. "You're not mad *at me*?" she clarified.

"Of course not!" Dirk yelped.

"How could we be?" Kirk mewled.

"It was us who fed *you*!"

"A guest is entitled to the very best a host has to offer, such has always been our belief."

Unable to help herself, Patience looked around the cramped cabin and wondered, "do you entertain often?"

"Never before!"

"You're the first!"

"How are we doing?"

"We are always looking to improve!"

"What would you rate this visit, on a scale of one to seven?"

"Kirk, I'm wondering if maybe we ought to employ an even-numbered scale."

"Why's that?"

"Oh, no reason. Seven works for me!"

"So, dear guest, with one as the best and seven as the worst, how would you rank our performance as hosts today?"

"Um..." Patience fought down a burp. "One's the best?"

"Which one?" Kirk asked.

"Oh come now Kirk, of course she means you."

"Don't sell yourself short brother! My feet were dragging when it came to ferrying in the peas, that certainly-"

"No no," Patience cut in like a compliment, "sorry, that's not what I mean. I meant...I was asking if one was the best score on this scale."

"Oh, ha ha!"

"Ha ha!"

"Yes it is!"

"Well," Patience beamed as best she could from flat on her back, "then you two are a one!"

"Zero!" the brothers shouted together, and collapsed with laughter.

"Which," Kirk gasped, "is how much food we have left!"

"Ha ha!"

"Ha ha!"

Patience watched the Serkises climb to their feet, clutch each other by the elbows and dance around the living room. Suddenly the summertime snow falling outside the window behind them was the least of her questions.

S I X

THE REASON THESE TWO CANUCKLEHEADS DIDN'T HAVE any food (beyond 'Patience ate it all') became immediately apparent, leaving only the mystery of how the hell they'd acquired so much in the first place.

Kirk and Dirk were, apparently, *allegedly*, fur traders. In this they were resounding failures, due to their inability to acquire any fur in a halfway reliable manner. Or rather, their unwillingness. The brothers were more than capable trackers, and dead hands when it came to marksmanship. What they lacked was the will to point their rifle at something cute and fuzzy and shoot it in the face. Ordinarily, this wouldn't even be a laudable quality in a person; it would just be baseline human decency. But in two self-identified fur traders, this was certainly a tick in the 'weaknesses' column. Lucky for them, tracking was all the way at the top of 'strengths'; so refined were their skills, they could identify a sick or wounded animal purely by the marks of its passage. These they would pursue from a respectful distance, until such time as the critter finally died a natural death. At which point, the Serkis brothers would whisk the carcass off before any predators had a chance to desecrate it. They were, in brief, the ultimate scavengers of Lake Ontario.

And that was where they left it. Patience looked from one to the other. "Don't you have to, like, cut the animals up? To get the fur?"

"And the meat, sure we do," Kirk nodded.

"The meat and the fur," Dirk concurred.

"Ok…" Patience raised her eyebrows. "So *that* doesn't bother you?"

"What?"

"The…" she pantomimed vivisection.

Kirk tilted his head. "The slicing?"

Dirk titled his head the other way, at the same angle. "The dicing?"

Patience shivered. "Yeah. That."

The brothers laughed together. "Oh, certainly not!" Dirk boomed.

"All part of the job."

"And we've never gotten any complaints, eh?"

"Well, there was that one time."

Dirk looked skyward. "Which time?"

"With the moose."

Patience, Ambrose

"Ah, right."

"The moose?" Patience inquired.

Dirk nodded to Kirk. "You can tell her."

"That's awfully generous, but it's your story to tell."

"You tell it far better than I do."

"Well, it's awfully generous, just like I mentioned."

"My pleasure."

"Mine too. Ok." Kirk turned to Patience. "One time there was a moose that we thought was dead, but it wasn't."

"…"

"…"

In the nicest way she possibly could, Patience asked, "…and?"

"And that about covers it."

Dirk placed a hand on Kirk's shoulder. "May I?"

"By all means."

"You did a tremendous job."

"Did I miss a trick?"

"Just the one."

"Oh, about the moose noise?"

"That's the one."

"Rats! Or should I say 'moose'?"

"I think it's pluralized as 'mice'."

"Is it?"

"They are."

"I never knew that!"

"You didn't?"

"That two mooses are mice?"

"Which two?"

"Any two."

"Not the one that made the moose noise."

"If there'd been another one, though."

"Then what?"

"They'd be mice."

"Really?"

"Yeah!"

"I never knew that!"

"*You* taught *me!*"

"I'd put it more along the lines of, we're always learning from one another."

"I couldn't agree more."

"Bring it in, brother."

"With alacrity!"

The Serkis brothers hugged.

"But then what do you call two mouses?"

"Mice."

"They're the same?"

"Not technically, I guess. They do look it though."

"Mice and mice?"

"You can just say 'mice'."

"Mice?"

"Yeah!"

"But how do you know if I mean mooses mice or mouses mice?"

"I don't know what you mean."

"That's just what I was afraid of."

Patience knew then that she would never, ever, hear the end of the tale of the moose that seemed dead but was not. Which was fine by her. Just then all she wanted was sweet, glorious sleep. She feared that she would only dream of terrible mouse/moose chimeras. But, she admitted to herself, that'd be an improvement over that world of obsidian revelries into which she gazed, each time she sought her brother. And which seemed increasingly to reach for her, unsought.

S E V E N

THE TASKS WERE SIMPLE, THOUGH THEIR PURPOSE LAY beyond Ambrose's understanding. His charge was simply to act as an extension of Bulstrode's will. Be the gust of wind which splatters a newspaper across the window of a barbershop, alerting a man mid-trim to a significant headline he might otherwise have missed. Be the guitar string that breaks, forcing the troubadour to take five, and ultimately skip the song that would have kicked off the bar fight. Be the rock which slips from beneath a running foot, turning the ankle to which it is attached and confining the foot (and the rest of its human) to bed at a time when their presence out in the world might have served a purpose contrary to Bulstrode's mysterious ends.

That was what it always came down to, of course. Bulstrode had given Ambrose a tool in life, so that Bulstrode could use Ambrose *as* a tool in death. And who has ever explained the purpose of a hospital to the shovel which first breaks ground on it? How could one begin to? Because what the hell did a shovel know about the practice of medicine?

Ambrose understood the dynamic, and his role in it. Understood it all too well. Far better than his sister did, as she scuttled about in the snow, imagining herself to be foraging to replenish the empty pantry of her hosts. Ambrose could feel her musing on the power of these headwaters, awe-struck by the deafening pops of summer ice shifting on the lake. *That,* Patience imagined, *is power.* Horse-sized floes tossed on an imperceptible current dead-set on making its way downstream, carrying with it all the shit it could. Like fireflies, Ambrose saw the births and deaths of Patience's little misapprehensions.

Power was not a thing unto itself. That was what Patience could never realize, from so near the soil. Power was nothing more than the weight of what could be credibly dangled over others. Whether they knew it or not.

It was something Ambrose had. For the first time in his life. And all it had taken was his death. Ha, ha.

But Ambrose recognized it for what it was. He had labored beneath its shadow for too long not to. Bulstrode had given Ambrose power over the living, however indirect, to distract from the power Bulstrode held over him.

Power taken was freedom. Power received was misdirection. This was the fact.

Which was why Ambrose simply observed his sister, in those interludes when he was not doing Bulstrode's bidding, or else amusing himself with a jaunt through history (for as terrifying as it could be, serving as the emissary for a demon, let it not be said that the gig was without perks). There were still fleshy little emotions of which Ambrose became aware, from time to time. Feelings of abandonment, of rage, of profound sadness and loss. He was not beyond awareness of phenomena such as these. Feeling, perhaps, but not awareness. And besides…she still reached for him, did she not? Her efforts were genuine, were they not? To answer: she did, and they were. Yet Ambrose could not help but feel…betrayed. There was that, and he was aware of it. Betrayal.

It was precisely that intensity of, oh alright, *feeling* which gave

Patience, Ambrose

Ambrose the strength to simply observe. Yes, he increasingly found he saw ways to nudge Patience in the directions which would lead her to greater feats of focus. He could be the wind, the rock, the string. He could train her without her knowledge, and she could yank the tether to free him from Bulstrode's piggy little clutches. There was no body into which he could be returned…but he could be freed from this place. By Patience. And the bond their mother had given them.

Ambrose could see precisely how to make Patience do this.

Yet that feeling of betrayal stayed his hand. For it would be he that *gave* Patience the power she needed. Which was to say… he would be exercising control over her.

Which would solve nothing. Even if it pulled Ambrose from this horrible little well of death and nightshine, it would not address that feeling.

If the choices were between watching his sister life a full life, forgetting him, perhaps making performative little lunges across the tether, and dying an old spinster, thus consigning him to an eternity at Bulstrode's right hoof…or *forcing* her to act on his behalf, without her knowing she had been so forced…Ambrose happily chose the former.

This put him starkly at odds with the nation he called home. All the more reason to choose as he did.

Having said that…

Ambrose left his sister by the lake, as she lost interest in her foraging and toddled off to watch the ice crack. For down in Louisiana (if it made sense to think of it as *down*, from such a vantage as this), there was a plantation owner named Barry, and there was an Overseer named Hilditch. And a thought occurred to Ambrose regarding these two men, and how they might be nudged, step by step, into murdering each other.

Mercy was a gift from power. The granting of it, at any rate. And gifts came only at the pleasure of the giver. This, too, was a fact.

PART THREE

HER GUIDE THE RIVER

in the blink

b   l   i   n   k

ISABEL WAS RIGHT. THE BELL WAS A-RINGIN' IN THE FAR OFF land, only that land wasn't so far off for him anymore. He was, indeed, the thrumming of the bell. Bong gong, ding dong, there he was, rattling through ribcages, rumbling up to the heart from the naked soles. Count the peals to learn the hour; they never end. The far off land was one in which the tyranny of time had been overthrown, a coup against chronology. One would be tempted to say this happened long before he'd arrived, but that was precisely the sort of thing one still burdened by the yoke of sequentialism *would* say. Such things made little sense, to those in the blink. Which, in turn, made little sense to Ambrose.

Could he still be called Ambrose? If one so chose. If it made things easier. Was he still a he, or had he been reduced to an it? That was perhaps going too far. That was perhaps overstating the case. Perhaps not. Certainly, it didn't matter. To label something doesn't alter its fundamental being. Embrace an anchor, call it a life vest, leap from a long pier. See how that works out.

b   l   i   n   k

THE BELL ARRIVED IN SUBOPTIMAL CONDITION. THE CASTING had been shoddy, the packaging insufficient, and the handling, one could safely assume, rough. Such was to be expected from English ironmongers, Pass and Stow grumbled to each other. Never send an Englishman to do a Colonist's job. So they melted down the bell and recast it, adding a pinch or three of copper to the concoction. The inscriptions remained as they were, though. "Proclaim LIBERTY Throughout All The Land Unto All The Inhabitants Thereof. Leviticus XXV v. X." A noble sentiment from a good book, one in which it would be unseemly to tolerate a crack. So a pinch of copper in the recast. This pleased the Assembly, which pleased Pass and Stow.

The bell a-rang from the belfry of the Pennsylvania State House on July 8th, 1776. The Declaration of Independence was to be read, to proclaim LIBERTY throughout all the land unto all the inhabitants thereof. So it seemed, to those for whom heeding the ringer's summons was an option. Their laborers stayed home. For as cuddly as the tenth verse in the twenty-fifth chapter of Leviticus may sound, one need only look a score and some verses later in the very same chapter to find the dreadful harmonics of that bell a-ringing for Independence. There was no need to immortalize, for example, the forty-fifth and forty-sixth of the third book's verses along the skirt of the bell. "Moreover of the children of the strangers that sojourn among you, of them shall ye buy, and of their families that are with you, which they begat in your land: and they shall be your possession. And ye shall take them as an inheritance for your children after you, to inherit them for a possession; they shall be your bondmen forever." This wasn't something that needed reiterating. Freedom, independence, this was news. This was something that needed to be said, for it was not something that went without saying.

"I yield slowly," Chief Justice John Marshall once confessed, "and reluctantly to the conviction that our Constitution cannot last." Then, as all humans are wont to do, he died. July 6th, 1835, to be precise. The Pass and Stow bell pealed for his funeral, cracking once again in the process, two days later, on July 8th, 1835. Fifty-nine years to the day from its declaration of the Declaration. Marshall's successor, Roger Taney, would decide the Dred Scott case, denying even free black men American citizenship, twelve years after that (albeit not to the date – but wouldn't *that* have been something). Not symmetrical enough to be a truly head-spinning series of coincidences, but there's a certain slanted poetry to it, is there not? Consider this, then: twenty-three years elapsed between the bell's being hung and fixed in the Statehouse steeple, and its a-ringin' to announce the reading of the Declaration of Independence. It was, further, twenty-three years that passed between the signing of that document and the birth of Patience and Ambrose.

Coincidence? Naturally. Time often rhymes, which was perhaps why it was of no use in the blink. The lives of others, upon which one could eavesdrop as easily as glancing from a tall, well-scrubbed window, would drown one in poetry should their chronology be honored. Best to divest them of their lyricism. For one's own sake.

b l i n k

MORE RHYMES IN TIME: JULY 4TH, THE DATE OF THE NATION'S birth as it was (albeit twenty-three years later) of Patience and Ambrose's, was also the day upon which two of the nation's founders passed from the scene. "Thomas Jefferson survives," John Adams sighed with his final breath, which just went to show how much *he* knew: Jefferson had died five hours earlier. Five, incidentally, was the number of years in the future that another founder and ex-President, James Monroe, would die. Also on July 4th.

Many would take this to be a mark of divine favor; apparently, God blessed His most favored nation by grinding its luminaries into dust on the very dates that nation ought, by whatever right it could be said to possess, to be lauding its own existence. Poor William of Ockham, long in the grave. That old razor of his would no doubt had revealed contempt a more logical motive for the Lord than veneration. But then, the razor would have had a bit of work to do on The Big Man Himself.

But pour one out for William and leave him to rot, for there are clues enough in the Good Book. "For unto me the children of Israel are servants; they are my servants whom I brought forth out of the land of Egypt," the fifty-fifth verse of the twenty-fifth chapter of Leviticus insists, concluding, with a bluster that rings of compensation, "I am the *LORD* your God."

Here, perhaps, is the root of that hunger which happily mistakes contempt for affection. Behold the world in which freedom means having only one master.

b l i n k

THE MYSTICAL, MORBID QUALITIES OF THE NATION'S BIRTHDAY have scarcely been exhausted, though: July 4th of the year following the synchronized expirations of Adams and Jefferson saw the demise of slavery in New York, as initially laid out in the Gradual Emancipation act of 1799. One would do well, though, to remember those dreadful harmonics of the bell yet a-ringin'. What freedom meant as a concept, between its giant, implicit air quotes, and what it meant as a law to be applied to the real world, was an unbridgeable chasm into which all would sooner or later tumble. What lay at the bottom? *Was* there a bottom to be found? Perhaps that was where Ambrose was. Falling, falling through the unlit shadows.

b l i n k

TWO YEARS BEFORE THAT, THE STILL-EXTANT ADAMS' SON, then the current president, expatiated to Congress upon the connection between liberty and power, a connection most wholly encompassed by the word *is*. "Let us not be unmindful that liberty is power," he lectured, "that the nation blessed with the largest portion of liberty must in proportion to its numbers be the most powerful nation on Earth." This he did with the aim of exciting the federal assembly to enact internal improvements in the vein of those undertaken independently by some of the states. His favored example was the Erie Canal, which would only that year complete construction. He also mentioned the University of Virginia, though he did not, in his catalogue of internal improvements, mention the old hickory tree at the southern end of Pleasance Square. That horrible tree was, after all, rather low down on the list of noteworthy beautification endeavors, and besides, the era of beautification had come to an end. Consigned to the past were the Hellenistic pretentions to elegance in all things – the age of the utilitarian was at hand.

b l i n k

AGGY HUNG FROM THE INTERNAL IMPROVEMENT AS HER FATHER had before her. He who once was Ambrose saw this happen as though he were there. In a way, he supposed, he had been.

b l i n k

"TERRIFIC WORK!" NO-GOOD BULSTRODE SHOUTED, HIS VOICE wholly filling the deathwell. The creature was no longer making pretenses to hoghood, was something else entirely. Truly, he didn't have to shout. Ambrose had no choice but to hear him.

The work had nothing to do with the bell. With the improvements. These were personal explorations. Though it hardly made sense to speak of the personal. For Ambrose was uncertain of his personhood. He had been here so long. Decades and centuries. He had always been. In a way. He supposed.

b   l   i   n   k

THE ERIE CANAL, WHICH SQUIGGLED ITS WAY ALONG NEW YORK state like the infamous crack in the famous bell that was still a-ringin', albeit somewhere else, linked Lake Erie to the Hudson. The impact this had on American trade could scarcely be over-stated. Suddenly, shipping goods to the wealthiest outposts in the Midwest was both financially and logistically enticing. Within years, the population along the canal surged, most notably in and around New York City, which almost overnight snatched the mantle of economic and social center of the nation, much to the dismay of once-bustling ports like Philadelphia and New Orleans, Boston and Baltimore. This massive influx of cash, which naturally precipitated a comparable influx of humanity, created a number of small logistical crises. The city spilled out of itself, shoddy wooden shanties sprouting up in higher and tighter clusters to support the demands of a hungry workforce flooding the financial and trade districts. Speaking of flooding, a biblical deluge was something from which New York City might have benefited just then: the rapidly increasing population taxed the city's doddering infrastructure, requiring water in quantities that far outpaced the city's ability to provide. Sanitation suffered, the most dramatic consequence of which was a cholera epidemic in 1832. There was also no fire department to speak of, unless one wanted to greatly overestimate the capabilities of the disparate, and often unfriendly, factions of ill-trained volunteers.

This sort of evaluative error was one absolutely no one would make again after December of 1835 (the year Chief Justice Marshall died and the liberty bell cracked, not that that matters, not that it rhymes), when a dry-goods warehouse in Hanover Square caught fire. The night was cold, and the firefighters were tired from having extinguished a blaze the previous night. To call the response sluggish would do a disservice molluscs everywhere. When the severity of the spreading flames finally mustered the firefighters to their self-appointed duties, each faction arrived on the scene to discover a number of their rival firefighters along with them. A grand squabbling began, primarily as to which group would have first crack at pulling valuables from the fire and "misplacing" them. There followed feats of strength, young men attempting to impress one another by unlatching their horses and dragging the hose trucks nearer the flames themselves. By the time they deigned to favor the inferno with such attention, it had passed the point of requiring an audience – the blaze was self-affirming, needing only the aforementioned shoddy wooden shanties to feed its giddy expansion. At any rate, the freeze of the night had locked the hoses with ice. Desperate to rob the inferno of its fuel, the firefighters took to preemptive damage control, evacuating anyone in the path of the flames (and naturally relieving them of some of their precious valuables in the process), attempting to rob the fire of its fuel by, um, blowing up the buildings in the path of the ever-spreading inferno. It was ultimately the east river that halted the conflagration, and only after the fire had torn through thirteen acres of land, devouring seventeen blocks and over seven hundred buildings. The fire crippled New York's economic gains; in the aftermath of the disaster, all but three of New York's twenty-six insurance firms folded, much to the delight of the more solvent agencies in Connecticut.

The most lasting legacy of this conflagration was, perhaps, the famous grid system in which Lower Manhattan's streets were reconstructed (with a water supply being made a far higher priority). The tragedies were, fortunately, of a primarily economic sort. Not to downplay the misery of destitution, but, well, better off-bread than dead, eh? Alas, there were three fatalities in the conflagration, a body count manageable enough for most papers to address with no small amount of detail. These details included the names of the deceased, which were indeed widely disseminated through the press. Two of them are best entrusted to the pink mists of history; time being little more than a heuristic employed by limited human minds, their misfortunes may still be considered fresh, even ongoing.

The third name, though, was of indirect importance to whatever Ambrose could be considered, by virtue of being exceptionally relevant to someone who had once been still was would be quite important to him. He recalled her almost as dimly as he had recognized the name of the third deceased.

Praisegod Pinchwife, a man alone in the city, trapped by, and so consigned to, the flames.

b   l   i   n   k

OH YES, HERE WAS A FEELING OCCURRING, READY TO be noticed. Was it satisfaction? Was it a chef's kiss, a thumbs-up, a bit of enthusiastic footwork in the face of good news?

It was, it was, it was. It would have been bald-faced fibbery to pretend otherwise. However removed from his mortal form Ambrose may have been, to see the man who had sold him down the river fully consumed by fire, and to see this happen of its own accord, without Ambrose's needing to do any nudging… well, it warmed him. Warmed the both of them, really. One more so than the other, perhaps, though at that moment it would have been difficult to say which of the two that was.

b   l   i   n   k

WHO COULD POSSIBLY APPRECIATE THE LETHARGY with which news spread across the colonies better than Ambrose? By 1822 America had more regular readers of newspapers than any other nation, yet the daily rag remained a parochial affair, with publications in even the largest citites failing to crack circulation above four thousand. To be fair, though, news could travel no faster than the paper it was printed on, in which case, why not take an extra twelve hours to give it a bit of provincial topspin?

Indeed, the speed at which information was disseminated had scarcely increased in living memory, at least in a manner appreciable to the average citizen. An early, blunt-force attempt at faster-than-horse communication was made by launching a cannon relay along the Hudson – one cannon fired, the next in line fired the moment the sound from the first cannon reached it, the next being signaled similarly, and so on down the line. Though the only message this heavy-artillery daisy-chain was capable of conveying, of course, was 'kaboom.'

A not-entirely irrelevant sentiment, one supposes, when one

considers the seismic impact the death of Praisegod Pinchwife may have had on some people in the auspicious year of 1835.

Which Ambrose certainly did. He considered that in a manner which slowly brought his sister back into the storm of thoughts which now constituted him. Truth be told, his attention as regarded Patience had flagged. Just as her attention to him had. Yet suddenly, she returned to the front of Ambrose's thoughts. Which, as that was all he was…said quite a lot.

b l i n k

WATCH THE NEWS SPREAD IN EVERY DIRECTION, LIKE ink through an exposed vein. Tragedy in New York, three dead, here are their names. Drink deep of their misery, for it is far from your own. Enjoy.

1836

O N E

ONCE UPON A TIME SHE'D HAVE FELT BAD ABOUT PULL-
ing the trigger. That was before the hunger had really set in. Now
all that stayed her finger from that inestimably overpowered little
sliver of metal was the want of a clearer shot.

Such as here, such as now. Patience, having long since discovered that the virtue to which she answered could be lethal in the
right circumstances, crouched on the small wooden platform
she'd nailed to the base of the most powerful of the maple's
boughs. She loved using maple trees to set her stands; the sturdy
bark made a steadier go of swinging her heavy tools around
twenty-five feet up. At present, she'd yet to fall either during or

after the process of hanging the small two-by-two platform, but she'd resigned herself to the likelihood that it was simply a matter of time.

Here and now, though: she crouched in the stand as she had for the past day and a half, quietly provisioning herself with nuts from the pantry and berries she'd picked on the way out here, the barrel of the Springfield flintlock resting upon her raised knee. Gaze fixed down the length of the rifle, she watched the young buck graze, oblivious to her presence. Which was precisely the way things had to be. Her firearm was fairly accurate by the standards of the day, but only to a range of fifty, perhaps sixty, *maybe* seventy yards if fortune so fancied. To attempt the shot when the quarry was any further – ninety-some yards, just as a for instance – would be to waste a perfectly good shot in more ways than one.

So Patience was as advertised; she waited, watched, finger resting lightly on the trigger, breath so slow it hardly lifted her chest, blinking only when the dry Ontario winter stung her eyes more than could be endured. Waiting for the deer to draw nearer, until it was well within range.

Some time later (the precise amount of time was irrelevant, and so she'd ceased making an effort gauge it), the hardy rack of veal on wheels grazed its way into the flintlock's effective firing range.

Patience pulled the trigger.

Her least favorite part now: the plume of smoke that belched from the mouth of the rifle, obscuring her vision, sometimes for up to seven seconds on windless days such as this one.

She stared helplessly into what her brother (whom she sought most every night…well, at least several times a week, but had not wholly found in, gosh, quite some years) might have called a mist, waiting for it to clear, waiting to see if her aim had been true, or if the buck had made its escape. In which case, it would be cabbage stew for dinner once again.

In moments such as these, Patience was nearly tempted to pray.

At long last, the mist parted to reveal the buck wounded, the shot having pierced it above the right shoulder. It pumped its mighty back legs, attempting to push itself to some kind of safety. The antlers on its head, still sheathed in velvet, had suddenly grown heavier than its neck could support; they plowed through the soil, catching on half-buried roots and heavy stones.

Patience grimaced. A clean shot was a salve to her conscience; at least the beast went quickly. These drawn out affairs were distasteful (and, once upon a time but no longer, disturbing), not least due to the necessity of her delivering the final blow with a blade rather than another shot. Ammunition was exhaustible, after all…whereas a sharp blade and a woman with the will to wield it were anything but.

She paced the buck, holding some fifteen steps behind, letting it bleed out a bit more, letting it lose its will to fight for life. Never again would she make the mistake of approaching a wounded deer that had yet to be bled of that fight; the last time she had, the horn nearest her had torn straight through her arm, the scars from which she still bore high on her left bicep. She was convinced that there remained a certain degree of strength she'd yet to, and likely never would, recover from the injury. Dirk and Kirk insisted she was still plenty strong, and a lot of other nice things besides.

Yes, Patience had run away and joined the Serkis: 1816 had

proven a dismal year in countless ways, yet those manifold miseries could be seen to possess a pointillistic sort of good fortune, if only one would (and, indeed, was privileged enough to be able to) take a great many steps back. For 1816 had brought her to the Serkis brothers, just when her need for a friendly face was greatest. Why not *two* friendly faces, then? Thus did a year of survival lead to a year of repayment, as Patience devoted 1817 to retroactively justifying the brothers' uncountable kindnesses, chiefly by restocking the pantry she had accidentally emptied. Yet foraging would only provide so much, and so she dug up their old rifles (far shoddier affairs than the Springfield she would purchase in 1835, the year of the fire in New York, the year before this one in which she paced the wounded buck at fifteen steps remove) and taught herself to hunt, through trial and error and error and error and finally more error, and then something that resembled, but was not, success. Determined to achieve the genuine article, Patience determined to remain through 1818, and the brothers were happy to have her. By the time she mastered the art of the subsistence kill, yielding enough surplus meat to be cured, smoked, and stored, she'd rather fallen in with the brothers, as they had become taken with her. She ceased to be a houseguest, and slowly, without ceremony, beneath the awareness of any of the three parties, became a member of the household.

After that, it had been a matter of living her life, that most impossible of all tasks.

Finally, the buck lost its will, collapsing to its chest and breathing its last. Patience dashed forward, relieved to finally have the chance to visit her mercy upon the sacrifice. She made three quick, deep slashes, and the buck was history.

T W O

THE SLAPSTICK TUMBLEDOWN IN WHICH THE SERKIS BRO-thers had been living when Patience met them was no more. She'd encouraged them, with a needling that certainly evoked the stabbier associations of the word, to take greater pride in their lodgings. And so, with her help, they did, rebuilding their quarters, and piece by piece, year after year, expanding their domicile to take advantage of all their land. With some help from the Serkis' "neighbors" (who remained as geographically distant, yet socially proximate, as ever), Patience constructed a sugar house and learned its operations, boiling and distilling sap from her beloved maples to make into syrup, which could then be taken to markets in southern Ontario and northern New York and sold for a not-inconsiderable profit. The money would then be put back into the homestead's infrastructure. While never becoming a full-fledged *business* – their chief concern remained subsistence – Patience helped the Serkis brothers assemble a comfortable surplus of specie, for which they were eternally grateful. Naturally, they insisted, it was by rights hers; they considered themselves mere debtors to her generosity. Such was how the Serkis brothers expressed their gratitude – by all but refusing the proffered largesse.

To wit: "Oh, I couldn't possibly," was how, for twenty years now, Kirk greeted any plate of food Patience placed in front of him, sometimes even if *he* had been the one to prepare it.

Patience had ceased replying to these *pro forma* demurrals quite some time ago. As always, she set some fresh venison in front

467

of each brother and sat down in her own seat, taking up a glass of the cider she'd taught herself to ferment. It had been her own innovation, to add some of their hoophouse-grown ginger to the concoction, an addition that was well received at home and at market.

"Staying warm in the woods, let's hope?" Dirk wondered.

"Plenty warm," Patience replied, a slight fib to avoid the consequence of the truth, which would be Kirk and Dirk making a gift of their entire armoires.

"Bit of strange news," Kirk announced.

"Oh," Dirk jumped, "we'll go straight in, shall we?"

"Terribly sorry, it needn't be so! We might dillydally around the shrubbery."

"I don't expect that'll be necessary."

"I'd simply hate to jump the broom, as it were."

"The gun?"

"In the closet, I expect."

"I'm sorry?"

"No, *I'm* sorry!"

"Whatever for?"

"Giving you the impression an apology was necessary when it most certainly was not."

"How kind of you!"

"Fellas," Patience cut in.

"Yes?"

She smiled. "Is all well?"

"Yes! Well…"

Patience glanced at Kirk. "What's the strange news?"

Kirk jumped, as though it was he who expected some sort of odd information. "Well, funny you should mention it, only I have some strange news for you!"

"Came lately in today's paper," Dirk jumped in.

"Whilst you were out fetching us our venison."

"Absolutely terrific by the way, such a terrific meal."

"Stupendous, even."

"Here, here!"

"Or," Kirk pounded his paunch, "here, *here*!"

"Ho ho!"

"In my tummy!"

"I espied your amusing statement!"

"I appreciated your laughter commemorating the same!"

"I was but obliging my natural response to mirth!"

What perhaps astonished Patience the most about these spasms of ballistic *bonhomie* was how endearing she still found them, even twenty years on. The brothers' giddiness for life, their savoring of its blessings, their imperviousness to its cruelties, was equal parts naïve and inspiring. The energy they had brought into Patience's life was hardly an antidote to all she had already suffered, nor inoculation against the sicknesses with which life would inevitably afflict her. It was…a kind of opiate. A high that never diminished, no matter how many hits she took.

That there was something hopeless about spending twenty years under the influence of even a metaphorical opiate had certainly occurred to her. It had been easy enough to ignore, though, given the sappy outlets she'd found for her natural sense of industry. And of course, if she were to find herself in a low mood (which she often did…and it was hardly a coincidence, that these depressions coincided with her futile turns towards the tether), a boost was only a conversation away.

Typically, anyway. Which was why it was so unnerving that

the Serkises would announce that they had strange news, *strange* being implicit each time they opened their mouths. Patience suspected that strange was, in this instance, a euphemism for bad.

"Are either of you ill?" she inquired nervously.

The Serkis brothers halted their conversation and nearly crashed headfirst into one another, so hasty were they in rushing to Patience's side.

"No no no, absolutely not!"

"We are fit as fiddles!"

"Say," Dirk wondered, "are fiddles simply the most fit of all the stringed instruments, or a-"

"Hang on," Patience interrupted, knowing that to remain silent would be to condone a dialectic on the relative fitness of stringed instruments (with an all-but-guaranteed detour into the woodwinds). "I'd like to hear the news, please."

Kirk nodded. "The news, yes, of course."

"Though it might perhaps be a more amenable arrangement for you to read it?" Dirk suggested.

Kirk brandished the latest edition of *The Ontario Rag* (the actual name of the paper), which Patience had neither seen nor heard him take up. This was a common enough occurrence, these little magic tricks, as each brother served as the other's perpetual misdirection. "Indeed, for the journalists employed will likely be possessed of more tact than either of us!"

"We are not known for our impeccable comport, as pertains to journalistic practices!"

"Only why should we be?"

"It is hardly as though either of us should see our names on the masthead," Dirk mused while brandishing the paper that his brother had only a moment ago been brandishing. Again, the

470

handoff had utterly eluded Patience.

"How does one approach the bedside manner of a John Took?"

"What'd he take?"

"Who?"

"John!"

"A newspaper apprenticeship, I imagine."

"Oh, you're referring to John Took, author of the article detailing the great fire of 1835, are you?"

"Indeed I am, thank you for remembering!"

"The pleasure is all mine!"

"Fire?" Patience interrupted. "What fire?"

"The one that killed your halfbrother-fakefather!" Dirk exclaimed. "Oh, heck!"

Patience had one million questions. Rather than ask them, though, she lunged forward and snatched the paper (which had once again passed to Kirk's hands) and read as quickly as she could.

T H R E E

THERE WERE NO DETAILS IN THE ARTICLE ABOUT WHAT her halfbrother-fakefather, whom the article identified as Peter "Praisegod" Pinchwife, was doing in New York City at the time of the fire. Not that it could possibly have provided all of the answers Patience sought. A bit of context from which to extrapolate would have been appreciated, though. What had become of him, after she had last seen him in Pennsylvania? Had he returned home? Gone to the Estate to confront Drummond about his dreaded "race-mixing"? Had he found a way to make his peace with the fact, or had he distanced himself from his Pinch-wife progenitors? What had become of Mary, of Ezekiel, of Flann?

These were questions with which she had never importuned herself, in the score years she'd been with the Serkis brothers. But now, knowing that the answers would forever elude her, curiosity grew bold.

"This is…" she mumbled, still staring at the page even after she'd thoroughly scourged the words upon it with her increasingly boggled eyes. The descriptions of the inferno were apocalyptic, almost ecstatic. They were also written by *The Ontario Rag's* own John Took, which rather called into question his unattributed accounts of the blaze. But nevermind that – if they bore even the scantest relation to truth, then the fire must have been a truly faith-shattering experience. She tried to imagine Praisegod, cornered in a building, on his knees, hands clasped, hurling prayers vainly into the flames as hell itself cinched tightly around him. Oh, what a terrible conclusion for such a penitent man! Patience had never imagined herself as having a great deal of sympathy for Praisegod, yet to know that he had met his end in such a nightmarish fashion stung her. She didn't know whether or not he deserved it…but in either case, she'd never have wished it upon him.

Yet something deep within her – that part of herself which pulled the trigger on a buck in the crosshairs – spoke more plainly. And what it said was *good riddance.*

She spent the remainder of the day with the news, turning it over in her head, struggling to make sense of her own curiously shaded reaction to it. Yes, she finally conceded, she was hardly sorry to hear that *any* Pinchwife had met their demise. All were bastards undeserving of her sympathy, and Praisegod was no exception. Yet…she still felt something for him, in the manner if not fact of his annihilation. And at precisely the same time, she regretted the lack of reckoning visited upon him.

He ought to have been forced to confront his misdeeds, to articulate and atone for them. Granted, death by hellfire certainly seemed to qualify as punishment…but it was hard to view it in that light. For it had not been Patience (or, perhaps more pointedly, Ambrose) visiting said hellfire upon him. Which left her wondering if she was fixated on redress less for its own sake, more for how it would have made *her* feel. Enlightening to recognize, that was. Terrifying to accept.

These were not the sorts of things she could discuss with the Serkis brothers. It wasn't that they didn't understand where Patience had come from; she had shared each and every detail of her life with them, even the most fantastical facets. And the brothers, bless their oversized hearts, had never betrayed anything other than absolute belief in what Patience had told them.

Which was, in a way, the problem.

Oh, how Patience missed her brother. There had been a few times in the years since his…his passing, that she had been almost positive she had felt him. Yet no matter how many times she reached for him, no matter how carefully she marshalled her attention, she had never truly found him. Which told her it was only her grief playing havoc with her mind.

But two nights after she had learned of Praisegod's death, the knots into which her brain was tying itself had shown no signs of loosening on their own. She needed to unburden herself, with someone who might understand what she had gone through, how that spoke to what she was thinking now.

So, feeling faintly ridiculous, but knowing there was nothing to lose, Patience sat on the edge of her bed and focused. She closed her eyes, took a deep breath, did her best to focus without effort. To luxuriate in the ease of the...thing. What word had Ambrose used? It had been one that sounded odd coming from him. It w-

Enterprise, Patience's mind supplied, in a voice not entirely her own.

"Thanks," she whispered out loud.

She opened her eyes. Stared across the empty room, to the far wall. Which was just a wall. Nothing else.

...alright.

Slowly, Patience closed her eyes once again, and focused. Sat back as best she could, attempting to unmoor the seat of cognition from the center of her head. She relaxed. She surrendered. She let the *enterprise* wash over her.

Once she awoke from her accidental nap, she sat once more at the head of her bed and tried a new approach.

She focused as hard as she possibly could.

And, wonder of wonders...almost immediately, she felt something stir.

So shocking was the sensation that Patience snapped her eyes open and shot to her feet.

She frowned at the far wall for a moment. Was that...seriously what had locked her out of the connection that was rightfully hers for all these years? That she hadn't been applying *enough* effort? When Ambrose's whole *thing* had been that she apply as little as possible?

Boy, if that was the case...she was gonna have some stern

words for him. After she got out all of the much warmer ones she wanted to say.

Once more, she sat on the bed and shut her eyes. And *focused*.

It was like trying to use a limb that had fallen asleep. Or... no, not quite. Not at all like that, actually. It was more like trying to regrow a limb that had been amputated, that she might grab a thread of fire and *pull*.

Patience felt sweat beading on her forehead. A head that was going hollow. Empty? Dizzy. Lightheaded. She was holding her breath.

She let out an explosive sigh, sucked in more air, and reminded herself to *breathe*.

It was like trying to think of a word, it was on the tip of her tongue, she could *see* what the word *looked like* but it wasn't *speaking* to her yet...

...it was like reaching for a beloved keepsake that had rolled under the armoire, she could *feel* it bumping up against the tips of her fingers, she just needed to find a *little* more stretch in her arm, just reach a *fraction of an inch* further...

...it was like remembering the word why you came in the room the billfold the keepsake the knot the loose end loose pulling grip pulling releasing.

It was only then that she saw the folly of Ambrose's instruction. The first step was to try, try as hard as possible. It was only once one had done a certain amount of work, that one could understand the limits of a shoulder to the wheel.

So she opened her mind wide to see what gloomy winds might catch her sails.

F O U R

WHAT WAS MORE DREADFUL; THAT IT MIGHT BE A TOWER, a dismal edifice in its own right? Or that it might be but a single column, bolstering an even more gargantuan construction? In either case, the purpose was clear. This was an object of worship. All hail.

Okay, maybe not *all*. That's the rub, right? Not all hail, just a few at a time. But 'some hail', that's not an injunction, it's a weather forecast. Who's gonna respect that? If you leave the door open for some of the people to not hail, how many people are going to volunteer for the hailing? 'Hey, save me a kneeling spot, I wanna make sure I'm in the bunch that hails!' Actually, you know what, probably a lot of people would do that. There's a sucker born every minute, but how many people are born every minute? And how many suckers are there? Do the math, it doesn't check out. There would need to be dozens of suckers born every minute to explain the sheer…*proliferation* of suckers in the general populace, right? Unless, and this is something to think about, some of those suckers…are *self-made* suckers. Unless, at the end of the day, there are self-made suckers always on the lookout for something new to hail. Do you follow me? In a way, it's a beautiful opportunity they've got. If you don't live forever, and most folks don't, you never *really* see the effects of your causes, or how your causes are still just more effects. Immortality makes you jaded, see what I'm saying? Having a, uh, a, a *cap,* you know, a limit, not having to take in the whole thing, that's kind of a blessing, when you really think about it. No no,

I'm serious. Think about it.

Listen...

...

We've got an eavesdrop-

prrrrrrrrrr...

Patience opened her eyes to find a nightmare-black cat sitting on her chest, staring directly at her. From the back of its throat, and yet somehow much, much deeper, of a lower register than any cat could ever hope to reach, a purr rumbled forth like approaching thunder.

prrrrrrrrrr...

Patience tried to sit up, but found her prostrate body (when had she fallen to the ground? She hoped desperately that the landing had been soft) unresponsive. Arms, legs, head, nothing. Even her jaw refused to open, her vocal chords obstinately refusing to scream.

Quite unfortunate, as she would have liked nothing better than to scream just then. Because the cat was getting heavier. And heavier. And heavier. Patience's ribs felt on the verge of buckling into her innards.

"Whoopsie!" called a voice from Patience's hip. "Innocent screw-up in progress here, signals flipped like a griddle chip!" A frog hopped onto her clavicle, between her head and the cat's. "No need to crush the poor ribbit," the frog told the cat.

The cat didn't get any lighter, but it ceased to grow heavier. It also, as Patience's eyes adjusted to the dark, turned out to be not a cat, but a groundhog. A purring groundhog.

It turned its glowing red eyes down to the pitch-black frog, clementine-sized, with its webbed forefeet turned coyly inwards. It struck Patience as, in some strange way, familiar.

"She was spying on us," the groundhog whined.

"Hardly by choice," the frog sighed. "Swept our way in a blowabout, nothing more."

Patience didn't realize paws could be accusatory, but an accusatory paw was just what the groundhog pointed at her. "She's gonna take my ideas."

"Come now, let's not do this again."

"Agripides!"

"Yes, yes, Agripides, how *could* we forget about that disreputable chappie, when you're oh so fond of reminding us?"

Again, the accusatory paw. "She's gonna take my ideas and not give me credit!"

"I'll see to this," the frog placated the groundhog. "The boy'll be getting restive, eager to hear the end of your interminable extemporizing I've no doubt. Off you go."

Remarkably, off the groundhog did indeed go, vanishing with nothing but a quiet *pop* sound.

The frog sighed and turned to Patience. "You must forgive our dear He's so v-"

Using her newly reclaimed mobility, Patience tucked her elbows beneath her and hoisted herself into a half-seated position. "Our dear what?"

Suddenly finding herself flat on her back yet again, Patience once more tucked her elbows beneath her and hoisted herself into a half-seated position. "What the f-"

"Ah," the frog mused, "yes, yes, my mistake. Some of my sort don't go in for a name that suits the parlance of their particular realm considers it an ind…oh, apologies most sincerely tendered," it mumbled as Patience once again tucked her elbows and hoisted herself into a half-seated position. "Point is, those sorts of names don't exactly roll off the tongue, and even if one should find a tongue as roly-poly as mine, the human cochlea's only got so much spin, you see."

"I...don't."

"No? More succinctly, then: our IP-infringement-fearing friend's name, properly pronounced, is such a sound as might briefly separate any human that hears it from their consciousness."

"Ok..."

"Well, the bit to clock is is very sensitive...oh, I really am sorry, it just sort of slips out. *The entity in question*, we'll call it, fancies intellectual property among the most elevated of the virtues, a rather skewed sense of priority dating back to the Agripides incident. Mycenaean fellow, you'll never have heard of him, which I dare say is rather the point got it into...oh do please excuse me, *the entity in question*, let me back up a bit, *the entity in question* rather loves the sound of its own voice, which puts it in a rarified company of one, you see what I imply by so saying, at any rate the dunderhead would often rather hold court than go out and accomplish anything worth crowing about, much rather sit around and blather on about the nature of accomplishment itself in fact, the entity in question makes a mockery of our whole lot if you ask me, but ribbit ribbit ribbit, now *I'm* vanishing into my own navel! The frog and short of it is got it into...*the entity in question*, I'm so dreadfully sorry, cannot apologize enough, *the entity in question* got it into its head that Agripides, Mycenaean fellow I mentioned from a moment ago and who, until now, one might be forgiven for believing to have been a superfluous detail, slipping from the narrative as he did, at any rate, Agripides somehow, I suspect with the aid of some particularly gnarly plants which make for the funniest of all cigarettes, but I'm hardly qualified to speak on matters respiratory, at any rate, Agripides somehow eavesdropped in one of *the entity in question*'s excruciating, utterly unsolicited symposiums. *The entity in question* divined this by perceived similarities between Agripides' own philosophical treatises, the readership of which undoubtedly consisted of no more than Agripides himself, his mother, and *the entity in question*. A simple enough matter to ignore, would have resolved itself in short order by way of simply being cast back to the pink mists, as your dear brother might phrase it, this is the point I stress. So what does do? What does *the entity in question* do, apologies? Do you imagine it smote Agripides? Or do you imagine that it obliterated the entirety of his culture? If the latter, congratulations are in order, for that is precisely what *the entity in question* did. One minute we have the Mycenaeans at the top of their game, beset with riches both cultural and material, and it's worth mentioning one of my sort was running a game of its own there. In the next instant, *ribbit!* The populace vanishes. Surely the highest body count associated with a plagiarism accusation, at least until an incident in the twenty-second century when a man named Norm Twillig will supply an airplane manufacturer with safety documentation he lifted whole cloth from the manual for an entirely different plane, which naturally corresponds not in the least with the airplane in question, and so will prove of little to no use when the flight crew is really up against it!"

"..."

"You're right, I suppose it is a *bit* funny."

"I'm so confused," Patience finally announced. "I'm just trying to f-"

"Oh, no need to be so vexed! I am No-Good Bulstrode.

Patience, Ambrose

Where once I was a pig, I am now a frog. Simple as that. Well, there is a bit more too it — last fellow I tooled about with has long since noshed his last kebab, got too old to breath, but such is the fate of all you lot. I'm sure your brother mentioned me."

Patience realized the stratagem at once: Bulstrode was *trying* to confuse her. He was a wall between herself and her brother. Recalling that Ambrose had mentioned that the pig could read minds, Patience got straight to the point: she glared long and hard at the now-frog's bulbous, darting little eyes and asked "where is he?"

"Rather engaged at the moment."

"With what?"

"I do believe that this evening I have tasked him with plucking the most beloved facial kerchief of an unremarkable cobbler from the line upon which it is drying in Murfreesboro, Tennesse, to be whiskéd into the woods! The kerchief, not the cobbler."

"…why?"

"It is but one essential step towards a great end."

"What's the end?"

"Oh, you needn't concern yourself with it. You will be long dead."

Patience shook her head, then closed her eyes and *focused* again. Focused and pushed.

She felt Bulstrode making himself a bulwark, between herself and Ambrose. A knot tied in the tether. And no matter how hard she pushed, the little shit didn't budge.

"First notch on the docket," Bulstrode rumbled, "it's *tremendously* uncouth to think me a shit of any size."

"Well," Patience replied, "quit being a shit and I'll stop thinking it."

Bulstrode's bulbous gullet inflated and deflated like an indecisive whoopee cushion. "You find yourself," it finally replied, "between events of great historical import."

"Oh, fuck yourself, *between* events."

The frog frowned. "What a deceptively unpleasant person you are."

"I'm not *between* 'events of great historical import'," Patience snarled. "I'm *living* them."

"You've none of the perspective required to make such a statement, erroneously or otherw-"

"You have too much of the wrong perspective."

"Ah, but does that not sound like the utterance of one wi-"

Patience closed her eyes and felt once more for the knot that was Bulstrode. Seeking and finding, she focused…and did not push, but tugged. Gently, just as Ambrose had suggested.

The process of undoing the froggy blockade was not at all like the loosing of a knot, of course. But all the same, it was precisely that.

"Look at the time!" Bulstrode squawked, suddenly panicked. "I must get to hopping, your brother and I have quite a bit of work to do, none of which will be in the offing if bloviates…if *the entity in question* bloviates Ambrose into a whole new oblivion! Toad-le-oo! RIGIBBLEDRI-"

The frog vanished.

Scratch that; the frog had been banished. By Patience. Punched back up the umbilicus, into the deathwell.

Without leaving her bed, Patience followed him through, marveling at the ease of the enterprise.

F I V E

MAXIMS BY WHICH TO SEE THE WORLD: TO PUT THE course of human events into language is to render them sensible. To render the course of human events sensible is to reduce them beyond recognizability. To reduce them is to refuse them. Thusly do historical narratives supersede the events they purport to describe.

Oh, but that's rather gloomy, isn't it? A more colorful illustration of the concept: imagine time as a three-year-old child sat amongst countless baubles and bangles, each more enticing than the last. These doodads and geegaws are, of course, eras. The child snatches them up, largely at the behest of whims it is hardly cognizant enough to comprehend, let alone examine, and smashes the toys together, sometimes hurling them across the room, sometimes shoving them in its mouth. Behold, the majesty of the ages.

One last approach: chaos is the simplest (and yes, most reductive) watchword. Hold it close, for to embrace it is the surest inurement to its wrath.

How to make sense of one's place in this? How best to hold resignation at some kind of manageable distance?

Is it not obvious? Tend the tether. Tie no knots. Open all the doors and windows. Guard yourself, but only against those undeserving of your fire.

Speak to me, Patience thought.

b l i n k

AMBROSE FELT HIMSELF PULLED, AS HE'D ONCE BEEN PULLED from the womb, though this time life demanded him from the other side. Whereas his first summons was one he was loathe to heed, separating him from his only friend as it would have, this was one to which he was desperate to assent. There were those who would have him stay, of course, and the frog and others would have their way. He had no body, he had neither heart nor mind. Yet he was. Strange. He was strange.

The tether, though, the mystic chord of not memory but of of of *something*, he knew not what, had no desire to diminish it with language. Had no need to. It was what gave him life, gave as it got. In a manner of speaking, of course. Ha ha, tee hee.

Had he still a face, he would have forced it into a smile. He had been uncertain of whether or not his sister would ever pull him from this timeless place. Had, indeed, considered shunting her in that direction, in spite of his resolution not to. Yet it had never been necessary (save providing her with the word *enterprise,* for which Bulstrode had knocked Ambrose briefly back to the turn of the eighteenth century). She had done this herself.

Swimming upstream. Such was the experience of trying to ride the tether. No, more, language once again blanches at the task of expressing a simple enough concept. What, then? It was akin to swimming straight up a waterfall, a friend standing at the base, a hand clutching one's ankle, holding one down. Gravity made flesh. An encumbrance, little more. Some friend.

Was this Bulstrode? Was this *the entity in question*, whose true name Ambrose could hear – his faculties no longer constrained by the limitations of human hardware – and so be underwhelmed by? Or was it something else? Or didn't it matter, because whatever it was, was secondary to the consideration of *what* it was, i.e. an encumbrance, e.g. gravity, i.e. something to which he was no longer subject, e.g. the finality of death, perhaps?

He swam upstream, up the waterfall, kicking and flailing and thrashing until his ankle slipped its shackle, and even the thundering current could not hold him.

S I X

HER HEART SWELLED TO THE POINT OF BURSTING. HE WAS with her. It was unmistakable, it was true, it was Ambrose.

"I'm so sorry I let you go," she whispered to her empty room, knowing her brother could not reply to her, knowing he had no means of communicating at all. How she knew, she didn't know, but she knew it as she knew that he was with her: unmistakably.

Was communication necessary, though? She wasn't certain that it was. Or, at any rate, she wasn't certain that verbalization was, would be, *could* be. How far behind the heart and mind did words so often lag! Wars, begun and ended because of slow words. Guns placed in chin hollows, full-brothers sold down the river by half-brothers, mothers and Fathers strung up by bastards. Nothing good. This was the way of things, though. There was a hole between the thing and the hopeless inadequacy of the noise to which it answered. What rushed to fill the gap? Nothing good.

It was ok, though. Because Patience and Ambrose were, as

485

they had not managed to be since their earliest days, since the timeless embrace of the womb, beyond language. This was life at its purest, life before life, life before the world had a chance to claim its portion. For all of the language and movement, sound and fury, war and slavery, bloodshed and cruelty…there were still little gifts that the world could give. They were simply beyond words.

So Patience tended the tether from her end, and Ambrose from his, and they met in the middle, filling up the nothing, leaving only the good.

"Ambrose," Patience said.

Patience, Ambrose replied.

And from worlds apart, they were together.

1838

O N E

IT CAREERED WILDLY BETWEEN ENDEARING, FRUSTRATING, AND concerning, with that last option fast becoming the default. Or, rather, *slowly* become the default. Because it had been a touch over two years since Patience had pulled Ambrose from the deathwell, and the Serkis brothers were *still* setting a place for him at the dinner table.

Patience had tried, more times than she could count, to explain to them that Ambrose was not *physically* here. Each time, Kirk and Dirk nodded enthusiastically, insisted they understood, and hustled off to the kitchen to prepare a four-portioned supper.

In their defense, it wasn't as though Patience had ever

succeeded in explaining to them just what the arrangement was. It would have been reductive to say that Patience was carrying Ambrose around like a second conscience, for their thought processes were so tightly intertwined now as to be indistinguishable. Which, she (and therefore they) supposed, implied that they were both in control of Patience's body. Which they weren't – Patience remained at the helm. It was simply that Patience now thought *with* Ambrose. Which meant that the only things she ever did were those things that she and Ambrose had decided to do based on their single, shared thought process. For they were not two distinct minds in a single head. Which was why Patience wasn't *entirely* at the helm; she was no longer *entirely* Patience. But…she was also never ceding control to Ambrose, just as he never did to her…

As always, the problem was language. For from the inside, the twins understood the situation perfectly well. The challenge was in communicating that to Kirk and Dirk.

Although, in whatever the opposite of the Serkis' defense was (in their offense?), there was nothing ambiguous about the fact that Ambrose did not now, nor would he ever again, have a physical body to plop at the dinner table and fill with yams.

Patience sighed as she sat at the table. "You set an extra place again," she tutted.

Dirk turned to look at Kirk. "Did we?"

"If she says we did," Kirk replied, "then we must have."

The two turned to look at the extra place they had set.

"Ah!" Dirk exclaimed.

"An extra place!" Kirk added.

"For Ambrose, no?"

"Afraid not."

"Then who?"

"The extra place?"

"Yes."

"Oh, yes."

"Excellent." Dirk nodded. "Yes what?"

"To Ambrose."

"Oh, terrific!"

"I don't believe he's coming, though."

"Oh, pity!"

Kirk turned to Paitence. "Shall we set his portion aside?"

Patience just planted her elbow on the table and rested her head in her hand. Two years of this.

It would have been going too far to say she had grown weary of the Serkis brothers. After all they had done for her, all of these years they had spent together, Patience had nothing but love in her heart for these two screwballs. But...well, she was at the point now where it became necessary to think thoughts like *it would be going too far to say I've grown weary of these two.*

The truth, she suspected, was as simultaneously simple and complicated as the state of affairs inside her skull, for the one directly informed the other. Reunion with Ambrose had rearranged her priorities. She felt at once deep fulfillment, one which came at the cost of a new, unfamiliar emptiness. For she had attained what she had considered the work of a life. Yet the life remained.

Long had she imagined what she might do, if she left here. Much of that time had been dedicated to reaching for an option beyond the one that had presented itself immediately, which Patience and Ambrose had at once recognized to be *the* answer. For it was obvious, was it not? It was inevitable. It went beyond

Patience merely wanting to know what Praisegod had been doing in New York City during the fire; it was difficult to imagine a tremendously exciting or surprising answer to that question.

It likewise went beyond needing to head off that vague sense of guilt Patience felt around Praisegod's death. The guilt was not on his behalf, that she might have inadvertently started him down the path that ended with his name as one of three in another nation's newspaper. No, Patience felt guilt that she had never forced her half-brother to confront how rotten, how awful, how hypocrticial he was, how his greatest cruelties were the periodic generosities he had reserved for Patience alone. That he had been just kind enough to make her miss him.

No, what ultimately charted the next step for Patience and Ambrose was another need beyond words…though if language truly *had* to be roped into the proceedings, one could do worse than calling it *simple curiosity*.

For they wanted to know more of where they had come from. For each, they had been raised in a fiction, and subsequently aged into a mystery. Their mother's name had been Aggy, and their father's name had been Drummond. The only other facts that Patience and Ambrose knew about their parents were violence. Yet there had to be more to learn. And if there was…

It would be found at the Estate.

Oh, alright. Maybe it was fear that had kept them here for so long. Fear that there was nothing more, save two names and a legacy of horror and tragedy.

If he sets an extra place at the table tomorrow morning, Patience thought to herself, *then we'll go.*

Patience blinked the mist out of her eyes. What a frivolous ultimatum. As certain as hinging one's departure on there being weather, *any* weather, tomorrow. Of course Kirk and Dirk would set an extra place at the table. On the off chance Ambrose crawled out of Patience's ear with an appetite. That was just who they were.

Oh, she would miss them.

She smiled across the table at her two hosts. Who had become as true a family as any she had ever known.

"You feel good about working the sap house," she asked the brothers, "right?"

Patience would not have believed it but for seeing it with her own eyes; the Serkis brothers said nothing. They stared at their plates, and managed a smile in unison. For they may have been two deeply absurd men, but they were not fools. They understood at once the unspoken subtext of that question: *without me.*

Dirk was the first to meet Patience's gaze. "I'd say we certainly do."

"That's quite right," Kirk added.

"Thank you for asking."

"Thank you indeed."

Dirk nodded at his meal, then stood up (*without excusing himself,* quite unusual for him), and stepped outside.

Patience watched him go, then looked to Kirk.

The remaining Serkis brother was doing his best to force a grin at her, but his eyes kept sliding back down towards his meal.

In short order, Dirk returned with an astonishingly ornate glass decanter, covered in little puckers and protrusions which caught the light of the room and splashed it all throughout the amber liquid within.

It was as breathtaking a batch of booze as Patience had ever seen; what truly moved her, though, were the smears of dust she could see left in the spaces between the embossments Dirk failed to clean as he wiped the decanter down with his sleeve. Wherever this whiskey had been, it had been there for quite some time.

Which, given the Serkis brothers' penchant for eagerly parting with the literal shirts off their backs, let alone the content of their cupboards…well, this was something else beyond language.

Dirk shuffled off to the kitchen, and came back with four glasses.

Patience smiled, the corners of her lips twitching with the effort of it.

Neither Dirk nor Kirk made any grand show of this new arrival to the repast. There was no spiel explaining specifically what this liquor was, where it had come from, when it had been poured, nothing of that sort. Because its ultimate significance was clear.

For the first glass or two. Then everything went swimmy. Oh, they all got blindingly drunk; even Ambrose, unbodied phantasm that he was, was dreaming up pianos to dance on. There followed a hangover the likes of which Patience had never imagined she would be lucky/unlucky enough to experience. It was nearly enough to keep her at the Serkis place for another day.

But the brothers set a fourth place at their belated breakfast. And a deal, even one never committed to human speech, was a deal.

T   W   O

THE RIVER HAD SEEMED SOMETHING WONDROUS WHEN THE headwaters had been a mystery. There was that feeling of adventure, of promise, that had come from drifting upstream, from coming ever nearer to the source of this elemental power. As though there would be something to learn there, some truth that could be applied to one's soft little human life.

Which was ridiculous, of course. Ridiculous in theory, ridiculous in hindsight, and *especially* ridiculous as one was tromping the other way.

Following the river downstream was a disillusioning experience. At every turn, it revealed itself to be precisely what it was; a natural phenomenon, water and soil and gravity. All things flowed downstream, yes, and the shit was included in that. But the filthification of the waters was not as linear as Patience had imagined it to be, in her half-catatonic journey up. From the back of the horse the Serkis brothers had given her, she marveled at the way the flow seemed to periodically clean itself. The means by which it accomplished this were utterly mysterious to her, but the results were unmistakable; for however filthy the waters became, at irregular intervals Patience could glance down and find herself staring at flitting fish and the bed of pebbles beneath them.

She couldn't help but wonder, as she rode southward, well-provisioned and, yes, it must be said, well-armed...she did wonder what her horse's name was. It had been one she'd never actually seen ridden by either of the brothers – they were no more eager to climb atop an animal than they were to shoot one – so she couldn't simply rack her memory for an instance of its name being shouted. And in truth, she would likely have come up short on that score; this piebald beauty rode like a dream, her trunk rocking steadily as she traversed some astoundingly rocky roads. One does not shout at a horse like this.

It seemed disrespectful to give her a name. As disrespectful as it was unimportant. So Patience called her nothing; this left room for everything.

Patience wondered if she would know the way back to the Estate. It had been so long since she had last been, and she had been coming from the other way. From the south. From downstream. So she wondered, but she did not doubt. For all of the ways the river split and wandered, she never once doubted.

Over countless days on the road, she found it difficult not to think of the hunting rifle strapped to the horse, equidistant from Patience's ass and the horse's. She wondered if she would use it on Drummond, on Martha. To think these thoughts were to have already put them to Ambrose, and to have her ambivalence echoed back to her. There were arguments for and against the weapon. That fact was, in and of itself, perhaps an indication that the *for* column had a bit more going on in it than the *against* did, and that was a column that came pretty pre-stacked. In any event, Patience would need to get her head around the idea of pointing her rifle at another human being. That wasn't something she'd ever done before. And if the need arose...

Ah, but there was something else to consider. There could well be a need. For Drummond wasn't likely to be well-disposed to seeing his dear daughter again.

In a way, things would be so much easier if he started shooting at her. It would clarify the interaction. Kill or be killed. So much neater than some big, messy conversation.

The days and nights passed, whisked along by the river. The sound of its endless passage was Patience and Ambrose's third companion. Sometimes at a murmur, sometimes a roar. Even when Patience set up camp some half a mile off from the water, they could hear it. In their dreams, if nowhere else. Their singular dreams, of bright fires and depthless darks.

T H R E E

THE ESTATE WAS ABANDONED. PATIENCE COULD TELL AS soon as she crested the furthest hill which marked the boundary of the property.

Weedy thickets choked the terraces, dulling the hard edges of each ziggurat step with a brown, withered fuzz. Those grasses must have been poking out through each and every stone in the wall, Patience marveled. The tenacity of ruin never ceased to amaze her.

She recalled her departure from this place, so many years ago. How she had passed no fewer than half a dozen dark bodies out working the orchards. Well, there was not a soul to be seen out there now, though the trees themselves were still alive. Patience sniffed as the wind carried something sour in her direction; it was then she noticed a ring of black mush surrounding each of the trees' trunks. Apples, unpicked, fallen from the bough and rotting where they landed.

That started to give Patience a sense of how long the place had been abandoned. Or, at least, untended.

The difference between *abandoned* and *untended* occupied more and more of Patience's mind as she drew nearer and nearer the Estate itself, near enough to make out the individual flakes of paint peeling from the barn, near enough to see that one of the windows on the second floor of the house had been punched out.

She had a feeling. Not necessarily a bad feeling. Just a feeling that felt quite at home, in this landscape of grey grey dull grey.

Patience made a few practice arm-swings, seeing how quickly she could whip around and slip the rifle from the cords with which it had been lashed to the very back of the saddle. Not quickly enough to constitute a quick-draw. So she checked the safety of the rifle, then set it to rest on her lap, holding it there with her elbows.

She was aware of an unusual shade of embarrassment, one which she smiled upon identifying; this was what it felt like, to be teased from inside one's own head, without the bile of self-doubt. No, this was just Ambrose mocking her caution. Which was to say, his. So Patience laughed and thought a few pointed comments right back at him. Which was to say, herself.

Then she stopped laughing, for the way her voice echoed around the wild property unnerved her.

Clomping along the dry, caked dirt at the foot of the Estate proper, Patience, Ambrose, and even the horse turned to face the steps up which a fearful Aggy had once, twice, three times in a vanished century been summoned, down which Patience had been called by Jesse, only to be immediately spirited up again by Drummond.

Patience took her right hand from the reins, and rested it on the butt of the rifle. That did little to soothe her ever-mounting unease. But *little* was better than nothing.

She glanced at the stairs, at the spots that looked to have gone soggy with age, at others which would surely have snapped under a hard wind.

If she was unaware of how her present echoed her mother's past, there was no confusion as to the jeering similarity it bore to her own history.

It came to her like the long-forgotten name of a childhood friend: Patience saw Aggy walking slowly, tremblingly up these steps. To what would lead to the end of her life, and the beginning of Patience and Ambrose's.

Her brother's abilities – the *blinks*, as he called them – had been greatly diminished for being removed from the deathwell. Yet, to his surprise as much as Patience's, he found himself able to touch something that had not fully evaporated from this place. Their mother's terror. When she had been just a child. Oh, she had been just a child.

Patience spurred her nameless horse onwards. Up onto the steps. She didn't think about it; she simply did it.

The steps groaned beneath the weight of the horse, who seemed no more delighted by the arrangement than the architecture. Patience was in a far brighter mood, astonished her mount was taking the steps at all, having expected the horse to blanche at the command. If anything, she worried about letting loose another laugh. Because now her horse was wholly on the porch, Patience slouched and clutching the creature's neck to keep from putting her head through the wooden overhang.

It was quite remarkable, that the horse hadn't put a hoof through the steps. Had been an idiotic risk to run, in hindsight. But Patience felt protected in some sense. Impossible to say which sense that was. But it was manifestly true, in some fashion if not others.

"Yip yip," Patience whispered as she clutched the rifle on her lap, ducked her head still more, and spurred the horse into the house.

F   O   U   R

SOMBER THOUGH IT WAS TO BE IN THIS AWFUL PLACE, PATIENCE took no small delight in parading her horse around the first floor. Oh, if only Martha could see Patience now, tromping a splotchy mount over her precious rugs, knocking over tables laden with tea sets and serving dishes gathering dust, smearing the trim of the doors with dirt-caked fingers as Patience eased herself through each of the frames. All told, the interior of the Estate was in better shape than she would have expected. It didn't app-ear to have been gutted by bandits or conquered by squatters. Save a few bookcases that looked to have been violently divested of their literary loads, ornate portrait frames hanging empty on the sitting room walls, and a cupboard door or two hanging crooked in the house pantry, it looked as though everyone living here had one day simply, peacefully up and left.

Which seemed...unlikely.

Having satisfied herself that this first story was as dead as history, Patience guided her horse back to the main entryway and dismounted. "Good girl," she whispered as she stroked the steed's muzzle and ran its reins around the raised volute of the banister post.

She held the rifle in both hands, not quite socking it into her shoulder but *certainly* not resting it by her hip…and mounted the first step to the second floor.

The smell hit her instantly. She wretched once, stumbling backwards onto the first floor as though shoved. This was smell as an object, a viscous fishrot pudding funneled directly through the nostrils and into the brain. She could taste it, brine and tang by way of curdle.

Words failed. As always. This was a stench for which Patience had no frame of reference. The natural sciences could hardly have done better, she imagined.

Patience grabbed the knife sheathed just above the left stirrup of her saddle and cut at the blanket lain across the horse's back, peeling off a long strip to wrap it several times around her mouth and nose. Stank and tasted of horse, so it did, but that was a trade-off Patience was happy to make; at least the horse it stank of was alive.

Feeling suddenly ridiculous (thanks, Ambrose-half), Patience nonetheless took up the rifle once again and made a second go of the steps. As if the rifle was necessary; death had already touched this place. Done quite a lot of touching, in fact.

Despite knowing precisely what (if not *who*) she would find at the top of the stairs, Patience failed to identify the sound that hit her like a wave before she was halfway up the staircase. It was a low, ponderous *hmmmmmmmmmm*. One that Ambrose recognized on her behalf at once; flies. The crackling indecision of one million and one flies, debating with which end of the buffet they'd like to begin.

Patience paused just four steps from the top, eyes nearly level with the second story. She was surprised to discover the butt of the rifle pressed tightly into her shoulder. Absurd. Shaking her head, she forced herself to lower it, briefly freeing her left hand to pull the strip of saddle blanket higher up the bridge of her nose.

She took the final steps in a quick burst. The top one complained the loudest of all. Patience knew precisely how it felt.

It was impossible, she found, not to let her rifle lead the way down the narrow hall, its doors all arrayed on Patience's left, little square windows on the right. How many times had she walked up and down this hall, going from her bedroom to Martha's?

She recalled standing here, outside her bedroom door, decades ago. Thinking about floorboards as she glanced nervously to Martha's bedroom *there,* at the end of the hall…through the pale, peeling door, beneath which flies now spilled like a thick mist.

Patience swallowed hard, wondering if it might not be advisable to run down the stairs, leap directly onto her horse, cry 'yip yip,' and never come back.

She could do that. But if she did, she would *never* come back. She would never know who was dead in that room there. And simple curiosity would drive her mad.

A thought appeared in Patience's mind. Gratitude, that losing a body meant losing one's sense of smell.

Patience smiled at that brother-thought, which was no less her own than the word *asshole* now appearing in response.

Just a half-dozen uneasy steps delivered Patience to the door. Even through her long trousers, she felt flies spilling from beneath the door, buzzing around her ankles.

She fought the urge to gag, then pressed her hand into the warm wood before her – so beset with rot that it yielded like flesh – and pushed.

The door swung open, creaking with an appropriate theatricality.

Almost at once, darkness swarmed Patience as flies poured out into the hallway, landing on her eyes, alighting on her hands, bleeding into her makeshift mask and crawling into her nose, over her lips.

The urge to use her gun had never been so powerful.

And the sheer idiocy of that impulse focused her.

She leaned the rifle against the wall just outside the door, then turned her shoulder to the swarm and pushed onwards into the living night. No matter how wildly she flailed her hands, it did almost nothing to part the horde before her. She reached for where she remembered the window to be – which, more to the point, she recalled having thick, royal blue curtains.

It was impossible to make out the color, but the curtain was certainly just where Patience remembered it. She grabbed hold of it, once more fighting the urge to vomit as she felt dozens of flies squishing in her grasp, and *yanked* as hard as she could.

The rod popped off the wall, flooding the room in overcast daylight. The flies buzzed their displeasure.

Patience managed to fight the curtain free of its rod, grabbed two handfuls from the top, and swung it like the cape of a matador.

That did it. As long as, by *it*, one meant *cleared a cubic foot of flies for a second or two*. Still, with enough frantic waving, Patience managed to clear enough space to spot what looked to be a human form in the far corner of the room. Waving faster and harder, she struggled further into the hungry void, until she felt the bed unexpectedly thumping against her shins.

They had moved the bed. Patience found the mental space to be distantly annoyed by that.

And then she saw it.

She froze, stopping her flapping for just an instant. In which time the flies rushed to fill the vacuum, once more obscuring the body from Patience's vision.

Shaking her head, she resumed flapping, redoubling the speed and force thanks to a burst of terrible adrenaline. She risked a few more steps forward. Cautiously, as though approaching the edge of a cliff.

Slumped in the far corner of the room were the earthly remains of some poor man of dark complexion, rotten and bloated, his skin peeling away in fat, grisly strips. Something had punched a colossal hole into the base of his throat, swelling around the edges, into which what remained of his face had collapsed. There was not much that remained.

That hole looked like the work of a mighty blunderbuss, fired at close range. Perhaps from the bed. Perhaps whoever this was had attempted to surprise whoever had been in that bed, tried to attack them as they slept. But perhaps whoever had been in that bed had been awake. And perhaps they had kept a rifle under their bed, knowing that the day their property would set upon them was a *when* day, rather than an *if* day.

Where the weapon had come from, where it had gone, who had wielded it, Patience could certainly guess.

But as to who that man in the corner was…she was fairly certain. Perhaps it was spooky knowledge from Ambrose, or perhaps it was simply that she recognized the spread of his shoulders, the relative decency of his clothes, and his hands. It was not that there was anything wildly distinctive about them, no telltale scars or markings. These were simply the hands that had wiped clumsily at the mouth, in the instant before that mouth had told Patience the truth. About who she was, and where she had come from. She would never forget those hands. Would never forget anything about that final night she had spent here on the Estate. The first night of her real life.

Her hands suddenly became too heavy to wave the curtain any longer. The flies once more closed around all that remained of Jesse, the mouth of a many-eyed tomb.

Patience stood motionless amongst the flies as they closed around her too, a vise of starless hunger. For there were things, she had discovered, that were worse than this.

F   I   V   E

PATIENCE AND AMBROSE SAT ON THE PORCH, STARING OUT AT the property as the evening drenched it in impossible beauty. It was that color – gold and purple, orange and blue – which made a memory of all it touched. Birds sang softly out in the trees on the far side of the clearing; they were smart to keep their distance from the house. Perhaps it was simply her mind playing a trick, but Patience would have sworn she could still hear the flies.

The horse wandered around the yard, munching on those tufts of growth that had sprouted where there had once been only the hard-pack soil of a path. Its reins dangled freely down its neck; if she wanted to run away, Patience was happy to let her.

The unified twins studied the land before them, doing their best to imagine their mother living here. Their mother, who was never anything but a child. They tried to picture her tilling the soil, harvesting tomatoes, fetching water. But neither knew what she had looked like. Even Ambrose, who had seen her beneath that hateful tree for but a moment, could provide nothing.

So in their mind's eye, she was simply a shape. A shadow haunting a dead Estate.

Which was unacceptable. That was an unacceptable fate for their mother. So they stopped imagining. They simply studied the land before them, and watched the nameless horse nibble contently at it.

After some duration Patience and Ambrose could only guess at, both having been lost to the same distracted void of thought, the horse clomped over to the steps and blew a raspberry at Patience, its tail swinging in a slow, steady rhythm.

She considered waving the horse off, maybe even chasing it away. But she didn't. Because there was somewhere else she needed to go. That simple curiosity would *demand* she go. It was where Drummond would be, assuming he was still alive. It was the only place he could be. His was such a small little world, after all.

The horse blew another raspberry. *She makes a good point,* Patience and Ambrose conceded together.

They camped that night in the orchards, and hit the road before daybreak.

S   I   X

THE INN THAT PATIENCE HAD TWICE PATRONIZED ON HER WAY between the two Pinchwife properties was not only still standing; it had been carved out of the woods and expanded. Such was the magnitude of the transformation that Patience only recognized the place at second glance, from the low sloping roof of un-evenly-set tile. For as much extra space had been built on around the back, apparently that bit of handiwork on the original structure hadn't been deemed worthy of a revisit.

Patience left her horse by the hitching post, opting not to in any way restrain her, and stepped into the inn. Or, rather, what was now the main lobby, a little head to the much larger body of this turtle-shaped edifice.

At the desk sat a middle-aged man, who appeared to be about the same age as Patience.

"Oh, *Christ,*" Patience said out loud, in the moment she recognized she too had probably lived more than half of her life at this point.

The man behind the desk glanced up from the leatherbound book he had been scribbling in and cocked an eyebrow. "Hello?" he auditioned. Satisfied, he cleared his throat and committed to "hello."

Patience ducked her head in silent apology for a moment – 'Oh, *Christ*' was probably not what a proprietor hoped to hear when a patron stepped into their place of business – and offered the man behind the desk a smile. "I stopped in here a couple of times. Years and years ago."

The man behind the desk smiled. "Bigger than you recall, yeah?"

"Yeah."

"Yeah," the man replied, "it's nice and new. All those extra rooms. Went in…ah," his eyes ran a quick lap around the room, "two…near on three years back. Stop on the Long Island Rail Road went in somewhere makes us a good place to, ah, stop." He shrugged. "That was dad's strategy. No doubt you met him, if you stopped in years ago."

"Big guy," Patience prompted, "clean-shaved, but with hair out like this." She held her hands above her head and splayed her fingers out wide.

The man threw his head back and laughed, slapping his knee on the way back down. "Spitting image! Yeah, that's him. Mhm." He nodded thoughtfully, then planted an elbow on his desk and scratched at his chin. "You don't seem at all sour about him."

"…no," Patience replied. "Why would I be?"

"We just…um, he wasn't really known for being decent to your type. That wasn't…you know, he just didn't support you. As a…" he waved his hand vaguely through the air. "Well. You know."

Patience fought back a smile. Ah. So she wasn't 'passing' anymore. For all it could mean for her, being a black woman alone in this country, for as much terror as there was in the realization…she found it strangely gratifying, to be recognized for who she was.

She was aware of Ambrose trying to take credit for it. As though his melding with her somehow darkened her. She swatted that away with an ever-bigger smile. "Well," she finally said, "I guess he took pity on me for being a kid alone on the road."

"No, that doesn't sound like him at all."

"Well, he was perfectly decent to me."

"Do you wanna know where I stand on it?" the man asked.

Patience's eyes narrowed of their own accord. She forced them back open. "On what?"

"On your kind."

"…are you not going to rent me a room?"

"No!" he laughed. "No, I mean as in, *yes*, of course." He leaned back, folded his arms, and stared at the corner of the ceiling. "Because where I stand on it is, you know, I think slavery isn't great. For sure. For *sure,* it's really unfortunate."

Knowing that her thoughts, and so her hands, were one with Ambrose's…Patience was very glad she'd left her rifle on the horse.

"But," the man continued, liberating one hand to waggle a finger at the ceiling, "I will say this. I mean, I'll just say this." He cocked a thumb over his shoulder. "We wouldn't have all these extra rooms without it, you know. Slavery. We wouldn't have, uh, the railroad, too. Which brought us the Long Island Rail Road. And there's tobacco and stuff, too. Cotton. Cott…those two aren't connected. But, I'm just saying. Good stuff comes from slaves. They do good work. And that's how we got…" he cocked another thumb over his shoulder, then shrugged. "Probably. I don't know. My dad did the money stuff, I don't really know." He nodded at his desk, then looked to Patience. "You know what I'm saying? You get it."

Patience said nothing. Just stared at him.

"I'm just…" he raised his palms towards Patience, as though fending off a verbal assault. "All I'm saying is…" he lifted one upturned palm. "Is slavery great? No. Not in my opinion." He lifted another upturned palm. "…*buuut*…is this *nation* great? Yes." He nodded as his shoulders crawled up towards his ears. "So, you know…" He crinkled his lips at Patience and juggled his upturned palms, the scales of justice working overtime during a 7.1 magnitude earthquake.

Patience gave him a moment to hear his words echoing back to him. The man behind the desk took this moment to continue juggling his hands up and down, up and down.

"I just want to be clear," the man insisted, finally reeling his hands back in, using his right paw to point at himself, "*I* don't have slaves. I would *never*, you know?"

"They're just good for business," Patience filled in.

"Yes!" The man clapped and pointed at Patience. "You get it! They're good for the economy. Yes. I knew you'd get it eventually."

Patience nodded. Then turned around and walked back outside.

The man behind the desk had absolutely no reaction to her departure. Which spoke volumes more than he had already said.

Back out in the night, Patience turned her face up towards the sky, now clearly visible thanks to the hack-and-slash work done to clear the front of this property of verdure. She closed her eyes, took a deep breath, and thought to herself that she would *not* use the rifle on that man behind the desk. She would simply get on the horse and go.

It was one of those thoughts that was both a pitch and a promise. She felt Ambrose reluctantly sign on. That done, the singular twin got on their horse and hit the road, in search of a suitable spot to camp for the evening.

S E V E N

SOMEONE HAD REBUILT HER PRIVY. THE NEW STRUCTURE WAS about half as tall again as the original, painted a pale yellow for reasons known only to whoever had made that fateful decision. But the little culvert she'd dug underneath was just as she'd left it, when she'd bid the farm a less-than-fond farewell over twenty years ago.

Patience leaned on the pommel of her horse's saddle and smiled sadly at the new privy. It was inevitable that someone would have rebuilt it – her original construction, surely rotted-through long ago, had been the work of a child. And as charming as it could be to, say, allow a preternaturally gifted kiddo to sit at the piano for an evening and amuse company, Patience could appreciate that it was nobody's first choice to let the world's littlest architect call the shots on the shithouse.

Still…she couldn't help but feel a little pang of disappointment at seeing the pride of her early years, arguably the project that had given her the self-confidence required for everything that had come after, replaced by an admittedly superior struct-ure.

Ah, well. It was a short-lived pang, one replaced by a cocktail of confusion and mirth as she turned her horse to get a closer look at what else had changed on what had one been Praisegod's pig farm.

The stables where Praisegod had kept everything (and every-one) he considered chattle was missing. Whether it had been destroyed or deconstructed was impossible to say for certain, though Patience was leaning towards the latter; she saw no deb-ris, no piles of old planks or stacked-up gates. All that remained to haunt the premises was a starkly-delimited rectangle of grass, brighter and springier than that found anywhere else on the property. Years of natural fertilization, finally getting its time to shine.

If that was a powerful demonstration of the use to which large quantities of shit could be put…over on the spot where Praise-god's house had once stood was a striking counterpoint.

The Estate. Someone – and here Patience was able to quickly narrow the field of who *someone* might be – had torn down the late Praisegod's abode, and in its place erected an exact replica of Drummond's Estate. Had Patience not just seen the ruins of the original teetering amongst terraces, she could well have imagined the Pinchwifes had taken their old home apart, loaded it up into carts, and rebuilt it atop their departed son's acreage.

While that didn't rankle her quite as much as the rebuilt privy, there was something ghoulish about seeing the Pinchwife Estate reanimated on the land of someone who had wanted nothing to do with the place. But the dead cannot withhold consent. No doubt the young man now running the inn would present that as one of the things that made this nation so great.

Patience leapt off her horse, marveling at just how lifeless the property was. She had, in her youth, taken the ambience of swine and sow for granted. She had been raised amidst such vitality. All that life! Alas, all in the past. Gone were the stinks and snuffles and snorts; now the only claim on Patience's attention came from the giggling of the river, the wind slinking through high boughs, the elderly woman running straight towards her with a large axe clutched tightly to her breast.

Patience's jerked to a halt. She started to reach for her rifle, then stopped. "Mary!"

Mary's legs locked in mid-air, landing on her heel and sending her stumbling for several steps. By the time she recovered her balance, she got knocked for a whole new loop upon recognizing who it was she had been running at. "Patience?!"

Patience smiled. "Hello, Mary!"

Mary carefully dropped the axe, being sure the head fell away from her, then hustled as quickly as she could to Patience.

Patience, Ambrose

MARY LED PATIENCE TOWARDS THE REPLICA OF THE EST-
ate. As they walked, she filled Patience in on the broadest possible strokes of her life since last they had seen each other in Reading, Pennsylvania: she and Praisegod had lingered there until
news of Washington D.C.'s sacking made its way to them. At
that point, Praisegod insisted on heading west, which prompted
Mary to take loose inspiration from Patience and abandon him
under cover of night. Unlike Patience, she returned to the pig
farm, full of hope that she might yet find Ezekiel and Flann
there. It took her several long, arduous months (the misery of
which was palpable in Mary's many ellipticals), but by 1815 she
found her way home, to be welcomed by Ezekiel and Flann into
the dreamy equilibrium they had established there, working and
living in modest comfort. Flann pretended to be the one to
whom Ezekiel and Mary were indentured, so that those few who
called unexpectedly sensed nothing awry (nothing, that was, beyond the abberation that was an indenture-holding Irishman in
Gurewitch county. In time, Ezekiel met a lovely woman named
Anne at one of their rare trips to market; in 1821, she joined the
farm. Flann had had to purchase her indenture, which had been
an emotionally squishy arrangement for everyone save the man
making the sale, but fortunately the discomfort passed almost
the moment Anne came home, and was wholly forgotten by the
time she and Ezekiel jumped the broom. Flann passed in his
sleep in 1829. In 1834, Ezekiel and Anne had a son, whom they
named Philip, for no greater reason than they liked the sound of
it. Then in 1835, New York burned, and Praisegod with it.
Shortly thereafter, Drummond and Martha had appeared, banging a brand new drum.

Patience, recognizing a conversational cliffhanger when she

saw one, took the reins and recounted her trek to the north, through the impossible mid-summer snow, and the life she made with the Serkis brothers. She also spoke of Ambrose; there was no sense keeping anything from Mary. To Patience's astonishment, Mary took the strange tale on board as easily as if it had been no more miraculous than a description of changing a horseshoe. Her only challenge came in accepting that Ambrose was within Patience, that she was speaking to the child whom she had pulled from the river, and handed to the man who had sold him away. Even as Ambrose's thoughts (and forgiveness) expressed themselves through Patience, Mary said nothing more than that it was a pleasure to meet Patience's brother, and that she was sorry. So very, very sorry.

It had been a long walk to the new Estate – Patience and Mary had lingered, savoring one another's company – but when they arrived, Mary led Patience up the steps as though she owned them. Patience was only too happy to come tromping up after her, thumping hard on each plank.

A shadow appeared behind the screen of the open front door. Ah, but here were two new additions to this Estate: a screen on the front door, and a sense of welcome.

The shadow yanked open the screen and stepped outside. Sunlight dribbled itself over the featureless form, filling in the blanks of Ezekiel. "Girl!" he shouted, as he tottered out the front door and lifted his age-withered arms as high as he could.

It was funny, for Patience to recall how much that word had rankled her as a child. When it had applied.

She smiled and rushed to embrace him. "How are you, Ezekiel?"

"Where you been, girl?"

Before she had a chance to tell him, a woman appeared in the door with a young giant squirming in her arms.

Patience brightened. "This must be Anne and Philip!"

Anne said "how do you do?"

Philip burped and fell asleep.

"You should hear where she's been," Mary grinned as she slapped Patience on the shoulder. "Quite a tale."

"Love a tale!" Ezekiel cried. "Come inside!" And he led the way, into the Estate.

Patience paused, taking a moment to fully digest the sight. She laughed all the way into the sitting room.

E I G H T

THE FURNITURE SEEMED NEW. NEW ENOUGH THAT PATIENCE was hesitant to sit on it. She'd never sat on *new* furniture before, not even new-*ish* items like these. They couldn't have been more than two or three years old, she guessed, based on the timeline she was able to piece together from what Mary, and subsequently Ezekiel, had told her.

It took a bit of getting used to, sitting on new furniture without periodically reminding herself that she was sitting on new furniture. This was a mental roadblock she hadn't expected to be so fully halted by, but life was full of surprises.

After some hours of bringing one another up to speed on their lives, though, Mary finally revealed that new drum that Drummond had been banging on when he arrived here.

At that point, Patience's mind went fully, ecstatically blank. She blinked, reminded herself to breathe, and blinked even harder. "He's a *what?!*"

Mary smiled and shrugged. "He's an abolitionist now."

Patience threw her head back and laughed. "Wh…WHAT?!"

The others didn't seem to find this nearly as hilarious as Patience did. Granted, they had never met him before he'd shown up here…and Patience had just told them all what role he had played in her life, beginning with the creation of it. None of which was likely to dispose them to joining her in laughter.

Fair enough, she conceded, wiping tears from her eyes, even as gales of giggles continued to knock her about the couch.

"Drummond Pinchwife," she tittered, "the abolitionist. That's perfect. That's *perfect.*"

She glanced up at everyone else in the room. At which point she finally put her finger on something that had been, um, sitting poorly with her the entire time they'd been in the, ah…*sitting* room here.

Nobody else was actually sitting down. Not in the way you would expect someone to, after hours of catching up with an old friend. Mary was perched awkwardly on the arm of a high-backed chair; Ezekiel had lowered himself onto an ottoman, when the seat to which it belonged was fully available; Anne stood behind a loveseat, hands resting on its back, while at her side a palpably bored Philip propped his chin in a low swoop of the same.

All at once, Patience grew self-conscious of her luxuriant posture. "So," she asked as she straightened up, "where do you all live?"

Ezekiel gestured around the room. "Here. Inside the home."

Patience wanted to press the point – if they lived here, why were *they* the ones tiptoeing around like guests – but there was a simpler way to get at the same concept. Particularly when she was confident of already knowing the answer.

"Who *owns* the house?" she asked.

Everyone's shoulders fell, even young Philip's.

"Mr. Pinchwife," Mary replied.

The honorific left room for Praisegod's face to appear in Patience's mind. She felt Ambrose chase it away, and flushed with gratitude. "You mean Drummond?"

"He prefers *mister*," Anne sighed.

"Oh, I'm sure he does." Patience scanned the room for any evidence that Drummond or Martha actually lived here. Precisely what she was looking for, she couldn't say, but surely there would be *some* artifacts testifying to their presence, right? Filigreed dining sets, or monogrammed pillows? Patience saw nothing. More to the point — she *recognized* nothing. It was true that she had spent almost all of her time on the real Estate (although she supposed that *this* was the real Estate now; the other one was merely the *original*) trapped on the second floor. But even so, she would have said she'd gotten a fairly respectable sense of Martha's decorational aesthetic. If one had to describe it in a single word, it would be *too much*, because it was twice what was called for.

Enough was the word for this living room. It was tasteful in its resplendence, if such a thing were possible. Too simple for the Pinchwifes, but perhaps too gaudy for their indentured servants. Perhaps that was a product of some compromise.

Patience frowned. Yes, with the exception of fortunate little Philip, the people before her remained indentured servants. Yet they lived in the house. Yet they didn't sit, seemed vaguely anxious at being near the furnishings at all, even as they evinced no such anxiety about tromping around the house itself...

What the hell was going on here?

"Where *are* Drummond and Martha?" Patience asked, refusing to let the names catch in her throat.

Mary and Ezekiel glanced at each other. The look that passed between them was unreadable, but its meaning was unmistakable, like hieroglyphics on how-to tablet for human sacrifice. In unison, they turned back to Patience and, slowly, each raised a finger towards the ceiling.

"They…" Patience couldn't resist smiling, "…they live upstairs?"

"Yessum," Ezekiel nodded.

"And they never come down," Philip volunteered, sounding quite a bit older than he ought to.

"*Almost* never," Anne confirmed.

Patience nodded. "Do you go up?"

"Only to leave food on the landing," Mary replied. "And to change the chamberpot."

Patience blinked and shook her head. She opened and closed her mouth a few times, auditioning words and finding none up to the job.

"Sounds like it is prison," Ezekiel said, reading Patience and Ambrose's minds. "But it is their choosing of this life."

"Works for us though," Mary was quick to clarify with a hollow smile.

Patience nodded and matched the grin. "When's the next time food goes up?"

"Ah…" Ezekiel grunted himself to his feet, then toddled to the empty doorframe to peek at the grandfather clock in the next room. "Six o' clock. Two hours and some." He turned to Mary. "Best to begin the meal shortly."

"Two and a half hours to…" Patience leaned forward, planting her elbows on her thighs. "What all are you making for them?"

Mary fixed Patience with a glare that Patience remembered well. It was the one that preceded a whap upside the head.

Patience flapped her mouth once, then leaned back into her seat. "I'm just asking. It's an odd arrangement."

"So is sharing a brain with your ghost brother," Mary replied. "You don't see me questioning it."

"That…is a very good point." Patience laughed.

"If we do not cook them the good food," Ezekiel explained as he hobbled his way out of the room, "they will come down, and they will complain. The good food will keep them upstairs."

"Mhm." Patience smiled and stood. "Well, I'd like to take it up to them tonight."

Ezekiel, Mary, Anne, and even Philip all took turns glancing at each other. Once they'd satisfied themselves with their omni-directional gawp, they turned as one to look at Patience.

"That'd be really funny," Mary observed.

And so it was decided.

N I N E

PATIENCE GOT KICKED OUT OF THE KITCHEN IN RELA-tively short order. The issues were twofold; first, Ezekiel and Anne, who did most of the cooking, had a system of working together already in place. It was something of a dance, really, tightly choreographed enough to make the addition of a third party – however gifted they were in the kitchen – a challenge.

Indeed, it was Patience's personal experience preparing food with the Serkis brothers that made her such a poor fit here. She had her own way of doing things, one that couldn't easily be unlearned.

But that wasn't entirely the second of the two issues. No, that came from the simple fact that, for all of the years that had passed since Patience, Mary, and Ezekiel had lived under the same roof…they found the bonds between them strong enough to almost instantly snap them back into their old dynamic.

Trouble with that, of course, was that Patience had been a child at that time.

"Put that down," Mary snapped from the doorway.

Patience turned to frown a question at her, the knife that had prompted the comment still in her hand.

"You're gonna hurt yourself."

"Mary, I am a grown woman."

"What do you need the knife for?"

"I'm…" Patience glanced around the counter before her. Spotting an onion, she reached out and pulled it towards herself. "Onion," she announced.

"Ooh," Anne cooed, half-reaching for the filched bulb, "I was about to cut that."

"I can cut it," Patience insisted.

"You may simply take it from her," Ezekiel told Anne, not bothering to look up from his own chopping.

Anne turned to her husband. "I don't know her that well."

"I do." Ezekiel used his knife to gesture from Patience to Anne. "Give her the vegetable, girl!"

Patience smacked her lips in disappointment. "I can cut it!"

"I just have a way it works for me," Anne explained apologetically, as she slowly extended her arm for the onion.

Patience sighed and turned to Mary in the doorway.

"This is why I stay out," Mary shrugged.

"I know how to cook," Patience grumbled, putting the knife back down on the counter. She stepped out of the kitchen, and moped her way back to the sitting room.

Philip was there, sat on the loveseat, playing with a doll that looked quite a bit like the sort Ambrose had expected to find Doctor Mayhew playing with, before he'd gotten to know the old warthog. Stitched out of fabric, with an oversized head and unnervingly large features. It was, Patience couldn't help but notice, a white doll.

She sat next to Philip on the loveseat and smiled. He waved the doll through the air in a lazy figure-eight. A sideways figure eight.

Infinity.

Her smiled faltered, but she managed to find it again just before Philip looked up at her.

"What's it like having an extra person in your head?" he asked.

"I don't know," Patience shrugged. "I think we've always been sharing a mind, in a way. My sibling and I." She smiled. "What's it like having *one* person in your head?"

Philip swung his doll through a few more thoughtful cycles before responding. "It's hard," he finally said.

Patience nodded. She wasn't entirely sure what to say to that, except nothing. Which was, sometimes, the only thing one could say.

T E N

PATIENCE PUT TWO RATHER UNAPPETIZING BOWLS OF WHAT Ezekiel affectionately referred to as "chicken mess" (a stew of some description, and *mess* was certainly as good a one as any) on a thin tray, woven from some flexible wood Patience could not identify. She included two spoons, and a single kerchief which she was assured would be more than enough for both of them.

Thusly outfitted, she carried the Pinchwifes' repasts to the stairs, helpless but to smile at the topsy-turvitude of it all.

She planted her foot on the first step, then looked up.

Martha stood at the top of the stairs, looking down. The narrow dress she wore was backlit by the window behind her; Patience could make out a tangle of loose threads at the hem.

"I expect you'll be coming up now," she croaked.

"You could always come down," Patience replied, lifting the tray in her hands slightly, "if that's preferable."

"*Bah,*" Martha declared, as she summoned Patience with a wave of the hand. As though Patience's ascent was some honor the Pinchwife Mistress was reluctantly bestowing.

Patience remained just where she was.

Martha's head reappeared from over the banister. "Are you coming?" she called.

"Ask me nicely," Patience responded, surprised by how distant she sounded, even to herself.

"...excuse me?"

"A *please* would be terrific."

Patience, Ambrose

Martha uttered the most miraculous *harrumph* Patience had ever heard, as her head retracted behind the banister. She reappeared bodily at the top of the stairs and grimaced down at Patience. Her eyebrows and lips rattled at the conversations she was no doubt having in her head.

Patience just kept on smiling. She hated to admit it, but the chicken mess did smell quite good.

"Okay," Martha finally grunted. "Bring the food up, girl… *please.*" She'd hardly finished that last word before she spun about on her heel and stormed out of view once more.

Patience laughed to herself as she began to climb the steps. The last of her smile had died by the time she reached the top.

She could hear the flies again. Coming from the master bedroom, at the end of the hall. For it was precisely that hall Patience now turned down, in time to see the last of Martha's dress being slurped up by precisely that doorway.

There were no pillars of flies pulsing in and out of the half-open door like a heartbeat, of course. Patience knew the flies weren't there. Even as she saw them, heard them.

She tried to focus on the smell of the chicken mess wafting past her nose. Something too kind to be consigned to a kingdom of flies. But that was life.

Patience set her jaw and stepped slowly but confidently towards the door at the end of the hall.

She stepped into the room and discovered, first and foremost, that there were no flies. Which wasn't to say that she no longer heard them.

Her second discovery was that the bed had been moved back from where she had knocked into it in the original Estate. It was where she had remembered it being. Long ago.

The third discovery, most predictable of all, was that Drummond Pinchwife lay sprawled across the bed, taking up the entire mattress. He was quite a bit heavier than the last time Patience had seen him, quite a bit paler. It was hard to dismiss the notion that he was simply coming to more closely resemble his personality.

Patience stepped into the room, drifting to within just a few feet of the side of the bed. "Hello, father," she growled.

Martha slumped into a chair in the corner of the room, allowing herself to be swallowed by shadow.

Drummond grimaced over at his wife.

She threw up her arms. "She had the tray. I don't know."

Rumbling like a landslide, Drummond pried his eyes from his wife and stared up at his daughter. With no small amount of effort, he mushed his features into a lightless smile. "I forgive you," he said.

That was bait Patience refused to take. She took a slow, heavy step nearer the bed. Her knuckles popped as her fists clenched around the handles of the tray. "Do you want your food?" she asked him.

"The Christian thing for you to do now," he continued, his smile growing toothier, if not larger, "is to forgive me. And I know you had a *very* Christian upbringing."

"If you want your supper," Patience warned, "you had best be careful." The room was starting to spin around her – she'd underestimated how difficult this would be. She willed the world to steady, willed her forehead to quit sweating.

"*Careful,*" Drummond repeated. He gestured limply to the bed on which he sat. "I am careful as can be."

Patience didn't know what to say to that. She said nothing,

and it was all she could say…but this was a different sort of nothing than she had said to Philip just an hour or two ago. This was nothing as a surplus of something. Nothing as a consequence of everything.

Drummond considered Patience as he might a mysterious blob smeared across on the sole of his nicest shoe. "I have made my penance. I do not ask your forgiveness. I simply mean to point out what the precepts of a charitable lifestyle dictate your next action be."

Patience wanted nothing more than to dump the soup across her father's belly. Overturn the tray, and pray the mess was still hot enough to scald him.

Yet she couldn't. Even now. Even in his weakness, even in her strength. For there were too many flies. She had not the strength to move, for all the flies.

Drummond pushed himself further upright. "He came to us before he left for the city," he announced, at a volume just beyond one suited for speaking indoors. "My son. My *son,*" his voice broke with the repetition. His upper lip flared, revealing a row of yellowed teeth. "Were it not for you, he never would have felt the need to…" he lolled his head towards Martha. "What were his words?"

"I don't remember," Martha mumbled from the shadows.

Drummond glowered at his wife and made a *thhh* noise, like a cat. But he said nothing in response to her.

"You say *son,*" Patience managed, furious at the tremble she could not keep from her voice, "like you only had one."

"Yes. Yes, I know Jesse told you." He lifted his hands and made a show of inspecting his soft knuckles. "And do you know what became of our beloved Jes-"

"You shot him in your bedroom," Patience interrupted.

That pulled Drummond's gaze up to her own, his eyes wide enough to show white all the way around. He blinked, and forced a smile. "How is the old Estate, then?"

"I don't want to know," Martha mumbled from the corner.

Drummond let his arms flop down to his sides. "Well I do, Martha!"

The Pinchwife woman curled her nose at him, then turned her sad, idiot eyes towards Patience. "Was he kind to you?"

Patience cocked her head slightly.

"My son. Was he k-"

"Have you ever," Patience immediately snapped back, "asked that of Mary or Ezekiel?"

"Don't you dare talk about my son!" Drummond blustered, in the fashion of a performer wrestling an unexpected improv back towards the script he had painstakingly memorized.

"When did you know?" Patience asked Martha.

She stared blankly back. "Know what?"

"That I was your husband's daughter?"

"Don't talk about my...don't talk *to* my wife!" Drummond roared, deigning to lift his torso gently from the pillows.

Martha sighed. "Within hours of your birth."

"I mean when you were teaching me," Patience replied, doing her best to burn the tears from her eyes before they slid down her cheeks. "When I lived with you. For *years.*"

"I knew all the while," Martha replied, her expression frozen in neutrality.

Patience felt the fragile little handles of the tray breaking in her ever-tightening grasp. "You could have asked me how kind your son was then. You could have said something."

"It seemed imprudent then. It was not my place you tell you what you so clearly did not know."

"Yet you're happy to ask me now."

Martha flinched slightly. "It seemed imprudent then."

"Yes. Well, he was alive. That certainly complicated it for you."

Martha rose halfway to standing, then crashed back into the chair. "How dare you? Praisegod was m-"

"Peter," Drummond corrected.

"Praisegod was my *son,"* Martha snarled. "And you took him from me!"

"He *left* you," Patience reminded her. "Years before my arrival."

Martha stood all the way up this time.

"Sit down," Patience ordered her.

"Get out of my house," Martha ordered right back.

"Sit down, Martha."

Mistress Pinchwife took a step forward.

"I will hurt you," Patience whispered, standing straight with the tray still in hand, her body wound so tightly she heard her shoulders *crack*.

One step was enough for Martha, it seemed. "...you would?"

"I don't know," Patience confessed. It was apology and warning, both at once.

Martha studied her for a moment...then sat back down.

Patience looked down at the bowls on her tray. Chicken mess. That just about summed it up. She didn't know what she was doing. All she knew was that an unexpected flood of anger was ripping through her...and she was deeply disappointed to have left her rifle outside.

"This is all in the past," Drummond rumbled, obscured from Patience's view by the tray in her hand.

She moved the tray to the left, slowly revealing Drummond's face once again.

The fear in his eyes was delicious. For as much as it terrified Patience too…oh, it was lovely.

"We now know full well," Drummond whinnied up at his daughter, "that slavery is an evil. It had taken our son from us. Thus, we oppose it!"

"Mhm," Patience smiled. "I heard about that." She sat down on the side of the bed, as though visiting with a loved one.

If it wasn't quite intentional that she sat squarely on Drummond's knee…well, she wouldn't be losing sleep over it. Over other things, yes, but not that.

"Ah!" Drummond roared. "Careful, you heifer!"

"Drummond," Martha tutted.

Patience nodded at Martha, then turned back to Drummond, balancing the tray of stews on his lap. "Tell me precisely wh-"

"I don't want that there," Drummond growled, turning his nose up at the tray teetering atop his belly.

"Tell me what it is you do," Patience continued, "which makes you an abolitionist."

"We oppose slavery." He smirked. "Do you not know what an abolitionist is?"

"Yes, but what do you *do?*" Patience pressed. "Do you write pamphlets? Attend gatherings? Agitate for the cause? What do you *do?*"

Drummond looked to Martha. Back to Patience. "Abolitionist means that you oppose slavery."

"Yes. *How* do you oppose it?"

"Strenuously!"

"Drummond is scarcely mobile," Martha submitted, gesturing to the blanket-covered legs.

"Mhm," Patience chuckled, glancing down at her own lap.

She heard the *cl-clink* of Drummond snapping up the spoons from the tray. "I've taken hold of the spoons, Martha! She is unarmed!"

Martha and Patience sighed at Drummond.

"Attack!" he cried.

Patience leaned over the bed, balancing by digging a fist into Drummond's gut, and slapped the spoons from his hand.

"Ach!" He followed the spoons with a frown, as they soared across the room and clattered against the wall opposite the door. "Well, now you'll have to fetch us new spoons."

"Drummond," Martha rumbled. "Shut up."

The Pinchwife Master spun slowly around to face his wife, his eyes and mouth both hanging wide open. He spun his beached carp astonishment towards Patience, but she was looking out the window beneath which the spoons had come to rest.

She could see Mary outside, sitting on a low stone wall, while Philip skipped around her in a serpentine loop.

"Where are the others?" she asked.

"The others?" Martha asked.

"The people you owned."

"Sold 'em," Drummond purred.

"And was that before or after you decided you were an abolitionist?"

"After."

Patience pinched her lips together and shook her head until it was facing Drummond.

He shimmied a touch more upright in the bed, using his hands to stabilize the tray. "Can't own slaves if you're an abolitionist," he explained, as though to a child, "because being an *abolitionist* means you've seen that it's evil."

"So rather than free them," Patience clarified, "you sold th-"

"Well, this house wasn't about to pay for its-...and *besides,*" he interrupted himself, "they're not slaves, they're *servants!*"

"I didn't use the word slaves."

"But you were *thinking* it," Drummond insisted, tapping the side of his head. "And that's just as bad."

Patience narrowed her eyes, felt her mouth fall open into a soft 'o'.

"We're sorry," Martha insisted, urgently enough to lift her a few inches from the chair. She settled back in quickly. "We're very sorry. Aren't we, Drummond?"

"Sorry," Drummond spat. "Martha, her spoons are on the floor. She's powerless."

"Drummond."

"You're sorry," Patience parroted flatly back to Martha. Just so she could hear it. Hear how small a word it was.

"Yes, yes. Aren't we sorry, Drummond?"

The man of the house shook his head. First at the soup, then at his daughter. "No. You know wh-"

"Drummond!"

"No, dear, I am *not* sorry! In fact, I'm pr..." he frowned at the tray threatening to spill on his lap. He picked it up, and handed it to Patience. "Here, hold th-"

With one quick swipe, Patience swung a palm up and over-turned the tray in Drummond's hands, spilling the chicken mess onto the swell of his stomach. "Ah!" he shouted in surprise.

"AAHH!" Martha shrieked, which was *way* too much.

Drummond shook his head at the broth-and-chunky rumpus now dribbling down to the mattress in a hundred little runlets. "Well, the joke's on you," he groused at Patience, his voice trembling with emotion, "the soup wasn't hot anymore." He tossed the tray against the same wall as he had the spoons. "So that didn't even hurt." He risked a wounded little double-take up at Patience.

She stood over him and stared. Fearing what might happen, if she permitted herself to move just then.

Drummond shook his head up at her. "I'm not sorry. I only did what my father did, and what his father did before him." He jabbed at himself with a fat little finger. "*I'm* the one who broke that chain. *I'm* the one who saw it was wrong. So frankly, I deserve some credit for that."

"Do you regret what you did to my mother?"

"Do *you?*" Drummond folded his arms, a sickly little smile flashing across his face. "Because if I hadn't done it, you would never have been born."

"And my brother," Patience reminded him, her voice small, like a firing pin.

"Whatever."

"Not whatever."

"And Praisegod would still be alive," Martha mumbled from the corner.

Drummond waved that away, keeping his eyes on Patience. "Do you wish you hadn't been born? Is that what you're saying to me?"

Patience remained silent, staring down at him, her fists trembling by her sides.

"As I thought," Drummond nodded. "So…if you'll only see your way to an apology, and a *thank you* for my having given you life, then you can be on your way."

"Drummond," Martha all but sobbed in the corner.

"What?" He threw his arms out wide and glared at his wife. "What is it, Martha? WHAT?!"

Martha buried her face in her hands.

Drummond turned his glare to Patience. "I don't…" he raised his fingers for air quotes, "…*feel bad.*" He let his hands fall across his soup-sogged belly. "I don't feel bad about your mother, just like I don't feel bad about *her* father. I hung him from the same tree I did your mother, did Jesse tell you *that?*"

"Just don't hurt *me,*" Martha whimpered to Patience. "I'm sorry. I am." She pointed a trembling finger at her husband, but withdrew it before she vocalized the thought that had obviously prompted the point.

"I refuse to be made to feel bad," Drummond insisted to the empty space over the foot of his bed, "for seeing the err…the *very few* errors of my ways, and becoming an enlightened, modern man. I'm…" he shook his head. "I *refuse.*" He looked back up to Patience with a perfectly transparent mask of fury on his face.

At first, Patience took this for empty bluster. But upon closer inspection of that purple, quivering visage…she realized that it was something so much more horrible than that.

It was conviction.

Patience still wasn't certain what she had hoped to get from Drummond, what satisfaction she had expected to find up here. But what the old bastard's face finally communicated to her was that, whatever it was she needed to hear, it would not be coming from him. He genuinely believed himself a good man. Better than good, in fact. And that self-righteousness made him bullet-proof against anything she could throw at him.

Yet...to Patience's astonishment...she found herself not in the least bit troubled by this. Oh, make no mistake, his mulish sanctimony was *enraging*...but it was too fragile to truly disturb her. Why else would he feel the need to hide himself away up here? The world would shatter him.

And what was a fragile little man like that to her? A man with no love in his life? No fire, save that which he smothered, lest it light something other than himself?

He was...nothing. Absolutely nothing. And so, unworthy of her attention.

Undeserving of *their* fire.

She and Ambrose smiled at that thought. Couldn't help it.

Drummond grimaced at her smile. "Something amusing?"

Patience considered responding...then decided that her ever-expanding grin was already more than Drummond deserved. Was, indeed, more than words could have expressed.

"Stop smiling!"

A laugh burbled up from deep within Patience. She did nothing to stop it.

Drummond pushed himself nearer to upright. "SILENCE, DAMN YOU!"

Patience's giggling all but doubled her over. She clapped a hand across her aching sides.

"LISTEN TO ME!" Drummond screamed, his voice cracking, his face now turning red. "SHUT UP!"

"Ah..." Patience wiped at her eyes. "Best of luck with the abolitionism," she grinned, with a wink and another slap on the leg.

"AAH!"

She turned and left the room, borne aloft by Drummond's re-criminations. Because she and Ambrose were done here. They were done.

"Bitch!" Drummond shrieked. "You're going to apologize to me! Come back here!"

The further down the hall Patience got, the more her father started to sound like just so many flies.

E L E V E N

SHE WANDERED INTO THE KITCHEN TO FIND EZEKIEL AND ANNE pulling apart, breaking up one of those little intimate moments Patience was dimly aware of lovers having with each other.

"Sounded like there was some excitement up there," Anne said with a hesitant smile.

"The tray!" Ezekiel grinned, pointing to Patience. "No tray! I surely did tell you, the loud thud was the tray."

Anne laughed. "I never said you were wrong!"

"I knew this sound to be the tray," Ezekiel insisted.

Anne patted her husband on the shoulder. "So," Anne asked Patience, "did you…um…" she shrugged. "I don't, uh…did you get what you wanted out of them, I guess?"

Patience chewed on her bottom lip. "I don't think I did. But… I don't know if there was anything I wanted."

"Oh."

"Then why did you go up?" Ezekiel wondered.

Patience thought about that…then smiled.

Ezekiel nodded, then glanced out the window. He, in turn, smiled at his son, playing with Mary out in the yard.

Patience, Ambrose

Patience planted her hands on her hips, and stared at her feet for a moment. A smile flashed across her face. "Would you be upset if I burned the house down?" Sure, Drummond was unworthy of her fire…but still.

Anne cocked her head to one side. Ezekiel slowly cranked his head back towards Patience.

"Um," Anne replied, "…yes?"

"Not with you in it," Patience clarified. She pointed to the ceiling. "With *them* in it."

"…"

"I wouldn't stop them coming out. I just want to see if they *would*."

"We live here," Ezekiel reminded her.

"I know," Patience quietly replied. "There's a place we can go. A better one. It's up in Canada."

Ezekiel glanced down at Anne. She met his gaze, then looked back at Patience. "Is that where you're going?" she asked.

"…ah," Patience nodded.

"I don't mean it like that," Anne was quick to add. "You don't *have* to leave. It's just…"

"They are safety for us," Ezekiel said, taking up the baton. He did nothing to indicate he was talking about the two Pinchwifes upstairs. He didn't need to. "No one bothers us. Because we keep them. It is a safe place here, for raising a child."

"Yeah," Patience granted, "but who comes around to catch you out?"

"People come around," Anne sighed matter-of-factly.

Patience considered pressing the issue…but ultimately left it. Drummond wasn't worth the effort. She nodded. "Okay." Smiling despite herself, she flopped her arms out and said "figured it couldn't hurt to ask."

Ezekeil and Anne laughed. Which, when a dear friend comes around and asks to burn down your house, is really all you can do.

Other than letting them, of course.

T W E L V E

PATIENCE POLITELY DECLINED HER OLD FRIENDS' OFFER TO stay the night – genuinely tendered though it had seemed, Patience didn't trust herself to sleep under the same roof as Drummond without setting that fire after all. So to the evident confusion of Mary and Ezekiel, Patience said her goodbyes out on the front porch, even as the sun was crawling towards the finish line of the horizon.

"You can come back any time you like," Mary told her as they broke their long embrace.

"Thank you," Patience replied, and meant it. She stopped just short of saying she would take Mary up on that offer – she wanted to be able to mean *everything* she said here.

"You will be okay," Ezekiel told her as he stepped forward, his arms outstretched.

"I know," she replied with a chuckle.

Anne and Philip were much quicker farewells, of course. They hadn't the same history. Yet they sent each other off with warmth regardless.

Patience descended those familiar steps for the final time, swung onto the horse who had waited faithfully on the yard, and got on her way. She didn't inconvenience herself with a look over her shoulder.

That night she camped in the deepest, darkest part of the woods her horse could manage to reach. Within half an hour, she had a fire, set in a makeshift pit just before a stump suitable for sitting. There Patience sat, on the log, in the woods, with the fire.

She stared into the flames, seeing Ambrose in them. Seeing herself, and knowing that to be Ambrose's mind flickering alongside hers.

When this body dies, Patience thought into the fire, *we'll finally be together again. All the way together.* She smiled, and took up a stick to poke at the edges of the little inferno. *First time since the womb.*

The fire popped.

Patience nodded. *I wonder where we'll go,* she thought. Which was both a continuation of the last thought, and the beginning of a new one.

T H I R T E E N

SHE HADN'T MEANT TO COME HERE...YET SHE SUPPOSED, as she paused just outside the open gate and laughed beneath the massive brass sign which named the place...it was inevitable that it would bring her here.

She just couldn't say for certain what that *it* had been.

Carefully, suddenly sensitive to just how fragile a human body was, Patience slid off her horse and walked through the gate.

The experience of stepping into Pleasance Square, of entering this half-block almost wholly swallowed by the shadow of the old hickory at its southern end, was heartbreaking in its banality.

The square was just a square, and the tree was just a tree. People floated past, oblivious to the generations of trauma that had… oh, but that wasn't true, was it? For it was all too likely that at least a few of the well-dressed toffs taking their twilight constitutional in the square had attended a lynching or three here.

It wasn't inconceivable that one of them had been at Aggy's, or at her father's.

Patience felt her right eye twitch.

Slowly, one trembling step at a time, she approached the old hickory tree at the southern end of Pleasance Square. Because there was nothing else to see here. Nothing else that could have called her.

The nearer to it she drew…the less like a tree it seemed. Its bark seemed to…it was almost as though the leaves were…

She reached her hand out towards it. Carefully, ready to pull back, in the unnervingly plausible event its mighty trunk should split open and swallow her arm.

The sounds of the world around her hid, one by one. The birds ceased their songs, the wind ceased to blow. All she heard was the sound of her heart beating in her chest, and the sound of swarming flies.

Her fingers touched the tree.

She snorted her breath out through her nose; it was only then she realized she had been holding it.

Patience ran her hand along the grain of the bark, now applying her whole palm to the trunk. It was unnervingly warm. It even seemed to…breathe? But that was obviously just her imagination. Though there was power in this haunted hickory, that much was certain.

Just as there was power in every tree. For it was from their pulp that men made paper, and it was upon that paper the fates of people like Patience and Ambrose were written. Paper had made of them slaves, and perhaps one day it would make them free. Or it would banish them from the country. Or order their wholesale extermination. There was no greater power in this land than a pen put to paper.

The bark of the hickory yielded slightly beneath Patience's hand, as her fingers curled into soft fists. She failed to notice.

Drummond and Martha might have another child, Patience thought. Or people like them would. Slaveowners and overseers, but also the people who came to the square for a lynching and said nothing. They would all have children. Those children would themselves have children. And those children would have children. And yea unto the seventh generation, the children would have children.

And one day, if the right sort of hand finds its way to writing the right words on any old piece of paper, the slaves would be free. And the seventh sons to the seventh sons of the slave-owners and their accomplices would be good, upstanding, enlightened people, who would gaze across the expanse of history and dimly acknowledge the inhuman practice for what it was. They would shake their heads at the cruelty of their forebearers, even as they refused to accept the vantage that cruelty had afforded them. That was the past, they will say. It was a different time.

But the lives already ground into the mill will be gone, long gone. And those seventh sons of the seventh sons will have no place from which to shake their heads but atop the remains of those long-gone lives, never wholly appreciating that their fortune rises to meet them amidst monuments of human suffering.

Or perhaps they will appreciate this perfectly well. Perhaps they will see the bodies upon which they dance, and think themselves decent for shaking their heads and singing *that was the past. It was a different time.*

Patience flinched and yanked her hand back from the tree.

As though, yes, okay, as though it had bitten her.

She frowned up at its naked canopy, towards the heavy boughs from which their mother must have swung.

b l i n k

AND THEY KNEW. JUST AS SHE HAD WANTED THEM TO KNOW, just as she'd never believed they could. They knew.

Patience and Ambrose knew that their mother either loved them or liked them a whole lot, or at least had some sort of positive feeling towards them, even if their father was more a bastard than either could ever be. They knew she was a failure in her maternal obligations, having not the slightest idea how to sooth their blistering hearts save to bring them nearer one another, and that not a day would go by that would bring her reprieve from that; she would not allow it. They knew that she hated herself for how she had given up on whatever they had been in the womb, how she had abandoned them in her heart purely to protect herself...most of all, they knew what she herself was only now discovering, late in the day but hopefully not *too* late, that defining love by imagined ends rather than immediate means could only close one off. All roads ended in a great, lightless contraction, and good fortune could only be constructed on the graves of those who had suffered sufficiently to shore up the foundation. All of this, Aggy knew to a near-moral certainty.

And so, her children knew it.

But Aggy had given her children each other, and she had given them their names, and she had given them half a chance.

They saw, through her eyes, the price she paid for that. They saw as the rope swung over the bough, as the mill ground her under.

F O U R T E E N

PATIENCE AND AMBROSE CLOSED THEIR EYES AS AGGY'S filled with darkness. Tears stung at the corners of the black.

Those tears streamed down their cheeks and fell to the ground.

The roots of the hickory reached, and found.

And thus, the tree watered itself.

1839

ON OCTOBER 2ND OF THE FOLLOWING YEAR, A YOUNG BOY named Calvin Buckworth tripped on an exposed root and tumbled into the old hickory tree at the southern end of Pleasance Square. It was a gentle collision, hardly worthy of note, were it not for the splinter driven into the hand that he had lifted to break his fall. Just a modest little wink of timber, one that became infected with a speed for which no physician could account. The infection, though quick to develop, was slow to spread, yet unstoppable even after the arm had been hastily amputated. The boy died, in more pain than any human should ever be forced to endure, on October 9, 1839. It was the tree's one hundred and forty-sixth birthday.

The End

Also by Jud Widing

Novels
Go Figure
Jairzinho's Curbside Giants
The Little King of Crooked Things
A Middling Sort
Westmore and More!
The Year of Uh

Stories
Identical Pigs

Made in the USA
Middletown, DE
19 September 2024

60643738R00324